Not All a Dream

What Reviewers Say About Sophia Kell Hagin's Work

Whatever Gods May Be

"A riveting novel with a twist of romance, *Whatever Gods May Be* is a fun and exciting read, hard to put down."—*Midwest Book Review*

"*Whatever Gods May Be* by Sophia Kell Hagin is brilliant! This is one of the books that leaves you just wanting to say 'WOW!' Kell Hagin writes about war with a freshness that keeps the heat, the fear and the violence in the front of your mind as you are turning the pages, glued to the action. There is nowhere to hide in this book, it is full on."—*Lesbian Review*

"There are twists and turns throughout the book and to give any one of them in a review would be a disservice to the reader. Suffice it to say that each twist and each turn is believable and will keep the reader turning pages as fast as she can. Kudos to BSB for departing from their norm and publishing this book. This book deserves a wide audience, if for no other reason than to say to lesbian publishers, your readers want more than what is being served up to them now. This book is a start."—*Lambda Literary Review*

"*Whatever Gods May Be* is an exceptionally fine first novel. Jamie Gwynmorgan, its heroine, grabs the reader by the heart in the first few pages, and never lets go. With great character development and an exciting plot, this is sure to be a novel considered for the GCLS award for Debut Author."—*Just About Write*

"This is a story about survival and resilience as a young soldier thrust into marine basic training, and then into war. The central character is wonderfully drawn by Hagin, and convincingly portrays the vulnerabilities of a self doubting young woman, and the pressures and responsibilities she faces as more and more is asked of her. There is grit in the telling of events, and Hagin sets a blistering pace in the action, that at points I could hear the gunfire going off in my head."—*Lesbian Book Review*

"This physically and psychologically intense war novel has balls. The blood of battle courses through this novel's pages with an astonishing relentlessness; the harrowing experience of prolonged interrogation becomes horrifically riveting. This isn't a novel for the faint of heart. It is a novel for fans of straight-up war stories, with a dash of the supernatural on the side."—*Gay Calgary Magazine*

"The blood of battle courses through this novel's pages with an astonishing relentlessness; the harrowing experience of prolonged interrogation becomes horrifically riveting."—*Pride Source*

Omnipotence Enough

"I think any lover of thrillers will enjoy *Omnipotence Enough*, but readers of the earlier books will feel a special investment in this last journey. Well done, Sophia Kell Hagin. I look forward to your future novels, for the adrenaline and compassion and all the future woman crushes sure to come."—*C-Spot Reviews*

"The personal narrative with Hagin's rich use of language has been my great love of all three books in the series. Jamie Gwymorgan is the thing that carries you through the work and she is one of those characters that you find yourself thinking about long after you have finished the book."—*Lesbian Review*

Shadows of Something Real

"This novel is a thriller, but also a romance, so much the sweeter for Jamie after all she's survived. Adele (Lily's sister and just as bad-ass as the rest of the family) is the emotionally open woman Jamie needs. Thankfully, all these women are humanized by their flaws. This book is chock-full of evil politicians and corporations, high-tech gadgetry and life-and-death struggles. Highly recommended, even to folks who don't tend toward massive woman crushes like me."—*To Be Read Reviews*

"Hagin has taken command of the words on the page and shown such a richness of language. ...It was another brilliant read, and I am waiting to see where her wonderful imagination will take us next."—*Lesbian Review*

By the Author

Whatever Gods May Be

Shadows of Something Real

Omnipotence Enough

Not All a Dream

Not All a Dream

by

Sophia Kell Hagin

2021

NOT ALL A DREAM

ISBN 13: 978-1-63679-067-1

This Trade Paperback Original Is Published By
Bold Strokes Books, Inc.
P.O. Box 249
Valley Falls, NY 12185

First Edition: October 2021

Credits

Editor: Cindy Cresap
Production Design: Susan Ramundo
Cover Design By Tammy Seidick
Cover Concept By Sophia Kell Hagin

Dedication

for Susan

thank you, thank you, thank you
for washing ashore with me

I had a dream, which was not all a dream,
The bright sun was extinguish'd, and the stars
Did wander darkling in the eternal space,
Rayless, and pathless; and the icy earth
Swung blind and blackening in the moonless air;
Morn came and went—and came, and brought no day…

—from *Darkness*, 1816
by George Gordon, Lord Byron

Chapter One

The way I would love her

I never liked the company Christmas party, an optional event I nevertheless felt obliged to attend since *everyone* would be there and absences were noted—as in (typically with one eyebrow arching askance) "Oh gee, I didn't see you Friday night…"

The company spent some bucks on these shindigs. Upper-crusty hotel ballroom, open bar, nonpoisonous hors d'oeuvres, live band. Two hundred people dressing up to party on down. If I'd been into penalty-free boozing and flirting with men, I might've enjoyed it. But I wasn't, and I didn't.

So I sidled in late to nurse a glass of chardonnay and nibble bacon-wrapped dates and cheese straws through perfunctory chats with the people I saw daily (most pointedly my boss and my boss's boss) before departing as inconspicuously as possible for the Saints, the downtown dive bar where I recovered by dancing with my own kind—acquaintances and strangers alike—until closing. For four years of company Christmas parties, I did this.

The fifth year was no different—except for the eye-catching stranger who stood at the far side of the ballroom. Each time I glanced at her, I found her gazing back at me with a slight smile while, leggy-tall and graceful in a sleek black dress, she conducted conversations that inspired men and women alike to laugh and, every now and then, daintily dare to brush her forearm. A newbie from the Framingham facility, I figured, made curious by the customary welcoming gossip about, among other things, the Lesbian.

I forced my eyes to quickly move on, unsure afterward if she was really as attractive as others' deference and my glimpses alleged. Once when she looked over at me, out of politeness I did kind of smile back, but she never came by to talk—and, as the only dyke in Hetville, I knew better than to rile the boys by approaching one of theirs.

As usual on company Christmas party night, I left as soon as I reasonably could and drove directly to the Saints, arriving overdressed, relieved to be liberated, and hoping to bump into somebody, anybody willing to share a joint in the alley out back. I was in luck, too; the place was full of familiar faces, and DJ Donna's picks kept me boogying.

Hanging with the usual crew, I happened to be standing with my back to the dance floor when, from somewhere among the undulating women behind me, came a tiny tap on my shoulder and a voice I didn't recognize—"Hi there…"

As I turned, at first I didn't recognize her face either. She'd robbed me of context by changing from sleek black dress into jeans and a long-sleeved blue T-shirt that matched her eyes and celebrated her perfect B cups.

"Will you dance with me?" she asked.

When she smiled, a little self-consciously this time, I smiled back (again), said, "Sure," and stepped toward her. Without another word, we began to move together, to sync up. I didn't yet know her name, but I already understood that I would never love anyone the way I would love her.

CHAPTER TWO

COHERENCE

Cordelia, my beloved Cordelia, spent her final summer on our screened porch mostly, tiring and thinning as her discomfort deepened into remorseless pain and frailty. With the last of herself, she relished our unspoiled eight-tenths of an acre of scrubby, diminutive woodland and the creatures who visited and feasted here. And even as her body failed, this disciplined woman long committed to meticulous planning took on one more project.

"I'm not taking on anything, Hester," she humphed when I suggested one afternoon that she might rather ease back and watch the pair of cardinals winging through our trees. Her gaze swerved from her tablet screen to catch my eye with a resistance-is-futile flare. "I'm finishing up."

Many times she demanded I recite the List, item by item: the financial essentials filling the upper drawers of her rolltop desk, the three passwords that accessed all other passwords, the phone numbers I must keep memorized. Etcetera. She made sure that the car and generator were in good order, that the solar panels on the roof continued performing as promised, that the water softener was replenished, the septic system scoured, the chimney and dryer vent scrubbed, the boiler and air conditioning units serviced, the trees trimmed, the leaves raked. Etcetera.

In response to the pandemic that had raged before her diagnosis, Cordelia had insisted on building a huge stash of supplies. Food primarily, but also medicines, hygiene and cleaning agents, batteries, firewood, tools, and an apparently haphazard assortment of spare parts. After her diagnosis, even as the pandemic ebbed and supply chains once more approached normal, she kept right on stashing.

Forgoing both my usual tease ("Control freak!") and the irritation I had too often let creep into it over our years together, I went along with this one online order at a time, trying to ignore a nagging qualm that some odd derangement might be infecting her at the end. Instead, I watched her, and a few times I surreptitiously videoed her in the last of the sort of mundane moments I was already desperately missing.

She knew, of course. Cordelia always knew. "No, Aitch," she laughed too weakly, "I'm not demented. Just getting you ready for the season."

Almost like every year, even before the pandemic, when we'd stock up for months of storms. Around here, these typically begin with September's hurricane threats and roll into winter nor'easters that augur but rarely actually deliver power outages—though now and then we'd get snowed in for a day or two, the price of residing on a private road with erratic plowing arrangements.

Enough supplies for a month, Cordelia had always urged, plenty more than ready.gov's half-baked advice. But then, that last summer—

"Time to get serious," she announced right after telling me she'd bought a large commercial freezer (adding to the small one we already had) and explaining where in the basement it would be located. "Ever hear of food buckets? I say we go for the three-and-a-half-gallon size. Five-gallon would be too damn heavy for an old lezzy like you."

I couldn't help looking away from her when she said "you." I was already mourning the loss of "us."

Initially, Cordelia wanted two months of food, then six, then a year "at least," all recorded on a detailed spreadsheet. She poked around survival prep websites between tapping in food orders and reorders. On the heavy-duty shelving she had installed in our basement storage room I stacked cases and more cases of cans and jars alongside, yep, three-and-a-half-gallon food-grade plastic buckets filled with rice, flour, dried beans, rolled oats, powdered milk, powdered eggs, and plenty of powdered cocoa, all heat-sealed with oxygen absorbers into mylar bags.

Around mid-September, she moved into the guestroom on the daylight side of the basement, a compactly finished space brightened by a six-foot span of high south-facing windows and French doors that open to a somewhat larger den with north windows and direct access to the garage as well as to the driveway nestled about halfway down our property's northwest-to-southeast slope. "Easier to get my dregs out of here when the time comes," she said.

On the first of October, once the hospice nurse left, she asked me to play her favorite greatest hits album—"The oldies, the one that starts with ABBA." As "Take a Chance on Me" began, she asked for a food stash count.

"Twenty-four cubic feet of frozens, three hundred twenty cases of cans and jars, thirty-two food buckets packed to the brim, all sealed up tight," I told her.

Cordelia nodded and fell asleep holding my hand. Sometime later, after I'd snuggled into the bed alongside her, she half-roused during "Dancing Queen," though her eyes didn't open, and she murmured, "Will you dance with me?"

"Sure," I said softly, close to her ear, and kissed her.

Eyes still shut, she made a small, satisfied sound, like she'd nibbled something delicious. Then she almost smiled, slipped back into sleep, and never woke up again.

Ever wonder what happens to your awareness when you die?

One possibility: You simply wink out.

Poof! Done.

Or you might linger a while, lifting away to watch from the ceiling or the stratosphere or wherever, akin to what's reported by some of the people who survive cardiac arrest. Your heart has stopped, but the neurons in your brain continue to fire, releasing large amounts of chemicals that induce high-level cognitive activity during which your brain's various energy frequencies synchronize and your brainwaves achieve coherence.

Not—keep in mind, *not*—the regular old coherence that's all about congruity or logical consistency. Oh no, this kind of coherence occurs when different waves of energy form up and move together with close-order-drill precision. Like what a laser beam does.

Cordelia and I went to a lecture once when we were young and the physicist Philip Morrison was still alive, and I heard him say, "As above, so below."

Watching Cordelia die, I kept on talking to her, stroking her hand, until I eventually went quiet, wondering if she wanted that high-level cognitive activity, that coherence. Wondering if she was aware of me, of herself. Wondering if she was dreaming. Wondering what she was dreaming.

I thought about "above" (did she want me to?)—about the Milky Way that arced over our driveway, about the black hole lurking invisibly at the

Milky Way's center with a mass that's becoming ever smaller even as it grows heavier and denser, its inexorably intensifying gravity able to pull matter and light past its event horizon toward the singularity at its center, and there's no escape *ever*.

The Milky Way's black hole will grow smaller heavier denser, smaller heavier denser, until it's an unimaginably smaller-than-small, heavier-than-heavy, denser-than-dense point that evaporates—or, who can say, maybe turns in on itself—and out bursts enormously powerful high-frequency radiation. Coherent radiation. Like what a laser beam does.

And down here, down "below?" Did Cordelia experience a final burst of coherent, high-level cognition as she crossed her life's event horizon?

And then what?

Then the theories—every damn one of them about above as well as below—collapse beneath the weight of anomaly and ignorance.

Cordelia crossed her event horizon in the soft light of a waxing half-moon while I waited for her next too-ragged breath, the one that didn't come *ever*. In the ensuing silence, I held on to her hand until well after it felt irretrievably cold, but even now I wonder how long her coherence persisted before she evaporated forever into the incomprehensible.

CHAPTER THREE

SOON

Naturally, we'd discussed what I'd do After. I said I'd wait a while—"recover," I called it—then sell the house and move ten miles down the road to Seaside Point in Provincetown, that well-appointed "concierge condominium community" of almost-final resting places at the tip of Cape Cod for old farts from all walks of life.

Cordelia did the math and declared that, yeah, I *would* be able, barely, to afford the outrageous four-figure monthly fee. "Assuming you don't live too long," she said with that distinctive vocal fry she reserved for when she didn't believe a word I'd uttered.

But I did. Sort of. Without "us," I believed I'd be ready to relinquish the house we'd designed and built, trade it in for two small, boxy rooms and the proximity of other lonely old farts. A decent bed, small sofa, maybe a couple of chairs around a bistro table would be sufficient.

Not enough windows, of course (there's a cemetery next door), and perhaps too many neighbors miffed at hearing so much of ABBA and the Bee Gees—but at least space for a mid-size flatscreen and a few shelves for selected keepsakes.

Ah, well.

I can stow our gazillion photos and videos on a flash drive or two, back it up in a digital cloud somewhere. But how do I pick through all the totems and talismans of our private culture? What about the birthday cards and Valentine's cards and Christmas cards and hey-I-love-you cards stuffed randomly in various drawers, waiting for me with their neglected memories? Or Cordelia's clothes, so familiar, from which I can still sometimes get a whiff of her…?

And where better than the realm of "us" to remember the lasts? The last time we danced together in the living room, the last time we walked down to "our" beach, the last time we sat in the dark out on the porch watching the fireflies light up our trees, the last time we made love.

Did Cordelia know I'd be too enamored of the vague scents lingering in this house, of the shimmers and echoes just out of my sight, just beyond my hearing? Too enamored of sleeping in the basement guestroom bed, of lying there too long upon waking as I listened to her favorite music, aware till it physically hurt that everything I looked at was also what her eyes beheld before they closed forever?

Inevitably, repeatedly, life's banalities pulled me away. But none of it—not eating, not sleeping, not paying bills or grocery shopping ("Remember, Aitch, you're s'posed to save the food stash for emergencies")—no, none of it diverted me for long. And then I'd wander the house again, wake up in the guestroom bed again. And again.

So I stayed here, pretended to myself with Soon: Soon I'll sort my memories, and our stuff. Soon I'll sell the house, join the old ladies at Seaside Point gossiping over their shrimp scampi, singing along with the accordion-playing chanteuse from Wellfleet.

Soon.

And hell, maybe I would've done all that. Eventually.

But it's way too late now.

CHAPTER FOUR

NEVER KNOW WHAT MIGHT BE WORTH WITNESSING

If you were alive and sentient when the Bal Diwas Incident went down, I bet you damn well remember the moment you learned about it—where you were, how you heard, what you did next.

No surprise that I was alone on that now infamous fourteenth of November. Scarcely past the exhausting litanies of condolence, already devoted to an assortment of rituals I'd conjured to keep Cordelia from fading. Only occasional glances at a TV weather channel linked me to the rest of the world.

But that morning, my chosen TV weather channel had been transmogrified by newsreaders bumbling wide-eyed and disbelieving over the words they spoke, reporting with maps, then seismographs—but no video.

Even now, I can hear the quiver in their voices. Immense explosions. Power grids, communications, internet, and transport systems crippled by at least one electromagnetic pulse that arced from the Caspian Sea to Kathmandu. Rumors of firestorms, rumors of vast, viscous plumes of black smoke billowing from some of the largest cities on earth.

As one of those fortunate enough to have been nine to twelve time zones away from where it happened, I'd been oblivious, of course. Still asleep, like most of us in the West. Didn't feel a thing.

Everyone who's ever described to me the moment they learned of Eleven Fourteen talks about a kind of two-fer experience. First, disbelief— no, can't be, I must've got it wrong—and then feeling quite literally physically ill upon grasping that, oh dear god, it really happened.

For me (and, I suspect, most others lucky enough to reside nine to twelve time zones away from the ground zeros), shock gave way to numbness as each freshly horrific *BREAKING NEWS!* announcement piled on. Like getting shot up with procaine by the dentist, my body seemed to lose sensation and become clumsily oversized and alien as I listened to reports of one military after another leaping into high alert, one stock exchange after another closing, air traffic halting country by country, borders slamming shut.

Accident? War? Where exactly and is it over yet? What if it cascades all across the globe, cascades right into every neighborhood on every continent? Is civilization coming to an end?

Do you remember how the "world leaders" staged themselves in front of their gold-fringed flags and tried to reassure, some of them visibly trembling as they resisted going off-script? Too bad; without a damn script, they might've blurted something worth hearing.

I'm not sure, even now, what disturbed me more at the time—that the potentates and their politician lackeys knew the answers but weren't saying, or that they stood there genuinely clueless. Either way, even in my numbness I resented how they kept lamely muttering "Unprecedented" without ever quite providing this attention-grabbing adjective anything to modify.

Soon enough, I had more personal questions: Could this be why Cordelia insisted we build such a ridiculously large stockpile of damn near everything? And what was I supposed to think about the fact that Unprecedented went down six weeks *to the day* after she died?

I studied my favorite photograph of her. "How the hell could you have known?"

Cordelia grinned back, ever thirty-seven years old, ever beautiful, the gleam in her blue, blue eyes ever impishly playful—and said nothing.

"Right," I muttered at her. "Sometimes coincidence really is just coincidence. Right."

If she'd been here, she'd have urged me to switch from the weather channel to one of the news channels. So I did. Not that it mattered. This news was everywhere.

Hour after surreal hour, tremulous assurances looped into a hypnotizing mantra about no radioactive fallout here—no, no, not nine to twelve time zones away—while I, we, waited for more information, for photos, for video. The skies were clear above the Outer Cape, the air November-crisp but not yet nipping. And hardly any wind here in this place twenty miles out to sea that's almost always at least a little windy.

I remember that quite clearly: hardly any wind.

❖

What happened when the numbness wore off was predictable, I suppose. And it wore off damn fast as soon as those first few endlessly recycled videos appeared.

Burned, sobbing children. Smudged mothers' thousand-yard stares. Before-and-after aerial camera footage of places I, for one, had never heard of: Island City's unrecognizable ruins ablaze, Gwadar Port's gleaming container cranes now melted and mangled, utter obliteration where the Tarbela Dam once held back the Indus River, flames licking the blackened rubble of what had been the Red Fort—or was that once the Azadi Tower?

And over it all, dismally dominating every single frame, the heavens had already lowered into an eerie purple-brown dusk. Wow, I whispered, grateful to be hunkered nearly half a world away.

No more than a dozen videoclips, but they triggered a worldwide freak-out. Remember all the reports, the images from undamaged places thousands of miles from any of the impacts? Hysterical crowds wailing prayers. Inebriated men roaming city streets, torching buildings, shooting guns, looting cars and stores, attacking women.

Even those overwintering in my half-empty North Truro neighborhood were affected. This became evident when loud bangs echoed through the hollow alongside the house—firecrackers rather than gunfire, I could only hope. Perhaps, I mused, some of the older folks were recalling those absurd mid-twentieth-century duck-and-cover drills, fretting about the suddenly real possibility that they'd never see another Fourth of July.

But then—did you notice how the freak-outs seemed to ebb after that incident at Indianapolis International Airport, the one where passenger-posted phone videos recorded several crazies inexplicably attacking the flight crew during takeoff minutes before the plane crashed?

I have two theories: Repeatedly watching those videos—including the later ones showing the enormous widebody jet cartwheeling wing over wing down the I-70 interstate until its full load of fuel burst into a colossal fireball—sobered us into behaving like adults. Or, alternatively, ever since Indianapolis the media has been menaced into suppressing reports of the worst of our tantrums.

Anyway, by comparison, my freak-out (yeah, there was one) seems pretty minor:

While those first devastating images replayed ad nauseam on my TV, I spiraled back to a moment a week or so before Cordelia died when I peered at her, silently contemplating my own end and the hand I might take in it. I reckoned I'd stick around as long as I could sense her lingering energy—like the waves from the wake of a passing boat—and when the last of her energy had entirely dissipated, *then* I'd be outta here, too.

Cordelia understood, the way she invariably understood what went on in my head. "You promised me, Aitch," she said.

I sucked back most of my tears and tried to smile at her, acutely aware that we had only a few smiles left. I'd assented to not leaving "before my time," but I knew she appreciated the temptation. "You're strong," she encouraged me, her once resonant voice shriveled by the imminence of her departure. "Never know what might be worth witnessing."

Over our forty-five years together, Cordelia and I had talked plenty about Why We're Here. It's not about "winning," we agreed. "Win what exactly?" Cordelia would ask. We didn't want babies or billions. Nor approval or fame or martyrdom to the chimeras of some brittle, ephemeral ideology.

"I have no clue why I'm here," Cordelia would always end up saying at some point. "I'm just an involuntary guest, but I try to make the best of it."

I needed more, though. "Maybe we're here for the sake of our passions," I once proposed, "since passion is how we embrace beauty— and, if the poet got it right, how we also embrace truth."

"Orgasms are beautiful—and true, too," Cordelia teased me, her eyes sparking as she slithered closer. "I do kinda like the notion that our larger purpose is orgasms. Definitely a hypothesis worth testing."

I nudged my hip between her legs. "As long as everybody gets one."

Cordelia nudged back. "Only one?"

Another time I suggested, "Maybe we're here simply to love and observe."

"So," replied she-who-never-forgot-anything, "we're here to lovingly observe the passions arising from beauty and truth embraced?"

"Mmm, wait," I said. "More than 'observe'…"

"To bear witness, then."

"Well, yeah," I said after a moment. "And witnesses testify, right? About how the beauty we witness is true and how the truth we witness is beautiful."

"Nice mix, Aitch. Corny but nice. A witness testifying to love, passion, beauty, and truth. Everything but the kitchen sink. I say we go with that."

"You are incorrigible," I told her.

"That's because I can't resist the way you bear witness." Cordelia smiled—god, how I miss seeing that smile. "Your oral testimony is so—" Her smile broadened into a grin. "So beautiful." And then she kissed me softly, slowly…

Standing in the middle of our living room in the early After of Eleven Fourteen, I had to chuckle just a little: Cordelia's taste for irony was unbounded. Literally.

Then, in a blink, there she stood a few feet away, breezily shaking her head as her smile, *that* smile, flashed, tangible enough to yell at.

"Dammit, Deels! Why the fuck aren't you here with me for this crap?!"

In the tiny sliver of that second, I felt like I could step across some threshold and be with her. Just a step…

But, of course, I blinked again. And was alone again.

So I waited. I stood in the middle of our living room and blinked and waited for Cordelia who didn't come back. For days, I returned to that spot in the living room and stood there, blinking, waiting.

Thing is, life makes its claim. Like gravity.

So what if Cordelia's dead?

So what if at least 200 million people were immolated in mere minutes and the count continued rising daily in seven-figure and eight-figure increments?

I still had to pee every couple of hours or so.

The electric company still meticulously counted monthly solar net metering credits and wanted whatever was owed after that paid by the due date.

And in Truro there was, still, but one way to deal with running out of ground beef or frozen yogurt or grapefruit.

Even though Cordelia was dead.

Chapter Five

Back to Normal

When was the last time you considered what you really know? Not the manipulations of word and sound and screen calculated to mold your beliefs, your desires, your purchases, your votes—calculated by algorithms massaging gigs of data about where you live and where you go, how much you're worth, with whom you communicate, the apps you use, all that you buy and watch and photograph and write and say and search for and wish for...

What do you *really know* because you've seen it with your own eyes, heard it with your own ears, smelled it with your own itchy nose?

Not much, I bet. Not much at all.

At first I was naive enough to assume we'd eventually learn the truth about Eleven Fourteen—why, who the hell started it, what it will fuck up and for how long.

No more.

We'll never be told the full story—not even close, and not least because Eleven Fourteen appears to have incinerated many of the arrogant fools who let it happen, while those able to skitter away will forevermore deny any involvement. Plus we all should damn well recognize that the extant potentates have, by commission and omission alike, fake-newsed the hell out of plenty of what's happened since.

Pardonable, I suppose, given how scary-fast swarms of people were engulfed by what our nation's fourth president once called "the turbulency and weakness of unruly passions."

Doesn't take much for such swarms to upend that delicate economic, political, and social balance so essential to potentate privilege—especially when the swarms come armed with an arsenal of blunt internet instruments. Not to mention assault weapons.

Don't get me wrong. I have no fondness for potentates or their lackeys. Plenty of evidence points to them being profit-obsessed psychopaths engaged in collusive criminal enterprises that take too much from too many—the necessarily evil result, ultimately, of *any* construct that relies on hierarchy.

Yet isn't hierarchy inevitable?

"It's survival of the fittest in an evolving world," Cordelia used to retort impatiently after encountering Pollyanna social media posts about how we should all live hierarchy-free. "So at any given moment some will be more fit than others. And that, like it or not, is a hierarchy."

Then she'd cite what she considered the most basic, no-alternative rule imposed upon all life on earth, regardless of provenance: "We have to eat each other to survive, and who gets eaten by whom—well, c'mon, that's *the* hierarchy. And it makes us all murderers. No matter what. The really lucky ones get away with their crimes and become 'the rich,' the unluckiest get eaten, and those in the great unwashed middle get by."

Whereupon she'd indulge in pause-for-effect. "But sure as hell, Aitch, none of this was my idea. So I'll try to cause as little damage as I can while doing what's necessary to stay safe and score as much time with you as possible."

Sharing that ethos, Cordelia and I finagled luck and perseverance into an agreeable niche wherein we worked together using our brains, ducked the worst of the rapacious male gaze, and managed not to misuse the people we dealt with.

About a third of the way along, we dared to launch a home-based business comprised of only the two of us. That and being female cost us a lot of money, but (full disclosure) by luck and perseverance we were able to modestly and mostly legally support ourselves, pay off our debt, and even build a small stash of savings—all of which put us among what Cordelia called Society's Comparatively Free Peasants.

Not bad for two out dykes living on the jagged edges of an eroding middle class through the increasingly feudal decades before and after the turn of the millennium.

Which accounted for my quandary in those early After Eleven Fourteen days.

Yes, the existing hierarchy was shamefully corrupt, jiggering rules to its own inequitable advantage. Yes, its outrageously greedy potentates had to be constrained. But at the price of the sort of unruly passions that propel widespread urban violence and cartwheeling jetliners?

I inclined to No. As did the potentates and their lackeys. Thus the need for a prophylactic media campaign designed to distract us all from Eleven Fourteen's consequences. And to tamp down expectations about what the future holds.

It came straight out of some junior lackey's Advertising 101 notes: Forego rational, informative messages for emotional, sentimental ones (kids and babies help); keep it simple by using words and pictures that are easy on the mind and easy on the eye; make sure attractive people do the talking, preferably with easily remembered slogans that rhyme; employ lots of repetition, lots of repetition.

I called it the Soon We'll Be Back to Normal crusade. You saw it every time you watched a politician speed-talking as dully and drily as possible through the Eleven Fourteen scary stuff that simply couldn't be dodged. The first of these that I recall was delivered in a low, parched baritone: "The Bal Diwas Incident resulted from hostilities, not accident."

Then—

Did you notice that before you even had a chance to contemplate the implications of what you'd just heard, you were bombarded with divertissements? Vignette about gallantry and/or love. Spiel about why "everyone" is so breathless over the really cool benefits of cutting back on [fill in the blank]. Sports highlight acclaiming the "heroism" of some steroid-drenched catch or pass or jump or hit.

I was sufficiently pissed off by the way they did this that, for a few weeks early on, I resisted by browsing arcanely specialized websites in an attempt to gather scraps of "real" Eleven Fourteen information and then try to make it all into something.

Alas, I didn't manage to make it into much. But from what I can tell it's more than most people know, even now. Because the official version(s) of what happened are beyond mendacious.

Have you realized, for instance, that at least 100 and maybe as many as 200 "mid-size" warheads were detonated across northern India, all of Pakistan and Afghanistan, and most of Iran? Yes, *at least a hundred* warheads, perhaps twice that—not the twenty or thirty we first heard about.

And all those urban ground zeroes span an irregular 1,000-mile by 600-mile swath while abnormal weather across south Asia on November

14 (a low-pressure system over the North Arabian Sea that spawned easterly winds) pushed the effects of the explosions farther westward into additional geographies already forgotten because they were too economically inconsequential to matter.

Then there was that oft-repeated line about "Only a tiny fraction of the world's nuclear arsenal was deployed in a limited area." Indeed, those 100-200 detonated warheads don't add up to even two percent of the nuclear warheads in the world. So we have more than ninety-eight percent to go.

And the hey-it's-not-so-bad claim that the area affected by Eleven Fourteen constitutes less than three percent of the planet's habitable land mass? Keep in mind that this "tract" is larger than the size of Alaska and includes at least seven percent of the world's arable land. That's approximately 250 million formerly arable acres, once capable of feeding hundreds of millions of people. But no longer. And nobody wants to talk about it, even now.

There was more, all of it worthy of squinty-eyed skepticism.

About how, yes, okay, although international finance and trade *have* been affected and will experience "some trivial inconveniences," supply chains will nevertheless see only slight disruption.

About how reports of another, or maybe the same, highly infectious virus with pandemic-level mortality rates at the edges of the ground zeroes "were recklessly exaggerated and should be regarded as unreliable"— especially any speculation that this so-called Eleven Fourteen Virus might indeed become pandemic, since "an effective *new* vaccine is currently in the late stages of development."

About how, unlike the atmospheric impacts of a significant volcanic eruption, "the effects of this tragic incident have begun to dissipate and will remain largely imperceptible beyond the Incident Impact Zone."

All of that sounded damn dubious to me, and I had plenty of questions about supply chains and transport systems and food and medicine stockpiles and what the hell does "atmospheric impacts" mean, anyway?

But here's where I dead-ended, because beyond discovering that the United States no longer maintains a federal grain reserve, I just couldn't get any useful details. Not via an internet that was being overtaken before my eyes by the carefully contrived distractions of Soon We'll Be Back to Normal.

❖

Certainly I grasped why, all around me, Normal was what everyone yearned for. Why social media interactions seemed suddenly even schmaltzier and more cloying than before. Why once squabbling children sought to sleep in bunches. Why restaurants and bars were jam-packed with people in dire need of a crowd, any crowd, and so many got so drunk so often.

But I comprehended this from a distance, almost abstractly—the price of never being very good at Normal, especially the relating-to-others part. Even when I was a little kid, I couldn't quite pull off the girlfriend stuff that everyone else seemed to so easily and enduringly slide into. A new girl would arrive in the neighborhood at the beginning of summer and we'd be best buddies till school started in the fall. A couple of weeks later, she'd be treating me like a distinctly unappealing stranger.

It got better—or, I suppose, I did—later, when I was grown, escaped from the claustrophobic suburbs of Chicago and trying to connect with the lesbian community in Boston. I had real friends and relationships, too, in that volatile way horny young dykes do, and even now there's one or two left from those days to whom I've remained thinly threaded.

But I hadn't seen them in years and, truth is, they were never more than acquaintances, the last of the people who once upon a time had a crush on me and who stuck around after I found Cordelia because they ended up with a crush on her. All the people I had a crush on are long gone, lost in the folds of time.

During the twenty-seven years we lived on the Outer Cape, Cordelia and I occupied a kind of no-man's-land between the year-rounders who depended on the local economy and the summer people who were, ultimately, just visiting. We were year-rounders but didn't make our money locally, nor did we leave in the winter—thus both camps regarded us, semi-suspiciously, as outsiders. Especially the locals.

To the extent we had contact with other Outer Cape people, it was Cordelia who developed and tended those few relationships. And, yes, everyone—those we'd stayed in touch with from back in the day and the newbies alike—had been kind and caring as she was dying and after she was gone. But they had a hunger for Normal even before Eleven Fourteen that only intensified after Eleven Fourteen—a hunger I couldn't share.

I mean, how the hell could anything ever be Normal again?

Thus I politely declined the you-shouldn't-be-alone invitations to Thanksgiving dinner, Christmas dinner. Cordelia and I would do the holidays like we nearly always did: just the two of us. Simply a matter of cutting the recipes in half.

CHAPTER SIX

ENTROPY

God, how I wanted to see Cordelia the way I'd glimpsed her when I blinked that day right after Eleven Fourteen and she appeared before me for one smiling second. But I had to settle for my own desperately contrived ghost-sense of her, like a shadow only lighter, an echo only fainter. Remembered wisps of who and how she used to be—her touch, her laughter, what we'd talk about, where she'd sit, the meals we'd share, the TV shows we'd watch together.

Not once back then did I dream of her either, though I hoped, I waited. But no.

Until the morning right after Christmas when I woke to the sound of a single word. "Entropy," someone said. Someone female.

"Deels?"

I asked it out loud, wishing I was sure that, yes, Cordelia had spoken to me, yes, even if only in a dream of my own making.

"Deels, was that you?" But damn, I couldn't be sure.

So was she trying to tell me something? Was *I* trying to tell me something?

"Yeah, thanks, that's great," I grumbled as I began to pace from room to room and talk to the diaphanous, wavering image of Cordelia I'd taken to imposing on the empty space she'd occupied for so long. "I get one word? *One?* Not even a whole sentence?"

No reply.

I tried again, loudly: "Entropy, my ass!"

No reply.

On the theory that I needed to show Cordelia how I was in fact *not* breaking down and becoming disordered, I spent the next three days cleaning the house, starting at the top and working my way down. I even cleaned the garage.

And though I didn't throw out any of Cordelia's stuff, by the end of the third day the garbage cans were overflowing. So on the fourth day, since Truro has no garbage collection, I decided to make a quick run to the town dump.

Innocuous, right? But for me it changed everything.

CHAPTER SEVEN

DUKA

One day back when she seemed healthy, no end in sight, Cordelia discovered a twenty-something kid working for a local builder in Provincetown. "Ten feet up a ladder on Commercial Street, clearly playing on Team Sappho," she noted at the time. "A little taller than me, maybe even five ten, and a hell of a lot stronger than me. Also quite talented with a nail gun."

She got the kid talking and detected what she called "stand-your-ground aspiration"—which she contrasted with the unquestioning, common variety conformity to which so many succumb. Cordelia preferred people who've found their ground, or at least recognize the general area where it's located, and strive accordingly. And she preferred women to men, especially around her house. So she inquired whether this "appealingly high-spirited" stranger might accept small home improvement projects on the side.

The kid's answer was yes. The kid's prices also ran slightly lower than her (mostly male) competitors, her work was very good, and she completed it when she said she would.

So Mariana Duka Canché became our fix-it wiz. Small project by small project, we realized we'd found ourselves a genuine jill-of-all-trades, accomplished at not just carpentry but also masonry, all manner of metalwork, fixing engines and motors, even a little plumbing. And besides all of that, she was an apprentice electrician working toward qualifying as a journeyman.

She built storage drawers into our upstairs bedroom knee walls, climbed higher on ladders than either Cordelia or I dared to replace damaged cedar shingles and install new light fixtures. She rebuilt our decayed front steps, repaired a bunch of porch screens, and constructed the storage area in the basement where I later stacked all those food buckets and cases of cans and jars.

As you might guess, I forgot about home improvement projects when Cordelia got sick. I'd forgotten about Mariana Duka Canché, too—until I was driving to the dump that day after my first Cordelia-deprived Christmas, the rear of our twenty-year-old Subaru piled high with garbage bags. Half a mile from the house, the car sputtered out right in front of the ramshackle cottage on the corner where our private lane meets South Highland Road—and kept right on sputtering when I tried to restart it. So much for Cordelia's scrupulously scheduled maintenance.

As I sat behind the wheel cursing and fumbling in my pocket for my wallet and the AAA card I hoped I'd remembered to put in it, Mariana Duka Canché appeared at the car window with tongue-tied apologies for not contacting me after she'd read Cordelia's obituary in the local media.

Oh jeez another one, I thought, ducking and shrugging past the I'm-so-sorries until she finally took a breath and I had a chance to change the subject by gesturing toward the shabby cottage with its ugly flat-roofed addition, a structural hodgepodge I had often wished somebody would demolish. "Do you live here?"

She nodded with an expression harboring—what? Regret maybe, or frustration? The building's large studio space had attracted her, she said.

I concede I was only half-listening—until she told me, frowny and thin-lipped, that she'd moved in right after last Labor Day. Something—her face perhaps, or the tone of her voice—made me pay enough attention to realize that her hair's cropped black tangles had been too long neglected, that she'd lost weight. I looked at her more carefully.

The robust, muscled frame I remembered seemed almost gaunt beneath layers of frayed sweatshirt and worn denim. Shadows darkened her deep-set eyes, her broad cheekbones claimed new prominence—and for the first time, the discreet hook high on her long, narrow nose struck me as downright baroque.

Perhaps life at the low end of what had been, before the pandemic, a highflying economy built on well-heeled tourists and owners of pricey second homes was taking its toll. At that moment, I figured Mariana Duka Canché wanted to tell me so, and I girded; over the years, Cordelia and I regularly heard versions of this same story of failed fantasies, imploded dreams, and desperate bargaining with the fates for just one more chance.

Instead, I was peppered with questions about my Subaru and an offer to look under the hood. Not long after I managed to release the hood latch, Mariana Duka Canché offered a diagnosis. "Maybe the fuel line or plugs, but let's start with the air filter." She barely paused before continuing. "An' yep, it's pretty clogged. Y'know, I think I got one of these. Gimme just a minute."

With a long stride, she darted into the ramshackle place and returned a moment later with a tablet-sized rectangle that she snapped into position somewhere on the other side of the hood while I recalled when I'd last seen her: late May. We'd hired her to erect our basement storage shelving but opted not to burden her—or us—with any mention of the terminal diagnosis Cordelia had received only a few weeks earlier.

Although the intervening months seemed to have diminished those appealingly high spirits that once attracted Cordelia, Mariana Duka Canché's skill as a mechanic remained as honed as ever. In a few minutes, she'd fixed the car and refused several times to let me pay her, not even for the part she installed.

"Okay," I said, "then how about coming over for dinner? Sunday maybe? I'll roast a chicken with potatoes and veggies."

Her eyes flared, which I took to mean that she was as surprised by my invitation as I was. But she smiled and agreed. And come Sunday I managed to do a decent two-bird version of Cordelia's roast chicken dinner.

I didn't learn a whole lot more about Mariana Duka Canché that day. I'd already noticed her upper Midwest inflection: strong rhotic as well as flat, nasaled vowels and anything ending with an -ing pronounced with a long ee sound—so, for instance, "anything ending" becomes "anytheen endeen." I suspected northern Illinois or perhaps Wisconsin, not far from my own beginnings. But before I could broach the subject and ask, she informed me that she preferred being called Duka.

"'Mariana' is just too damn frou-frou for someone like me," she declared with brusque edginess, pronouncing her first name the way someone who speaks Spanish or Italian would. Mah-rrrr-ee-*ah*-nah.

Maybe on another day I'd learn about the source of that wound. And yeah, I thought as I watched her, she's right: not remotely femme, not cute. Her face veered from marginally handsome, when her jaw and that nose encountered the right light, to just plain...plain. And you never knew from one glance to the next what you'd behold.

Besides, upon being reminded, I had to admit that Cordelia *did* always call her Duka.

So I quietly apologized. For about half the meal, our interaction stayed a tad starchy, taking refuge in safely shallow topics—the weather, the pros and cons of buying a used car versus a new one when the Subaru finally gives out for good, what the ramshackle place's landlord was like—until I confessed how much and how erratically the world had clouded for me since That Day when I found myself face-to-face with the diagnosis that sealed Cordelia's fate.

Then I managed to change the subject (to food) and cajole Duka into accepting a large second helping, which she polished off so thoroughly that I persuaded her to take home the other chicken I'd roasted, along with a quart-size container of roasted potatoes and carrots and onions and celery—an exceptionally generous gesture even in those early days after Eleven Fourteen, but hey, she looked like she needed it and she seemed so young and too close to the edge and I liked her.

"I'm guessing you don't cook a lot," I said. Takes one to know one, I didn't say.

Duka dipped her head—a nod, I surmised—and, after acknowledging that she pretty much lived on peanut butter and supermarket bread, rewarded me with a small, reciprocal confession: She'd gotten stuck in an "it's complicated" with her sort-of girlfriend Essie, who'd gone off to Florida with plans to return in time to pony up half of the ramshackle place rent, which was due to nearly triple come next May. But Essie had begun to prevaricate.

"She's staying with one of her exes, really getting into West Palm," Duka mumbled, then glanced at me—warily, I thought, but not, I knew by then, wary of me as the words spilled out. "Essie says she an' this ex are just good friends now, no messing around. Says I should move down there so the two of us can get our own digs. But I don't wanna live in Florida. I like it here."

The next time I saw Duka, a few days later, she was in front of the ramshackle place hitching a snowplow to the front of her truck. "They're saying as much as a foot overnight," she told me when I slowed down the Subaru to wave and say hi.

I'd spent the morning with Cordelia's '70s greatest hits, so this was news to me. Until then, the winter had been bleakly cloudy but pretty mild; we'd seen only a couple of dustings of snow. Hence I hadn't lined up anybody to clear the driveway. "You do snowplowing now?" I asked her.

"Since last winter." Duka straightened and patted her large gray pickup truck. "I'm kinda hoping we get more snow than last year so this baby'll pay for its keep."

"I can help with that a bit if you've got the bandwidth for another customer," I said, then on impulse added, "And if you do my driveway last, I'll feed you." Because I'd enjoyed cooking up Cordelia's recipe more than I'd anticipated. Because my anti-entropy campaign might benefit from cooking again, which Cordelia always insisted was more satisfying when done for two. "What're your feelings about meatloaf, mashed potatoes, and broccoli?"

Duka cleared my driveway one other time, too (homemade chicken and veggie soup, Cordelia's Irish soda bread), before that mid-January day when I saw she'd finished plowing but hadn't rung the bell seeking her fifty bucks and my promised spread of blueberry-walnut pancakes, pear compote, and too much bacon. As I opened the door and called out hi, she looked up with one of those time-halting glances that instantly becomes an indelible memory because so many thoughts coalesce around it.

I didn't know I was seeing what might be my last clear, sunny day *ever* as the northwest wind chased a few lingering clouds out to sea and the sky's blue arched with an almost electric intensity over the crackling-white, unsullied snow that draped the undersized woods around my house.

I did know, somehow, what Duka would tell me, a next step along the inevitable path she'd travel and where, ultimately, it would bring her—not specifics, but the gist, the bottom line. I should not have known this; I don't know why I knew. But I did. I knew how I'd respond and how she'd respond to my response. I knew that down the road a bit I'd briefly regret it, then I'd un-regret it, and then I'd be grateful in an accepting-my-fate sort of way.

Soon enough, though, the knowing faded. Not that I forgot it exactly or chose to disbelieve it. More like it was overshadowed. Overwhelmed.

CHAPTER EIGHT

BLACK COLD

In retrospect, I realize that the dimming began almost immediately—certainly by the time I got around to noticing how extravagantly those crimson sunsets backlit the trees on the high western slope of my property.

I remember that noticing. Within a month of Eleven Fourteen it nagged, or tried to: Pay attention! That red means something, that red's too damn red...

There was another hint, too: The app on my computer tracking how much electricity the solar panels on my roof were generating displayed smaller and smaller bars on its graph—notably smaller than all the prior years.

But for long stretches I was too distracted to check the app, to focus on anything beyond sustaining memories of Cordelia and plodding through another day's chores. What little energy that remained got dragooned by my itch to search websites for arcane bits of information about Eleven Fourteen and its aftermath.

My website searches had always been superficial—just the parts of the internet declared safe by my cybersecurity service provider. No dark web, certainly no hacking (hell, I wouldn't begin to know how to hack anything)—but sufficient to earn a living as a writer of analysis-tinged technology marketing bullshit.

After Eleven Fourteen, my usual online search habits helped me pretend for a while that maybe I had control over something, that at least I might be able to see past all the Soon We'll Be Back to Normal hype.

Ah, well.

Network by network, server by server, site by site, all but the most frivolous and banal parts of the internet were 404ed or stuffed with unclever, obvious malware that sent my security software into tizzies. And Eleven Fourteen death toll reportage entirely disappeared.

Meanwhile, a fawning living-better-modestly theme infested everything from news and documentaries to dramas, comedies, and commercials. Nor was there any escape, other than the OFF button, from the excruciating PSAs explaining yet another new-but-no-big-deal regulation that claimed to make life easier and/or fairer—hint hint hint about how much harder and scarier and less fair life was becoming, and no relief in sight.

Reality doesn't bite. It gnaws.

As reality gnawed on me, I finally surrendered to it: I was too tired, too alone, too relict to achieve control over anything. I ceased rummaging through what was left of the internet, abandoned the scant social media presence I'd maintained after Cordelia died, and never quite got around to checking my solar panel app or considering the implications of overly brilliant red sunsets. Instead, I turned up the volume on Cordelia's favorite music, which somehow always kept time with the unfaltering throb of my ache for her, and let myself just, well, drift...

So in late January I was as spooked as everyone else when a thick, somber daytime shade swept the whole of North America and less than a week later shrouded its upper two-thirds in complete darkness (so much for solar power) followed almost immediately by cold.

Really *deep* cold.

The black cold, everyone called it, and on the coasts especially, it colluded with the wind, which, around here, rarely eased below thirty miles an hour and regularly gusted to twice that.

Step outside for more than a few minutes without dressing for arctic conditions and you risked your life. People died from the black cold while waiting for buses and subways, they died on snowbound sidewalks, in their cars, their garages, even their houses—though after the first couple of weeks, the shocking media reports waned.

Maybe everyone swiftly mastered the new art of black cold attire. Maybe they stayed indoors. Or maybe the media tamped down reporting all but what seemed like a continuous dribble of celebrity freezings.

❖

Certainly, the black cold did a number on the Soon We'll Be Back to Normal crusade, whose pundits initially insisted we were experiencing nothing more than "a brief stretch of record-setting stormy weather across the northern tier of the country."

Thus about a week after daylight vanished from virtually anywhere north of the fortieth parallel, I began to spot reports of local authorities across New England urging their citizenry to "shelter in place" rather than attempt travel to warmer locales. As the black cold intensified, these shelter-in-place warnings grew more widespread, more frequent, more strident.

Explanation-wielding "experts" started appearing on screens everywhere to tell us how vast amounts of very hot black carbon smoke and particulates from the Eleven Fourteen ground zeroes had lofted high into the earth's atmosphere—lofted fifteen, twenty, thirty miles above us, all the way through the troposphere into the stratosphere and even the mesosphere.

Like a volcanic eruption, they said. But a whole lot worse, they said, because so much black carbon smoke had so quickly wreathed the entire planet. Over a period of about two months, many areas experienced "unusual" darkness and, because of the loss of light and heat from the sun, suffered "exceptionally" cold temperatures.

Why had some areas gone so much darker than others? The experts trotted out a parade of occasionally contradictory theories. But not to worry, we were told—this fluctuating "haze" would "soon" shift away from [fill in your location here].

Mid-afternoon video out of Atlanta, for instance, showed almost-daylight—in the form of a dingy gloom just shy of tripping on the city's sensor-activated streetlights.

The Outer Cape, however, was one of those places that Eleven Fourteen's black carbon smoke had fluctuated *to* rather than *from*. Layer on February's typical thick coat of winter clouds, and conditions here went very dark, very cold—as well as very windy and snowy, thanks to a parade of nor'easters that strafed the eastern seaboard and triggered an "uncommon" number of power and especially communications outages.

"Soon" seemed to recede into the black cold, as did "Normal."

And once again, out of irritation as much as anything else, I went looking for more. Despite the earlier frustrations and dead ends, I began where I'd left off—the much-depredated internet. Since I couldn't afford to risk the destruction of a bad malware infection, I concentrated on financial and insurance industry media, the least moronic of what remained available online.

I diligently trailed the few digital crumbs I found to reports from actual scientists who'd conducted relevant, peer-reviewed climate simulations and studies—reports with live links to entire academic papers.

Of course, I downloaded all of it. I even paid exorbitant subscription fees to access peeks behind the Soon We'll Be Back to Normal media curtain, eavesdropping on climatologists, economists, fixers, and their bureaucrat flunkies. Better than nothing, yet it quickly turned into not nearly enough. As the black cold gnawed on and on, I kept wondering what to believe.

Unlike the prevailing view that the black carbon "haze" would soon disperse and Entirely Back to Normal was mere months away, the climatologists' studies and simulations implied that while some black carbon smoke would rain out of the atmosphere, too much may have risen high into the stratosphere, well above any rainclouds.

As time passes, suggested the climate people, Eleven Fourteen's black carbon smoke and particulates would spread out more uniformly but dissipate only very slowly, staying in the stratosphere for years, for decades, darkening the skies, lowering temperatures—and doing immense damage to the atmosphere's ozone layer, thus exposing humans, other animals, and plants alike to dangerous levels of ultraviolet radiation.

Buried in dense pages of arcane climate analyses I found opinions asserting that even those far from the ground zeroes should wear protections against UV radiation—wide-brimmed hats, UV-blocking sunglasses, gloves. Another paper focusing on the black carbon fallout recommended everyone run air filters indoors and don facemasks whenever venturing outdoors. For the foreseeable future. Even if you're nine to twelve time zones away.

I confess I was skeptical—until the day I turned on the porch light outside the living room and saw a fine layer of tiny black dots sprinkled across the snow. "Jeezus, Deels," I found myself whispering, "back to the goddamn facemasks again." Fortunately, we still had plenty; Cordelia had bought boxes of N95 facemasks years ago when we'd had that anthrax scare, and we'd managed to use them sparingly through the pandemic. I also decided to turn on the air filters again, despite the impact on my solar-starved electric bill.

I didn't hesitate, however, to believe what the experts said about coastal areas, which would experience stronger winds for years to come—the result of widening temperature differentials caused by land masses growing colder much faster than large bodies of water. So here in North

Truro, twenty miles out to sea on a strip of sand dune that narrows where I live to a mere two miles across, our newly feral winds would rarely relent, at least not anytime "Soon."

Even worse was what I read about "nutriment" as I hunkered in my darkened basement guestroom. Although nothing I saw made it explicit, it lurked between the lines: People had begun to hoard out of fear that Eleven Fourteen's aftereffects had threatened agribusiness's ability to keep us all fed—and they were probably right to do so.

CHAPTER NINE

WHY AM I BOTHERING?

Through the whole of February and into March we were in darkness. I saw no daylight at all. Not even a vague, feeble glow somewhere in the southern firmament. The Outer Cape's night sky also remained entirely, implacably opaque. No stars, no moon traversing the windows along the back of the house, no Milky Way sweeping over the driveway.

Which I've missed most—the moon or the Milky Way—is a toss-up. In the few weeks before Cordelia died, I'd step outside at night once she slid into sleep and walk the hundred or so feet to the end of our eerily shimmering shell driveway, then back, and do the circuit again and again, staring up at the Milky Way, trying to breathe, my mind unable to form words or even thoughts. Not lucid thoughts, anyway.

After Cordelia was gone, I maintained the habit—my way of impossible-hoping as I paced the driveway: Maybe it hasn't happened yet, maybe she's in there sleeping, just sleeping...

Nor did I give up when I came back inside to an empty room. Maybe she's in the kitchen, feeling better...

I'd blink. I'd pause. Maybe she went up to the second floor, to the study...

Alas, the outcome never varied; I don't appear to be the sort of person who attracts ghosts. But I kept walking the driveway anyway, unable to give up impossible-hoping—until the Milky Way disappeared and the extraordinarily cold air froze all my maybes into an unyielding No.

Anybody assessing me then would probably have decided I was depressed, since even my appetite for chocolate withered. To me, though, it seemed more like I was just running out of motivation. Nothing struck me as worth seeing, or hearing or doing or thinking.

And yes, I was sorely tempted to stop. Simply crawl into bed and stay there for good. It would have been *so* easy. Yet I shuffled on, grumpily acquiescing to the life instinct—that determined, involuntary, incessant rote always tantalizing me with memories of making love with Cordelia, prodding me one more time, just one more time to get out of bed in the morning and do whatever it took to stay warm and fed.

Whatever it took was neither cheap nor as easy as it used to be, since by February the prices of propane, gasoline, electricity, meat, dairy, fruits, vegetables, and anything with a grain in it had more than doubled from what they'd been before Eleven Fourteen.

But I was addicted to staying alive. The life instinct is like that.

Thus I retreated nearly full-time to the best-insulated part of the house—the basement guestroom where I'd already been sleeping for months. I lowered all the thermostats below the usual frozen-pipes-prevention level, down to forty-two Fahrenheit, and except for dealing with essentials (including regular water pipe inspections), I spent entire days in the guestroom bed, swathed in several layers of clothes, burrowed under nearly every blanket in the house, lighting only the room I occupied only during those brief stints when I wasn't sleeping.

And the pipes and I lucked out, since none of the power failures exceeded thirty hours, during which I was able to make do by moving upstairs to the living room, keeping a fire cranked in the living room's woodstove, and minimizing what the propane-fueled generator powered.

As for food, I counted the black cold as an emergency and relied on Cordelia's stash, though I didn't consume a whole lot of it inasmuch as my appetite had withered and I typically ate only once a day.

During this surreal stretch I had vivid dreams, but not of Cordelia. I dreamed of Raskolnikov, easy to recognize given that he hadn't changed at all since I'd met him fifty-odd years earlier, when I was in college living alone on a miserly budget and he inhabited one of the reading assignments I'd decided to tackle during a caliginous, single-lightbulb winter break.

He lived like me, though I suppose it's more accurate to say I lived like him: cold and alone, hungry and imagining (or not) bad guys with a propensity to loom in darkened doorways.

Through that first winter without Cordelia, it was Raskolnikov who crossed the threshold into here-and-now hallucination. Several times I woke to glimpses of him staring at me from, you guessed it, the guestroom's darkened doorway, even when I hadn't dreamt at all. He never spoke, but I felt like he'd been looking at me for a while.

After a time, I started to wonder if maybe he was lurking in the den just beyond where I could see him. His presence seemed real enough that, finally, one turbid day I decided to get out of bed and take a look.

I'd pulled back the bedcovers, had flashlight in hand, both triple-socked feet on the floor—and heard Cordelia's voice behind my left shoulder. "Damn, Aitch, you've always been *ridiculously* credulous."

I whipped my head around so fast I pulled a muscle in my neck. And yes, there she was. Just for a second. She sat cross-legged on the bed smiling, healthy and clear-eyed and not in pain. And wearing those jeans I've always loved.

"Aw, Deels," I said as she dissipated.

I didn't see either of them again, not dreaming, not waking. And, ooh, a few times after that, despite my addiction to the life instinct, I came close to leaving.

And I had the means. Almost immediately upon Cordelia's diagnosis, she was prescribed painkillers and we were both given prescriptions for anti-anxiety meds, all of which I dutifully filled and we both mostly declined to take. After Cordelia died, the hospice people gathered up and took away all their liquid morphine leftovers—but they didn't know about the other stuff stashed in the upstairs refrigerator, and I didn't tell them. So I had all I needed to dose myself anytime I wanted with alprazolam and oxy, then follow up with a fat amaretto chaser.

And a question, *the* question, had emerged from the omnipresent shadows: Why am I bothering?

I had no answer.

But—

Some two or three weeks after Cordelia died, I'd been discovered by my new neighbors—Melinda Reid and Annie Chin, both energetic, forty-ish nurse practitioners. I liked them, which made me want to cry because Cordelia would have liked them as much as I did. She would have described them as winsome. Our long-held fantasy about having lesbian neighbors right across the street in the house closest to ours had come true at last—but too late for Cordelia.

Seeking relief from pandemic-induced exhaustion and PTSD, Annie and Melinda had taken jobs at the health centers in Provincetown and Wellfleet, and they were eager for friendly relations with everyone, something they accomplished quickly. With me, their version was scrupulous adherence to the idealistic adage, Don't Forget to Check on Your Elderly Neighbors.

I admit I sometimes avoided them back then, before Eleven Fourteen. I struggled to engage them by myself, *only* myself, resisted that glimpse through others' eyes of the immense, yawning emptiness that accompanied me everywhere. Better to stick to my established neighbors protocol— the occasional friendly wave or brief chat as I cruised by on the way to somewhere else.

But after Eleven Fourteen, they found an excuse to drop by every week or so. And quickly enough after Eleven Fourteen, I didn't mind.

One afternoon in the early days of the black cold, Annie and Melinda noticed my single basement light and ventured over to make sure I was okay. I took too long to answer the door (for a weird moment, I considered that Raskolnikov might be knocking, and damned if a phantasm was going to get me to open the door to a blast of arctic freeze). So, of course, once I grasped my foolishness, I almost literally pulled them inside and began babbling increasingly embellished versions of "I couldn't believe my ears when I heard you out there."

This only reinforced their instinct to worry about the Old Woman across the street who was, perhaps, not entirely all there. I needed the better part of ten minutes to convince all of us that, in fact, I was. Mostly, anyway. Offering them something hot to drink helped (they chose homemade chicken soup over tea or coffee, so I added some bread and cheese). That's when I learned how severely Eleven Fourteen was dinging local healthcare.

"So many people are leavin' the Outer Cape that the Health Center's scalin' down and consolidatin'," Melinda explained (Melinda filled the room—any room—in body and voice and did most of the talking, while tiny, modest Annie smiled, nodded, and noticed everything). "No urgent care or walk-in services anymore at the Wellfleet Center. Annie and I are the substitutes. We're 'mobile care providers.' Doin' it online, by phone, and with a medically souped-up SUV. Best part's the gas allowance."

Melinda started ticking off the names of long-time Outer Cape year-rounders who'd departed—names I should have recognized but mostly didn't—along with occasional color commentary about who'd gone where. Including too many who had died at home. In the black cold. From the black cold.

Be sure to cover up against the UV radiation, they said, and do you have a facemask? Oh yeah, I responded, brandishing one of my N95s. Let's exchange phone numbers, they said, even though phone service was dicey.

I suggested walkie-talkies and gave them one from Cordelia's walkie-talkie six-pack. After I promised, yes, yes, to stay in frequent touch, they scurried back home again, and not ten minutes later sent a text: *Just checking our cell connection.* Next, we chatted via walkie-talkie to ensure the channel I proposed actually worked.

Annie and Melinda weren't the only ones keeping me from obsessing about *the* question.

For years I'd been on wave-and-chat terms with Lizbie Watts, who lived in the house southeast of mine with her husband, a couple of kids, a dog, and a coop full of chickens. Then, one day before Christmas, she sent her daughter Mirrie over with some fresh eggs—apparently just to be nice. So, of course, I reciprocated (easy to do thanks to Cordelia's stash), and my relationship with Lizbie and Mirrie grew from there as we exchanged more and more of what Mirrie, who was maybe ten or eleven, called "food stuff."

Meanwhile, I'd developed a habit of sorts with Mariana Duka Canché: Every week or so I'd pretend to be Normal, light a fire in the woodstove, then cook a meal and overfeed the two of us.

Duka responded by periodically dropping by with something related to our most recent conversation, which usually focused on local black cold horror stories, black cold survival strategies, and rumors she'd heard about life "over the bridge" off-Cape. She showed up once with half a cord of hardwood that she wouldn't let me pay for; another time it was bundles of oak twigs (the only kindling I can reliably light). And she'd do things like check the generator's oil and battery or stack firewood in the garage or traipse my garbage to the dump.

Early on, I passed along the advice about covering up against elevated UV radiation and wearing a facemask, and after giving her a couple of N95s and a nag or two, she took me seriously. I never saw her outside again without a mask and, during the day, sunglasses, wide-brimmed hat, and gloves. "Even got my buddy Toby doing it now," she told me.

I don't remember when the winter's ferocity induced me to ask if she was getting by all right in the ramshackle place—especially if she was keeping herself warm enough. I hadn't quite realized I'd begun to worry about this until I caught myself quizzing her somewhat overzealously. How cold do you let the place get when you're away working? What about overnight? Are the water pipes staying unfrozen? How many blankets do you have? Do you use a space heater?

Looking mildly amused, Duka explained how she'd cocooned into the ramshackle place's warmest room—yes, with plenty of blankets and a space heater and the landlord paid the electric bill, not her—and, no, the pipes hadn't frozen yet. "So far, so good," she said, her amusement ripening into a grin.

I grinned back. Yep, the Old Woman is indeed a nag, and do you maybe want to stay the night since the woodstove fire will be keeping the whole house toasty till nearly morning?

Oh no, she'd go on home. Her place did need conscientious tending, she said. But, she also said, she'd like me to have a key. Just in case.

"Not even Toby Snow has a key to where I live," she admitted. "We work together, y'know, an' we're pretty close, but I don't get along so good with his girlfriend. An', uh, Essie left her key behind."

When I said me too, the deal was done: We'd exchange keys. Just in case.

All of which meant that if I ceased operations right there in my house, eventually Melinda and Annie would come snooping. Or Duka would show up and unlock the door to my rotting remains, which seemed unfair to do to someone anticipating a nice roast, or at least a polite smile.

And, wimp that I am, Plan B would have to wait; damned if I was going to do it alfresco or even in the car during the worst winter I'd ever experienced in my life.

❖

An afternoon came in mid-March when, by flashlight, I took a break from the infuriating tedium of figuring out my taxes (oh yes, all due on April 15, disaster be damned) and witnessed the thin red line on the Fahrenheit thermometer outside one of the dining room windows reach all the way to zero. A few hours later, Duka showed up.

"Did you see it?" she asked excitedly as I quickly shut the door behind her. "We gotta celebrate!" She smelled of cold and burning oak as she wagged a little baggie in front of me. "Tobyweed," she proclaimed, talking way too fast while she yanked off her boots. "Really good stuff, grows it himself. I thought maybe, uh, maybe we could—"

I couldn't help but laugh, though I didn't find a temperature of zero all that exciting. "You'd like to keep celebrating, but Toby's girlfriend—"

Duka's nod came with a sneer. "Loo-weeeze."

Well, now—I hadn't vaped anything since…?

Since sometime last summer, when Cordelia still functioned at about sixty percent. Okay, I decided, but no music. "So we're celebrating zero? Degrees, that is?"

"We're celebrating *the light!*" Duka nearly shouted as she bounced on her toes. "We saw daylight! Toby an' me. Around noon. Just a kinda lighter fuzziness overhead for a few minutes. Woulda never trusted it if I'd been alone. But Toby saw it, too. It was *real*, I swear!"

I believed her.

A few minutes later, I held high Cordelia's favorite vape, stuffed with Tobyweed, and offered a toast: "Let there be light." Then I put the little black oval cylinder to my lips and inhaled before passing it on. "Now," I urged her as I exhaled, hoping Duka would do the talking so I wouldn't have to, "tell me where you were when you saw the sun."

She obliged, egged on by my (largely involuntary) chortles whenever she inserted a snark about Loo-*weeeze*.

The third time I drew from the vape, or possibly the fourth or the fifth, something loosened in my shoulders first, then in my head, between my temples; I became about fifty pounds lighter and, as I recall, slightly airborne.

Right around then, Duka asked me how I was doing.

"Okay," I said. "But, god, I miss her." And then I kept talking. And eventually I talked about maybe leaving.

Shaking her head, eyes glistening, Duka put down the vape. She tried and failed to speak, her voice cracking before she pulled in a deep breath, let out a sigh, and spoke very softly. "Please, Hester, don't go yet."

I guess it was what I needed to hear.

Chapter Ten

Is *this* worth witnessing?

Duka's friend Toby claims people placed bets on whether the sun would ever be seen again, on when this much-hoped-for "Solar Advent" might occur, on where (only counties north of the Mason-Dixon line need apply). Prizes, some of them sizable according to Toby, would be awarded for the first documented Solar Advent photo and video.

Rumor has it that one of the half-dozen remaining citizens of Seneca, Nebraska, of all places, took the honors—at twenty-nine days. A week after Duka's and Toby's forty-three days, my own Solar Advent arrived, smack dab on the vernal equinox—which seemed ironic in that squirmingly visceral way a Diane Arbus photograph is ironic.

I'd just finished my midday house temperature and water pipe check, pausing on the way from the kitchen back down to the guestroom because I noticed that some of the snow thickly pasted on the dining room windows had finally peeled away. For the first time in weeks, I could get a look outside at the white pines along the back of the house.

Soon after we moved in, Cordelia and I planted five of these fast-growing Cape Cod natives, rare here ever since the early European immigrants cut virtually all of them down for ship's masts and house timbers. We watched ours flourish over the next couple of decades to tower majestically above our south-facing roof, so high that we had to keep them trimmed to prevent them from blocking sunlight to our solar panels.

But when I peered out the dining room window on the vernal equinox—at high noon, no less—the black cold seemed as opaque as ever and I saw squat. So I switched on the outside floodlights, which actually somehow worked, and beheld an iced-over combat zone.

The black cold's wind and snow had bent, broken, and glaciated our white pines into rough, frozen tangles that cost them more than half their height. Beyond these ravages, I saw similar damage to the nearby oak and pitch pine scattered across the rear of the property.

I switched off the floodlights. To save my costly kilowatt hours. To save my sanity. The world outside reverted to the same abject darkness as my dining room. With an urge to tears swelling in my throat and beginning to burn, I turned, intending to follow my flashlight's beam back downstairs to the comparative warmth of the guestroom bed.

And that's when I saw it—as I turned: a small grayishness in the southern sky. I flicked off the flashlight and watched the small grayishness slowly dilate into a hesitant, faint glow behind my broken trees and maybe, possibly glint for a moment off the ice sheathing them. The first natural light I'd seen in fifty days.

"Look at that, Deels," I murmured to my memories. "Qualifies as terrible beauty, don'tcha think?"

And silently, in that squealy private place one tries to hide even from one's own awareness, I half-wondered the question I couldn't bring myself to ask the figment that was all I had left of Cordelia: Is *this* worth witnessing?

❖

My Solar Advent, such as it was, faded after about an hour, and the black cold claimed the next day as it had claimed so many days before.

But the ensuing week seemed almost balmy, temps only a few degrees below freezing. I used the "thaw" to venture forth—first to the garage and an attempt to start the car, which grudgingly obliged, then on to the post office over very poorly plowed roads, where I retrieved weeks of mostly junk mail, and finally to the supermarket in Provincetown, which, given the extended break in the cold, should have been far busier than it was and far better stocked than it was.

Even so, I bought all I could, especially milk, meat, frozen veggies, potatoes, and rice. I crossed paths with several people I knew, too—a normal experience for most, including Cordelia, but unusual for me. Everyone was more than friendly, though—as relieved as I was to see that, yes, we all had a few neighbors left.

Not that this was quite explicit. But I engaged every person I came upon—acquaintance and stranger alike—and they engaged me. We crossed aisles to ask after each other in a deliberately casual way, like this is no big deal.

Yet it *was* a big deal. I saw tears in people's eyes as they groused about how difficult it had become to pay for food and fuel, as they spoke of family, friends, neighbors gone now, to Florida or the Carolinas or an urn on a mantel somewhere.

When I ran into Lizbie Watts, she suggested we team up in future to run errands "to save a few bucks." As soon as I agreed, she murmured, "Thank the fates we decided to stay."

In addition to tending her egg-laying chickens and the greenhouse her husband had built across the back of her house, Lizbie taught fourth grade at the Truro Elementary School, and as she told me stories relayed by her students—of entire families of relatives who'd disappeared within days of departing the Cape, no phone calls, no cars or luggage discovered later, nothing—her usually sturdy, quietly matriarchal bearing faltered.

We were joined by Sylvie Costa, the young woman who helped take care of Toby Snow's mother. She, too, needed the therapy of retelling stories of clients, customers, and co-workers at her father's oil and gas business, where she also worked—stories about whole caravans of people who'd ignored the shelter-in-place warnings and were found frozen to death in their cars.

"By the dozens," Sylvie Costa said, her eyes wide. "Right there on the interstates. And I know it's true. I've seen the pics, the ones all the cops share that never get published."

As Sylvie spoke, Isabella Franzi came up behind me at the supermarket's poultry section and grabbed the second-to-last roasting chicken while she tried to outdo Sylvie with tales of how those lucky enough to "make it south" suffered outrageous exploitation and violent vigilante roadblocks and worse along the way, only to face unabashed intolerance at their destinations and find themselves herded into migrant camp tents and shacks.

"Like dust bowl Okies," said fifty-ish Isabella—whose temperament, wardrobe, and palette wholeheartedly embraced chiaroscuro. She owned a gallery on the east end of Commercial Street in Provincetown that devoted the bulk of its wall space to her photographs, especially the ones she took on her impressively sleek sailboat; her house in the newer, pricier neighborhood just southwest of mine made me suspect she was a closet trust fund baby.

"But, crap, staying in the city *just* isn't an option," Isabella continued, turning with a bit too much flourish to the quite attractive woman accompanying her (someone, usually a quite attractive woman, nearly always accompanied Isabella). "Isn't that right? With those gangs roaming the streets looking for whatever they can get?"

"Well," Isabella's companion offered, "it's to the point in Boston where nowhere's safe. Not even your own house in a decent neighborhood."

I figured there was more to that story, but I didn't hear it till much later. Instead, in typical sweeping-flare fashion, Isabella filled the almost uncomfortable pause by introducing Lizbie, Sylvie, and me to Phoebe Benevides. Younger, blonder, and less contrived than Isabella, Phoebe had retreated to her parents' second home near Isabella's place. "Good thing I kept some clothes there and can work from home," she said, "though my internet service has been spotty since, y'know…"

We all nodded. Phoebe meant the black cold, of course. Her place in Boston's South End had burned near the beginning of the black cold, but she managed to make the drive to the Cape "almost hypothermic but unscathed." She'd lived in her parents' house alone since then, "But at least Mom and Dad are safe in Boca and my sister and her husband and kids are safe in Newton."

Phoebe struck me as the sort of well-kept, upscale high-flyer who'd scuttle back to her urban wonderland as soon as possible. She also needed to talk to anyone who'd listen—perhaps because she needed to steer conversation away from whatever it was that incited the unyielding tension in her face.

So we heard all about the secret nationalization of the banks during the black cold—"when no one's looking, not because anyone would object, but to avoid panic withdrawals." About how nationalization of all sorts of other industries would be essential to "preserving American life as we know it." And about how, despite the Outer Cape's shortages and hyper prices, after Eleven Fourteen we were safer "way out here at the end of the world."

No one disagreed, though the chatter quickly reverted to local matters, and Phoebe went quiet as the others speculated about the businesses and people who would and would not return for the coming summer. Isabella was noncommittal about her gallery, while Lizbie wondered whether the school would be able to open in the fall, since, she said, enrollment had already crashed.

Nevertheless, we mostly smiled our hope, we reassured. We needed the succor of each other's presence, and on this day at least, for a few minutes at least, that's what we got.

Even so, ain't nothin' fer free…

CHAPTER ELEVEN
WHAT HAVE I MISSED?

Our "thaw" heralded another nineteen inches of snow—wet and heavy this time and nearly twice what had been predicted. It piled punishingly overnight atop the layers of earlier, unmelted snowfalls. I heard at least two nearby trees snap—smaller ones, I hoped but had no way of seeing—and I pondered how much more weight the roof over me would tolerate.

Much sooner than I anticipated, Duka arrived to plow the driveway and share the meal I'd planned for us—roast chicken, this time including carrots, potatoes, and onions, but no celery. The supermarket didn't have a single stalk, hadn't had any since before the black cold, and the manager couldn't even guess when it might appear again.

"Everything okay?" I asked Duka from the basement den doorway. She'd finished plowing and had also shoveled out the path to where I stood—but she stayed next to her truck peering upward as she waved a flashlight in the general direction of the roof.

"Might be a good idea to get some of that snow offa there," she replied, then started walking to the rear of her truck. "The smaller two-story section in back is pretty high, but I got a roof rake that'll reach most of the rest from the ground—well, from those drifts—along the front of the house. Gimme a few minutes."

I'd already learned that "Gimme a few minutes" meant Duka would accept no payment for what she was about to do. And usually these favors really did require only a few minutes.

But not this time—because she cleared the entire roof, even the "pretty high" south-facing part at the back. This she accomplished (without accepting even the meager assistance I could offer) by lugging the extension ladder out of the garage, positioning it atop the enormous, ice-hard drifts that had settled along the front of the house—drifts made even larger by the snow she'd already raked—and then angling the ladder's fully extended twenty-eight feet flat onto the roof so she could climb to the peak, rake in hand, and reach the south-facing side.

Almost two hours later, as I took her jacket and she removed her snow-encrusted boots, I asked again. "Everything okay? I didn't expect to see you till—"

She shrugged, her face carefully expressionless. "That's what happens when too many customers decide to dump your ass since they won't be around anytime soon, so who cares how much snow piles up in their driveways an' parking lots. 'An', oh by the way, we're canning your property management services, too, cuz we're selling the damn house ASAP.'" She shook her head. "So much for making money off a snowy winter."

Duka didn't exactly invite touching; I had the sense that she battled a reflex to flinch or even jump away if the wrong hand—just about any hand—came too close. But that afternoon, on instinct, I reached lightly, commiseratively to her shoulder and she allowed my hand to rest there without reacting.

"Let's get you dry and then warm," I said, unable to ignore the *uh-oh* roiling up my esophagus from that squealy private place one tries to hide even from one's own awareness.

❖

I'd never seen Duka consume more than two beers in an evening, but she did that night.

I reckoned the suds substituted for sobs. One hint: She brought Tobybeer, home-brewed to impressive potency by the man himself. So I could try it, she claimed—but hey, she walked in with *two* half-gallon growlers. And although she kept repeating "I shouldn't be doing this," she polished off the first growler in less than an hour.

Sometime during growler number two, she confirmed what I'd already supposed: Her upset concerned more than lost customers.

"Got a Dear Jackass message this morning," she muttered. "Essie won't be coming back from West Palm. Not fucking ever."

And *snap!* Instantly, I found myself on the other side of grief, outside looking in at Duka's misery, my throat and chest surging with *Aw, sweetie* as I watched her try so hard to stay poker-faced. Here, right here, is where we all blank about what to say beyond the usual trite crap that so crudely exposes our self-consciousness and fear...*there but for the grace of...*

I tried to keep it simple, told Duka how sorry I was. I offered food, made eye contact as I sent my hand to her shoulder again, a gesture she accepted, even possibly leaned into a bit. I did my minimalist best, hoping what I said would invite her to talk without making her feel like I demanded or needed anything.

And although Duka's not much of a talker, her face can be quite eloquent; from it one can learn, as I did that evening, when to shut up—whereupon, sometimes, Duka *will* really talk.

Initially, she said nothing else about Essie, shifting instead to how the property management business she'd launched with Toby was a lost cause, how so many customers owed her money. Address by address, she ticked off the delinquents, most from South Truro's Viagra Village subdivisions, the ones exclusively devoted to oversized second homes owned by people who bitched a lot about how much they paid the town in property taxes. "I'll never see a dime. Some of 'em didn't even bother t' ask for their keys back."

"Maybe it's just temporary," I offered, succumbing to the desire to say something, anything positive. "I mean, if they want you to keep their keys..."

The way Duka stared at me made me wonder if I'd naively failed to perceive some obvious truth about the world that was known to everyone but me, and I was about to ask—What have I missed—when, abruptly, her eyes flicked away.

"Was in the cards, uh-course," she sighed as she poured beer from the second growler into her glass. "Essie was jus' playing with me. An', dammit, I *knew* that." A long swig, another sigh, eyes shimmering. "Essie likes t' play. An' play...an'...an'..."

"And you're not really a player, are you?" I said—gently, I hoped.

"Guess not." Duka hunched her shoulders. "Kinda seems like it should be fun—till, y'know..."

"Yeah, till you actually try it."

Duka looked at me again, tears brimming in her eyes. "I don't think I know how t' be happy. I pick wrong. Wrong women. Wrong way t' make a living. Even managed t' put the wrong fucking gas in my fucking truck." She slapped the center of her chest with the flat of her hand. "Me. Can you believe that? *Me*...the wrong fucking gas...like I can afford that..."

"Whoa, back to that wrong women thing," I said. "Maybe you're—"

"I'm a *drag*, Hester—an' *not* the entertaining queenie kind." Gesturing expansively, she lifted the second growler with one hand, emptied glass with the other, and, glass clinking unsteadily against glass, poured out the last of the growler's contents without spilling a drop.

"You're not the one who's a jackass here," I said, but I don't think Duka heard me. Her dam had burst; words gushed out of her, cracking and breaking as they tumbled into the air around us.

"It's official—I...am...a...*drag*. Essie told me that at the airport. I'm a damn fool, too, cuz I trusted her, told her all kinda shit. 'Bout Waukegan. 'Bout how I didn't have money for tickets t' her hoity-toity charity stuff an' I hadda work cuz me an' Toby are trying t' make a business, y'know? Oh no problem, she says. But then I'm no fun, then I'm a drag. An' she gets all pissy an' says 'at least do Instagram, do Tik-fucking-Tok.' But really she got pissy cuz I wouldn't do a threesome with her an' some gender-wiggly unicorn she found."

Down went the last of the second growler in a single audible gulp. "An'...an' then she gets all up in it, worrying her friends'll look at me an' think...*eww!* Cuzza my, uh...¿Cómo se dice?" Duka's face screwed into a grimace. "Oh yeah—my 'checkered past.'"

Certainly I couldn't actually prevent Duka from driving home. The woman has five inches, probably thirty pounds (of muscle), and roughly minus-forty years on me. Nor was she immanently persuadable; sloshed as well as sober, she sought explanations, reasoned arguments.

"You are too drunk to drive anywhere, Duka," I said slowly, articulating each syllable as she loomed over me swaying. "Not. Even. Up. The. Street."

"I'm fine."

"Show me."

When she failed the test we negotiated—stand up straight, feet together, close your eyes and keep your balance while bringing the tip of your index finger to the tip of your nose—I caught her before she toppled and we negotiated again: She'd stay the night upstairs in the master bedroom, where no one had slept in more than six months.

I helped her navigate the stairs and the intricacies of buttons, sleeves, and pant legs. I coaxed her into swallowing a few aspirin, tucked her in, put a glass of water on the bedside table, left a robe draped on a nearby chair, made sure a nightlight showed the way to the bathroom.

And maybe because she'd already nodded off...maybe because I'd had time to peruse the delicate black lines of the spiderweb tattoo that emerged from her untrimmed pubic bush (where the spider hid?) to radiate asymmetrically from just beneath her belly button to her left hip's iliac crest...maybe because there was no denying the jagged scars on her abdomen, on her back, five of them...whatever the reasons, I leaned over her and ran my fingers gently through her hair a few times, the way my grandmother used to do with me.

But my head was spinning—"selling the damn house ASAP," *eww*, Waukegan, those scars, that tattoo, checkered past, wrong women, those scars...

What have I missed?

CHAPTER TWELVE

CONSIDERING

At 6:49 a.m., the coffee table in the living room suddenly began beatboxing. I was so startled by the blitz of clap-whoosh-pop-hiss-click that I nearly dropped the small basket of clean clothes and towels I'd just carried up from the basement. By the time I identified the source of the sounds—Duka's phone—the device had gone quiet, but on its screen I saw four letters:

T o b y

Night owl that I am, I shouldn't have been awake at that abjectly early hour when, in another era, the sun would already be brightening and warming the world around me. At *this* 6:49 a.m., however, the black cold had relented only slightly, and all I dared hope for was a terse midday twilight that might last for more than an hour or two.

Briefly, I'd attempted to sleep, even dozed off a bit after I put Duka to bed upstairs. Not for long, though. The house remained warm from the evening's woodstove fire—an almost Normal environment excellent for after-dinner cleanup and ferrying loads of laundry between washer, dryer, and folding.

I crept upstairs to the second floor once to check on Duka, who hadn't moved at all. For a heartbeat I worried, an effect of those peeks age gives you into how thin the membrane really is between alive and not. *She hasn't moved at all.* But yes, Duka was breathing fine, slow and deep and steady.

That night I thought often about Waukegan, the small industrial city on the shores of Lake Michigan some twenty miles from where I grew up, long past its prime when I was a kid and little improved since. Could

Waukegan be the site of Duka's "checkered past"? Perhaps where she acquired those terrible scars and the tattoo I couldn't help but regard as provocative?

And did it matter if I never found out?

When Duka's phone burst into breathy percussion, I tossed it in the laundry basket I was carrying and continued upstairs to the master bedroom having already promised myself that I would asking nothing—yet.

My houseguest had curled fetally onto her left side but remained well asleep, undisturbed by the hallway light I'd switched on, snuggled into the bed, the room. *Like she belongs here*, I thought, though it seemed more like a whisper in my ear than a notion in my head.

Rather than wake her, I placed her phone on the bedside table, taking my eyes off her while I did this—and found her staring at me when I glanced over again.

"Good morning," I said.

Duka stared at me in silence, her face utterly impassive.

I thought, You don't know where you are yet, do you? I said, "How're you feeling?"

Something flickered in her narrowing eyes. Something hard, gladiatorial even.

Fear?

Mmm, maybe for an infinitesimal. Then she softened, recognizing me and, I realized, registering the room for the first time. That's when she finally blinked, her gaze carefully traversing the bedroom and its high, angled ceiling before she nodded.

"I'm, uh, not too bad." She blinked again. "Oh shit." Her face and shoulders scrunched into a cringe as she remembered more. "I'm sorry. I didn't mean to get drunk like that. I'm so sorry—"

I waved off her apology, adding a small laugh. "No biggie, kiddo. Really." Because, really, I liked having someone else in the house all the night through.

She studied me to make sure, not quite willing to relinquish her scrunch just in case, which made me laugh again. "Really," I repeated.

She smiled back, relaxing some, and indulged in a small wriggle under the blankets. "Nice room. Super comfortable. Haven't slept so good in, um…a while."

I took this as a compliment. Duka did not, I was quite sure, want to get out of the bed Cordelia and I had slept in, made love in for forty-five years.

"Sorry I woke you," I said. "It's pretty early, at least by my standards, so I was trying to be, uh—"

"Stealthy?"

"Well, as unclunky as a clunky person can be. I figured you might want to have some clean clothes to put on when you woke up. Also, you got a call a few minutes ago. From Toby."

Duka groaned, allowed herself a single yawning sigh, then picked up her phone, tapped it several times, said "¿Qué onda, Tobes?"—and three beats later lurched upright in the bed, her face as stone-bleak as I'd ever seen it.

❖

I had hoped Duka would stick around long enough for breakfast and conversation, which I wanted to steer away from our usual here-and-now topics—the bizarre weather, the horrendous price increases, the much-reduced hours at town facilities, the latest rumors about which local businesses have shut down for good and who else had decided to go south, the shortages escalating from can't-get-it-way-out-here to can't-get-it-anywhere.

Instead, just this once, I wanted to talk about origins. As in: I'm guessing from your lingering Midwestern accent that, like me, you come from somewhere near Chicago—Waukegan, perhaps? And that would neatly, smoothly slippy-slide into details about Duka's "checkered past" and that spiderweb tattoo and those cruel scars…

But less than two minutes after her three seconds on the phone with Toby, Duka was dressed and racing out of the house, blurting something in Spanish that, according to the rushed translation I managed to elicit, involved a blacksmith's house and wooden knives.

"Gotta get to my place," she nearly shouted without slowing down. "Rápido."

"What happened?" I hollered after her.

But she was already in her truck, its tires spinning as she skidded it in reverse out of the driveway.

And although I had no obligation to follow her, I did.

❖

Even before I parked my old Subaru behind Duka's truck, which she'd left roadside with the headlights on, I could see that half of the ramshackle cottage where she lived—the large flat-roofed addition built long ago as an artist's studio—had collapsed beneath the snow load it bore, pancaking so completely that most of it stood no more than four feet high. And a large portion of the rest tilted precariously toward the rumple of ruins.

I recognized a few neighbors among a small clutch of flashlight wielding people converged in front of the mess. Several of them, including Melinda, were dragging large black construction bags of god knows what from the edge of the wreckage to the middle of the cottage's snowy driveway. But no sign of Duka. I angled the Subaru so its headlights contributed to the scant light at the scene, exited the car masked, covered up, and carrying a flashlight (as most everyone had been habituated to do by then), and called out, "Where's Duka?"

All of them looked over in response; the Gibsons and the Silvas waved, as did Lizbie Watts and her kids, Mirrie and younger Nate, who was clearly frustrated at not being allowed to treat the scene as a playground. Annie pointed toward what was left of Duka's abode.

But only one person answered aloud—a woman I didn't know.

"Inside," she snarled too loudly, inclining her head toward the destruction. "With *my* Toby. Getting him t' freeze his nuts off an' risk his life fer a few fuckin' tools an' batteries—an' uh-*course* those precious mobiles or sculptures or whatever the fuck they are."

Loo-*weeeze*, I presumed. A bottle blond, I discovered as I came closer, wearing too much makeup and an (unmasked) expression as irate as her smoker's voice was grating.

Adding batteries, mobiles, and/or sculptures to my mental list of Duka curiosities (the tools, at least, made sense to me), I ignored Loo-*weeeze* and approached Annie, who appeared to be, if not in charge, then at least deferred to by the others whenever she said anything.

"Nobody saw it collapse, but the people next door heard it," she told me. "One of 'em called Toby, who got here just as Melinda and I were passing by on our way home. He was afraid Duka was inside, but then we noticed her truck wasn't here—"

"She stayed at my place last night," I said.

Annie nodded. "Yeah, she told us as she went tear-assing in there. Flashlight in one hand, construction bags in the other, Toby right behind her. They've been shouting back and forth and to us, hauling stuff that can be saved to that spot—" Annie gestured at a tunnel-like gap in the wreckage. "Melinda, Lizbie, and a couple of the guys have been moving the stuff clear, but Duka and Toby haven't come back out yet and nobody's sure where they are exactly—in the cottage, we're hoping, given the condition of the studio."

Following my flashlight's beam, I scanned what was left of the splintered structure. "Has it been making those creaking and cracking noises for long?"

Frowning, Annie nodded again. "I wish they'd get the hell out of there." She looked down the street toward South Highland Road. "Been almost half an hour. I'm surprised the fire department hasn't shown up yet. Or at least a cop."

Within a few minutes, both a fire truck and a police cruiser did arrive. Troglodyte that I've been for the twenty-five years I've lived in North Truro, I didn't know any of the firefighters, though one looked vaguely familiar. Nor did I recognize the lone police officer, a woman with three stripes on her parka's sleeve. But Melinda and Annie greeted each one by name, briefed them with clipped precision, and steered them to where Duka and Toby had crawled into the remains of the building.

Which was, by then, where I was standing with Lizbie, Mirrie, Nate, Loo-*weeeze*, and the Silvas. We'd all been pointing our flashlights into the opening and taking turns calling for Duka and Toby (everyone besides Loo-*weeeze*, who, in an oddly canine yowl, called only for Toe-*beee*). The cop—Higgins, according to her nametag—immediately marched over to usher us aside in that officious-polite way cops can be so good at.

"A safe perimeter," I heard her say more than once while the contingent of Truro firefighters lumbered around the ruins, their oversized lightsaber flashlights slashing the darkness. Finally, the one who'd seemed familiar to me—and ostensibly the boss—rather imperiously directed a younger, far more fit firefighter to venture into the opening where we'd been standing. He began to reluctantly obey, then backed out again as Toby, then Duka emerged dragging more construction bags, at which point Sergeant Higgins attempted to herd them, too, behind her "safe perimeter."

Instantly, Loo-*weeeze* enveloped Toby, who was unquestionably skinnier than the last time I saw him. He's a good-sized guy, big-boned and taller than Duka, but next to Loo-*weeeze* he seemed almost small as she possessively stroked his thinning blond hair and push-pulled him toward the street. "Hi, Hester," he managed to say just before he succumbed to her demand for his undivided attention.

Duka, though, refused to be pushed or pulled. "Uh-uh," she insisted. "I got more shit bagged up just inside an' I need to go get it." She turned around to re-enter the structure, but Sergeant Higgins, who's closer to my size than Duka's, blocked her way.

"Please, ma'am." Sergeant Higgins's voice had stiffened from officious-polite to the cold-implicit-threat-of-force tone cops too often find necessary to "maintain the edge." One of her hands rose like she intended to push Duka away from the ruin while her other hand hovered near the weapons on her hip. "Move. *Back*."

Both of them right, both unwilling to relent. To create some sort of distraction, whatever it would take to untangle them as they stood inches apart, eyes locked, I violated the "safe perimeter" and started walking toward them.

"Excuse me," I said from about six feet away.

No one noticed.

The long, silent moment continued; neither Duka nor Sergeant Higgins budged. Everyone else had frozen in place, too—except me. I'd decided to keep going. As I moved closer, Duka, utterly motionless, murmured a single word which I suspect only Sergeant Higgins and I could hear: "Don't."

One Mississippi, two Mississippi—and while I pondered whether that lone word had been directed at me or at Sergeant Higgins, the sergeant stepped aside.

With impressive efficiency and speed, Duka managed to arrange temporary shelter for her stuff a half-mile away in a recently vacated garage-like commercial space at the North Truro Tradesmen's Center. Aided by Toby, Melinda, the Gibsons, and Lizbie's large, bearded husband, Sam Behr, the well and septic guy, she carted most of it over there in a caravan of pickup trucks. I went along to help because something told me not to go home yet, and lugging a few bags beat listening to Loo-*weeeze*, who stayed behind to flirt with the boss firefighter.

"Before Eleven Fourteen, the Tradesmen's Center had a long waiting list, but now two of the four buildings are empty—which is why Greg Silva's giving me a couple months gratis," Duka murmured to me after thanking him profusely. "He's hoping I'll ante up the rent he wants after that. And I'd love to—dude's offering a great discount. But I'm not optimistic."

Nor was she optimistic about where she'd shelter herself. Too many friends and acquaintances had given up their rented digs to go south. A few others had already doubled up and tripled up, leaving no room for more. And while all around us for miles plenty of dwellings sat entirely empty, they were also entirely inhospitable—heat and water shut off, alarmed against squatters, defended by distinctly unfriendly private security and the cops.

"I hear the cells at County're warm enough," Loo-*weeeze* sneered at Duka after we'd returned to what remained of the cottage, now encircled by a line of yellow Danger Do Not Cross tape. "So when you break inta one o' those waterfront mansions, I'll be more 'n happy t' send along a LEO t' bust your ass."

Nearly everyone else had left by then, although the boss firefighter had stuck around to hang out with Loo-*weeeze* in his truck (giving me the chance to finally recognize him as the same pulpous, rarely seen man who lived across the street from me to the northwest). And for the second time in one day, I beheld that way Duka's face has of going bleak and hard and somehow almost gray—but she ignored Loo-*weeeze* and kept on loading her truck with the last of her stuff.

Of course, I probably should have ignored Loo-*weeeze*, too. Again. But I'd had enough of her, so I elected to don my best wide-eyed old woman demeanor and ask if her knowledge of the cells at County had been acquired firsthand.

This paid the dividend I'd hoped for: Loo-*weeeze*'s face squinched for a second or two and she refused to look at me, brusquely announcing to Toby that "I…am…outta-here-with-you-or…*fuckin'*…without…you."

Meanwhile, Duka, who'd kept her back to Loo-*weeeze*, couldn't quite tamp down a smile. She'd wiped it away, though, before she turned, patted her now thoroughly discomposed buddy on his back, and said, "Go on. I'm cool. Thanks big time, Tobes, for helping me out with this. An' say hi to your mom for me."

She stood very straight and waved as he climbed into his truck, but as soon as his vehicle was out of sight, her broad shoulders slumped and she squinted sidelong at the remnants of her cottage and studio. Like a cornered animal, I thought. She opened her mouth to speak, but managed only a wheezy "Damn." Then, after a pause: "I had such hopes for this place. The studio was perfect for what I was trying to—to…"

And that's when I did it.

I invited her to stay in my house.

Might as well have zapped her with a cattle prod. Duka jumped, literally, into moving and talking all at once.

"Oh no no *no* I couldn't you've already been so kind no don't worry I'll have something lined up by tonight not a problem I'll be *fine…*"

And she kept on babbling like that while she scurried back and forth, flinging the last of her bagged-up stuff—clothes and the like—into her truck. Finally, I grabbed her arm as she hurried past, which had the surprising effect of twirling her around to face me.

"Your options are limited," I said, keeping my eyes on hers in a way that, yes, was my version of an old-lady demand: You look at me now, you pay attention now.

"Loo-*weeeze* yells at Toby every time she sees you talk to him," I continued. "So if you accept his offer to stay at his place, you'll be living in Bitch Central. Wouldn't put it past that woman to decide to kill you in your sleep. Or maybe she'll wait till Sylvie Costa comes by to help his mom and you're all there—you, Sylvie, Toby, his mom. Because 'off the deep end' is Loo-*weeeze*'s wading pool. As for that Tradesmen's unit, it's barely heated. Certainly way too cold to sleep in. And so is your truck—even if you park it inside your Tradesmen's unit."

"Fuck," Duka rasped. "Fuck fuck fuck."

"Not so bad," I consoled her. "Considering."

"Yeah? Considering the fuck what?"

"If you'd come back here last night, you'd have been in there when the roof collapsed."

"I'd have raked the damn roof, so it wouldn't have collapsed."

"But you took the time to rake my roof instead. Which means the least I can do is give you a place to sleep under it."

Duka shook her head more in surrender than objection.

"C'mon, kiddo. We're talking just for now, okay? Just a few days or weeks or whatever. And it's bloody *cold* out here, so how 'bout we go home and warm up with some hot cocoa?"

CHAPTER THIRTEEN

STILL

I felt her whisper before I heard it, a waft of warmth and the sweet exquisite balm of her so close. So achingly close. *You did good, Aitch. I'm proud of you.*

I sighed. "Why don't I ever see you for more than half a second, Deels?"

You have to open your eyes.

"I'm afraid you won't be there."

Risk it, she murmured as I felt her softly kissing my tears. *Please.*

So I did—and there she was, in her favorite blue silk PJs just like all those mornings when she lay waiting for me to rouse, kissing and murmuring me awake when she finally got restless and a tad impatient because, c'mon, it was time for breakfast.

I turned toward her, watched her blue, blue eyes gleam as her face creased into a smile. You're dead, I thought. And instantly this thought fell away, not because it evaporated or disintegrated but because it didn't matter; the rules of life and death simply didn't apply.

And I could touch her.

I could kiss her.

I could close my eyes and open them again and she was still there, still warm and soft, and her scent hovered around me as she held me firm and reassuring while I cried and cried. She was still there, still, as we kissed again and touched each other and so easily, smoothly found our rhythm together and, moving together, entwining, lifted each other, first her, then me, all the way to what Cordelia called Home…

As I climaxed, I closed my eyes—and caught sight again of what I'd already forgotten: Cordelia is dead and I am dreaming. Yet I heard the same delighted laughter that invariably rippled out of her when she'd brought me to this magnificence.

"Haven't lost your touch," I mumbled as I dared to open my eyes again.

I remembered every minute of my life with you, Cordelia said, perhaps in reply, perhaps not, because although she looked at me, she seemed to behold, well, more.

"I wanna stay with you, Deels."

Cordelia's smile meandered from wistful to wry; hiking up on one elbow, she shrugged into her shoulder. *I wish I could tell you it works that way.*

"You knew what would happen, didn't you?"

Not really. I sensed something—a kind of mental itch. And I did whatever it took to soothe that itch. She leaned in to kiss my forehead. *But it won't be enough, Aitch. Everything's about to get worse. Harder. Scarier. A much different world than the one I got to live in with you.*

"Yeah. Complete with a ragamuffin roommate sleeping in our bed. Did I mention her scars? And that tat?"

She'll talk to you when she's ready. Cordelia broke into a grin. *Hell, Aitch, you know that. She's already passed all your tests.*

"Almost all. There's Waukegan. And how she keeps telling me she'll be moving out soon."

Oh no, she'll stay. And you're going to need her as much as she needs you. You'll see.

"I'd rather not. I'd rather be with you."

Cordelia remained silent, her grin retreating to a contemplative smile as she gazed at me and stroked the side of my face. Finally she spoke, slowly, casting each word separately adrift. *However...This...Goes... For...You...*"

However this goes for you...

Which is to say, for me.

"So I'm not done yet, huh?" I asked.

Seems not, Cordelia said, her voice gentle, calming. *But you'll know when. Unequivocally.*

"Will I be afraid?"

Yes.

"Will I be brave anyway?"

Yes. But mostly you'll just be very tired.

"At least," I said as I played with Cordelia's regally elegant nose, "I haven't got a whole lot left to lose."

You might be surprised, she replied as she rolled onto her back and pulled the bedcovers around us both. *C'mon,* she urged me, *it's early yet.* Cordelia patted her shoulder where every morning for years I'd cuddled into her, nestling my body along hers, my head on her chest, inhaling the scent of her as I felt her heartbeat beneath my head.

I snuggled against her, fell back to sleep soon after she wrapped her arm around me, and woke up alone.

CHAPTER FOURTEEN

I SHOULD HAVE REALIZED THIS
WOULD TURN INTO A TEST

By the third week of April on the Outer Cape, the cold had waned just slightly and the black had relented to a dim brownish gray.

At its "sunniest," our new version of daylight featured a marginally brighter blur that oozed across the southern sky. For the first time in two months, the app that measures the roof's solar energy production displayed bars on its graph. At least Duka had found a way to rake the snow off the solar panels without damaging them. But the app's bars were scrawny—not even 200 watt-hours in a day from a 7200-watt-hour system.

I wish I could tell you that the snow had warmed into rain by the third week of April (a time formerly warm enough that I could turn off the heating system).

But no: Storms bearing lightly sooted snow regularly darkened our perpetual gloom—ominous hint that Eleven Fourteen debris lingering high above the clouds might keep our air too chilled for anything like a typical summer season. These storms didn't require another roof raking, but they spawned days dark enough that the solar app showed no bars at all.

Duka seemed gray, too. She was grim and quiet as she grieved the loss of her dreams—the almost-girlfriend with whom she'd live happily ever after in the almost-affordable cottage with its almost-perfect studio that made her feel almost like a real sculptor while her almost-realized business venture with Toby almost paid the bills.

Hardly surprising, I suppose, that she so often returned "just one more time" to rummage through the debris.

I found I could anticipate these moments because shortly before she'd say something about going back for another forage, her face would darken even more than the beclouded skies above us. Whenever I noticed her shadowed like that, I'd practice regret avoidance and invite myself along, sometimes before she said anything at all.

This was not what she wanted, but I exploited her instinct to be kind to an old woman—and her remarkable ability to respect a rational argument she hadn't thought of herself as long as it's calmly presented.

Thus I suppressed an impulse to go screechy, as in: Goddammit, Duka, how the hell do you think I'll feel if I say nothing and then you run off and get yourself maimed or killed in that goddamn pile of crap!?

Instead, hoping my old-lady-*awww* would mitigate the worst of my old-hag-irritating, I tried gentle: Wouldn't another trek to what's left of your cottage be easier/nicer/less uncomfortable with hot drinks and some food?

Yes.

And safer while you're crawling around inside structurally dubious rubble if you use one of Cordelia's walkie-talkies to communicate with someone *who's close by?*

Yes.

In the end, I mostly huddled in Duka's truck maintaining walkie-talkie contact, then helped her lug whatever she retrieved (typically a small tool or two, occasionally scraps of wood or steel or glass) to her Tradesmen's Center unit, where an eccentric hodgepodge of materials had begun to overwhelm her well-organized storage of mechanic's tools, electrician's tools, carpenter's tools, blacksmith's tools, and spare parts.

Early on, when I asked about what I saw there, I got a mumbled reply about crafting found objects. When I asked where she'd actually found some of her found objects, she waved her hand a tad dismissively. "Hell, Hester, leftovers are everywhere around here these days."

She said it too carelessly, with an almost-wink and just the slightest edge. What the fuck does it matter, I thought she meant, which is but a single sour note away from What the fuck does anything matter—a feeling I knew too well. Except I have forty-odd years on her. No, kiddo, I thought, you're way too young for that.

So I kept doing what seemed obvious: Hope that at least during Duka's absurdly dangerous ventures into that wreckage, my presence might moderate the worst of what struck me as her impulsive lurches between finding something worth living for and the seductive relief of not living at all.

❖

Duka's confession came during her fifth week in the house, the day after Truro's town meeting had been canceled because it lacked the twenty-five people required for a quorum. So much for voting through an article that would have the town take possession of those properties with tax delinquencies exceeding one year.

I'd begun the morning after the non-meeting around nine as usual, multi-layered in cotton and wool against my reluctance to turn up the heat, sitting at the dining room table with a small breakfast of nuts, dried fruit, and hot cocoa pulled from Cordelia's stash, and grateful that the gray chill allowed me to see anything at all as I gazed out the windows.

Almost May and the broken remnants of our white pines and oak trees remained so encrusted with ice and snow that they were unrecognizable; our once-wooded eight-tenths of an acre looked like it had been bombed.

One more time, I took inventory based on the size and shape of the ragged snarls before me and what I recalled used to be there: You're dead, you're dead, maybe you've got a chance if the weather ever gets warm again, if the sun ever actually shows itself again—and whatever does survive will need decades to regrow.

Almost May and not a green shoot in sight—at least not from my dining room window. This is when things are supposed to improve, I thought. As in warm up. But it's worse than even grim little me expected it to be—

And one more time, I silently played out scenarios...

What should I sacrifice to afford the ever-escalating costs of fuel and electricity?

How much longer might my savings last if I rely more on what's left of Cordelia's stash and less on supermarket dairy, poultry, and grains? On the other hand, how much longer might Cordelia's stash last if I use my savings to supplement it with supermarket dairy, poultry, and grains?

And what will life really be like when I finish off Cordelia's supply of chocolate?

None of the scenarios I could imagine ended well.

"I don't know what to do either." Duka's hushed voice came from the darkness of the small adjoining hallway.

Every second or third day since her arrival, Duka would interrupt whatever she'd been up to for the previous few hours and briefly join me in the dining room, cradling a cup of much-coveted, obscenely pricey coffee while she updated me about the latest house project she'd insisted on undertaking "since you won't let me pay you any rent."

But not on this day.

On this day she sat down across from me and frowned at her coffee like she was studying tea leaves.

"You first," I said when she'd settled in.

She shrugged, looking at me with an isn't-it-obvious? expression.

Okay then, I thought, guess I better take the conn.

"Cordelia got it right," I said. "About the importance of having what you need to sustain yourself through an emergency. She even grasped that an emergency can last for a long time. But *this*—"

"Yeah, *this* emergency seems like it won't be letting up for, well, years."

"For years," I repeated. "I admit I'm having a hell of a time with that. I look at what's already happened and I think, 'Nah, it can't get worse than this.' But *then*…"

"It's this house, Hester." Duka spread her arms inclusively. "An' that pantry you got downstairs—which, by the way, I don't ever mention to people an' I hope you don't either. Your house is seductive. Makes the world seem steady, regular. I actually daydream here, like about making truly functional kinetic sculpture—like, say, small-scale wind turbines." She gazed out the window. "But then—then I know, I *feel* I'm in the kind of jeopardy I could never've imagined before Eleven Fourteen…"

"You're young and strong, Duka. Great skillset. You could go anywhere." I leaned forward to study her. "I just don't get why you've stayed on the Cape. Why haven't you followed Essie to Florida? Most of the caravans are getting through now, according to Melinda Reid. Dear Jackass letter be damned, I'd wager Essie would help you find somewhere to stay. She might even have the brains to keep you close. So you wouldn't be arrested for vagrancy and shipped to one of those migrant camps Isabella Franzi talks about."

Duka hunched in on herself, head bowed over the coffee cup she was again clutching. "Told you already," she said, her voice constrained yet razor-edged. "I don't like Florida."

I examined her for a few extra seconds before I took the plunge. "What about Waukegan?"

A strange sound came out of her, a gasp maybe, and she bucked to her feet, shoving the chair back with her legs—yet instead of marching out of the room, perhaps out of the house forever, she froze.

I'd heard her mention Waukegan just that once—during the only time I'd ever seen her drunk—so I suspected something about it was a big deal for her. But hell, *this* big?

"I'm sorry," I said, watching her carefully as she stared down at me. "I'm just trying to understand."

Seconds passed, more seconds. Finally, she blinked. "I—" Turning her face away, she gulped the kind of gulp that hurts your throat and can be heard across a room. "I will never go back there. Ever."

"Why?"

She sat again, elbows thumping the table, head down, and more seconds passed—until: "Bad things happened to me there." She rubbed her cheeks—too vigorously, I thought—before she looked up and her eyes, too hard, too bright, drilled into me. "I didn't do any of the shit they said I did. That they convicted me for. I was *innocent*. An' they damn well knew it, too."

Ah, well.

I should have realized this would turn into a test—of me, not Duka.

As that word—CONVICTED—reverberated between my ears, I fought to keep my face impassive, neutral. She said she was innocent.

Whereupon I heard an echo of Cordelia's voice—*Damn, Aitch, you've always been* ridiculously *credulous*.

Even so, as I returned Duka's gaze, I believed her. "If you can't, I'm completely okay with that," I said. "But if you can, please tell me what happened to you."

Chapter Fifteen

Now that I've asked

You gotta understand," Duka began. "Both my brothers look mestizo, like my mother's people. In Waukegan, you pay for that. The schools, the landlords, an' especially the cops make sure you pay. Steve dealt by finding the army in high school an' enlisting after graduation, an' he never looked back. But Nicky—Nicky's a pendejo who plays the cholo, y'know? Always blaming his endless fuckups on gabachos hassling him, calling him dirty. Nothing was ever poor oppressed Nicky's fault."

Duka paused and glanced at me—to make sure I could handle what she was telling me, I suspect. And even though I had to guess at what "pendejo" and "cholo" and "gabacho" meant, it seems I did okay, because she continued.

"Then there's me—the youngest, only girl, almost güera cuz I kinda look like my Hungarian father. Enough to, y'know, pass. Mostly. An' even though I never much liked school, my father called me 'college-smart'— but nobody ever called Nicky college-smart."

Nevertheless, the nickname became an expectation which Duka dutifully met. She finished two years at the local community college— "buncha auto technician certifications, a little electrician stuff, also some art an' design courses"—and come autumn, she planned to continue the long, slow trudge toward a no-debt bachelor's degree by enrolling part-time at the nearest branch of the state university while she worked as a mechanic.

When her first-ever girlfriend, who attended a nearby private college and "came from something," invited her to spend the summer on Cape Cod at the family second home where they'd live rent-free and work summer jobs, "Saying yes was a no-brainer."

Duka's expression became almost pensive. "I spent the summer in Wellfleet, first time ever away from Waukegan. An', jeezus, the world opened for me. That summer I saw possibilities I never dreamed of. Met people who made me feel completely at home for the first time *ever*. Best fourteen weeks of my life." Then she sighed. "I was kinda bummed when I went back cuz Barbara had gone off to do a year at the Sorbonne while I'd be stuck at my parents' house, working at my uncle's garage, commuting to school down in Chicago."

Duka's voice had grown husky; her eyes glistened. "Shit, I came *so* close to staying on the Cape. *So close*. But I didn't. Left crack-ass early on that Thursday, got back to Waukegan late Friday, did a shift at the garage on Saturday, visited with my grandmother an' ran errands for her on Sunday. First day of classes on Monday, an' I come home to find these two Waukegan police detectives waiting on my parents' front step to arrest me for what's called calculated criminal drug conspiracy."

"That sounds bad," I said.

"Sixteen-year-sentence bad," Duka replied. "Cuz I wouldn't plead out on something I damn well had nothing to do with."

I was truly shocked, which had to have shown on my face. And in my silence. Duka actually sort of smiled.

"Yeah, I know," she said. "I didn't believe it either. Not when I heard 'guilty,' not when the judge said 'sixteen years,' not even when some prick courthouse deputy smirked that I'd have to do three quarters of that before being eligible for parole. Hundred 'n' eighteen days in the county jail, but it took that van ride downstate to DeWitt to make it real for me."

"DeWitt?" I managed to squeak.

"DeWitt Correctional Facility, two-hour drive into the Illinois hinterlands. Old, leaky, moldy, always way too cold or way too hot, crawling with cockroaches, mice, rats, an' creepy male hacks a lot more criminal than most of the inmates. Eleven hundred crazy bitches in DeWitt—some of 'em truly fucking scary, some of 'em the kindest, most generous people I ever met. Closed the year after I got outta there."

"How *did* you get out of there?" I asked in a stunned whisper.

"Fucking outrageous luck—in the form of the Illinois Innocence Project. I'd been in DeWitt for sixteen months when one of their attorneys visited me. That's when I finally found out what really happened."

She'd been framed, I guessed.

"Yep. The detectives who arrested me had just scored a big-ass heroin bust the day before that would cinch their promotions as long as they could turn it into class X conspiracy convictions of at least some of the gangbangers they'd been targeting. But they'd nailed only one dude— my brother Nicky. His 'bros' escaped, so the cops squeezed Nicky, who was so shit-scared of his bros that he narced me instead. As his sole co-conspirator. This set off the cops' bullshit meters, but so what? Just a little goosing an' they had that class X conviction."

She'd seen and heard enough growing up working-class ragged in Waukegan to be cynical about the criminal justice system, and her bail terms were so impossible that she remained stuck in the Lake County Jail, yet Duka simply didn't believe she could be convicted.

After all, even the cops had to concede she was a thousand miles away when the conspiracy was planned, and they found no evidence of any contact between her and Nicky in over a year, or between her and any of Nicky's "gang associates." And she'd been back from the Cape for only two days when Nicky managed to get himself caught selling a dozen kilos of heroin to an undercover cop.

What's more, Duka was miles away from the point-of-heroin-sale where the detectives busted Nicky that Sunday afternoon. She'd been doing those errands for her grandmother, and although she'd paid cash and saved no receipts, she was sure that security videos—from the supermarket, the panadería, the pharmacy, the gas station—would prove it, prove that she had done nothing that would connect her to Nicky's class X felony.

No matter.

"I pissed off the whole damn universe when I insisted on pleading Not Guilty," she said. "The prosecutor, the judge, the public defender who barely went through the motions. My trial lasted half a day. No security videos to save my ass. Plus the prosecutor showed slides of latent fingerprints on one of Nicky's heroin bricks that a crime lab tech swore under oath were mine. Then Nicky's testimony—" Duka flinched. "What Nicky did was worst of all. God, whenever I remember that my stomach turns."

About six months after her conviction, issues with other Illinois Innocence Project cases triggered an investigation of the crime lab that processed her case evidence. Nearly another year passed before it became clear that the same tech who testified about her fingerprints had tainted more than a dozen drug cases with dry-labbing and perjury—all to gain accolades and bonuses for his role in bringing in the extra money his lab received from the State of Illinois whenever it processed evidence that resulted in a conviction for controlled substance offenses.

"By the time I heard about all this, everything that tech touched was under review, including my case," she said, at last really smiling. "Only time in prison I ever cried, cuz I had hope again."

Belatedly under genuine scrutiny, the "evidence" against her began to collapse, and quickly. It started with an Innocence Project intern discovering the videos that would have cleared her had they not been "lost"—oh gee sorry.

"A wonderful word, 'exculpatory,'" Duka said.

Then one of Nicky's bros, who'd successfully dodged the cops that Sunday afternoon in Waukegan when Nicky got caught, was himself arrested for the murder of a cop at almost exactly the same time on that same Sunday—but fifty miles away in Chicago. To duck the Chicago murder charge, the bro insisted he'd been in Waukegan driving Nicky that Sunday afternoon—a story the bro's cellphone texts, previously undetected by the Waukegan detectives, corroborated. As did Nicky right after declaring that he'd lied to the cops and at his sister's trial.

Mariana Duka Canché was never involved with the gang, or its activities or the heroin sale that Sunday afternoon, or any of their drug sales ever, both said. Her fingerprints on the brick of heroin must be bogus, both said.

"An' finally, *finally*, that fucking lab tech says oh yeah, the Mariana Duka Canché case too. He admitted to faking my fingerprints on that heroin brick. Admitted he dry-labbed it, admitted his testimony was false. A lie. So ninety-nine weeks to the day after those cops arrested me, I was chained up one more time, marched into a Lake County courtroom, an' the same damn judge who sentenced me to sixteen years in prison vacated my conviction."

"And then you were free?" I asked. "Just like that?"

"Mmm, outta the chains an' outta the cage, anyway. They also vacated the fine that was part of my sentence, plus all the jail an' prison fees they piled on after they, y'know, threw away the key. But I was destitute. They'd taken everything. My truck, my four grand in savings, my phone, my laptop. Even my tools, which I needed to be able to get work an' would cost almost as much as my truck to replace."

"Please," I said, "tell me you got some kind of restitution."

Duka shrugged. "Not huge, but I ended up with a new truck, decent new set of tools, plus enough to settle my grandmother's last expenses.

An' I was able to pay back the money people put in my account while I was locked up. Helped out a couple DeWitt women I cared about, too—even had some left over. Also got my name off the inmate search database, my conviction records expunged, an' a certificate of innocence. So I can answer *no* when I'm asked if I've been convicted of a felony. Made 'em give me a passport an' a new driver's license, too."

She could have sued, she told me, but mediation was much quicker, taking only six weeks. She said she felt rich, except for losing her grandmother two months after gaining her freedom. She stayed in Waukegan for those two months, living at her dying grandmother's place.

"Worked out cuz, god, I missed my abuelita, who really needed the help—an' my mother was frigging impossible. She couldn't look at me without starting a screaming fight. She blamed me for her dear, special Nicky stuck in prison after I got out. Like I could actually *do* something about the fact that he'd pleaded guilty, then got caught perjuring himself about me. So I stayed away from her. But I got lucky again, cuz my uncle believed in me, let me work at his garage, even allowed me to use his tools till I got my own again."

Plenty of other people regarded her as guilty, though, so staying for even those two months had been uncomfortable verging on perilous; the cops who'd busted her not only didn't get in trouble, they got their promotions and made a habit of harassing her. As did the gangbangers who claimed Nicky as their own.

"Suddenly, Nicky's bros decide I owe 'em favors. Fix somebody's ride. Drop off a package. An', man, they didn't like hearing *no*. When I balked, they said 'You get a pass for now cuz you're the one taking care of Nicky's sick abuela.' But, y'know—volveremos, puta. So I had to ghost right after she died. Coulda gone anywhere, but I wanted what I'd found on the Outer Cape. What I dreamed about for ninety-nine weeks."

The day after the funeral, Duka packed a duffel bag, gathered up her tools, said goodbye to her father, her uncle, and her cousin, and started driving. South first, then west—to confuse any of Nicky's bros who might be following her. She exited the expressway and did a few loops through Chicago's southern suburbs—"just to be sure I'd thrown 'em off"—before turning east.

"Didn't stop for anything except gas till I got to Hyannis, where I picked up camping gear, hiking boots, plenty of food—" She shook her head, averted her eyes. "Set up my tent at the North Truro campground, as far away from everyone else as I could get. Then I just hunkered there, cooked my meals on my little camp stove, walked all over the National Seashore, the beaches. Just walked an' walked an' walked."

Sitting across the dining room table from her, I asked one more question—"How?" I reached my hand across the table to take hold of hers. "How the hell did you get through that?"

Her eyes swung back to meet mine. Really? they asked. You really want to know what I'm not sure I know myself?

I nodded.

Chapter Sixteen

The nick of time

Duka took a few breaths, like she was beginning a race, and as her hand gripped mine I understood: Now that I've asked, I must let her talk and talk and talk until she's talked out.

"I started out so angry, Hester. Just arrested, in shock, so damn scared I couldn't say anything but no, I didn't do what you're saying, no, Nicky's making shit up again. No no *no!*

"On the way from the police station to the county jail, I came within a second of full-on freak-out, just screaming YOU CAN'T DO THIS TO ME! But somebody else beat me to it an' I learned right up front: Whatever else you do, *don't* do that. Doesn't matter how righteous your upset or frustration—the more you freak, the worse it gets.

"Cuz the way it really works is not 'innocent until proven guilty.' It's actually 'assumed guilty until proven guilty.' You're in handcuffs, leg chains, at the mercy of goons with absolute power who don't care about anything except getting through another shift or, sometimes, the pleasure of treating you like shit just cuz they can. Beating you to the ground just cuz they can.

"No question I'd have to surrender physically to their commands. But I decided anybody trying to rape me better be prepared to kill me, cuz that's how I'd be defending myself—all the fucking way down with everything I have.

"Pretty soon after I got to the county jail, I was living by a kinda first principle: Do Not Show 'Em Anything—no matter what I felt inside, no matter how much anyone goaded me, humiliated me, cheated me, dehumanized me, hurt me. It was the only way I could see to shield the deep core of myself.

"I had a couple other survival rules, too. Careful who you trust cuz the place is fulla manipulative psychos who seem perfectly normal—prisoner psychos an' hack psychos, too. Also, save yourself from HIV, hep C, all the STD shit by never getting kissy or touchy with anyone.

"During those first hundred days in County before my trial, I had a faith: 'Soon this will be over.' Believed it so much that I pushed for a quick trial date—cuz, hey, I'm innocent, I shouldn't be locked away in here, treated like this.

"In jail, though, nobody's allowed to be innocent for long. I learned that if you go by the hacks' rulebook an' refuse to cheat, you end up like the runt of a litter of zoo animals—kicked around, trying to survive on scraps.

"I also saw that anyone stuck in the zoo for very long—runt or alpha—needs to find a new way to experience time, because every day locked up is an eternity. Infinite time, duration without beginning or end.

"Hints of what was coming—but back then I was entirely certain I didn't have to worry, because *of course* a jury would see that the charges against me were ridiculous an' I'd be found not guilty an' soon it'd be over. Only thing that helped me deal with the waiting was reading books, a new one every few days, the best of 'em actual literature that got you thinking, that swept you into another world, another time, away from being trapped in a cage.

"Then I'm convicted, I'm a class X 'offender' waiting to be sentenced, looking at a six-year minimum. An' I'm numb, I can't believe it. During those days between my trial an' my sentencing, I kinda imploded into that numbness. I was sure that somehow the verdict would be undone.

"Ha—magical thinking at its deluded best...

"Every night I dreamed of my regular life. Working on a car in my uncle's garage, going to classes. I dreamed of Barbara's parents' house in Wellfleet, of the Truro metal sculptor whose studio I visited that wonderful summer.

"An' then I'd wake up in the cell, in the noise, in the cruel, bleak tedium. An' I'd realize all over again, jeezus, oh jeezus, they *convicted* me, an' my brain would freeze into no no no, this is beyond fucked. This cannot be happening to me!

"I barely remember my sentencing. I heard the judge say 'sixteen years' an' the deputy said twelve years till parole an' my no no no went into hyperdrive, except at night when we were locked down, when I'd start counting. A hundred an' thirteen, a hundred an' fourteen, fifteen, sixteen, seventeen eternities already endured. To be subtracted from the four thousand three hundred an' eighty-three eternities I faced before any possibility of parole. Or five thousand eight hundred an' forty-four eternities if I have to do the whole sentence.

"Then I'm all chained up in a sheriff's van with four other prisoners on our way to DeWitt. I'm the only virgin, only class X, only one with a double-digit sentence. Somewhere during the ride I said 'For what it's worth, I'm innocent,' an' all four of 'em laughed an' pretty much in unison came back with 'Join the club.'

"By the time we got to DeWitt, my hope was gone. Just gone. All I had was Do Not Show 'Em Anything. Which I held on to like it was a frigging life jacket in the middle of the frigging North Atlantic. Do Not Show 'Em Anything.

"Once inside DeWitt, it was cage to strip search to another cage. Waiting an' waiting till they got around to us, listening to inmate tales of woe. About their kids mostly; almost all of 'em had kids.

"Then it's into a freezing cold segregation cell where you wait some more, essentially in quarantine, till you get through medical clearance. 'Twas a very long twelve days of Christmas. Get nightmares even now about stepping into that windowless beige box, facing the back wall till the cell door bangs shut behind me, an' I'm told to step back an' stick my hands through the chuck hole in the door, an' when I do they take off the handcuffs an' I pull in my hands just before the chuck hole cover slams shut an' the bolt thunks real loud.

"I'm locked in now, by myself, drowning in this glaring light, in this din—people yelling, crying, metal banging, toilets flushing—an' I'm looking around mute while my brain's screeching 'Tell me why I should live like this for one more goddamn minute, much less the next four thousand two hundred an' sixty-four days at least? At fucking *least*. Cuz maybe it'll be the whole five thousand seven hundred an' twenty-five days.'

"So I started thinking about how I'd do it in this cell that contained almost nothing. Rolled-up bedsheet seemed like the best option, one end tied to the towel hook bolted into the wall, the other around my neck—then jump, keeping knees cradled high, an' drop. But I figured for it to work, I'd have to wait till late, after the day's last count, before the one they do in the middle of the night.

"While I waited I started remembering my fourteen weeks in Wellfleet with Barbara. Even before I left the Cape, I understood Barbara would move on from me pretty fast; I was one of her adventures, an' if I wasn't along on her next one—well, nice knowing ya. That stung, but she was up front, no mindfucking. An' there was this, like, consolation prize, which was the Outer Cape.

"I'd been so tempted to stay on after Barbara left for Paris. Just ditch Waukegan an' school, which had always been my father's dream, not mine. Rent my own place, keep working on cars an' trucks an' getting electrician qualifications, maybe expand into carpentry. An' keep learning metalworking, blacksmithing, kinetic sculpture, even artglass. Coulda saved myself a lotta hassle if I'd stayed here, cuz then Nicky woulda never thought about accusing me of anything. Can't tell you how much I wish I'd stayed.

"But I didn't stay. Best I could do during that first eternity in the seg cell, an' every single eternity in DeWitt afterward, was to resurrect all I could remember about the Outer Cape.

"I'd go back an' forth—from bedsheet strategies to recalling bonfires an' bay sunsets an' the feel of working sixteen-gauge weathering steel. Finally, somewhere in there I thought 'Even if I'm locked in this very same hole for the full sixteen years, even *that* isn't forever. In sixteen years, the Cape will still be there. Weathering steel an' the woods, the beaches, the dunes will all still be there.'

"So I decided to stick around an' try. Then it was about how. How do I survive this for *at least* another four thousand two hundred an' sixty-four eternal days?

"I already knew the importance of Do Not Show 'Em Anything. I also knew I'd been one of the lucky ones in the county jail because my father, my uncle, my cousin, an' sometimes my grandmother an' my brother Steve would put money in my account, which meant I could buy stuff from the commissary once in a while. But hell, that couldn't continue for twelve more years, or what might be sixteen more years.

"At DeWitt I'd have to make a prison living in a prison economy, an' even if I could *get* a prison job, I'd need more than any prison job would pay. Cuz the State of Illinois doesn't give prisoners much for free— even charges for things like making phone calls, medical visit co-pays. An' anything that isn't free costs way more in prison than out here in the world. Way more.

"Which meant I needed a hustle. I'd seen the major options at County. Selling cellphone time, drugs, cigarettes, even pruno. Gambling, coercion, loan sharking. Trading sex and/or servitude for drugs, food, physical protection. Trading sex with a hack for extra privileges or to avoid getting dragged off to segregation. A few managed by styling hair or makeup, selling tarot readings, doing people's laundry, making fancy cards people could send to their kids, stuff like that. There were even a few bible-bashers promising Jesus for a pretzel.

"The most lucrative hustles, though, require doing business with hacks willing to smuggle in contraband. Drugs, cellphones, whatever. The hacks who do this risk less than you'd think, since regardless of what shit they pull, they cover for each other right up the hack food chain. An' the hacks who smuggle in contraband make plenty doing it. Fancy-car plenty, pay-off-the-mortgage plenty.

"But I had visions of getting caught doing a hustle like that, visions of my time at DeWitt stretching to the full sixteen years. An' during those first twelve days at DeWitt in that seg cell, I was naive enough to believe I could find some sort of decent-paying 'legit' hustle.

"Great in principle. In seg. Actually seemed doable after my medical clearance finally came through an' they moved me to a reception an' classification unit, where they decide your security level, offender grade, an' escape risk so they can choose where you end up, who you end up with.

"You get the regular prison uniform then—the white T-shirt, blue pants, canvas sneakers—plus a few more privileges, like phone calls an' commissary access. But it's not a real test of what it'll be like long-term cuz everyone in reception an' classification is on their best behavior, hoping for an okay placement. Also, I had enough left in my account to get by while the deciders decided what to do with me.

"They already know your crime, your sentence, whether you're a retread or a first-timer. So they haul you in for interviews to dig for details that aren't in their records cuz they're after information that answers one big question—are you predator or are you prey?

"They have bunches of rules about how prisoners can be classified. So an inmate with a sixteen-year sentence—especially a first-timer, a virgin like me—should be placed in a medium security unit. But they also have plenty of leeway to justify anything they decide. An' they decided to max me.

"After all, I was class X, way above-average sentence length, presumed gang ties (thanks, Nicky), dissociative tendencies (no tears during the interviews), lack of remorse, obviously a dyke, young, big, strong, not quite white enough (don't be fooled by the nose, pay attention to those beady black eyes an' how well she speaks Spanish)—but educated enough to be psychologically manipulative as well as a high escape risk.

"Nobody ever actually said 'We've marked you as a predator.' But I ended up in maximum security general population with a psycho class M cellie. M for murder an', unlike almost everyone else, she didn't hesitate to talk about the mess she made that landed her in prison for the rest of her life.

"An' no point in challenging where I got dumped unless I wanted to end up back in seg. DeWitt convinced me the word 'insolent' was invented by a prison hack. So there I am, cuffed up, holding my bag of stuff in front of me, an' the hack who escorted me shoves me into this seven-by twelve-foot box where Emilia has lived for a while.

"God, Hester, she terrified the hell outta me. Taller than me, forty pounds heavier, maybe thirty years old, an' *intense*. Also, I find out pretty damn quick, she runs one of the two top inmate crews at DeWitt—the really nasty one.

"I always thought Emilia was more powerful than the prison administrators ever realized. I know she owned at least two hacks that she'd blackmailed into obedience. She prob'ly owned more. Sure as shit, she could get pretty much any prison-world thing she wanted whenever she wanted it. For all I know, she put in an order for a cellie with certain characteristics, an' that cellie turned out to be me.

"Or, hell, maybe on that particular Tuesday my southern-belle-wannabe classification counselor felt like fucking over an unrepentant mestiza dyke who had the nerve to list her religion as Wiccan (because, as I learned at County, a 'holy' book is the only reading you get to have with you in seg, an' since a Wiccan Book of Shadows is pretty much whatever you say it is, I chose my copy of *The Women's Encyclopedia of Myths and Secrets*—an' got away with it).

"Don't know what other max units are like, but the one I lived on at DeWitt, G-three, was way overcrowded—ninety-six ticked off, fucked up women double-bunked into forty-eight single-person cells on two tiers surrounding a dayroom. What we lacked in space we made up for in drama. Only good thing was that the cells had windows. About four feet high, six inches wide. The window in my cell was north-facing, so no direct sunlight—but when I angled myself the right way, from my bunk I could see some trees an' a bit of sky.

"We called G-three the Garbage Can cuz everyone in there had double-digit sentences like me. Besides the six inmates who got to be unit janitors for twelve cents an hour, nobody else had a prison job, even though everybody I met or heard about had applied. None of us had been accepted into any of the education or even rehab or exercise programs either. We were classified as 'Unpaid Administrative Idle'—last in line for call-outs to the gym, the yard, the library, for every one of DeWitt's puny resources.

"Other than getting sent to seg forever or shipped off in an interstate transfer, the only way outta G-three came when the time remaining on your sentence dropped below six years. If you'd managed not to fuck up, you had a chance at moving to another unit an' finally landing a job an' some program placements.

"Meanwhile, the garbage in G-three stayed locked down in their cells for eighteen hours a day, allowed out in six 'opens' spread between seven in the morning an' eight at night. Our longest time outside our cells was two hours in the afternoon.

"Except for when the entire unit was mass-moved to an' from the dining hall for our three feedings, we were let out only one tier at a time— forty-eight inmates instead of ninety-six. Like double sessions in school. Meant your two-hour crack at either the yard or the gym happened with just the women on your tier, an' so did all your socializing an' hustling. Then there were a couple shorter, very regulated periods for showering, doing laundry, getting visits or a haircut, picking up your commissary order if you were lucky enough to afford commissary.

"So I'm trapped in this eighty-square-foot box with Emilia in chunks of two hours here, three hours there, then locked in with her for ten hours at night. An' damn, that woman was always talking, always in Spanish. To herself, on a cellphone to her kids, her mom, her man, the whole time winding herself up tighter an' tighter. I got the upper bunk, where I tried to read an' be invisible an' wondered when she'd wind up enough to stick me from below with a shiv.

"Emilia barely spoke or understood English, couldn't read or write at all, not Spanish or English. About three days after I arrived, she finally talked to me, asked me to read this letter from one of her kids. Then she asked me to write her words into a note back to her kid. I was rewarded with a big grin an' a command: 'You're better than Jazmin, so now you can teach me English.' That's when I discovered I had replaced one of her crew who'd been doing the reading an' scribing for her in the dayroom during our recreation periods.

"I started Emilia out with vocabulary, hoping that would be enough to get her going cuz sure as hell I didn't know squat about teaching English. I guess I did okay cuz she gave me time on her cellphone, extra soap, packs of ramen noodles, tampons, an occasional joint. Even showed me how to set up a prepaid debit card with my cousin back in Waukegan so I'd have someplace to stash hustle money that the hacks couldn't reach.

"I figured I'd found my hustle—reading, scribing, translating, teaching. Trouble was, Emilia monopolized my hustle. Best I could do was barter Emilia's handouts. But I was so relieved to be getting along with her that, okay, I'd take it slow, try to loosen her grip over time. God knows, I had plenty of time.

"But Jazmin was apeshit cuz Emilia had given me both her reading-an'-scribing job *an'* the teaching job she'd been hoping for, too. I got growls first, then insults, then threats.

"Last thing I wanted was to make a mortal enemy as soon as I hit general population, but that's what I'd done. So I tried to fix it, went to talk to Jazmin during a rec period—an' ended up sliced. She got me five times, front an' back, the two in front deep enough for an ambulance ride, emergency surgery, an' three days in the nearest real hospital handcuffed to the bed.

"I spent another couple weeks in the DeWitt infirmary before they sent me back to G-three. Emilia an' Jazmin were long gone by then. Word was the hacks planted contraband in their cells, slammed 'em with charges, threw 'em in seg—an' soon they were gonna be transferred to New Mexico.

"But the rest of Emilia's crew hadn't gone anywhere, an' some of 'em didn't like me much. Fortunately, they lived on the top tier an' I'd been put in a cell on the bottom tier, so at least I didn't share rec with 'em. Had to watch my back, though, during our mass movements to feedings.

"My second G-three cellie—Zoë—also was fucking crazy, but much easier to deal with than Emilia. Zoë also had a sixteen-year sentence an' had done a year, but she wasn't class X so parole was closer for her—about seven years away. In another year, she had a shot at moving outta G-three to a unit where she could get a job an' do some programs. The last thing she wanted was to screw that up. But she was single, no family help, so she needed a hustle.

"I frightened her in the beginning, I think—she was a little straight girl, a weird combination of OCD an' sleight-of-hand sneaky, an' when she looked at me she saw a big scary brown dyke. But I let her know I wouldn't mess with her stuff an' I wanted no papaya but my own, so we did okay together in our box.

"Pretty quick after I got back on the unit, people on my tier who didn't do much English asked me to translate, read, an' scribe stuff. Next thing I know, someone's asking me to teach 'em to read an' write English. Seemed like at last I had my hustle cranking.

"An' then I didn't. Cuz I just couldn't bring myself to make my 'students' pay.

"Most of those women had nothing. Hustles ranging from nonexistent to pathetic. No prison job, hardly any help from families or friends. Not even a way to get enough sanitary napkins, much less tampons—cuz god forbid the State of Illinois should give female prisoners more than one pad a day for free.

"During the rest of my time there I ended up teaching five women to speak English, another three to read an' write both Spanish an' English. I made some good friends who shared what little they had an' watched out for me, too. Twice they kept Emilia's old crew from jumping me on the way to the dining hall. Kept a couple of the pervert hacks from cornering me, too. I thought of 'em as The Meek Shall Inherit the Earth Patrol.

"Those women taught me that there's only one way to survive—in a group of people, a community, really, that you can trust. Cuz cooperation, sharing, an' trading depend on trust. But I still needed a hustle, an' I had this idea that I could come up with one that wouldn't require me to risk my parole possibilities on a bent hack.

"Cuz the bent hacks run a double racket—demand, say, five hundred bucks for a twenty-dollar contraband burner phone, wait a month or two for the inmate who bought it to rake in a fat profit from charging other prisoners to use it, then do a shakedown, confiscate the phone so the inmate has to pay the same bent hack all over again to bring in a new contraband phone. Round an' round, over an' over.

"I'd been back on G-three maybe a month, scraping along, when I heard one of my students bitching about her broken cellphone. Told me if I knew anybody who could fix it, she'd let me use it for fifteen minutes, call anybody I wanted. I thought of my grandmother. I thought, 'Wow, fifteen free, private minutes talking to Abi.'

"I took a real deep breath, counted how long I had yet to go in the G-three garbage can. One thousand eight hundred an' sixty-six days before I could even hope to leave the unit. Four thousand an' fifty-seven days before I had any shot at parole—eleven years an' change. I thought about how people build whole careers in eleven years an' change. How most people do careers where they have to, not where they want to.

"So I said 'Show me your phone,' an' she did an' I told her I could fix it if she could get me a soldering iron an' some wire. Took her a couple days, but when she got what I needed, I had her phone fixed in five minutes. An' with help from my cellie Zoë, my real hustle was born: repairs—cellphones mostly, sometimes media players or headphones. No bent hacks required.

"It wouldn't have worked without Zoë, who had a gift for finding, sometimes making, really good places to hide shit. Cuz I was paranoid about getting caught, didn't want tools an' materials in our cell for a single second longer than necessary. Zoë made a few hiding places in our cell, but mostly out in the dayroom, the laundry room, the phone bank—places that, surveillance cameras be damned, not even the inmates knew about an' the hacks never found. She'd move stuff to an' from our cell without anyone realizing. Plus she was a fine lookout.

"Since we shared the risks, we shared the proceeds. We never made big bucks like the people who worked the hacks, sold phone time, trafficked drugs. But I didn't need a lot like some who were getting played by their boyfriends or trying to help their kids—or just plain greedy. Neither did Zoë. Our hustle got us enough.

"Ran that hustle for almost six months an' never got pooched, though we had one really evil shakedown an' a few close calls. But then one day just before Christmas, with two hours' notice, Zoë got transferred an' I never saw her again.

"I had a day an' a night in the cell by myself before Tattoo Tammy, who everyone called TT, showed up—after fourteen months in seg for rupturing a male hack's testicle when he tried to use his dick to diddle her in the laundry room.

"Once upon a time, TT had been a hotshot tattoo artist, had her own shop. Lived up to her name, too: She was covered in ink. When she saw that I wasn't, she got downright sulky for maybe twenty seconds before reverting to what I learned was her normal state—spinning as fast as one of her tattoo engines. Even before New Year's Eve, she'd gotten her hands on the irons an' works she needed.

"But to ink her customers she also needed a bent hack to allow her to sneak into other inmates' cells an' stay there through a daytime lockdown period—something that took a while to negotiate. In the meantime, she was restless to work on some skin an' stalked me like a large, hungry cat cuz my skin was virgin territory.

"By then I was a damn mess. I stopped repairing anything after Zoë left, screw holiday season demand, because without Zoë it just wasn't the same hustle. If I resumed, hiding my tools an' materials would be on me— but I didn't have Zoë's skills or instincts.

"I was just starting my second year in DeWitt, an' at that point reading books wasn't doing it anymore. It got so I couldn't stop counting. I remember this one day—the numbers on this one day. Four hundred an' ninety-five days locked up, three thousand eight hundred an' eighty-eight days to go before I'd reach the possibility of parole.

"But jeezus, parole was looking like a pipe dream, because I knew as soon as TT's hustle got busted, which I figured was inevitable, I'd get slammed by the hacks for not snitching on her. Sixteen years it was gonna be—five thousand three hundred an' forty-nine days to go.

"So after four hundred an' ninety-five days of doing my damnedest not to show 'em anything, a year after I had decided to stick around an' try, I was done. I was thinking about bedsheets again. All the damn time.

"Gotta give TT credit. She sussed it out an' said 'Look, bitch, you can't stay clean an' safe in here, can't stay clean an' safe anywhere. It's all the fucking same. Same asshole quotient. Same rip-off quotient. Only difference is the kinda boot pressing on your throat. It's called survival of the fittest for a fucking *reason*.'

"Then she told me I needed a tat. An' I thought, hell, maybe it'll distract me from thinking about bedsheets for a while, so why not? I smoked a couple bongs, strong shit, told her I wanted a spiderweb where I felt most deprived, an' let her tac it on.

"I remember looking at it when she finished, all red at the edges, kinda sore, an' I thought—I decided—'You wanna convict? Okay, assholes, I'll *give* you a goddamn convict.'

"After that I got as good as Zoë at hiding shit an' went back to my hustle with a vengeance, even expanded into blackmailing bent hacks with smartphone videos of 'em whoring with working girl inmates or passing contraband. Damn, I liked the power of blackmail, making hacks squirm.

"I got more an' more reckless, insanely reckless, took all kinda risks. Not like I wanted to get busted, but I refused to be terrified of it. An' I knew a smackdown was coming for me. They'd find a way. An' I'd end up on the merry-go-round—in seg for months or years at a time, then out for a while, crazy as hell cuz seg does that to you, till I caught more charges, eventually charges that would extend my sentence way beyond sixteen years. I figured I'd die caged in a zoo.

"So I decided 'screw Do Not Show 'Em Anything.' I showed 'em anger, attitude, which I aimed at the inmate bullies an' especially the hack bullies I'd put up with ever since I was first arrested. 'Insolence' got me tossed into seg twice.

"An' then, two weeks after I came back from my second stint in seg, I got that visit from the Illinois Innocence Project attorney. Eight weeks later, I was free. In the nick of time, I guess."

CHAPTER SEVENTEEN

ONE HELL OF A HUSTLE

As she finished her tale, Duka's eyes lifted from her coffee cup and I saw her anxiety: Would I respond to this ex-con sitting across the table from me by throwing her out of my house?

I think possibly I managed a breathy "Wow" of astonishment, of dismay. What I remember most, though, is how completely the simple thought—she was innocent—overwhelmed my ability to say anything.

She was innocent.

If she hadn't also been almost miraculously lucky, she'd be imprisoned still, barely more than half way through that outrageous sentence. I felt my eyebrows lift, my head move slowly back and forth. She was innocent.

I reached across the table and placed my hands over hers. There may have been tears in my eyes.

Duka smiled. Hesitantly at first, then almost sympathetically, even knowingly.

"Abi and Abu, my mother's parents, started very poor," she told me. "Mojados with the usual hopes an' dreams. My uncle would joke that Abi's goal was to be 'lace curtain mestiza making American kids.' They weren't after felonious filthy rich. Just modest honest—willing to work hard for a decent, legitimate living, sliver of margin for the occasional misdemeanor like a speeding ticket, no having to always look over your shoulder trembling. An' they did it. So I got raised believing modest honest was the baseline, mine to screw up. Which I did not."

Schoolteacher-patient, she waited for my nod, then continued.

"In prison, though, I learned that most people gotta risk doing felonious shit just to get through the day. Being able to relax into a modest honest life is actually a rare privilege, prob'ly inherited from someone on the family tree who pulled off a big enough cheat to buy into that privilege. An' the original cheat gets obscured real quick by amusing family tales, so the generations inheriting that privilege are pretty much clueless about how incredibly lucky they are. An' if their luck happens to run out, they're disoriented an' helpless."

"Yeah," I whispered as I recalled my father's droll anecdotes about the small-town speakeasy his immigrant German parents operated during Prohibition.

Until that moment, I had assumed that once the black cold abated, things would slowly stabilize into a basic, no-frills version of the life I'd always known, and other than an ever-painful lack of Cordelia, it wouldn't be so different, really, than what came before.

Sure, the weather would stay freaky for a while and we'd face the hassles of supply chain disruptions. We'd endure shortages, maybe even inflation like the 1970s. And, hell, we'd probably be better off with price controls or rationing (after all, before Eleven Fourteen the country's citizens had gone quite insane, wasting at least thirty percent of our food supply while enabling forty percent of people to grow obese).

In the comfort of my almost-cozy living room I'd read all about what to expect after Eleven Fourteen—and figured that, hey, with a little fairness we'd get through it with enough to provide at least minimally for everyone. And when it came right down to me—well, no way would the cost spikes exceed what I could afford. No way.

Because, hey, with a little fairness, things would mostly keep working okay, not go *too* crazy, right? Once everyone calmed down, *of course* the rule of law would prevail again, even in the cities. We'd all keep stopping at stop signs. No one would break into my house and kill me for the contents of my pantry. I'd get my monthly SSI stipend as always, have to pay taxes and bills as always, be able to buy what I needed when I needed it. As always.

But—

But what if the world I'd lived in for seventy-five years, the only world I had any clue *how* to live in, was gone—exploded out from under all of us? What if I was experiencing a slo-mo, denial-infused descent into a new reality? A descent that *seemed* slow only because I was so unable to believe it—but maybe that new reality was actually coming on faster and faster as our descent approached terminal velocity...

And what, besides denial-infused habit and naiveté, allowed me to assume I'd be among those granted the "fairness" of a gentle landing (at terminal velocity, no less) when even before Eleven Fourteen this innocent young woman in front of me had been so nonchalantly declared a criminal and deprived of her freedom for the sake of promoting a couple of corrupt cops?

I studied Duka as her words echoed, heedless of how I seemed or whether I came off as rude. *If their luck happens to run out, they're disoriented and helpless.*

"You worry about me, don't you?" I said. "Like I worry about you."

This seemed to startle her. "You worry about—?"

"You. Yes."

Duka's laugh came out ragged and harsh. "You *do* get how that food stash downstairs ain't even close to enough to feed you an' everyone you share it with for as long as we all need it to, right? An' keeping it replenished will take a huge pile of money, Hester. A *shitload.* Cuz those spacious skies'll be way too cold an' dark for much of anything beneath them to grow long enough to be worth harvesting."

"Well, there *is* environmentally-controlled agriculture," I said, trying to sound hopeful.

"Nope, not enough," Duka replied. "Industrial-scale indoor growing adds up to a tiny fraction compared to what's grown outdoors. Like four thousandths of one percent. I got no doubt there's been plenty of greenhouses built since last November, an' plenty existing ones converted from growing flowers or weed or whatever to food—but it can't be enough. Not even fucking close to enough."

I admit it: I was speechless. How the hell did she know all that?

"Maize grown in the Midwest," Duka continued, eyes narrowing as she answered the questions I couldn't bear to ask, "down by ten to forty percent, an' soybeans down by, like, twenty percent—and it'll stay that way *for a decade.* The Chinese rice crop down at least twenty percent for three years, Canadian wheat entirely wiped out for god knows how long—"

"Where are you getting these numbers?" I asked.

"Remember that time when my phone had died an' I needed to check my email?"

"I remember."

"I noticed this article sitting on your computer's taskbar—'Earth's Future.' The one from *Atmospheric Chemistry and Physics*—so I clicked it up."

"Ah yes, one of my scarier digital crumbs. I recall downloading it, but I admit I've been procrastinating about that particular read."

"Sorry." Duka began to squirm. "Shoulda asked if it was okay for me to look at it."

I sighed, suddenly tired enough to take a nap. "I'm glad you did."

"Question is—how rich is rich enough to get a fair share of the food that *does* manage to grow? Best I can tell, the answer is: orders of magnitude richer'n you, Hester. An' you're orders of magnitude richer'n me. Which means I'm an early write-off. Plenty of people like me are already dead. People like you go a bit later."

"And as we starve—what?" No wonder I avoided that damn article. "We rob and kill each other for the last hamburger?"

Duka shrugged. She *shrugged*—and a panicky omigod omigod cranked up my heartbeat enough that I felt it thud in my throat, my ears, and I no longer wanted to nap.

"Be barter time soon." She spoke softly. "Lie-cheat-an'-steal time. An' yeah, maybe even—" She lowered her head and retreated to a whisper. "Worse."

"But you've decided to stay here," I managed to say, and I don't think my voice quivered. "Way out here on the Outer Cape where there won't be any food."

"Yeah. I'm home here. Know my way around. Not too many people. Lotsa, y'know—" She lifted her gaze and gave me a hard look. "Leftovers—unoccupied houses, unoccupied land, abandoned building materials, concrete foundations with nothing on 'em. An economy as much underground as above ground. Once I pick a spot, I got a better shot here than anywhere else."

"A *spot?*"

"For a greenhouse where I can grow food."

"You're going to buy property?"

"Hell, no. Cuz for a while anyway, I won't have to buy property."

I stared at her.

"Outflow," she said, schoolteacher-patient again. "Way more people leaving the Outer Cape than staying or coming in. So more Outer Cape businesses will collapse like mine already has. Things are already pretty skeletal around here now, almost a frontier."

"Yeah, I get that—real estate prices will tank even more than they already have. Like what happened to Detroit." Only worse, I didn't say, likely far worse than I'd allowed myself to expect. I sighed again. So much for ever selling the house. I wondered how long it would take Seaside Point to fade away, whether the accordion-playing chanteuse even lived in Wellfleet anymore.

"So I gotta pick a place—"

"For a greenhouse."

"Yep, an' soon. Takes warmer weather to build a structure, even if all I do is put polycarbonate or plastic over a foundation I fill with dirt—" Duka hesitated and her gaze fastened on my face, looking for something. "A new concrete foundation, though—" she paused again, her eyes narrowing as she blatantly stared at me, into me. "That'll need a decent stretch of fifty-degree weather. And there's signs it's on the way. After that, veggies'll take—"

"Mmm—about three or four months of growing time, right? Before they're ready for harvest." Now came my turn to hesitate and stare at her. "You're serious about this, aren't you?"

Duka nodded gravely. "Oh yeah. I just don't see any other way."

"To survive."

Another nod. "To survive."

Goddammit, I thought, suddenly deeply weary again. I am seventy-five years old and I do not need this, I cannot do this.

I contemplated excusing myself from the dining room table to put together that alprazolam/oxy and amaretto cocktail, then retreat to the guestroom bed downstairs to curl up and sleep forever. *Before* the stash in the basement ran out, *before* I actually experienced the hunger I knew others were already suffering, the hunger coming for me, coming closer every day. And perhaps as my cocktail took hold I'd get lucky and dream of Cordelia as I...

"Hester?"

How many times had Duka repeated my name before I heard her, before I realized I'd been gaping out the windows at the wretched remains of my white pines?

"As long as you understand what you're dealing with, there's opportunity in an economy that ends up mostly underground," Duka said, a strange, restless energy emanating from her.

"Sure as hell," she continued, "you'll always need 'official' currency for 'official' stuff, like taxes an' whatever rationed goods you're allowed to buy. For what'll be hardest to get, or get enough of, yeah, cash is great if you got shitloads of it. But if you're among the ninety-nine percent, it's down to bartering. So you gotta have stuff other people want. Stuff they'll trade for."

I turned to stare at her again, my mind jumbling. Before Eleven Fourteen, after decades of saving, eliminating debt, and living modestly with Cordelia, I'd thought of myself as someone with a decent amount of money and minimal expenses. I'd thought of myself as someone who could spend down unto death without risk of having to live out my last days cold and hungry in a cardboard box.

But now?

Now my income barely covered the ever-higher costs of food, utilities, gas, taxes; god help me if I had to contend with even a minor emergency. I hadn't yet dug into savings, but only because of what Cordelia's stash continued to provide.

Now I had to look at what Duka so urgently wanted me to see: Cordelia's stash wouldn't last forever. And food prices were escalating with each passing day, sometimes dramatically.

I remember inhaling slowly, hearing Cordelia's whisper: *Do it, Aitch...*

"Attached to the back of the house would be best, don't you think?" I said to Duka as I exhaled. "That direction is eleven degrees east of due south."

"I didn't feel like I had any business asking," she said, her head lowered. Like she was praying.

"You wanted to ask though, huh?" I pressed. "A couple hours ago, when this conversation started, when you told me you didn't know what to do. You thought a greenhouse right out there"—I tilted my head toward the dining room windows—"would be a damn good idea."

Duka nodded, her head lifting. "But, Hester, I'm broke. I can't even pay for the Tradesmen's Center space unless I come up with some kinda barter to dangle in front of Greg Silva—"

"I don't want any money from you, kiddo. I believe there's a better way to pool our resources."

The rest of what poured out of me was spoken by someone I'd never met before. "I bring this house and that old car, plus some income, some savings, and what's left of Cordelia's stash—for as long as all that lasts," I told her. "I'll also throw in what little physical effort I can muster. You bring your prodigious strength, your skills, your creativity and energy, your tools and truck, anything useful you've got over at the Tradesmen's Center. For whatever we need that's beyond the reach of your bartering abilities, we'll use my savings."

"Are you sure?" Duka rubbed her face. "I mean, I'm an—"

I reached across the table and again placed my hands over hers. "No matter how you count it or what happens next, I'm near the end of my ride, and if I try to go the rest of the way alone, very soon it'll get *very* uncomfortable. But you—your ride is just developing some momentum—"

"Well, it was. Till this Eleven Fourteen shit blew up my business."

"But you're young enough, skilled enough, and resilient enough to adapt. Especially if, like I said, we pool our resources—an arrangement that, by the way, I want to put in writing so it's crystal clear about your fifty percent stake—"

"No, Hester, that's wrong. That's too much. It's your property. Your savings."

"Fifty percent, Duka, and hell, I'm probably cheating you. Because if you're even a little bit right about what's ahead—and given the way my stomach twists into my throat whenever I think about it, I believe you *are* right—then we're gonna need one hell of a hustle. And we both know that's mostly gonna be on you."

CHAPTER EIGHTEEN

AS MUCH GARBAGE AND CHICKEN SHIT AND COW SHIT AS POSSIBLE

Our Final Greenhouse Plan called for several hundred square feet of plantings.

"In raised beds," Duka told me as I perused her scale drawings, done in pencil on graph paper. "Already found some good framing lumber. Been collecting seeds, too. An' some decent soil—though I need plenty more. Lizbie Watts knows a lot, said she'd give me a hand. Ever check out her greenhouse back there? I've been helping Sam install some LED grow lights in it. Damn impressive, what they got."

I smiled, nodded encouragement.

"If we can grow a decent supply of veggies, potatoes, an' peanuts, the money we budget for food can be spent on meat an' dairy," she continued, her dark eyes squinting. "So maybe we won't have to go to bed hungry next winter."

How many nights last winter had Duka gone to bed hungry? Too many, those eyes suggested as she mused about what lay ahead: "By next winter there'll be all kinda 'emergency' declarations an' new rules. Limits on how much can be bought at any one time. Some form of rationing of meat, flour, milk, gas, soaps. All of it with craploads of new surveillance, maybe even martial law, depending on how pissed off an' desperate all this shit makes people."

I smiled some more. Nodded some more. But about ten seconds after we agreed on the Final Greenhouse Plan, I retreated to my basement guestroom refuge, curled under the covers, and hyperventilated my doubt into a pillow.

By morning, I'd achieved full-fledged waffle. Not that I was ready to admit I wanted to beg off. More like let's tone it down, scale it back.

But when I came upstairs to do my little waffle dance, Duka was nowhere to be found. A few seconds later, I saw her standing outside some ten feet behind where we'd agreed to put the greenhouse, akimbo atop a tangle of broken, partially ice-covered tree limbs.

"Right along here," she shouted loud enough that I could hear her from the middle of the dining room. She wasn't after my attention, though. She was hollering at Toby Snow, who came into view as he made his way down the western slope of the property. "It'll be great!" she declared exuberantly as she raised her arms like she was embracing the whole back of the house. "It'll be fucking *great!*"

Tears in my eyes, I stared at her and counted.

Twenty-seven years since Cordelia had stood out there, arms spread wide, grin spread even wider. "This'll be *great!*" she had yelled to me across what back then had been a heavily-treed undeveloped lot, pushing me to say yes, yes, we'd buy the property and build on it the house where we'd grow old.

Now Duka talked of clearing away most of those irretrievably battered and broken trees, taking care to separate out the hardwoods, "cuz we'll sure as hell need all the firewood we can get next winter," tossing the rest into the hollow to be chipped and composted.

Two yeses, then. One coming in, one going out.

With help from Toby, Sam Behr, and Lizbie Watts, Duka had our greenhouse built and planted in just under seven weeks—a herculean effort that began with clearing the tangled masses of debris behind the house, then digging out and leveling the ground in preparation for an insulated concrete foundation. We had to wait a few days for the fifty Fahrenheit degree stretch of weather that Duka demanded for pouring and curing concrete—first the footings, then the four-foot-deep foundation walls.

The hardest part for Duka came next; she had to give the concrete four weeks to cure before framing.

So she cut and split remnants of hardwood and piled them into stacks of firewood. She made compost bins. She ran wires for greenhouse lighting and ventilation, laid pipes to deliver water and heat to the soil she'd be putting in the raised beds, installed a dedicated electric boiler. And showed me what she'd discovered in a sheltered, south-facing corner of the hollow: Huddled beneath gnarled-claw tree remains, bits of green flashed their neon-bright resilience—*alive! alive! alive!*

She pointed first to a few tentative shoots of wild grass. "Also, look under those dead pine branches," she called out. "Moss. Violet. Over there—that's blueberry, I think. An' farther up the slope—see it?—burdock. One of your rosa rugosa survived, too."

The sight of living green banished, for a while anyway, my recurring bouts of pessimism about our new After Eleven Fourteen world. Moss and grass and violet and blueberry hinted at darkness lifting, at least a little, even though the solar panels on my roof churned out little more than they had a month earlier.

See? Cordelia whispered in my left ear. *Something left to love.*

When at last Duka could frame the greenhouse, she finished in just a few days, erecting reclaimed cedar timbers that supported UV-resistant polycarbonate triple glazing with automatic vents, all carefully caulked, weather-stripped, and sealed. Then she installed LED grow lights, several oscillating fans, and night-time thermal blanketing. She even erected trellises and hanging trays that she cut from commercial gutter remnants.

I ended up paying cash for the fans, the electric greenhouse boiler, and the various town permits (which, in effect, were bribes; the inspectors signed off on everything sight unseen—saying, according to Toby, "that Duka girl knows what she's doing").

Every bit of the rest was, ahem (whenever I inquired, Duka would clear her throat), "leftovers." Anytime I poked for specifics, she'd shrug and say something about scavenging or bartering.

Between acquiring all the greenhouse materiel and making it into something, Duka must have found some time to sleep and eat (and perhaps pine for Essie), but I have no idea when. I made meals for both of us, hers packed in a little plastic tub; during those days, I rarely saw her actually consume anything.

Well before I wanted to begin my morning, she'd be outside laboring on the greenhouse, exploiting what murky daylight we had plus what the floodlights along the back of the house provided. When it got too dark for her to continue with detailed work, she'd trudge garden carts of soil into the greenhouse from a tarp-covered pile behind the garage that seemed to magically replenish itself. Many evenings she'd disappear for parts unknown (by me anyway), returning late enough and quietly enough not to wake me.

I found it impossible in the face of Duka's shot-out-of-a-cannon work ethic to just watch all this from the comfort of my perch at the dining room table. So, despite her remonstrations ("C'mon, Hester, you're doing more than enough already!"), I honored my promise to take on what physical work I could—and ended up in shit.

Literally.

Because one does not simply toss any old dirt into planting beds. One decides (again) not to pursue questions about where the hell Duka finds 700 cubic feet of assuredly clean topsoil, and then one "amends" that topsoil with compost.

Sounds innocuous enough, but when we're talking compost, we are in fact talking garbage—and shit. As much garbage and chicken shit and cow shit as possible, as shredded and/or broken down as possible, all layered into Duka's three wood-and-wire bins, each one a cubic yard.

Three feet wide by three feet long by three feet high. Times three.

This may not seem like a whole lot—unless you're an affirmed keyboard queen and your task is to fill each bin with green nitrogen garbage (fresh leaves and plant stalks, kitchen scraps, coffee grounds, crushed eggshells) alternating with brown carbon garbage (dried leaves and plant stalks, coffee filters, straw, hair).

In between these layers goes chicken manure gifted from Lizbie Watts's chicken coop and some of the cow manure Lizbie gets from George Malcolm, the so-called South Pamet Farmer who for years has kept several seaweed-fed cows that, apparently, produce "good" cow shit.

Oh, and since all this has to be transformed from garbage and chicken shit and cow shit to compost *in a month*, it's gotta get hot in those piles—so make sure everything's moist but not soaked, and keep it aerated by getting in there with a pitchfork to turn it over every other day.

I admit to a cheat: Our initial pile of compost was actually a separate, ready-for-primetime present from Lizbie that arrived in garden carts pulled by her kids, Mirrie and Nate.

"Use this to amend the first soil Duka brings into the greenhouse," Lizbie instructed. "If you're diligent, by the time the greenhouse is finished, you'll have three bins of compost all ready to go."

Cheat or not, I hadn't spent so much time outdoors in years, maybe ever, and I wasn't accustomed to the sustained physical labor. But Mirrie helped me enough that I could sufficiently pace myself, and my back, though often sore, never seized. Plus the kid, like her mother, is a fine teacher. "It's Mum's soil recipe, so you'll end up with a nice crop. You'll see."

About two weeks in, I noticed steam rising from my compost piles. A good sign. Soon after, I started adding the biochar Mirrie taught me how to make using a remarkably ugly-quaint contraption comprised of nested steel drums that we set up on a patch of gravel down in the hollow on the east side of the property, near where Duka had dumped the carcasses of my dead pine trees.

Producing biochar involves the pyrolysis of wood, which required a bit of heavy-ish lifting that took me some getting used to. First, we had to shove chunks of wood through a "leftover" woodchipper Duka "found," then load the chips into the big fifty-five-gallon bottom drum. Next, we snugged on a second slightly small-diameter steel cylinder, followed by an even smaller third cylinder.

Result: a whimsically chimneyed barrel stove that we'd light via the holes in the bottom drum and get burning at 500 degrees Fahrenheit for maybe an hour or ninety minutes, producing plenty of combustion but not much carbon.

Each burn yielded slightly more than a cubic foot of small, black, glistening chips that sound like broken glass when they cool and dry out. Since for weeks I didn't do much else besides composting and pyrolyzing remnants of my dead trees, I managed to generate fairly impressive amounts of biochar. Enough for all our soil as well as Lizbie's garden and greenhouse—the least I could do to pay back some of what we owed her and Sam.

"That stuff is gardening gold, y'know," Duka said when she heard I'd been sending Mirrie home with buckets of biochar. "But Lizbie an' Sam are crazy busy, an' they don't want Mirrie making it unsupervised—" She stopped herself when she saw me chuckling.

Mirrie had supervised me much more than I ever supervised her, and with her help I'd built the skills and finesse I needed to make biochar by myself during weekdays, when Mirrie was at school. "Does this mean I've found myself a hustle as a biocharwoman?"

Duka grinned. "For as long as you can stand it."

All considered, I stood it pretty well, even though the biochar had to be made outside through a May that, while starting out decent enough with temperatures that ran close to normal, took a record-breaking plunge as June approached—into cold, blustery, and occasionally snowy.

Yet the off-kilter weather might have helped me pay sufficient attention to making sure I didn't hurt myself. Because, for me anyway, the work was exhausting. I got away with it, though, aided by caution and lots of ibuprofen. And sleep. I slept more soundly and for longer stretches than any time since Cordelia was diagnosed.

In those many moments when fatigue gave me no choice but to stop and rest, I took refuge in a tent Mirrie brought over. We erected it near the stove, moving it as necessary to keep it upwind, and because of it I was quite effectively sheltered and warmed, especially when I had Mirrie for company.

I enjoyed my time with Mirrie Watts. The implications of Eleven Fourteen weren't lost on her, but she refused to be frightened and had a gift for steadying her little brother, Nate, who hated wearing a mask until she drew crayon decorations on it and made it part of a new superhero outfit comprised of a tan outback hat with a chinstrap, old deerskin gardening gloves, wraparound sunglasses, an almost ankle-length cape (aka Mum's green rain poncho), and one of Cordelia's hiking sticks.

Thereafter, Nate became Guardian of the Coop, a task he and his large mutt took very seriously. He also declared himself Second Safety Officer (Mirrie held the rank of First Safety Officer); in their presence *no one*, kid or adult, was allowed to be "UO"—Uncovered Outside. If you found yourself outdoors without your UV-blocking sunglasses, your wide-brimmed hat, your facemask, your long sleeves and long pants and gloves, then you heard about it—loudly and unrelentingly—from Nate or Mirrie. Or, god help you, both of them at once.

At the close of many of our biochar days, Duka, Toby, Sam, Lizbie, Nate, and often Melinda and Annie from across the street would gather round the stove with Mirrie and me and we'd cook a potluck supper over its fading heat. Loo-*weeeze* never joined us, but during the couple of weeks before the greenhouse was done, Sylvie Costa came by with Toby's mother, and we all finished off the hot dogs from Cordelia's stash, along with "leftover" hot dog buns, cans of baked beans, and bags of potato chips acquired by Duka.

By the end of May, about two-thirds of the greenhouse planting beds had been filled with Duka's soil. Looking back, I'm not sure how I managed to keep up with the soil amending; my back had gone into high squawk mode as I shoveled in the ripened compost I'd already boosted with biochar.

But manage I did, and on the first Sunday in June, Duka, Toby, Sam, Lizbie, and an especially eager Nate, Superhero of our Upper Hollow Circle neighborhood, carted the last of the soil into the greenhouse while Mirrie and I followed behind working in the remainder of my biochar-boosted compost.

"Yee-*hah!*" Lizbie hooted when we finished. "Couple of weeks for the compost and the soil to get to know each other, and this last part'll be ready for planting."

Duka scowled. She was pale, stiff, and hoarse; the circles under her eyes made her look either very ill or beaten up, and she'd started to forget little things, then become too angry at herself when she remembered. For days, she'd been grousing about blown schedules, even though we were within a week of her extremely ambitious deadline. "We gotta plant it all ASAP," she muttered to me as she stood in the middle of the greenhouse twitching at the prospect of delay.

"We're good, Duka," I soothed her, running my hand down her back as I recapped her plan yet again. "The crops that need the most time we plant first, right?" With my other hand I pointed behind her at the beds closest to the house where I'd done my very first soil amending almost three weeks earlier. "Those beds are ready to go. After that, we—"

"Yeah," she said, already in motion, "then we sow the quickies like spinach an' potatoes. Yeah."

I shifted my hand to her belly to slow her down. "In the morning," I said. "After you finally get some real sleep."

"But—"

"C'mon, kiddo." I had to take a couple of steps with her because she hadn't stopped moving. "You're wiped. I bet you don't even know what day it is."

"Uh-course I do." She halted. "It's—it's—"

"Time to call it a day, my friend. We'll start planting tomorrow."

CHAPTER NINETEEN

AL CONTRARIO

I admit it: Cordelia's stash had struck me as extreme unto absurd before Eleven Fourteen and seemed immense in those first months After—even for two people rather than one, even as it sporadically shored up Lizbie's crew or Toby's mom or Melinda and Annie when they ran out of milk or rice or wheat flour. The enormity of Cordelia stash was how, for months, I'd been able to hold on to It'll Be All Right.

In retrospect, I suppose that's why I'd avoided doing a stash inventory in those days right after we planted the greenhouse. I'd been too afraid. Until, finally, I opened the large freezer and realized there was hardly anything in it anymore.

Time to count.

So: I'd gone through nearly all the frozen food, two-thirds of the rice and flour food buckets, about eighty percent of my cocoa supply, and more than half of the canned stuff. As I stood in our basement storeroom, I realized I simply did not know how long the rest of the stash might last us.

"Jeez, Deels, this is getting serious."

One more time, I felt Cordelia nearby, just out of sight. One more time, my yearning for her caught in my throat, stung my eyes.

She hadn't been ready to go—not until those last couple of weeks, after she'd passed her eightieth birthday and no longer had strength to resist the deepening debilitation or the disorienting, drug-induced stupor that kept her implacable pain at bay. While she was still here, I had tried to say it all, and so had she. But I'd left out so much, forgotten so many moments...

Then came Eleven Fourteen, and how do I not tell her about that, even if I'm jabbering to a phantom? So jabber I did, especially since I was, invariably, all by myself whenever she came around.

"Look at me now," I said to her as I stood in the middle of our main basement storeroom squinting at the grim calculations on my tablet screen. "I've become the watcher of your shrinking stash and our deflating bank accounts, the keeper of compost and maker of biochar, the meal planner, the cook, the launderer, the housecleaner, the greenhouse sweeper and weeder and waterer… And not only am I terrible at all of it—it's not enough. I did the math and *it's not enough*."

Well, Aitch, you're impressively adept at biochar. Her voice seemed wispy, but it carried a light, teasing laugh—Cordelia's laugh. *Slacker.*

She was right, as always. Even though I'd continued composting, and went so far as to brew compost tea to spread on our soil, I hadn't made any biochar since we'd planted the greenhouse.

Which is why I marched down into the hollow east of the house every day for a week to pull scraps from the tangle of softwood debris dumped there, plow them through Duka's woodchipper, and do burns in our crazy-tilt pyrolyzer.

A couple of pails went to Lizbie, some I kept for our own compost piles, and the rest I planned to barter for whatever Duka and I agreed we needed most.

"We could ask Michael Oswald," Duka suggested when we discussed it. "He might want biochar."

"The guy on Highland Road who farms mushrooms?" I shook my head. "Annie told me he grows his exclusively on the trunks of dead oak trees, so that's doubtful."

"Michael also keeps bees. For honey mostly. But he has a garden for his bees—not huge, but he's prob'ly worth asking."

"Oooh, honey. I *like* that."

"Maybe George Malcolm, too. Lizbie says he's putting polyfilm high tunnels over his gardens, which means he might have interest in biochar."

"Yeah, I considered that. But he only trades his milk and wants *a lot* for it. I was hoping to get some fruit, maybe some spices like cinnamon and garlic."

"And coffee?" Duka asked hopefully.

"Yeah. Coffee too."

"Well, there's this guy in South Truro—Duncan Dorrance. Bugged out from New York to his manse by the bay, an' his high tunnels are done.

But his asshole quotient's higher than his tunnels, so I try to stay away from him. He sometimes does trades, though. Has access to stuff like fruit, meat, sugar, all kinda cheeses, soaps, weed, over-the-counter meds. An' coffee. Older dude." Duka paused to study me, one eyebrow rising. "Who can say? He might kinda like you." Another pause. "Or I could talk to Alison Perry. Y'know, at the Pond Village Market."

"Really? I've seen the Open sign when I drive by there, but the place always looks so dark inside. I wasn't sure it was actually in business anymore."

"Oh, it is." Duka offered up a quick, sly smile. "Alison had to adapt to the pandemic, of course, so she went takeout. Then, with Eleven Fourteen, the summer demand for bahn mi avocado an' pickled carrot sandwiches on gluten-free baguettes dried up. Now—well, she's no charity, but she can get you almost anything you want. Just ask, ante up, an' ye shall receive. She has deep off-Cape sources, though not a whole lot gets displayed on her shelves. We oughta be calling her place the Pond Village Black Market. Not that I'm objecting. Al contrario."

CHAPTER TWENTY

EL PURGATORIO

To me, Alison Perry had always been alternately see-through-me indifferent on a busy summer day and off-season almost-friendly. Maybe she'd been pretty once, but as she passed fifty, she'd gone saggy, slitty-eyed, and unrepentant tough-gray. One of those people, like so many others around me, whom I should have known better than I did.

Certainly I should never have missed the fact that, like Isabella Franzi, Alison Perry remained among Duka's few customers from Before.

"I do snowplowing for all her properties, repairs once in a while—the market, the café next door, the apartments in back, plus the three houses up the hill," Duka said, then blurted at the speed of light "An'sometimesotherbusinesstoo."

I suspected (as in *aha!*) that Duka both wanted me to notice that last bit and hoped I didn't. "Other…business…" I tried to sound offhanded. "Presumably related to 'leftovers.'"

"Not just leftovers."

I waited for the rest. And waited.

She remained mute. Nor would she look at me. Then: "Up till Eleven Fourteen, Hester, I played it completely straight. Never broke a single rule once I got out from under that conviction. But now—well, now I do the best I can. Y'know, under the circumstances. Which, uh, isn't always the same as being strictly law-abiding.

"I kinda figured that out, kiddo."

"So, yeah, I exploit the, um, gray areas, like with scavenging. An', yeah, sometimes I outright cheat. When it's necessary, like with the electricity. Depending on what's involved, I figure the details oughta be, uh, strictly need-to-know."

"Electricity," I repeated. "Curious you should mention that." I waited till she finally looked up in order to catch her eye. "This morning I got the first electric bill since we turned on the greenhouse boiler and grow lights. And since you installed those honking big lithium-ion batteries—"

Duka groaned. "I can explain, Hester."

"Glad to hear it." I watched her eyes skitter away to eventually settle on her nervously interlaced fingers. Stalled just a little too long, didn'tcha? I waited some more while her shoulders scrunched and her knuckles whitened. "Duka, tell me why the electric bill didn't go up at all for June. I estimate that the greenhouse roughly quadruples how many kilowatt hours we consume, and the solar panels aren't producing anything much. So…"

One Mississippi, two Mississippi—and her gaze rose to meet mine, yet she said nothing.

"So I'm guessing," I continued, "that you've found a way to pilfer electricity. Just for the greenhouse and the battery, judging by the amount of the bill." Clever, I didn't say.

She seemed to ricochet off my words, lifting onto her toes and talking way too fast as she paced a tight circle in the middle of the living room.

"They won't be able to tell who did it even if they come out here an' snoop around cuz—cuz I didn't tamper with anybody's meter," she babbled, "I cut into the line across the street in three places, all roundabouty an' disguised, y'know, an' the line in the middle, I shielded that one, got it coming into the greenhouse an' the battery stack, y'know, unseen, so they won't find it, an' also I got both dummy lines going toward Union Lane, an' they'll never be able to stick anything on you even if they suspect you, which they won't cuz…cuz…they won't…"

I should have been upset. Not so long ago—Before, when life was Normal—I would have demanded she disconnect an illegal electric power hookup. The downside risks, I would have told her back when life was Normal, were just too high.

"So—" I had to run my index finger along my lips to tamp down my grin. I swallowed a breath and tried again. "So you tapped into the underground power line across the street, and then you buried this illegal tapline, and—and what? You managed to tunnel your pirated tapline under the whole width of the street to get it over here?"

Her head moved down-up-down-up too quickly. "With that little tunnel boring machine Sam has. Mostly the same tunnels as for the closed-circuit alarms an' cameras we installed. I made sure it's all real safe, Hester. They won't figure it out cuz they'll find one of those other dummy taps first." Her hand flittered eastward. "Coming above ground after a few yards, camouflaged an' also all weatherproofed an' sealed, both of 'em going off into the woods to, y'know..."

"Right. Toward Union Lane."

I kept watching her—one Mississippi, two Mississippi—and as I watched her she started babbling again, which was when, quite abruptly, I kind of split into two versions of myself, two streams of awareness running in parallel...

One stream had me wanting to chuckle: 'Bout time the shareholders of that damn for-profit electric company did some sharing of their own, and let's just see how long we can get away with it, and what the hell, let's just see what they'll be able to prove when—if—they come huffing around here all indignant and righteous.

The other stream had me staring at Duka in amazement:

First she sells me on alarming the house—infrared sensors, cameras—but let's do closed-circuit and redundant, hard-wired so it can't be hacked. And let's expand it to Sam and Lizbie's place, and Melinda and Annie's, and Toby's, too, since you never know about the "Uns" (unknowns) on our street. Like whoever lived in the house rising above mine to the southwest, like "that asshole" across the street to the northwest—"y'know, the guy Loo-*weeeze* messes with, Bo Broderick who works at Coxswain's Bank, thinks he's boss of Truro's firefighters."

And then—*then* onto this neighborhood closed-circuit security system Duka piggybacks underground power lines rigged to pirate electricity.

As she kept on talking talking talking too fast, I also realized—

Okay, yes, some-damn-how I've acquired a roommate—although I'd begun to see us as forging something more like a businessy kind of partnership. Certainly she was what I needed—young and strong and hard-working and impressively, usefully multi-skilled...

I knew she'd added her old prison hustle—fixing electronic devices—to her ongoing repertoire of engine and motor repair and maintenance as well as anything electrical, carpentry, masonry, metalwork, snowplowing, and (almost always with Toby) plumbing. Now small tunnel boring. But there was more. And dammit, I needed to know what it was. To what degree had "scavenging," which she'd never given up, become larceny?

I needed her to tell me the truth, all of it and right then. I held up my hand. "Stop, Duka. Just stop."

She went silent. Her face blanked. And behind her blank, so determinedly rigid and controlled, I saw her fear, raw and clawing at her insides.

"Tell me, kiddo—" I said, lightly touching her forearm. She gawked at my hand in surprise, and my fingers felt her urge to pull away, but I kept them on her arm despite its high-frequency quiver. "Am I right in supposing that you don't tell me about some of the things you're into because you want to protect me?"

Once more, her head moved down-up-down-up too quickly.

"Do you think I'm going senile?"

At this, she laughed out loud, a sort of high-pitched hoot, and her arm stopped quivering. "Hell no, not you."

I smiled. "But I'm too old, too privileged to really understand— y'know, about what you gotta do sometimes."

This time she nodded slowly. "Also—" She wavered, shifting her weight from one foot to the other. "I don't like to, um, have to come asking you for, uh—"

"Ah, yes, for what it takes to get things that can help us."

"I'm trying to keep the pressure off you. Cuz it's—it's—"

"Financial pressure."

"An' I'm frigging broke, Hester." Tears brightened her eyes. "I'm sorry about that an' I'm trying to—"

I rubbed her arm before gently withdrawing my hand. "To spare me, shield me. But also because you don't entirely trust me not to judge you—"

"I don't entirely trust you to understand how godawful this Eleven Fourteen shit really is, how much, how bad it's changed everything."

"And what it might take to—to—"

"Survive, Hester. The word is 'survive.'"

"But when you don't trust me, *I* end up not trusting *you*—and god, I do *not* like not trusting you, Duka."

Her eyes flared and then her shoulders rose, fell—another way of nodding. "Our only chance," she said, "is to create a crew with other people. People you can trust to cooperate, share, trade fairly. An' all I have to bring to that, my only resource, is the work I can do. I try to be smart about who I trust, about how to make my work valuable, about where the margins an' edges are. Try to, y'know, anticipate."

"I can't promise to always see it your way, kiddo. But you have to risk telling me what you're up to anyway. And I have to risk—well, I have to risk going along with you. Even when it scares the crap outta me."

I waited for her to absorb this, which she did statue-stiff, head down, for a long moment. Then she lifted her head into another nod. "Okay, I get that," she said. "But I don't want you to ever end up in trouble or be in, y'know, any danger cuzza what I do. What I have to do."

"I appreciate that. Keeping me entirely in the dark isn't an option, though. So how about we find a middle realm—?"

Duka laughed. "Not bad enough to be damned to hell, not good enough to go to heaven. 'El purgatorio,' my abuelita woulda called that."

"Sounds about right to me."

Duka peered at me, eyes narrowed, for another long moment.

"Deal," she finally said and held out her right hand, which I took, and we shook on it.

"Excellent." I touched her arm again. "So I have only a few questions."

CHAPTER TWENTY-ONE

TAKES SOME ADJUSTMENT

We talked first about "scavenging" for "leftovers." Beginning with: When did you start doing that?

"End of last year around the holidays," Duka said as she sat down at the dining room table. "That's when customers started dropping us an' putting their properties on the market. At first, I was able to get some to agree to let me an' Toby take stuff in lieu of paying their bills." She gazed out at what looked like a thriving greenhouse crop. "Electronics. All kinda furniture. Appliances. Tools an' parts. The woodchipper, the new generator. Picked up a hi-def camera drone one time. Canned an' frozen food with good dates. Even a few jars of peanut butter."

"And after 'at first'? Then what?"

"We'd take shit from deadbeat customers who blew us off cuz they were walking away from their property, not even bothering to try selling it. Sure as hell they wouldn't be paying their mortgages an' taxes anymore. Or ever paying us either."

"And they didn't even want their keys back," I muttered, recalling the only time I'd ever seen Duka drunk.

"Yeah, those were the easy ones to, y'know, 'barter' with. Involuntarily, ahead of their creditors. Got the sinks an' lights I installed upstairs that way. Also all the sensors, cameras, an' control panels for the alarm system. Plus a lotta what went into the greenhouse—the cooling an' dehumidifying systems, the LED grow lights, other stuff from this *bum* in Wellfleet with delusions of marijuana-growing grandeur…not to mention delusions of leaping into Essie's bed. An' then, uh—"

She'd stalled, like a car starved of fuel, so I sat down across the table from her. "Then you expanded again, to deadbeat ex-customers whose keys you *didn't* have."

"Yeah. An' after that to scavenging places obviously abandoned, already mostly stripped of the easy pickings. Those're good for things like piping, wiring, fixtures, windows, well tanks. The last of business inventory sometimes—like some of our seeds, most of the greenhouse soil from a couple of those defunct landscaping outfits. Also found our lithium-ion house batteries that way, still in their packaging in a shed behind a pile of garbage, which was unusual—but you'd be shocked at what you can find in P'town these days."

"What's left of P'town, you mean."

Everyone had such high hopes for what was supposed to be a spectacularly profitable Outer Cape summer. But it turned into our first After Eleven Fourteen summer, and it was catastrophic. Just how catastrophic was most obvious in Provincetown. Memorial Day's three-inch snowfall turned out to be merely a forerunner of the blizzard-like squalls that obliterated two June weekends, and Commercial Street stayed gray and empty.

Many of the stores and restaurants that had managed to survive the pandemic never opened, and every day saw the demise of another of those that did. Public restrooms were again shuttered. Ferry service ceased. Once more, Carnival was canceled. Street cleaning and garbage collection were suspended. I heard gossip about both newspapers folding, about how many real estate agents were leaving town, about more and more locals deciding to pack up and go despite having endured here through the pandemic and then the black cold.

When that cemetery-side condominium complex for well-heeled hoaries, Seaside Point, stopped serving meals, rumors swirled about the place no longer having staff at all because hardly any of its few remaining residents had been paying their fees. No surprise, really, given how little the stock markets had rebounded from that calamitous November 23 nosedive.

Other rumors gusted around us, too. Several damaged cell towers would not be replaced anytime soon, so don't expect cellphone and internet service to resume pre-Eleven Fourteen levels anytime soon either. Is it true the supermarket has reduced its hours? How long, realistically, can it stay open at all? And what about the pharmacies? The health clinic? The bus service? One or both of the gas stations in Provincetown? Maybe also the one in Truro out on Route Six?

Into this downward spiral, jarringly, some new faces arrived on increasingly barren, dismal Commercial Street, especially around the Coast Guard station.

"Used to be, like, twenty Coasties over there," said Toby, distrust in his voice and his eyes—something I wasn't accustomed to from this very kind, essentially gullible man-child. "Sylvie told me there's gonna be at least a hundred now."

Others appeared, too—mostly men in civilian attire, all unsmilingly vague about who they were, what they were up to, or where they were living.

Their reticence churned up a new round of rumors among the persevering locals—chiefly that the newbies carried the highly contagious so-called Eleven Fourteen Virus.

Probably true(ish) enough, but I also pondered whether the rumors about its high mortality rate were fed by a certain After Eleven Fourteen jealousy, since virtually all of the newbies—civilians as well as Coasties—worked for one of the very few operations in town *not* losing the battle to survive: the Department of Homeland Security.

No question the old Provincetown was dying, and the old Truro, too. I listened for hints about what would come next as Duka described how she pulled a living out of the detritus.

"So," I asked her at one point, "am I right in assuming that whatever you don't keep from your, uh, 'scavenging' you trade with Alison Perry?"

"Among others. Greg Silva's nothing if not a trader—that's why I still have space at the Tradesmen's Center. For hard-to-find consumables, I mostly deal with Alison. She's a broker, like Greg. Isolates buyer from seller. So what one of 'em gets from me—I dunno where it goes, don't wanna know. An' vice versa with what they sell me."

"You trust Alison and Greg not to—to—"

"Fuck me over?" Duka snorted. "Mostly. They'll take more than they should sometimes. 'Specially if you mouse up an' don't haggle with 'em. Flip side is they got lotsa contacts—an' plenty of motivation to keep the parties involved separate from each other. So all of us can say we didn't know nuthin' 'bout no felony, officer."

A bolt of anxiety shot through my chest. "Damn, Duka, has that *happened?*"

"Nah. Not even close. One of Alison's buddies, an' prob'ly Greg's, too, is that Truro police sergeant—what's her name?"

"Higgins," I said, a little surprised at myself for remembering.

"I choose not to guess how Alison an' Greg keep the sergeant happy. As for me, I'm willing, at least so far, to pay for a layer of anonymity, a little distance from the darker side."

"And how dark *is* that, exactly?"

Duka shrugged. "Don't know much about Greg's gigs, but Alison's got all kinda hustles. Made a deal last winter with the Truro Distillery people, bought the Village Café next to her store, coaxed what's left of town government into letting her sell booze there, an' keeps it open late for anyone who likes to drink the local whiskey an' play small-stakes poker, then slide out the rear door straight into the arms of those very friendly ladies in the apartment building up in back, which she also owns. Far as I can tell, Alison's running the healthiest businesses in Truro."

"Jeez, and here I was wondering how that café place could be surviving as a tourist fish-and-chips joint when there's no tourists anymore."

"Yeah, well, Alison's just getting started. Toby told me she's also got a deal with some guys in Provincetown trying to keep one of the Commercial Street liquor stores alive. They give out coupons for her café that include free van rides back an' forth with one of the ladies. Toby says it's working cuz most of the liquor store customers are 'new people'— not just from the expanded Coast Guard station but also the Border Patrol an' other DHS dudes who wouldn't bother coming out to Truro without certain, um, incentives."

"And how do the Provincetown store guys make any money?"

"I'm guessing Alison has a stake in their business—an' according to Toby, who I know supplies her with black market ganja, she picked up a stake in the Truro Distillery, too, not just a sales deal. Nice way to set herself up for what'll be even more new-people customers as soon as that offshore windfarm construction gets final-staged outta P'town harbor."

I'd heard gossip from Melinda, or perhaps it was Annie, about a couple of possibilities in the Outer Cape's future—not merely a Provincetown airport upgrade to accommodate small jets and helicopters but also a 900-megawatt windfarm off the backshore—yet Duka's news smacked of decisions actually made by those with the power to see them through.

"You mean this windfarm thing is more than a distant maybe?" I asked.

"Front-burnered according to what I hear," Duka said. "Word is the windfarm work will start as soon as the pier's extended eastward an' the harbor's deep-dredged to handle bigger vessels—small-scale ships, also small LNG tankers."

"Whoa—" I interrupted. "Did I hear you say LNG tankers?"

"Yep. Propane, an' gasoline an' oil, too, coming straight into Provincetown harbor by boat—well, small ships actually. Other vessels'll bring in food an' other supplies, mostly for the Coasties an' their DHS accomplices. Also wind turbine stuff for the windfarm people. An' who knows? Maybe the rest of us'll be able to finagle a little something. Legally or not."

So: No more praying to a false god that the trucks hauling everything across the bridges and all the way down Route Six would actually make it out here with their cargoes intact. Sure as hell *sounded* like good news.

"When?" I asked. "How long will all this building and dredging take?"

"Haven't heard any dates—but it'll be a while. The fuel operation will come first cuz it's easier logistically. Since Costa Fuel is the only game in town anymore, Sylvie's dad is part of the consortium behind it. But Sylvie's the one running Costa Fuel day-to-day now, an' she says they're going for a floating transfer terminal that'll locate east of the harbor, off Beach Point. At least a year for the switchover, but she's all excited cuz she just got the contract to supply the P'town Coasties, an' she's chasing the windfarm's onshore fuel contract, too."

"Golly gee whiz," I said, "I suppose boosting the Coast Guard facility, bringing in a bunch of Border Patrol goons, and building an industrial-scale windfarm offshore just might keep Provincetown from disappearing, at least for a while. Any info about who the hell's gonna pay for all this?"

"Gummint, of course." Duka winked. "The part that gets away with printing money."

"At least," I murmured, "there actually *is* a gummint printing money, hyperinflated though it is for anything except paying taxes and Medicare premiums."

"Not everyone sounds as happy as you. People like Isabella an' that obnoxious friend of hers are freaking." Duka waved her hands in mock dismay and threw her voice into falsetto. "'All that riffraff marching around in uniforms? That's militarization! A windfarm? Cargo ships an' tankers—*tankers!*—in the harbor? That's heavy industry! Oh *no*, our views will be forever ruined! Oh *no*, what*ever* will happen to Provincetown's precious artistic heritage? Oh *no!*'"

"Ah, well." I sighed. "The Outer Cape's economy has to shift from harvesting tourists and rich people to harvesting wind and strategic geographic value. Takes some adjustment."

"They don't *want* to adjust. Isabella gets all weepy-eyed, which won't last long—she'll be pounding her fist hard-ass as ever soon enough. But her very important friend Phoebe Bigshot twists up like a neurotic pretzel cuz not everyone is raging about it *an'* she can't get high-speed internet every fucking second of every fucking day *an'* I haven't found the right remote yet for the fancy-ass garage door opener in her daddy's fancy-ass house."

"Hmm. Just about as tall as you, blondish, good-lookingish, well-tended, lives near Isabella?" When Duka huffed a contemptuous affirmative, I nodded. "Yep, I think I met her at the P'town supermarket once, back when they sold potatoes—"

"Very important tech princess, got burned outta Boston, yada yada." Duka flipped a hand dismissively. "Heard it all. Only good thing about that woman is she'll pay up front with fat wads of cash—like a junior Isabella."

I found this information vaguely disconcerting. How much did it confirm what I dreaded to hear about conditions not only in my Outer Cape environs, but also *out there*, beyond the rotary in Orleans, beyond the two bridges over the Cape Cod Canal? "So she hasn't gone back to the city yet."

"Oh no, Phoebe Bigshot's here fulltime, an' all pretentious about it, too. Like something must be seriously wrong with anybody who *doesn't* make six fucking figures working from home."

I shook my head. I'd had the impression when I met Phoebe that she wanted back to the city as soon as it became livable again; had she stayed because she deemed the city as yet too chancy for tech princesses? Was she no longer taking unstable internet connectivity in stride because she worried she might be stuck indefinitely in Truro?

Or was Duka exaggerating because Phoebe Bigshot had pushed every last one of her buttons?

"Acts like she's got plenty to burn," Duka grumped. "So how 'bout she buys up what's left of P'town an' makes it into a fucking living history museum? *That'll* keep the military-industrial corruption at bay an' show all us pitchfork peasants what for."

Yep, no button left unpushed.

"So where," I asked, determined to stay on topic, "does all this belong on my worry scale, one being no biggie, ten being my head will blow off? Starting with how the cops are responding to your, um, enterprising activities."

"Ha! They don't have time for anything as piss-ant as chasing locals who scavenge abandoned buildings. Outer Cape law enforcement funding's pretty much from the feds now, an' the feds want the local LEOs running alongside the Border Patrol, the Coasties, an' the other DHS bullies chasing after illegals who sneak in from Canada an' traffickers of anything illicit. Plus the local cops gotta make a show of trying to catch those guys who've been hijacking trucks on Route Six."

Talk of these robberies along the Outer Cape's only through road to the outside world was everywhere. Brazen and frequent enough to intermittently worsen the already skimpy supplies at Provincetown's supermarket and the surviving pharmacy, they put everyone on edge. Especially anxious were Melinda and Annie, who spent a lot time traveling Route Six, and Lizbie and Sam, who worried about sending Mirrie to middle school in Orleans—an eighteen-mile trek up Route Six. Even Alison Perry had been impacted.

Odd, everyone agreed, that not a single culprit had been identified, much less caught.

"How the hell," Melinda had griped, "do you escape a peninsula that's only twenty-five miles long, is at no point more than five miles wide, includes forty-three thousand acres of national park, has only one road out—and fewer than two thousand people still livin' here?"

"Maybe they *don't* escape," Duka had replied. "Pay-to-play is easy once you know which of the local cops are interested in the game."

CHAPTER TWENTY-TWO

CATASTROPHIC COUNTRY INDUSTRIAL

Our peanuts had showed up first—on the morning of the eleventh day after we planted the seedlings. Once both Duka and Lizbie confirmed that yes, the little green shoots I spotted really were peanuts, not weeds, I rejoiced. But Duka fretted about soil temperatures. "Figured we'd see the acorn squash before anything else."

Did that mean our squash crop would be a bust? Although sprigs of squash plants popped up soon after the peanuts, Duka's worry was understandable. During our first summer After, the weather continued to be, for lack of a better term in these misogynist times, a *bitch*.

And a deceitful bitch to boot. Following those three inches of snow on Memorial Day, we enjoyed seductive stretches of coolish but almost typical summer temperatures that encouraged hope—"See, it really *is* getting better!"—before another bout of freezing hit-and-run snow squalls. June and then July continued the gray, blustery weather pattern that replaced the black cold, and we saw no rain, only snow which actually didn't add up to much (snow squalls, after all, are more about wind than precipitation). We were on the verge of drought.

At least the electric power stayed stable, mostly. In fact, it went out often, but for periods brief enough that the generator managed to keep the greenhouse lights and heat running. Plus we were able to get the propane we needed, though it cost plenty and the Costa Fuel Company had taken to demanding payment on delivery.

About midsummer, Duka began talking about small-scale wind turbines again and about some guy she met who had "all the right credentials for putting 'em in the right place."

I watched her peer out the living room windows toward the wind-battered monstrosity of a house that loomed on the higher ground to the southwest. ("The Hulk," I'd started to call it ever since the black cold had wrecked the thick pine and oak mini-forest that once mostly hid it from my view.) Then her gaze slipped westward to the empty lot across the street, also more exposed than ever after the black cold ravaged its trees. A good spot for small-scale turbines, perhaps, if someone were to clear away the wood debris.

Unfortunately, I didn't own either of those properties—but hey, a girl can dream, right? *She wants to keep going, Aitch.* Cordelia's appreciative light laugh faded as soon as I heard it. *I do believe your girl has a vision.*

Some vision. Wind turbines rather than trees. Rough, low-slung structures. What Isabella Franzi once snootily described as "catastrophic country industrial."

I wanted to disagree, but my vision, such as it was, had glommed uncomfortably onto the greenhouse, and what I saw at first was huge and raw—essentially cedar timbers propped against the back of my house to hold up an almost-transparent polycarbonate cover that sprawled twenty feet into the yard's bedraggled little wilderness where my white pines once towered.

"Ugly," I thought as I watched the greenhouse foundation and its frame take shape, repeatedly burying the sentiment with unspoken words like "necessary" and "inevitable" and "beats starvation."

"Ugly," I thought again after we planted and I endured the glare from the greenhouse grow lights blazing through the window in my basement guestroom refuge where I'd never bothered to close the blinds until the day Duka brought in a backhoe.

Bu-ut, teased Cordelia. *C'mon, Aitch, admit it. But...*

Okay, dammit. *But* at least I no longer see all that scraggly, dying scrub oak and pine from the guestroom window every time I get in or out of bed. And, yeah, yeah, I don't have to suffer the sight of the Hulk dominating the southwestern sky whenever I sit at the dining room table or glance out the living room's back windows.

In fairness, the greenhouse did become less ugly the more I looked at it and spent time in it, less ugly as the lush, life-affirming greenery of trellised acorn squash—*healthy* acorn squash—filtered the light coming through the guestroom window, an effect that inspired me to resume leaving the blinds open because the new greenery gave the space where I woke up every morning such a wonderfully *not*-After feel.

By the time our acorn squash had grown that high, I very much needed the guestroom's *not*-After feel. Because by then the Outer Cape's summer season was about half over and already universally regarded as a disaster.

Chapter Twenty-three

On fire

Drought plus wind plus desperation; in retrospect, the inevitability of it all was obvious.

Eight weeks after Memorial Day, fire had destroyed twenty-three Provincetown buildings, victims of several arsons, accidents, and equipment failures that the diminished capabilities of the town's shriveled volunteer fire department could not prevent from spreading to nearby structures. One business owner had been arrested for torching his premises, and according to the gossip that flashed across the Outer Cape faster than any flames, another had been deemed a "person of interest."

Fires afflicted the other Outer Cape towns, too. A wind-driven blaze in South Truro, allegedly accidental, spread to three more dwellings. I heard a lot about that damn fire, in granular detail, from Toby, who'd signed himself up as an auxiliary firefighter and responded to the call, as well as Duka, who went with him "to see what all this auxiliary firefighter shit is about."

Why secondhand reports of a fire on the other end of town should keep me from sleeping and then invade my stunted dreams I shall never know. Maybe it was the hushed and wide-eyed way Duka and Toby talked about how the flames awed them. Terrified them.

"They were alive," Duka whispered. "They had a-a—"

"A hunger," Toby said. "Felt personal, y'know?"

For at least a couple of weeks, our new fire precautions (a go bag, carrying around a walkie-talkie rather than relying solely on our shitty cellphone service) only provided fodder for the fires in my barely-asleep nightmares, which invariably jolted me hyper-awake again. Until, finally, one night I was just too damn depleted *not* to thud into heavy, dreamless sleep.

I woke up still tired but grateful for the greenhouse labor that had helped exhaust me. Even automation-assisted, it just wasn't the sort of work I was used to. I'd grown up with a small backyard vegetable garden, but that was long ago and I never knew much anyway. Duka's experience was far more extensive—and recent—than mine, so by default she was our Chief Greenhouse Officer, and I learned a lot by simply following her around during the meticulous inspections she conducted each morning and evening.

For a while, what I learned gave me a cautious, unspoken sense of almost-comfort: The greenhouse systems continued to behave, Duka seemed to have mastered the lighting, I'd gotten the hang of what to water when and how much, and the usual garden pests hadn't found our sheltered patch. I even learned how to pollinate acorn squash. All told, as June progressed into July and then August, our nine crops appeared to be doing well.

During those weeks, Duka also went fishing with Sam Behr, whose well and septic business had, like so many other local enterprises, fallen off an economic cliff. For years, Sam had fished for the fun of it in his old thirty-foot downeaster; after Eleven Fourteen he and Duka spent long days fishing out of necessity.

Thus we sometimes ate seafood—stripers mostly and occasionally a slab of bluefin if Duka didn't trade it for meat or eggs or fresh milk or oranges. Early on, the fishing seemed decent, but I heard Sam lament that "nuthin's where it's s'posed to be anymore."

At least seaweed had continued rolling onto the beaches. Sam collected it by the truckload both to feed Lizbie's chickens and to resell, usually to George Malcolm for his cows. Sam's seaweed money went to gas for his boat—until the cost of gas outstripped the price he could get for seaweed.

That was when he started trading a portion of his catch for the rest of the gas his boat needed. By then Toby was working at Costa Fuel (having ignored both Loo-*weeeze*'s flirtation with Bo Broderick and her squawks about Sylvie Costa) and gave Sam a good deal on the gas and "y'know, sea-credit fill-ups, too, which means Toby takes the hit if I come back empty-handed."

Hence, as the weeks passed, he and Duka ended up with less and less.

"I'd try hunting turkey or deer or rabbit or duck," Duka said glumly after nothing to show for a long late-July stint on the water, "even outta season without a license, cuz nobody's enforcing that shit anymore an' I'd

NOT ALL A DREAM

have good odds of getting away with it. But the black cold frigging wiped 'em out."

At least the day's greenhouse inspection went well, since I'd spent the afternoon conscientiously weeding all of the greenhouse beds and cleaning the floors. So I tried talking about how nicely our spinach was ripening, how I thought it would be the first crop we'd be able to pick and eat. Duka responded in grunted monosyllables. Until we returned to the living room—

"Sam talks more an' more about taking a seal like some of the others've done. Hell, for all I know he already has, since I'm not with him every time he goes out..." Her shoulders hunched as she plopped onto the sofa. "Tempting, I'll admit. But it's not just a federal crime—with all those Coasties patrolling off the backshore these days using goddamn drones, it's also way too easy to get caught. She didn't speak for maybe a three-count, maybe four, then snarled "*Fuck!*" before going silent for the rest of the evening.

Thus did my cautious, unspoken sense of almost-comfort end. Something about Duka's demeanor began to haunt those moments when I crawled into bed, closed my eyes...

To be fair, my sleep patterns had gone wonky as soon as I'd taken on morning greenhouse duty. For one thing, I continued to stay up night-owl late, never mind that I had to rise obscenely early to water and tend what we were growing. After that, I'd spend maybe fifteen or twenty minutes with Duka reviewing the day's have-to list and just chatting before I shuffled back downstairs to snooze for another hour or two.

At least our first crop was doing well as we neared the beginning of weeks of harvesting. No time to falter in my greenhouse duties, no matter how much I wanted to stay in bed.

So there I was, crack-of-dawn sleepy on a late July morning, doing what I always did—which included stepping outside the greenhouse for a moment via its back door to check how heavy the clouds looked and what sort of gray they'd impose on the world around me. When I happened to glance up at the Hulk like always, a movement at one of the bedroom windows caught my eye: Someone stood staring down at me, and damned if he didn't duck behind a curtain as soon as I did a double take and offered a small wave.

This startled me because by then I half-believed the Hulk had been vacated like so many of the houses around us—though Duka maintained that it was occupied; she'd noticed late-night activity on our closed-circuit security network's logs. "Ol' Paula's long gone, but *somebody's* damn well up there. The cams at Lizbie an' Sam's show three different vehicles going in an' outta the driveway, always between two an' four a.m."

In almost two months of early greenhouse mornings, I'd never once seen anyone at the Hulk's windows. And then he was there every morning, same time, same window, same furtive retreat, which I'd spot out of the corner of my eye even before I turned my head. One morning after a week of this, I didn't step outside the greenhouse—mostly due to a ferociously biting east wind, but also because I decided (what the hell) to conduct an experiment by peeking out a second-floor window to see if the occupant of the Hulk would appear.

He did.

He hovered at the window for half an hour, then disappeared.

That night, well after my usual one a.m. bedtime, I woke to the potent, intimidating sounds of angry howls, screams of fear, and yelps of protest. Human sounds—and male, I thought. I had no idea which direction they came from, but they were loud enough to wake me in my earth-insulated basement space. Something horrific was happening somewhere close by.

By the time I stumbled into clothes, our alarm system began to blare. Someone was on the property.

By the time I got upstairs, Annie had arrived at the front door. "It's at Broderick's," she rasped as she bounded into the living room. "A fight, I think. Two voices, one of 'em headed up there—" Annie pointed toward the Hulk.

Duka was already moving toward the door to the greenhouse. "Let's get out there this way."

Flashlights in hand, she and Annie quickly scanned the greenhouse and were about to step outside to take the path that led up to the west side of Upper Hollow Circle. As Duka reached for the greenhouse back door, she glanced up at the Hulk—and froze.

"Omigod," she gasped. "It's on fire."

I followed her gaze and saw the Hulk's first-floor windows, all of them, glowing orange.

And then, well, chaos.

Because not only was the Hulk on fire, so was Bo Broderick's place. Southwest and northwest of my house, respectively, and neither of them more than 150 feet away from where I stood.

CHAPTER TWENTY-FOUR

WHAT'S GONNA HAPPEN TO THE CHICKENS?

Certainly, I had no wish for bad things to happen to other people's homes. But with all my being I willed that wind to keep blowing those damn flames away from *my* house, away. And with all my strength, I dragged garden hoses around my property for hours to douse what ground I could. Especially the hundred-something upslope feet between our greenhouse and the Hulk.

And oh god, we were lucky, though too many others weren't.

Because even before the fire department showed up, embers from the Hulk propelled by a thirty-five-mile-an-hour northeast wind spewed onto a house on the other side of Upper Hollow Circle and quickly set it alight. By then, Broderick's place looked like an enormous, out-of-control homecoming bonfire—which had started slithering and slapping through the wood debris in the yard toward a house behind it on neighboring Alder Way.

That house ended up rescued, just barely, thanks to my Upper Hollow Circle neighbors, whom Toby organized into our own unofficial little garden hose wielding fire brigade.

I saw little of what they did, since I was relegated to upwind/downslope duty on the other side of the Hulk's flames. But I heard plenty over the walkie-talkie. I felt relief at how they kept an eye on each other—and even more relief when Truro firefighters showed up with the town's only fire tender, which brought water to precisely the right place in our hydrant-deprived location.

Farther west, however, firefighters' efforts to drag hoses a quarter mile from the only "nearby" hydrants up to Alder Way came too late to save a whole section of that neighborhood from the Hulk's wind-driven embers.

Ah, the wind. Even while it (mostly) shoved the flames away from me, first blowing them southwestward, then nearly due south, fire filled the sky, heated the air around me. Every now and then, the wind grabbed a clutch of flames and twirled them, whooshing them suddenly, aggressively toward me before whooshing them away again. A reminder, I thought: Dare at your peril to believe you know me.

We're as prepped as we can be, I kept reminding myself as minutes turned into an hour, three hours, more. Go bags already in the car, which was already turned around so we could drive away to the north-northeast, into the wind, no backing up required.

One shit-scary sweep of ravenous flame at a time, I stayed to spray more water, watching for the next mad whirl of fire, the one I'd run from.

But I stayed—mostly, I think, because I was able to sustain walkie-talkie contact with Duka and Annie and Lizbie. So I knew everyone was okay. Still okay.

The Hulk itself burned to its foundation before my eyes, but the large two-car garage on the southeast side of the house remained mostly intact, if quite charred on one side. When I heard Duka's voice sounding almost calm over the walkie-talkie as she repeated "knocked down," I dared to relax a little—and that's when it happened.

The Hulk's garage exploded.

The kind where balls of flame blow out the windows. All four in the garage facing my direction, even the one up in the loft, burst like that. I'm not sure whether the blast knocked me down or I just ducked; anyway, I ended up in a tight crouch with my arms over my head, covering my ears. Jeezus, it was *loud*.

I suppose I was disoriented for a minute. Numb. My thinking simply stopped at *Wow*. Then I got to *What the hell?* Then I thought *Oh god, Duka.* And then the others… Annie…Lizbie…Toby…Sam…

My hearing took a little longer. I'd made it to my feet, had begun bumbling toward the west path to the street, hoping, hoping Duka and the others were safe somewhere on the west side of Upper Hollow Circle farthest from the garage. That's when I realized my walkie-talkie was yammering.

"Hester! Hester, talk to me!" Duka yelled and yelled again.

And yes, she was okay. Fortunately, everyone was far enough away from the garage to remain unscathed. "But the houses across the street to the south—" Duka sounded screechy hoarse and out of breath. "All three of 'em—they're all burning now an' it looks like Sam an' Lizbie's place'll be next. We're sending the kids to you. On the southeast path."

I turned around to look for them—and saw a red glow about fifty feet from the greenhouse. "Got some burning deadwood back here, too," I hollered into the walkie-talkie as I yanked the garden hose and pointed its skimpy output at newly sprouting flames.

"No, dammit, you do *not* get this," I screeched at the fire.

Seconds later, Mirrie, Nate, and the mutt came running up the southeast path toward me. "Mum said to come over here," Mirrie called out when she saw me, her voice quaking. "But what's gonna happen to the chickens?"

At least I didn't have to answer that one, since just as Mirrie and Nate reached me, the entire Upper Hollow Circle crew, led by Lizbie and Duka, came scrambling down from the west side of Upper Hollow Circle and rounded the back side of what little remained of the Hulk; the flames, Duka said, had made the street in front impassable.

While Lizbie calmed down her kids, the struggle to contain the fire shifted to the lower, east side of the street and was joined by a Wellfleet tender and a pumper and the nascent signs of what passed for daylight. None too soon, either: The tender's first task was to quench the flames threatening the cedar shingles on the west side of Lizbie and Sam's place. Then the upslope area I'd been trying to douse received a Wellfleet firehose drenching.

Lizbie and Sam's little homestead was saved, as were their chickens. So, too, were my house and Duka's greenhouse, the little rundown ranch behind Broderick's on Alder Way, and several houses on the comparatively ritzy street south of ours where Isabella Franzi lived.

Only with the full ooze of murky high noon did we get a thorough view of the damage: Altogether, ten dwellings and four outbuildings had burned to the ground. Our Upper Hollow Circle neighborhood and nearby Alder Way looked like a war zone. The whole southwest end of our street was a smoldering, stinking, apocalyptically black ruin. I had a panoramic view of it every time I gazed out any second-floor window along the back of my house.

At least, we told ourselves, no deaths, no injuries. Of the ten destroyed residences, just two had been occupied—the same two, Broderick's place and the Hulk, where the fires started. For another day, we were clueless about the fate of the man in the Hulk's window—until a body was discovered in the Hulk's ruins.

By then we'd learned why Truro's bald, boorish deputy fire chief, Bo Broderick, had failed to show up at any of the three locations where the fire had been fought: He had vamoosed—with an undisclosed amount of cash from Coxswain's Bank Route Six branch, where he worked as deputy manager. And he wasn't alone; Loo-*weeeze* vamoosed with him right after a blowout with Toby over Sylvie Costa, whom Loo-*weeeze* accused of stealing her man (by his own account, her man responded by declaring that he should be so lucky).

"Broderick believed it," said an incredulous Lizbie. "Actually believed we'd all buy his bullshit. 'Oh sure, the Route Six truck hijackers robbed a bank—even though they've never *ever* hit anythin' except vehicles.' And, 'Oh sure, just coincidence that you send a late-night text to your boss wantin' a personal day for a medical appointment—and then your house just happens to burn down.'"

Within a week, we found out that Broderick and Loo-*weeeze* had booked themselves into one of the few hotels open in Hyannis forty miles up-cape, where they were busted with their loot and several empty bottles of Dom Perignon. Soon afterward, Broderick confessed to a convoluted scheme wherein he'd faked ownership of the Hulk in order to allow the man I saw in the window to stay there rent-free as payment for the gambling debts Broderick owed him.

The guy, who scared the bejeezus out of Broderick, was "an accomplished double duker who also smuggled coke, meth, and the occasional jerry can of gasoline." When he demanded the deed to the Hulk (yes, ol' Bo owed him that much), panic ensued; Broderick decided to grab all possible cash from the bank and make a run for it. When the guy realized Broderick had duped him about the Hulk, he set fire to Broderick's place, and the Hulk, too, but somehow got trapped and died in his own fire.

Or maybe Broderick killed the guy and started the fires to cover everything up.

Last we heard, both Broderick and Loo-*weeeze* were residing yet another forty miles up the road at the Barnstable County Correctional Facility. I'm pleased to report that when Duka was told this, she did not gloat. Snickered for a second, observed that at some point we all seem to have an Essie in our lives ("even Toby"), then once more mused about the possibility of clearing the charred debris of the Hulk and Broderick's house in order to convert their foundations into greenhouses. But she did not gloat.

I wondered briefly whether she might prefer living at Toby's now that Loo-*weeeze* was no longer an issue, but before I could wheedle the question into our conversation, she made it moot: "Never figured I'd be grateful to that woman for anything, but if Loo-*weeeze* hadn't been around, I wouldn't have ended up here. And I'm damn glad I ended up here."

"So am I, kiddo," I told her. "So am I."

Chapter Twenty-five

Not Enough

More than anything, it was the fires—and the various towns' imploding abilities to cope with them—that provoked a critical mass of concern about the consequences of losing tax revenue. How long would we be able to sustain functioning fire departments? Would the elementary schools close once and for all? The health centers? The transfer stations? The harbors? What about the water systems? What about the cops?

Even closer to home, my neighbors and I faced the challenges of cleaning up after the fire at a time when insurance companies no longer answered their phones and government oversight of such matters had nearly vanished.

However, in a sign that at least some government survived (so far, at least), a state fire marshal inspector showed up to check for toxic and carcinogenic substances (verdict: not too bad) and to make sure we had no propane leaks. He came and went in less than an hour. The town offered use of some equipment to cart away debris and an unsupervised landfill to dump it in—but the labor required had to come from us.

So it did. Not because we owned any of the burned properties, but because we needed to remove all the toxic crap we possibly could—especially the ash too easily riled by our Outer Cape winds—if we were going to continue living unpoisoned in our homes.

I suspect Truro's town manager (by then also the town clerk/treasurer/tax collector) figured we'd put in half a day and then wimp out. But our Upper Hollow Circle gang of eight—Duka, Lizbie and Sam, Toby and Sylvie, Annie and Melinda, and me—stuck with it through four foundation cleanups. This inspired a bit more help from the town's remaining maintenance crew.

"We're it," the three guys told us after emphasizing that we were on the receiving end of a big fat favor from the town manager, whom everyone called Town Hall Margie. "We're all that's left of the Truro Public Works Department."

Melinda was the first person I heard talk in specific detail about how so many people forsaking their Truro properties had created a revenue crisis that eviscerated town services and personnel—something brought to her attention during a home visit with the man who was the chairman of our local finance committee.

"No wonder the poor guy had a heart attack," she kept repeating, having learned all about how, ever since Eleven Fourteen, Truro property tax receipts, more than three quarters of the town's income, had been dwindling. "Not even the banks holdin' the forfeited mortgages are keepin' up with property taxes anymore. I've seen the numbers—it's beyond scary."

I tried not to sigh aloud as I listened to her. My long-time question(s)—when will our Ponzi scheme economy come crashing down around us, and when it does, how much government, anywhere at any level, will continue to function?—were being answered. Live. In real life.

And I admit I worried. The force of this demand—that the town take possession of tax-delinquent properties *now* and offer them for sale via a Land Bank Authority modeled on the one in Detroit—signaled that, yes, our Ponzi scheme economy was indeed imploding; it also signaled that, during the rest of my life anyway, money might never be the same.

Even FDIC-insured bank certificates of deposit like Cordelia and I had were worth less every day as measured by how much was needed to buy, say, a pound of coffee. Or fill a gas tank, something so expensive that I carefully planned any use of my car, waiting for errands to pile up, figuring out the most efficient routes, hooking up with Lizbie usually so we could split the cost of an excursion, similar to what Duka often arranged with Sam or Toby.

Beyond scrimping and the greenhouse, there wasn't much I could do but hope.

Hope that we'd pull a good first crop from our greenhouse soil, enough to feed us, and that the next crops would be good ones, too.

Hope that the potentates might remain sufficiently fearful of unruly passions run amok that they'd prioritize basic government functions like depositing social security stipends every month, maybe even see fit to pressure food producers and energy suppliers into reining in their greed.

But August would soon yield to September and another winter. Even if the "experts" turned out to be right and we were spared a second stretch of black cold, we'd face winter temperatures—and food supplies— "significantly below normal." So for how long, really, would we be able to sustain ourselves in this dreary, sunless After Eleven Fourteen world?

The more I thought about it, the more I realized I didn't know how to think about it. I had shelter, so far anyway, and our water supply seemed to be holding up—but in my whole life I'd never been truly hungry, much less nutritionally deprived. I'd never once worried about lacking the money to pay for food or fuel or electricity.

Because we'd saved enough, Cordelia and I. We figured we sat somewhere around the ninetieth percentile—about ten percent of old American farts had more than we did, ninety percent had less. Adequate for taking us through "the duration," we told ourselves. But as I gazed at the devastation upslope from my house, as I watched Cordelia's stash and our bank accounts wither, Not Enough loomed larger and larger.

And I wondered: If it's like this for me, what horrors have beset the ninety percent with less than me, the billions of even poorer people all over the planet? For that matter, besides me and the people immediately around me, how many of us were even still alive almost nine months After?

Once upon a time, I would've had a clue about that. But no longer; the "news" had long since devolved into pablum about "defending our borders" and endless complaints about lousy weather predictions. Hell, maybe I was better off *not* knowing how many of us were still alive almost nine months After.

CHAPTER TWENTY-SIX

REVERENCE

I'd never been a fan of spinach. Ominous-dark leaves, often wrinkly and stringy, bearing an almost bitter taste of minerals—unless they were cooked into a slimy glop that reminded me way too much of seaweed.

Cordelia's various spinach preparations improved my attitude some, but I believed this was only because she understood how to hide the insipid truth with ingredients that, some nine months after Eleven Fourteen, no longer graced our pantry or our refrigerator: fresh lemon and/or oranges, avocado, bacon, chickpeas, unpitted Greek olives, cheeses, spices—even, occasionally, delicate phyllo pastry.

Then came that day in early August—dark and cold like maybe we'd see some much-needed precip (even if it was frozen), but, as it happened, no, not a drop, not a flake or pellet on that day when Duka led me out to our thirty-odd square feet of greenhouse spinach and pointed. "These along here," she said, her hand casting a shadow over the green leaves as it blocked the LED lights above. "They're ready."

Deftly, she picked leaves from several of our dozens of spinach plants, stepped over to the sink in the greenhouse's small prep area to run water over them, and then placed a few in my hand while she popped a leaf into her own mouth.

Even though Duka smiled and nodded as she chewed, I girded at the prospect of an unappealing spinach dinner. At least, I thought, it'll be a solid hit of vitamin C and magnesium and all that other superfood stuff.

Thus did the first leaf of the first crop of anything ever grown on any property I'd ever owned find its way into my mouth.

And oh…my…god…

It was wonderful.

Sweet. Tender. Fresh fresh fresh.

I ate slowly, savoring each bite as we talked about how best to make a meal of the leaves Duka had begun to gather up.

"How 'bout we use some of that feta cheese I got from Alison yesterday?" she whispered as though she might be overheard by spies.

"And we still have some preserved lemon and soy sauce and balsamic vinegar," I whispered back. "Not a lot. But enough to make a decent dressing."

"Plus we can trade some spinach, too, like for Michael Oswald's honey and mushrooms…"

After celebrating with assorted spinach salad creations for a week or so, Duka and I dug up our first early potatoes. We decided to roast them, add lightly wilted spinach along with a tiny dollop of preserved lemon, cap this with a Lizbie egg each, then sprinkle it all with Wellfleet sea salt.

Reverence in her voice, tears in her eyes, a potato speared on the end of her fork, Duka said, "Good as anything Abi ever grew in her garden."

I agreed, of course, aware on a whole new level not only of what I was eating but of eating itself.

How much of the world's food-producing ability had been destroyed by Eleven Fourteen? If anyone anywhere knew, they sure as hell weren't saying. Nor did we have any idea about how badly Eleven Fourteen had disrupted the complex global supply chains we'd long since come to unthinkingly depend on for, well, almost everything. Except, of course, for one whomping hint: the persistent shortages of, well, almost everything.

No denying that by the end of the first summer After, supply chains of food, medicines, fossil fuels, you name it, that once so easily stretched all the way to the end of the Outer Cape had been severely throttled. Or maybe it was more accurate to say our supply chains had nearly dried up, like the flow of the Colorado River, so plundered upstream that it only rarely reaches the sea anymore.

Reason enough to feel reverence for a homegrown potato.

CHAPTER TWENTY-SEVEN

WHERE THE DEVIL IS

Although our seven remaining greenhouse crops were ripening nicely, my time walking the greenhouse with Duka had taught me there are no guarantees. So far we'd been very, very fortunate—but *shh!*, "don't wanna jinx it."

So I worried about the future in silence. After all, no guarantees the greenhouse's boiler would be able to heat both soil and air sufficiently to sustain a second grow as the air chilled toward what was likely to be an autumn as mercurial as the summer. And after that, god knows what kind of viciously frigid winter we might face, not to mention the possibility of another black cold.

I could see that these worries hounded Duka, too—but we didn't dwell on them, at least, *shh!*, not aloud, not yet.

Of course I should have done another count: Add up my meager income and savings, divide that grim sum by the prices of what was still available from local sellers, then add in what little remained of Cordelia's stash plus our expected greenhouse harvest, thinking all the while about what might be bartered for what...

But I didn't. Because, moment by harried moment, it was easier to stall than to count. Because I was so very tired.

And *then* because it became obvious that the rumored Eleven Fourteen virus, including its mortality rate, was real and probably as contagious as its pandemic-causing cousin.

We were, however, numb. Pandemic-numb and Eleven Fourteen numb. I heard more than one person say something like "What the hell, if it's gonna get me, then so be it" as they went on with their daily routines.

Hardly surprising, since nearly the only healthcare available on the Outer Cape came from Melinda and Annie. "We're down to almost-expired acetaminophen and Band-Aids," Melinda fumed. "Ever since the Border Patrol set up that tactical checkpoint in the middle of the Route Six rotary, none of our orders make it past Orleans anymore. I'm gonna have to drive to Hyannis again to get the supplies we need, then hassle with those idiots at the checkpoint. Damn, I hate drivin' back here with a car fulla the kinds of drugs people kill for."

As the days passed, the virus burned through the population of the Outer Cape alarmingly fast, infecting just about every person I knew and killing several of them, including Toby's mother, Sylvie's father, both of the Gibsons, and Greg Silva's wife.

"Whatever that damn virus is and however it traveled here, the special town meetin' shoulda been done remotely," Melinda railed. "I know Truro's broke and all, and of course we need to figure out what to do with so many tax-delinquent properties, but my god, facemasks don't help when people yank them off to yell at each other in an enclosed space. Has anybody who went to that meetin' *not* gotten sick?"

As far as I could determine, the answer was no.

Some of us ended up in much worse shape than others, though. I escaped with a relatively mild four-day case after which I felt quite normal—in time to deal with Duka, who spent a full three weeks flat on her back or rolled in a semi-conscious ball.

She probably should have been hospitalized, since her virus turned into pneumonia. But she refused. "If it's gonna kill me, let it kill me here," she wheezed. "Please, Hester, I-I'll stay in my truck if I'm contagious, but please don't let 'em take me away."

I'd recuperated sufficiently by then to assure her she'd stay right where she was, upstairs in the bed Cordelia and I had shared for so long (at least until Melinda or Annie demanded she be hospitalized—but I didn't tell her that).

Thus in between picking, processing, and storing the next round of our ripened greenhouse crops, I masked up, gloved up, and took care of her—kept her hydrated, regularly proned her, made sure she ate at least a little something, changed her sweat-soaked bedsheets, even helped her to the bathroom through those three days when she was too dizzy and weak to stand or walk without aid.

She did have the enormous advantage of youth, so her recovery, when it finally came, was quick and complete. Even so, she emerged scrawny and easily exhausted. Which meant, her protestations notwithstanding, light duty only.

"You're healed enough to supervise," I insisted. "*Supervise*, mind you. That means you keep me from making a mess of things *from a sitting position* for the next two weeks while our peanuts and sweet potatoes and broccoli and cabbage all pop."

And pop they did. For greenhouse neophytes, we'd done gratifyingly well.

Scores of servings of spinach, squash, broccoli, carrots, and cabbage. A potato and sweet potato crop topping two hundred fifty pounds. Thousands of peanuts, quart upon quart of strawberries. I became a veggie blanching-and-freezing expert and also acquired whole new skillsets: how to transform mashed potatoes into biscuits and pancakes and breads and pies and even cakes, how to press peanuts into oil, how to churn up peanut butter.

Meanwhile, Duka strengthened enough to collect and sort seeds, and kept on poring over spreadsheets, which she revised and re-revised as her greenhouse planning evolved. She talked (and talked and talked) about soil amendments and soil temperatures and crop rotation and companion planting and what might possibly benefit from trellising and how much more we could—realistically and maybe not so realistically—squeeze out of our 411 square feet of raised beds and rolling benches and hanging trays.

I smiled and nodded—and said nothing about the fret I saw in her eyes, the tension in her jaw. But I just couldn't ignore the *uh-oh* pulsing in the base of my throat.

Becau-ause, Cordelia whispered in my left ear, *the count. You were gonna do it more than a month ago, remember?*

There had been promises from on high—the flowery-vague type of which politicians are so enamored—that things would improve.

Yet ten months after Eleven Fourteen, very little of whatever endured of the world's production and distribution capabilities got past the Orleans rotary and onto the Outer Cape anymore.

Whatever did clear the rotary's thieving Border Patrol tactical checkpoint overseers faced the highway robbers of Eastham, Wellfleet, and South Truro. By Labor Day, this was semi-effectively addressed by "concerned Outer Cape citizens" (notably Alison Perry, Greg Silva, Duncan Dorrance, and a woman from Wellfleet named Hannah Atwood) whose small, cop-escorted convoys braved the journey down Route Six— greased by "donations" to Border Patrol "charities" and fat private detail payouts to the Outer Cape cop escorts—expenses that added significantly to the cost of everything on those trucks.

Entrepreneurial spirit being what it is, by Labor Day other supply chains—supply threads, really—had been opened by Alison and Greg via Provincetown harbor, by Hannah Atwood using the recently dredged Wellfleet harbor, by Duncan Dorrance out of Pamet harbor. Alison and Greg brought in stuff from Boston on ferries with ample room for cargo because they no longer carried scheduled passengers, and Hannah Atwood did okay in Wellfleet with somewhat smaller vessels. But silting limited use of Pamet harbor to high tide only.

Pricey, to be sure—yet water transport often cost somewhat less than road transport, while local goods locally traded typically cost less than either. Hence Lizbie Watts's inspiration: a weekend bartering day when anyone with something to trade could show up at the Truro Elementary School, now repurposed into the town's sole still-functioning community building, used for pretty much everything except police and fire functions.

Lizbie picked Saturdays, and her barter events were instantly popular, though far from cash-free. The first one came off like a classic pre-Eleven Fourteen farmer's market: Lizbie's beans and tomatoes and eggs, Michael Oswald's mushrooms and honey (gone in an hour), others offering lettuce, carrots, zucchini, goat cheese, sea salt, soap—all neatly arranged on tables. Since I didn't have a clue how much of our crop we ought to trade or how to value it, I merely helped Lizbie at her table on the first bartering day and traded nothing from our greenhouse.

Even before that first day ended, many deals were done on an elbow-bump in the school parking lot; rather than cart items to the school, traders showed cellphone images of what they had, agreed on terms, and exchanged goods off-site (thus did Duka negotiate a scavenged bicycle for a five-gallon drum of gasoline and spread word that she'd barter her services for "tell me what you got").

Such encounters produced new ongoing relationships—Lizbie ended up with regular customers seeking her eggs, for instance—even as Saturday bartering at the school continued, especially once the sparse selection was improved with Alison's "ferry stuff," which Lizbie soon dubbed "ferry gouging." Yet even Lizbie acknowledged that her Saturday barter events would have withered and died without Alison's ferry goods and the "insidious corruption" of Alison encouraging payment in cash at prices Lizbie called "beyond outrageous."

Ostensibly, those prices weren't quite so bad off-Cape. No consolation to those of us who lived here, however; ten months after Eleven Fourteen, food costs on the Outer Cape had risen at least an order of magnitude, often more. By mid-September, the majority of my comparatively high-end monthly social security stipend went to groceries, since, for example, a single gallon of supermarket milk cost almost forty dollars and one five-pound bag of wheat flour went for thirty—*when* these were available. Chicken had become rare, beef unattainable.

When I finally counted it all up, I appreciated why hardly anyone lived here anymore. And I found myself fully embracing what, deep down, I already knew—that Cordelia's stash had given me a profound sense of safety and protection—at precisely the moment when I had to admit a very scary truth: Cordelia's stash was gone.

"Jeez, Deels," I found myself whispering aloud, "looks like we'll be on our own this coming winter."

To tamp down the nausea-inducing clench that burbled into my throat, I finally counted, mapping what the greenhouse produced to the dietary requirements of people like me and Duka, who no longer had reliable access to meat or fish or grains or dairy or eggs—people for whom five kinds of veggies, two types of potatoes, one legume that pretends to be a nut, and a single small fruit crop might just have to be enough.

As I stared at my calculator, Cordelia became downright talkative.

Hmmph. That's what you get for clinging to a damn sandbar twenty miles out to sea.

"Gimme a break. You'd have done the same thing."

I would've counted more often.

"And how would that have made any difference?"

I'd have paid better attention to how long our supplies would last. And been less generous with the neighbors.

"Ha! You'd have shared as much as I have—and then brooded about it in more detail."

Where the devil is, Aitch. Gotta know where the devil is.

CHAPTER TWENTY-EIGHT

HAS THE TIME COME?

The thing about Saturdays at the Truro Elementary School, of course, is that unless you bring along a really big pile of cash and a willingness to get ripped off by Alison Perry, you need to *have something* to barter. Which means you must decide—in detail, where the devil is—how much of your 411 square feet of greenhouse harvest you'll consume and how much you'll trade.

No wonder that *uh-oh* kept on pulsing in the base of my throat.

We'd grown sufficient pseudo-grain (that is, potatoes) for the two of us for forty-two days—but we needed fifty or sixty days minimum to get us to the next potato harvest. And sweet potatoes? They wouldn't show up again for ninety days at least.

We had forty days' worth of our various veggies—but more carrots and a lettuce harvest wouldn't come in less than seventy days, while broccoli and cabbage were about a hundred days off.

We'd each get a helping of strawberries for twenty-seven days—but we had no other source of fruit and wouldn't see any more strawberries for months (and then for only another twenty-seven days, *if* we were lucky).

Our peanut crop would supply seventy-seven days of the plant oil we'd each need and sufficient peanuts or peanut butters for twenty days—but our next round of peanuts was a hundred or more days away.

"Damn," Duka growled defiantly after I recited all this. "I was fucking afraid of that. How's it look if we luck out an' manage to grow six crops of spinach an' six crops of potatoes a year?" Then she ticked off all the other best-case greenhouse scenarios crop by crop.

"Mmm." Crop by crop, I'd been tapping her defiance into the calculator on my phone. "Nope, not quite." I offered up the "good" news first: Spinach and potatoes almost all the time. Enough peanut oil to scrape by, the rest intermittent, strawberries twice a year.

Duka tried to smile.

I continued. "Bad news is, well, that's a whole year's worth of harvests, assumes absolutely nothing goes wrong ever—and we're left with zilch for bartering."

"Yeah," Duka muttered, her voice raspy from the lingering effects of pneumonia. "No whole grains. No eggs or dairy. No peas or beans. No herbs or spices. Sure as hell no fish or chicken or pork or beef or even a goddamn turkey. We're gonna have to find a way to expand, huh?"

She peered southwestward out the living room windows to the Hulk's foundation, where she dreamed of creating a greenhouse, then westward to where she envisioned a wind turbine spinning up the electricity we were still stealing from the power company.

I'd often seen her glance in both directions, her head at that certain angle—the angle of fantasy, the angle of hope. But this was the first time I ever heard her mention Kai.

She'd muttered his name just loudly enough that I suspected she was inviting me to notice. Okay, I thought, I'll notice: "Who's Kai?"

"One of the planning dudes for the offshore windfarm. Showed up sometime in the last month or so. Some kinda engineer or maybe a meteorologist. Knows all about how to site turbines using data an' wind roses an' software. Been kinda buddying up to Toby, who he's into, I think. Of course, Toby's inconsciente—y'know, oblivious. But I'm keeping it zipped cuz maybe I'm wrong an' I don't wanna step in it. Kai'll figure out Toby's preferences soon enough. Anyway, I like Kai. He's a keeper."

I must have said something in reply, but damned if I can recall what it was. Because that's when I happened to glance at my phone again—

3:17

Tue, Oct 3

Exactly one year and twelve hours since Cordelia died.

Suddenly I was back there again, at the instant I realized she was gone, awash in a current of *No!* buffeted by a countercurrent of agonizing emptiness as I waited, hoping for it not to be true but knowing it was true, holding on to her because I believed she might be hovering for a while, watching, wistful before she dispersed. Before she left me forever.

I was weightless then in a world without up or down or in or out as my hope surrendered to a gasping, searing melt of calamity that coursed out of my chest to claim all of me, every muscle, every nerve, every blood cell, every blink of my eyes: Cordelia was dead.

Precisely one year and twelve hours later, that gasping, searing melt claimed me again, and I embraced it unreservedly. It was all I had left of Cordelia. I wanted nothing more than to crawl into bed with it and go to sleep remembering her.

And at that moment I wondered: Has the time come?

I don't eat as much as Duka, but I eat enough. And my calculations, flawed and theoretical as they were, suggested that our 411 square feet of grow space would suffice pretty well for one person. *Just one.*

When you're seventy-five years old and deeply tired and the woman who centered your life for forty-five years is irretrievably gone and you're grieving for her still, always, you can't help but ponder why the *hell* you continue to bother with any of this shit—and that's when you can be very, very tempted by that alprazolam/oxy and amaretto cocktail.

Because if you stick around, all you're doing is feeding your grief and loneliness with resources that could sustain someone else who might have a future with more in it than grief and loneliness.

So yes, you have to ask: Has the time come?

But before you can answer, you notice the tears filling Duka's dark eyes. You watch her turn her head away from you knowing she doesn't want you to see those tears, and while you wonder whether maybe she's managed to hear you asking your silent question—Has the time come?—a kind of high-frequency vibration, somehow different than that hot, gasping melt, rolls through the middle of your chest.

Then it achieves voice.

A familiar voice, gentle, the one that always made you feel safe and warm, always...

Aw, c'mon, Aitch, you're gonna do this now? *Just a year later and there's not a damn thing wrong with you yet? What a waste* that *would be.*

And your eyes blink, a normal blink but slo-o-o-ow, a blink that pulls all the fragments and scraps of possibility gradually toward you, free of gravity, free of time, and you feel her smile as you grasp how all those fragments and scraps of possibility might fit together.

Okay, you decide, maybe not just yet...

Chapter Twenty-nine

Ten percent

"I need to talk to you," Duka said at the very instant I spoke exactly the same words to her.

A heartbeat ahead of me, she blurted, "You first."

I led her into the living room and pointed out the west windows to where the Hulk once stood and then to the property across the street to the west. "I found out those properties have been declared tax delinquent and the town has foreclosed on them. So they're for sale."

"You mean the Hulk?"

I smiled. "*Aa*-and…"

Duka's eyes went wide. "*An'* the property across the street where I keep picturing a wind turbine?"

"Yep. It's a double lot with a house over on Alder Way, the one that almost burned down, so purchase price is five thousand plus a hundred-dollar processing fee. As for the Hulk—it shares a border with this property and since the only thing left on it is the concrete foundation, it qualifies as an empty sidelot, which'll cost just a hundred dollars. As long as the current owners don't object and no one else grabs it first, I'll have the deed in my hot little fist thirty days after I sign on the dotted line."

Duka stood before me agape while I tried to recall if I'd ever seen her agape before.

"Fifty-two hundred altogether," she murmured. "That's a shitload of money, Hester."

"And a damn good deal, too—although just a start. We'll need plenty more to put a greenhouse in the Hulk's foundation. For the lumber and polycarbonate covering and soil and lights and heating and seeds—"

"Not to mention a wind turbine," Duka added almost absently as she stared westward out the windows. "So we can stop stealing electricity."

I gulped. Duka couldn't possibly build a real live wind turbine from what she scavenged. So we'd have to buy one—and how the hell much does a wind turbine cost? Better not to think about that. Yet. "What the hell," I said instead. "I'm willing to try if you are."

"Simón que sí, I'm willing. But you know we'll have to get through this winter first, right? Without much help from another greenhouse, cuz we'll need at least a couple months to build it an' make it operational."

"And then another three months for crops to grow. I understand. But I'd rather risk my fifty-two hundred bucks on that instead of contributing even more to Alison Perry's profit margin."

Duka rubbed her face with both hands, and behind her hands she was grinning. "Wow," she said. "That really jibes—"

"With what you wanted to talk to me about?"

"Exactamente. I got an offer. An' I said yes cuz there's not much time left an' I'll be paid ten percent of what we bring back here—gross, not net after costs. Won't have any say in what it'll be, except it'll be *food*, y'know? An'—"

"Whoa, wait." I put up a hand. "Not much time left for what?"

"For getting as much food in here as we damn well can."

"Before winter, you mean."

"Yeah, an' before food rationing starts."

"You believe our masters mean it this time?"

Duka's head flicked toward her shoulder. "Dunno. But it's what I'm hearing from, like, almost everywhere. Phoebe Bigshot. Alison. Greg Silva. Even Isabella. I, uh, kinda hate to admit this, but I believe it—I *think* I believe it—cuzza Phoebe Bigshot. She's a—whaddaya call it?—a market analyst, an' her contacts are telling her a federal food rationing program will be announced sometime in November. Before Thanksgiving for sure. An' word is it'll be harsh. That they'll come down hard on the black markets."

"So," I snarked, "*not* a chicken in every pot, then. What a shock."

I was one of those who believed food rationing should have been implemented as soon as possible after it was apparent that the world's supply chains had been clobbered by Eleven Fourteen, something that was overwhelmingly obvious within a couple of months of the event. God only knows how many of my fellow citizens would be alive if the potentates had cared about putting even a half-assed food rationing program in place during the black cold as much as they cared about their surreptitious bank nationalization program.

"From what I heard Phoebe say, the per-person amount is s'posed to, y'know, 'assist' with nutrition. Big frigging deal about 'nutrition.' So we'll all get, like, a certain amount of basics for a set price. Whatever the fuck that really means. Phoebe talked real fast an' complicated about how no, it's not price controls, about all these hoops you can jump through if you can't pay, but it sounded like a whole lotta politician bullshit to me."

"So you and Phoebe had a real conversation, huh?"

"Not really. But sorta, I guess. When I was repairing a window at her place. Mostly I listened, heard all kinda stuff. Like how the outfit she worked for collapsed last summer—so, okay, cut her some slack for her cabróna act. Now she's 'consulting' on some project—for the Commerce Department, I think she said—about industrial robots. While I was there she got a call from the suit who hired her. I admit I eavesdropped while she was working hard to make nice to him. Jeezus, Hester, she's smart. Knows a shitload about, y'know, *out there...*"

"Ah. The rest of the world, you mean. Beyond the Orleans rotary, beyond the bridges."

"Yeah. I hardly ever have time to think about that, to look up an' pay regular attention to bigger stuff like Phoebe does."

"And what she said has you worried about—"

"About how the rules around this nutrition-whatever program will flip the fuck outta the black markets. All kinda controls, a whole new set of food crimes, so prices'll go berserk. That wouldn't freak me out so much if we could count on actually getting what we're s'posed to. But I just don't believe it. Not way out here. We'll be skimmed an' cheated an' screwed like always."

"So this offer you mentioned—"

"Ten percent of nine hundred pounds of food. Nine hundred pounds cuz she figures that's what the boat can handle."

"The boat?"

"We'll be going across the bay to Plymouth. When I said yes, I thought of it as, well, an act of desperation—taking a shot at whatever I can get whenever I can get it, y'know? But *now*"—Duka allowed herself a slight smile as she glanced out the living room windows toward the Hulk's foundation—"I'm thinking it can help us through till we build a second greenhouse, also have something to trade for some live chicks..."

"Chickens, you mean? Complete with a chicken coop? When will you be able to—?"

"I've scavenged most of the building materials already. An' Toby says he'll give me a hand."

"I dunno, kiddo. You're not entirely back from that pneumonia—"

"I'm *fine*," Duka snapped in that brook-no-objection way I'd heard only once or twice before.

"Okay. I guess." All I could do was squint discouragingly at her. "So you'll do this trip at Alison's behest using Sam's boat?"

Duka shook her head. "Isabella Franzi's idea. Her boat, too. *Clarus*, she calls it. Has a shallow draft, so it can squiggle into all kinda places along the coast. Plan is for us to meet up with her contact to pick up the stuff off-Cape an' bypass all the Route Six bullshit—"

"I remember Isabella having a sailboat. Black hull, not huge. Sleek looking."

"Yeah, it's a thirty-one-foot racing daysailer. So it's fast—for a sailboat, anyway."

And then it hit me: Duka intended to travel back and forth across Cape Cod Bay during the coldest early October I could remember—on a *sailboat*.

I wanted to scream at her to not even fucking *think* about it. Which, I knew, would backfire. Big time. "Hardly more space than your pickup truck on a boat like that," I said instead. "And three times slower than a stinkpotter. Why not a faster boat at least? One with more capacity."

"Cuz *Clarus* has a real shallow draft. Plus the wind is free." Duka inhaled, exhaled. "Also, at least for now the Coast Guard an' the Border Patrol don't focus so much on the slow boats—like anything under sail. They chase speedboats instead, the ones they don't recognize, cuz those're likelier to be carrying the contraband they're currently after. Y'know, refugees, counterfeit cash, opioids, weapons, the occasional poached seal, stuff they decide is stolen."

"But if you're *not* carrying contraband—"

"Coastie missions are all about 'homeland security,' not safety. The crews now always include at least one Border Patrol agent—a La Migra skank who cares only about racking up interdiction numbers. So unless they know you, you get boarded. An' once you're boarded, the skanks almost always find something they'll claim to be contraband. Might even seize your vessel. If you object, they mess you up. Physically, I mean. But it's different for boats they recognize. Especially, like I said, the slow ones."

"So Isabella gets her boat into some sort of good-guy database like one of those government trusted-traveler programs?"

"Pretty much—though it's not official. You find out who's the Coast Guard station head honcho at the harbor where you're based, you make real nice, all eager to 'contribute' an' 'donate' an' all that crap. Y'know, a bribe by any other name. Then the lieutenant or master chief or whoever has your vessel checked out, listed as 'not of law enforcement interest.' Before you set sail, you let 'em know ahead of time. So no surprises when they spot you on the water, an' they leave you be. No skanking."

"Got it," I said. "Much slower traveling, but also much lower fuel bill—and way safer than driving, huh?"

"For now, anyway. It's easier to deal with the Coasties on the water than highway bandits an' the La Migra road warriors. On land, down to the Pamet River we're in a kinda safe space—but after that, if the bandits don't get you along Route Six an' beyond, La Migra skanks will, unless you have the right credentials—which better damn well be visible on your vehicle, like something medical or LEO or the windfarm company. Otherwise—well, if you're lucky, you're only delayed. If you're unlucky, you're robbed or beaten or arrested. Or killed."

"What about those speedboat pirates I've heard Lizbie fret about whenever Sam goes out to fish?"

Duka shrugged. "When Sam goes out now, which isn't often, he's after the last of the seals—dangerous unless you got an 'arrangement' with the Coasties an' La Migra, which Sam does. I don't go out with him anymore cuz I want *nothing* to do with the Feds. Not worth the risk for a mestiza girl, y'know? But Sam—hell, Sam's as lily white as they come. He takes the meat, pays off the Coasties an' La Migra with the hides. Lizbie doesn't like the risk, cuz basically Sam becomes a pirate when he hunts seal. But he plays by pirate rules, so for now he's okay."

"Pirate rules?"

"For the Coasties, vessels fall into two categories—friendly an' unfriendly. Boats the Coasties don't recognize are automatically considered unfriendly. Fair game cuz they tend to carry refugees—usually undocumented Canadians—or they're assholes from somewhere else poking around in new territory to traffic or steal."

"And 'friendly' boats?"

"Two kindsa those. 'Straight' friendlies, like Isabella's boat—they ante up minor 'contributions' cuz, theoretically anyway, they're not doing anything illegal. Then there's 'bent' friendlies—like Sam when he's out hunting seal—an' they gotta fork over full-fledged bribes cuz, y'know…"

I nodded. "They're doing something 'bent'—and paying the Coast Guard and the Border Patrol people—La Migra—to look the other way while they do it."

"Meanwhile, La Migra want those 'unfriendly' boats chased down. So they enlist their favorite bent friendlies to help 'em. Unofficially, of course. Kinda classic, I suppose: The pirates have become privateers."

"I dunno, Duka—sounds like there's a lot of gray area out there. Room for plenty of 'straight friendlies' that aren't so straight and 'bent friendlies' that aren't so friendly—and plenty of *very* bent and unfriendly law enforcement. Which makes this 'offer' of Isabella's sound awfully chancy."

"Yeah, well, nothing's risk-free—but I figure this risk is low enough, given the limited alternatives for those of us who don't have access to cargo aircraft."

"The roads or the high seas, you mean."

"An' La Migra putos are all over both. One of the P'town Coasties got all boasty with Sam recently about how they 'own' Cape Cod waters from the Crowell Basin to the Buell Seamount—a smartass way to say way the hell out to sea. Dude bragged that if they don't know you, they're coming after you. So for every vessel they scope—by eye, by radar or sonar or drone, by privateer, by fucking satellite sometimes—standing orders are to radio 'em an' leave 'em be only when the response is 'normative.'"

"And a 'normative' response is what exactly?"

"You ID your vessel, then yourself, confirm what you told 'em before you left the harbor about where you're headed—Plymouth, Boston, wherever—an' for what purpose. An', by the way, you tell 'em something like you're going for a doctor visit or business or a family matter. You do *not* say you're picking up nine hundred pounds of food."

"Because if the Coast Guard knows that, they'll stop you, board you, and take it?"

"Oh no, not them." Duka sniggered. "They're the *good* guys an' you're not doing anything illegal—yet. But, just coincidentally of course, some unfriendly speedboat 'pirate' will spot your vessel, chase you down, steal everything—an', oh dear, so sorry, the Coast Guard didn't have the means to assist, despite your distress call, because their limited resources were engaged elsewhere. Later, you'll see a Coastie with something that—just coincidentally of course—looks a whole like what was stolen off your boat. But you won't be able to prove shit."

"So," I said, "if you're carrying anything valuable on your boat other than what the Coasties have already seen when they declared your vessel 'not of law enforcement interest,' you better the hell not tell 'em. Even if what you're carrying is perfectly legitimate."

"Bingo. Which is why Isabella said she was traveling for family shit."

"So she's done this already."

"Once. An' they had no problems."

"They?"

"She went with Ellen Higgins."

"The Truro police sergeant?"

"Yep." Duka seemed to have a bad taste in her mouth, but she carried on. "I think Isabella figured the sergeant could flash badge an' gun if necessary to provide protection."

"What was she worried about?"

"Mostly the guy she was meeting up with, I think. But he turned out okay an' Isabella's all sanguine now. Ready to do it again."

"And everything was cool with the Coast Guard?"

"Just one radio contact on the way to Plymouth. Nobody at White Horse Beach 'cept Isabella's guy, zero Coastie contact on the way back." Duka half-smiled. "Not a speedboat pirate anywhere, either."

"So Isabella's buying food from—?"

Duka shrugged again. "Dunno."

"Stolen food?"

"Dunno. Don't care. I'm just crew."

"Ah," I said. "So, for ten percent of the cargo, it's don't ask, don't tell, look a little ferocious—and do what? Ninety-five percent of the heavy lifting, right? Which sounds like it might be okay—as long as you don't have to haul all nine hundred pounds onto Isabella's boat at once."

"Comes in small boxes, according to Isabella."

"*And* if it's not dangerous."

Duka ignored that. "First Isabella said five percent, but when I didn't jump for it right off, she immediately went up to ten. She's looking to make as many trips as possible before the rationing shit starts in November, so no time for haggling. Just wanted me to promise not to tell anyone she's bringing back huge amounts of food that'll be stashed in her house—"

"Except you just told me—"

Duka winked. "Shhh."

"Right." But I did wonder about how many other secrets Isabella might be harboring.

"Anyway, I told Isabella yes before she could change her mind. I figure she's paying for me not to throw her overboard an' steal the whole boatload. I'll be crew *an'* the pretend-protection Isabella thinks she needs. Which is fine by me."

"What about Ellen Higgins?"

Duka smirked. "Sergeant Higgins gets seasick. *Very* seasick. So her protective services are strictly land-based now. Works great cuz she moved outta the place she rented from Alison. She's Isabella's roommate now. Enjoying *all* the benefits, according to Phoebe Bigshot."

Well, there was one secret revealed. One less worry, too: Isabella had acquired the very best kind of land-based protection—an entire fifth of Truro's official remaining police presence.

Even so, in addition to the dangers of sailing a small boat in the dark across the bay during (a very cold and always unpredictable) October, other worries lingered: What happens if Isabella's food-laden racing daysailer somehow ends up boarded by the Coast Guard? Maybe the boat has a problem that requires a call for help; would Duka and Isabella end up arrested? Or maybe some so-called privateer doesn't get the word to leave *Clarus* alone. And then what? Would Duka and Isabella end up beaten? Shot? Drowned?

But I kept my mouth shut. Smiled encouragement. Because I had to risk going along with Duka's plan. Even if—when—it scared the crap out of me. That was our deal.

CHAPTER THIRTY

FIRST IN LINE

The trick was to hit the beach near the peak of high tide. This would bring *Clarus* within a few yards of dry sand, since its keel is only three feet deep when the centerboard's retracted.

In another era, I'd have used one of those boat-watching apps to track *Clarus* from the moment it departed Provincetown harbor, where it was moored—but like our electricity service, our internet access had become too spotty and unreliable, especially out on Cape Cod Bay.

"Twenty miles each way as the crow flies," Duka repeated as we stood, an hour before midnight, on the lightly rolling finger pier where Isabella kept her boat's dinghy tied up.

Shivering in the cold north wind, I nodded. Fifteen knots, Duka had said earlier—seventeen miles an hour, give or take, and expected to strengthen. The weather report, such as it was, also forecasted that temperatures could sink below freezing as *Clarus* sailed westward overnight across the bay. At least, I reminded myself, Duka had dressed appropriately: bright yellow sailing dry suit, neoprene dinghy boots, nylon-covered fleece watch cap, insulated sailing gloves, even an overjacket. Like she was ready for an arctic expedition.

Isabella hadn't been happy when Duka indicated I knew what they were up to—until Duka pointed out that I'd find out soon enough anyway. "I explained how you an' me have a deal that I don't lie to you, so I'd have to tell you where ninety pounds of food has come from. An' besides, this way you could drive us to P'town harbor, which saves us having to leave a vehicle there."

So drive them I did, Isabella lost in a frowny, mute back seat sulk until I turned onto the pier.

"Almost eight hours till the next high tide," I said to Duka after Isabella offered a clipped thanks for the ride and marched off toward her dinghy. Trying to seem unconcerned, I asked, "You think it'll really take that long?"

"Hope not." Duka glanced around the pier, then leaned down and rasped close to my ear. "In this wind we should make seven or eight knots tonight, even though Isabella wants to tow the dinghy—to make it easier to get her cargo aboard at White Horse Beach. So unless this fucks up royally, we should already be waiting offshore when Isabella's seller shows. Then we load what she's bought. Maybe an hour for that?"

Duka lowered her voice to a whisper so Isabella couldn't hear her. "Just found out when we picked her up—she's bought meat. Frozen, packed with dry ice in insulated boxes, thirty of 'em, one cubic foot of meat to a box. Which means I'll end up with three boxes, so I'm wondering about freezer space—"

"You're right. We'll need the second freezer. It's off now, but I'll switch it on so it'll be ready in time."

Duka straightened again and spoke more loudly. "I figure that'll be around, say, four tomorrow afternoon. Or, y'know…"

"Yeah. Could be later. You have the duffel with food and fresh water, right? And one of the walkie-talkies—for the last few miles."

She nudged her foot against the duffel and patted her jacket pocket. "Yes an' yes. I'll try to text you to let you know how we're doing, but, y'know—"

"Yeah, crapshoot reception. But I'll keep my phone close."

Once more, Duka leaned in to whisper. "I think it's a mistake to unload here in the harbor. Too many cameras, too many nosy Coasties. I suggested Cold Storage Beach, but Isabella's being stubborn, so we'll see. No matter what, I'll try to hail you on the walkie-talkie when we're nearing Long Point to let you know when we're back in the neighborhood."

It's not that I woke up early the day Duka was due back. More like I never quite went to sleep the night before—at least not for long, since I was on alert for a text (which did not come). But that wasn't the only reason: To my surprise, I'd become unaccustomed to spending the night in the house without someone else in it.

Although "sunrise" on a Truro October 9 is reputed to occur before seven in the morning, there wasn't sufficient daylight to walk around outside without a flashlight until after eight.

Of course, I could've driven. Certainly, the morning's swirling snow flurries made that damn tempting. But my car was low on gas and I had no clue how long I'd need that gas to last. So, checkbook and paperwork in hand, I planned to walk to our "new" town hall, now occupying a couple of unused classrooms in the Truro Elementary School a mere half-mile away from my house if I used Mirrie and Nate's shortcut.

I donned, as usual, my wide-brimmed hat and facemask and took the route Mirrie had shown me last summer—across her parents' property and along a path she and Nate had stomped out all the way to the abandoned place behind theirs, which, conveniently, stood at the end of a lane that led down to Route Six just next to the school.

I had to wait for town hall offices to open, but when they did, getting everything all approved and accepted turned out to be quite simple, thanks to the eagerness of Town Hall Margie.

"You're first in line for these properties, so once you sign the preliminary purchase agreements, the clock starts ticking on giving the owners and/or the mortgage holders one last chance to pay their back taxes, which they have to do within fifteen business days. If they do not, your purchase agreements are finalized," she told me. "And thirty days from now—which is, let's see, November eighth—the properties' quitclaim deeds will have been registered with the county and ready for you to pick up here."

And with that I was about to own the remnants of the Hulk and one bedraggled, slightly singed ranch on Alder Way with a usefully large double garage and double-size backyard where Duka yearned to someday erect a wind turbine.

Turns out I was only the fourth person (right behind Alison Perry, Greg Silva, and Michael Oswald) to yet take advantage of the new Truro Land Bank Authority's effort to revive the town's tax base by selling tax-foreclosed properties for a song and a promise to pay future property taxes. Which no doubt explained why Margie slipped so quickly into used-car-salesman mode.

"Since you're acquiring these," she encouraged me as she tapped a screen displaying a detailed topographical map of my North Truro neighborhood, "maybe you'd like to consider some others, too." Her finger poked several irregular polygons crosshatched with thin red lines. "As you can see, all these abut what you've just purchased. Hundred dollars a pop if the property has no usable existing structures, two-fifty if it has, say, a functional garage or a shed. Plus future taxes will be—" Margie cleared her throat. "*Very* low."

"The town has taken *all those?*" My question was rhetorical, of course, but I was surprised at how many properties—including every single one of the houses burned in our recent fire—carried the telltale red crosshatches of tax foreclosure.

Margie nodded. Margie smiled and talked more about how low taxes would be for years to come.

And yes, I suppose I got carried away. In my defense, I'll merely point out that Cordelia egged me on the whole time. Because, as she kept whispering, this was one hell of a good deal.

So...

Soon I'd anted up another $900 for more properties around the two I'd just bought. I departed the new Truro town hall with preliminary documents for upwards of nine acres altogether. Besides the Hulk and the Alder Way ranch, I was about to become the owner of the ruins of Broderick's house as well as six other fire wrecks and two undeveloped lots. A total of eight concrete foundation holes—each one a potential greenhouse, right?—and a significantly larger-than-anticipated swath of that higher ground Duka yearned for as a wind turbine site.

And it wasn't even noon yet.

CHAPTER THIRTY-ONE

PHOEBE

About a mile from my house stands, still, my town's quaint little historical museum. Among its many artifacts are photographs of an earlier Truro's undulating, moor-like landscape, long since stripped almost bare of its native oak and pine forests for the sake of colonists' ship masts as well as farmers' houses, fields, and firewood—a spartan panorama speckled with small clusters of simple wood buildings, cedar-shingled or clapboarded, hunkered between low-rolling hills against the gritty, unceasing onslaught of windswept sand.

The trees began to return later, oh so slowly, well after Truro's shipbuilders had departed and its farmers finally surrendered most of their fields to "summer people" and, later, to a national park. By the time Cordelia and I arrived, whole swaths of Truro had forested again—albeit on a somewhat more diminutive scale, I've always imagined, scrubby and idiosyncratic not only before the wind but also because those plows had ravaged what little topsoil our hill-and-dale sandbar had accrued since forming after the last ice age.

Even so, our own small parcel of second-growth Truro woods had been exquisitely rich with fireflies and frogs and rabbits and chipmunks and butterflies and squirrels and foxes and coyote and deer and all manner of birds...

Until the black cold.

I hated hated *hated* seeing the destruction the black cold wrought, and once Duka started building the greenhouse that so conveniently obstructed my primary views of it, I allowed the scale of my perception to shrink until I paid attention to little beyond what was right in front of me.

Later in the summer, despite what amounted to a drought interrupted only by occasional blitzkriegs of snow that blustered through here without ever adding much to the water table, I heard a couple of crows in the blighted hollow just east of my house.

Crows!

They stayed for less than an hour—but raucoused around down there in the dead tree branches long enough for me to notice even more bits of green than Duka had discovered earlier.

Perhaps because it's so effectively sheltered from the wind and also hosts our septic system's leach field, our hollow had not only nurtured the wild grass and burdock and violet and blueberry Duka had spotted in May, by late summer it also had revived two gangly, mangled oaks along with a tiny red cedar sapling, a few clumps of moss, and several colonies of dandelions, red clover, and fern. I even spotted what looked a lot like liverwort.

Yet our blackwater-fertilized hollow was the exception in a terrain ruled by ragged timber skeletons and desiccated underbrush. To our south and west and northwest, those skeletons were also charred by the early August fire that almost destroyed the whole neighborhood. Better to keep my head down than endure the sight of the ruined horizons that, for all their austere, sweeping drama, I simply should not be able to see.

Trouble is, sooner or later one has to look up.

It happened as I retraced my steps from the new town hall at the Truro Elementary School back toward Lizbie and Sam's little homestead, several officially stamped receipts for nine and a half acres of once coveted property folded in my pocket. Finally I raised my head to truly look around—and winced. What had I bought, *really?*

In front of me, the lane through this newer, glitzier neighborhood forked, and I had a choice: Stay to the right and return home the way I came, back toward the shortcut to Lizbie's—or take my own echoing question seriously and venture leftward, uphill past where Isabella lived to where the town assessor's map showed just one more too-big house at the end of the lane. If I picked my way across a corner of this last yard, I'd arrive at the southernmost and, at 118 feet above sea level, the highest-elevation property I'd just acquired.

The day seemed colder than average (though in truth there's no such thing as average anymore) and also, of course, darkly overcast and windy—a rambunctious, irritable north wind stronger than "expected," and likely even rowdier out on the bay where, I hoped, Duka and Isabella were sailing *Clarus* due east back from Plymouth.

"Please, please be careful, kiddo," I murmured as I began to walk up the steeper left fork in the road.

Duka is *being careful, Aitch.*

I didn't want to *not* see her there at my right shoulder, so I forced my gaze leftward toward all the broken, gray pitch pine carcasses and, several hundred feet distant, the older decaying houses along the unpaved road all those trees once would have so thoroughly obscured from any upper-crusty view. "Oh god, Deels, I miss you so much."

I'd miss you, too, if I could.

"Yeah. If you could."

Don't, Aitch. Not yet.

"But it just isn't the same place anymore. Like right over there. Used to be a beautiful little pitch pine forest. Saved from the fire, sure, but look—it's all dead anyway."

Not everything. C'mon, look again.

I would have retorted, *not* politely, but by then I'd passed Isabella's steroidal neo-cape with its OCD landscaping and reached the top of the hill, where, at the end of the lane, stood one last steroidal neo-cape with OCD landscaping that, yes, I'd assumed would be vacant. But I was wrong: A woman had appeared at the side door.

She stared unsmiling straight at me, her right arm out of sight inside the house, and maybe she was frowning, maybe her right hand even clutched a weapon I couldn't see.

Nahh, I thought, I hoped, not that bad around here yet…

But oh yeah, she certainly was frowning.

I approached her anyway with yet another hope—that she'd let me venture up her driveway and across about a hundred feet of what had once been her meticulously manicured lawn to the property behind it that would very likely soon be mine.

"Hi," I offered. When I received a silent, squinty nod in reply, I pulled down my facemask so she could see me and persevered. "Would it be okay if I—?"

"Nobody's home over there right now," she interrupted edgily from her doorway, her head tilting toward Isabella's house.

That's when I recognized her, although she looked older, thinner, more fatigued, and significantly less blond than I remembered from last spring, which was the last time—the only time—I'd met her. *You* live here? Really? I knew her place was near Isabella's, but *this?*

"Phoebe?" I said before my censor could rein me in.

This transformed her squint into a scowl that lasted long enough for me to wonder how much older, thinner, and more fatigued *I'd* become since last spring.

"I'm sorry," she began, oozing suspicion, "I don't—"

"We met once several months ago." I pulled off my hat and kept talking too fast, gesturing too energetically in the general direction of my house. "I'm Hester I live over on Upper Hollow Circle and I was hoping—"

"Oh! H-Hest—" Phoebe rummaged for something just inside her house and then stepped out of her doorway toward me, jacket in hand. "Um, Hester…you're the one who—" She stopped herself, shook her head almost imperceptibly, and tried again. "Duka—um, Duka Canché lives at your place, right?"

"Yeah, she does." I paused only long enough to inhale a breath and grasp that Phoebe did not remember me, though she'd connected my name to Duka. "I'm heading back home now, actually."

Phoebe descended the two steps to her driveway and began walking toward me while she donned her jacket. "To tend the greenhouse I've heard so much about?"

I half-smiled my deflection. "It does take a lot of time."

"Worthwhile though, huh?" She stood before me dressed in stretchy denim leggings and ankle boots, her dirty-blond hair blowing sideways, shirttail billowing beneath her designer leather jacket, hands clasped in front of her. Waiting. Almost childlike.

And I knew: Hell, as soon as I nod, she'll ask and I'll say yes because I'm too polite not to, and besides, I want to walk across her yard. So I proffered my smallest nod—along with another deflection. "But a lot more complex than I ever anticipated."

Undeflected, she launched, her words spilling over each other…

"I've been thinking about a greenhouse addition here." Her arm swung high and wide back toward her house. "Seems like the only way anymore to be sure of reliably having food. Maybe I could tag along and take a look at what you did? I'm a greenhouse novice, so I have a lot to learn. About all of it, everything, like what to plant and how much to water and when it's ready to eat, because I've been a city girl for years, and a greenhouse—wow, that's a mystery to me. Do you think I could hire Duka Canché to build one?"

If I nodded again, would she decide I was answering both of her questions with a yes? "Uh, let's see—no, I don't mind, although there isn't much to look at right now besides shoots of spinach, since we've only just finished planting our next round of crops." I paused, squared my shoulders. "And I don't know, you'll have to ask her, though I can tell you it'll cost plenty, assuming it's even possible to get the materials."

Finally, Phoebe smiled. I liked her smile more than I thought I would. But it stayed plastered on her well-proportioned face just a tad too long, and she was staring again. "You mentioned that we met," she said as we stood at the bottom of her driveway. "But I can't place where."

"The supermarket in Provincetown back when there was one. Right after the black cold. You were with Isabella—"

"Oh god, I was such a mess then." Phoebe buried her hands in her jacket pockets, her shoulders lifted into a hunch, and I swear she blushed. "That whole stretch is kind of a blur. On a scale of one to ten, how rude was I?"

I laughed. "You were fine. Very well-behaved. But I expected the woman I met that day to be back in Boston by now."

"Well—" Phoebe paused and lifted her face skyward. "From what I've been told, there isn't much Boston to go back to. Not safely, anyway."

"So you're staying." Since I was stating the obvious rather than asking a question, I pointed up her driveway before she could reply. "Shortcut to the greenhouse is this way."

"Really? Through the—?"

"Yep. Your yard to the property right behind yours. Were you home when the houses back there burned down last August?"

"Hell, yes, and I was scared shitless." Phoebe bowed her head and turned to walk up her driveway. "It was *so* damn windy. And these erratic gusts drove the flames right into the back fence. Took most of it, as you'll see. I figured I'd lose everything. So did Isabella next door. And we almost did." She trotted back to the side door of her house—to set the alarm, she said—and rejoined me next to her garage with a hat but no facemask. "Not much to steal here, but, y'know…"

I tried to make my nod sympathetic as I handed her one of the spare facemasks Mirrie had stuffed in my jacket pocket. "You haven't met Mirrie Watts yet, have you?" I asked. "Once you do, you'll never again go UO— Uncovered Outside."

Phoebe accepted the mask and put it on. "Guess I haven't thought much about how little I go out anymore." She glanced back at her house.

"Mostly I just wander around in there worrying about what'll go wrong next..."

Yeah, well, that deserved a second sympathetic nod. Living alone in Truro is hard enough; I'd freak if I had to do it in a house three times the size of mine. "Awfully big place to deal with all by yourself."

"Not for much longer. It's my parents' place actually, and they won't be back anytime soon. But my sister and her husband and kids will be moving in with me."

"Really? From, uh—?" I stuttered undiplomatically as I tried to recall what she'd said that day in the supermarket about her sister living safely in some well-heeled Boston suburb. "I mean, uh, is it really, uh—?"

"That bad? So Olivia says. And since they won't be bringing truckloads of food with them, we're gonna need a greenhouse. Also, the Nutrition Allotment Program should help."

"The rationing thing, you mean? Sounds like you have more faith in it than Duka does," I said as I pulled my hat on again and turned to walk toward the far back corner of Phoebe's parents' property. "She expects corruption to overwhelm it. Especially way out here."

Judging from the deep creases that instantly formed up between Phoebe's shapely eyebrows, she'd dismissed such a notion. Before she could begin the debate, I pointed to the charred northern end of the fence behind her house.

"Around there," I said, "and then I'm hoping we can hang a right."

"Hoping?"

"I've never tramped through here before."

"So why are you tramping through here now?"

Damn if I didn't careen right into that one. So do I tell her I just bought nine-plus acres of derelict, tax-foreclosed property? Do I mention my plan—perhaps better described as a hare-brained scheme—for foundation greenhouses, for small-scale wind turbines dotting the high ground behind her house? In a word: No. I figured Duka should be the first person to hear about what I'd done and why. Time instead for a lame joke: "To get to the other side?"

Phoebe's eyebrows shimmied. So okay, she wasn't fooled—but she calmly followed me while I clomped and crunched over the remains of burned trees and shrubs at the edge of what would be my new property—until I halted and pointed again.

"There," I said. "The roof with the solar panels, behind and just to the left of that foundation."

"Yours?"

"It is. You'll be able to see the greenhouse once we get a little closer."

"I like how your place is all burrowed into the slope. Protected from the wind." Even before she beheld the greenhouse itself, questions started pouring out of her. A take-charge, almost impatient Phoebe pushed for details, lots of them. How many square feet of planting beds? What were we growing? Did we use LED lighting...?

I answered her as we made our way along the property I'd just bought that lay kitty-cornered to hers, past small bits of debris that escaped the cleanup bulldozers and shovels—charcoaled chunks of wood and strips of tattered asphalt roof shingles and small strands of scorched, twisted metal, all of it plastered into windblown piles of water-stiffened ashes, much of it lying at the bottom of the lot's topless house foundation.

I answered until my eyes got stuck, unable to look away from the chaotic muck and how it mounded against the jarringly rigid, perpendicular planes of concrete at the foundation's far corner. Because shit, I'd bought *eight* of these. Eight foundations still dusted with ash and strewn with burnt, splintered debris, all still infused with god knows what kinds of melted-down, poisonous waste.

What the hell had I been thinking?

As I stared, my stomach must have three-sixtied at least once for each of those foundations.

Whaddaya think Duka will say, Deels?

I think she'll be speechless. Hell, Aitch, I'm speechless.

You coulda said something while Margie was, y'know, seducing me.

Why would I? I really like what you did.

"You okay?" Phoebe asked me, which is when I realized I'd slipped into a kind of daze and missed much of what she'd been saying—something concerning a conversation with someone at the Department of Agriculture. Something worth hearing, worth asking about...

But Phoebe was asking me—again. "Hester, are you okay?"

"Mmm—I guess." I sighed at the pile of debris-laden ash. "But there's a good possibility Duka will kill me when she gets back."

"Why?"

"Long story." I shook off my stupor and kept walking. "Ending as yet undetermined."

Phoebe stayed silent for a moment as she eyed me. "It's about food, huh?" she said as she got her first look at the greenhouse—and before my eyes her demeanor flipped from upbeat to forlorn. "Every goddamn thing is about food now." She angrily kicked a burned tree branch. "I mean, I knew it would be expensive out here—the price a woman's gotta pay for comparative safety, as I saw it—but *this?* I was *so* damn naive. Because this is approaching a price I can't afford."

The sudden despair in her voice gave it away: She meant "a price *even I* can't afford," and she seemed both affronted and horrified at the inexorable reality of it.

"When it comes to food," I said, "I think anybody who isn't a farmer or a hunter-gatherer is hopelessly naive." I gazed at the polycarbonate-covered frame stretching across the back of my house. "I'm a lifelong desk jockey who's spent the last several months working in there, and despite having only barely begun, I have learned one thing with utter certainty: It's not enough. Not even for just me and Duka. Food takes a hell of a lot of work. And worry. And luck."

Phoebe easily kept pace with me, but her voice shivered. "Whaddaya mean—'not enough'?"

"I mean what we're able to harvest from that greenhouse can provide some but not nearly all of what we need to meet our nutritional requirements. And, oh by the way, that's only if nothing goes wrong. Like if something happens to the greenhouse lights or heating. Or we screw up the soil. Or lose crop to pests."

This shut Phoebe up for maybe a minute, maybe longer. Then:

"So I can live somewhere close to one of the world's remaining, much-attenuated supply chains—in or near a city, the farther south the better—but I survive there only if I have sufficient resources to fight off very aggressive, dangerous predators, which I don't. *Or* I can live somewhere so remote and detached from any fucking supply chain any-fucking-where that just the minor predators bother with it—but I survive there only if I have sufficient resources to grow my own food, which I don't."

She may have had tears in her eyes.

Be gentle, Aitch, Cordelia whispered.

Chapter Thirty-two

All the way here

W e're not doomed," I said to Phoebe. "But unless this rationing thing gets real before winter *and* Duka's all wrong about it—"

"You mean the Nutrition Allotment Program?" she replied, brightening some as she spoke. "It's already real. It'll be announced soon, maybe even by Thanksgiving. Online account sign-up will start in January, and the first round of allotments are s'posed to be available to account holders within a month after that."

"So, realistically, it won't help much this winter, huh?"

"What I know, such as it is, comes from the command-demand research project I just finished. Interviewed a couple of people at the Department of Agriculture who're working on it. Seems like it's part World War Two rationing programs, part European Public Procurement Online system. You sign up via the internet, select your NAP provider from a list, and the system spits back options for receiving your allotment."

I shook my head. "Who the hell would qualify as a NAP provider around here? Please, please tell me it won't boil down to Alison Perry. Or Hannah Atwood in Wellfleet. Or risking our lives on Route Six to get to and from the supermarket in Orleans."

"I wish I knew, Hester."

"Also, how do you sign up if you live in a place with unreliable communications systems?" I raised my arms, palms up. "Like the Outer Cape."

Phoebe shrugged her silent dunno, then asked, "So, um, is that why Duka has such a low opinion of NAP?"

"I'm sure it's on her list. Duka's something of a cynic."

"About government."

"About how human beings wield power. And too often abuse their power. She'd tell you, I think, that this NAP thing is fine—in principle. But it's being implemented by people—"

"Who'll do a half-assed job."

"Yeah, that too."

"And succumb to the temptation to lie, cheat, and steal."

"Or get cornered by powerful others into lying, cheating, and stealing in order to survive." I winked at her. "Like when we turn to Alison for something no one else has and we choose not to ask where it came from or how she got it."

"So Duka's assuming the worst."

"Or trying to be realistic. As in: The so-called 'allotment' will turn out to be like my monthly social security stipend—too puny to be adequate—and *then* we'll end up receiving only part of it, whatever's left after all the cheats in line ahead of us claim their bits and pieces. Better than nothing, but certainly not enough. And in the case of NAP, unlikely to be reliable. What we'll really be able to count on is what we've grown ourselves, what we're able to trade with each other."

"That's just great," Phoebe growled as we walked up my driveway. "Especially given what you said a few minutes ago: 'It's...not...enough.'"

"Right. So we grow more."

Her voice shriveled to a hoarse whisper. "I don't know if I can do this."

"If you stay here and you figure out another option anytime soon, please let me know."

Even before I finished fumbling my key into the front door lock on my house and punching the alarm system into submission, Phoebe had mostly regained her balance. Mostly. "No escaping the predators, I guess." She still whispered, but her hoarseness was gone. "Not ever."

"Yeah, I'm afraid that's true. But even the lowliest prey can develop effective survival strategies."

"Keep telling me that. I may be starting to lose the plot."

We stood now in my living room; I signaled Phoebe to follow me across the room to the door that opened onto the greenhouse itself, a space about two-thirds as large as the first floor of my house.

"God, it's huge…" She waggled her head as if a cobweb had caught in her hair. "And you say it isn't enough?"

"I did the math—over and over," I replied. "This is four hundred and eleven square feet of planted space, and by my calculations, if it's planted year-round it'll provide enough food for one person, including some small extra for bartering—but by itself it can't feed two people. So we're seeking ways to create additional resources—"

"Such as the Saturday barters at the school." Phoebe didn't disguise her skepticism. "According to Isabella, Alison Perry is well on her way to monopolizing those."

"Mmm, I suppose Alison does lean more toward the predatory than—"

Whereupon something clicked.

"Oh," I blurted. "Is that Isabella's plan?"

"*What?!*" Phoebe spun to face me, her expression almost ferocious.

Oooh, I wondered, have I stumbled onto something? "To take on Alison, I mean—beginning with persuading Sergeant Higgins to, um, recalibrate her loyalties." I smiled up at Phoebe, determined not to be cowed. "Have I got it wrong?"

Phoebe stepped back. "Uhhh…maybe not…"

"Given their living arrangements, I assumed the sergeant is involved in Isabella's 'venture.' But I didn't realize till right now that you're involved, too. An invisible investor?"

"Shit."

I thought Phoebe might bolt back to her house right then, but she didn't.

Instead, she wilted. "I was hoping things would be better here," she rasped, "because, well, it's so remote, and surrounded by water, and there's a lot of wealth here—used to be anyway, and—and—"

"And maybe you could do like you did during the pandemic—just kind of snuggle in for a while with your work-from-home job that gave you enough money to wait out all the volatility across the bridge. But then you discover that even way out here it's way more fucked up than you ever anticipated."

Phoebe's single motion combined a nod and a defeated hunch. "I truly believed that after a year Boston would be recovered enough. But it's gonna take a lot longer. Years longer. Even now, even in suburbs like Newton or Wellesley, something really awful happens almost every day. People fighting over food in supermarket parking lots. Muggings. Hit-and-runs.

Shootings. The few stores that're still around keep their doors locked, and nobody will deliver anything. It's all *so* much worse than I ever…"

I risked placing my hand on her forearm because it seemed to me that Phoebe needed somebody to touch her.

"What happened to you?" I asked in a hush.

She spoke so softly I could barely hear her. "They were gonna kill me."

"Who?"

"Those—those two guys." Phoebe's face had scrunched and she swallowed hard. "They just rammed right through the deadbolt on the door and kicked me to the floor before I could even say anything…"

Skinheads, she called them, and during the second week of the black cold they invaded her South End condo with a plan: stuff themselves with her food and drink, then force her to drive from cash machine to cash machine and use her credit and debit cards to withdraw all her money. "Then back to my place so they could eat the rest of my food and 'fuckfest' me. That's how they put it—'we're gonna fuckfest the hell outta you.' Then they'd kill me. 'No witnesses,' they said. They wanted me to know what was coming. They got off on seeing my fear."

"Omigod, Phoebe," I croaked. "Omigod."

"Right off, they found the booze—a bottle of scotch, bottle of vodka, eight or nine bottles of wine—and drank all of it. Which is what saved me. That and whatever else they'd guzzled earlier. Didn't take long before they were shitfaced. Way too drunk to get it up or even locate a flashlight when the power went out about an hour after they broke in. I told them all I had for light was one of those kerosene miner's lanterns, and then—then I got lucky."

The lantern sat on a small table near the front door, and Phoebe hoped that as she lit it, she'd see a chance to escape. But when she rose from the floor where she'd been cowering to rummage for a match and light the thing, the skinheads stuck with her.

"The big bossy one who'd been waving around this handgun in between gulps of booze—he blocked the door, yanked the matches out of my hand, and actually managed to light the lantern himself. But something about the way the light flickered bothered him and he put the lantern down on the table by the door, then demanded that we leave and start driving around to cash machines."

Phoebe lowered her head; again I strained to hear her. "He stepped into the outside hallway while the smaller guy, who was behind me, pulled out his gun and yelled at me to pick up my wallet, keys, and phone. So I did—and then, as I turned to grab a jacket from the coatrack, he pushed me and my shoulder hit the doorframe, so he grabbed for me and I raised my arm, y'know, to defend myself. Took him so much by surprise that my arm knocked the gun out of his hand and it landed right in the doorway."

She hadn't done it on purpose, she said. "It just happened. When he reached down for his gun, I stepped back, picked up the lantern, and whacked it across his back. That broke the lantern glass, and the kerosene splashed all over him and caught fire. He ran out into the hallway burning and screaming, and I scooped up the gun and started shooting it. Shot both of them, I think. They went rolling down the stairs and even before they hit the bottom they were both on fire, both screaming. And the stairwell carpet was burning. Fire was already climbing the walls."

There was, she noted, a fire extinguisher just feet away in her kitchen, and maybe she'd be able to find it in the dark, maybe it would've been enough to stop the fire, maybe she could have saved them, saved the building. But—

"I admit it: I wanted them to never be able to hurt me again. I knew that the building, probably most of the block, was empty except for me. I also knew the fire department response time had slipped to at least twenty minutes, so if I couldn't put out the fire myself with my kitchen extinguisher, a structure that old with such flammable stuff in it, like the damn stairwell carpet, would be lost. And, wham, just like that, some other version of me took over."

She snatched up her laptop and the small duffel that weeks earlier she'd stashed with her important papers "just in case," then, aided by light from the burning front stairway, scrambled to her second-floor condo's rear stairs, which brought her down to the alley behind the building and, some fifteen feet away, her car.

"I jumped in the car, locked the doors, and drove the hell outta that alley before I called in the fire. And then I kept on driving."

"All the way here," I said.

"All the way here," she said.

CHAPTER THIRTY-THREE

YOU NEED HER BIG TIME

For her sake and for mine, I didn't want Phoebe to leave. She seemed a bit shaky after what I still think of as her confession, and besides, she was the best way for me not to obsessively worry about Duka and Isabella, who I fervently hoped were by then pitching and heaving their way across Cape Cod Bay back to the Outer Cape.

But since Phoebe was done talking about Boston, I made us salads—lettuce, carrots, broccoli, a bit of spinach, and, yes, peanuts, all from the greenhouse, dabbed with a little of what was left of my soy sauce dressing—plus we split one of my early, semi-successful attempts at mashed potato pone.

Of course, I expected her to be polite about the meager food I provided (after Eleven Fourteen, one was always polite about any offered food, no matter how terrible it might be)—but Phoebe flew right on past polite into outright exuberance; she even lathered praise all over my dubious pone.

"Wow," she kept saying. "All of this from your greenhouse."

"Almost all," I corrected her.

While we ate, we kept poking at our phones, attempting to send texts—me to Duka, she to Isabella. One bar triggered a "maybe we'll get lucky;" two bars inspired leap-to-your-feet excitement. But to no avail as we waited, though we kept what we waited for inexplicit.

For the sake of conversation, I moved on to the wider world—what remained of it, anyway. "Somebody," I ventured, "mentioned you'd been working on a robotics project. Is that the same one you talked about before—?"

"Yeah. A chunk of a larger joint study on industrial production requirements," Phoebe explained. "For the Defense, Commerce, and Agriculture Departments. My piece involved using data analytics to help determine what sorts of robots will be needed over the next two years, and what can actually be supplied, for various industries, tasks, and so on."

"So Defense, Commerce, and Agriculture are explicitly driving markets now—commanding the demand."

"Yep. And commanding quite directly and specifically, too. Because Defense, Commerce, and Agriculture now decide, well, pretty much everything. Even has its own acronym now: DCA. In the report I just finished, the current focus—for robots at least—is on energy production, environmentally controlled agriculture, and law enforcement. So much for *competitive* market analytics, which is what I used to do for a living. And since I've just finished my part of the study, I am now without employment. Or income."

But wait, Cordelia murmured. *Even the mighty-ish—or at least those with mighty-ish bank accounts—fall slowly enough that they can "invest" in the* Clarus *cargo.*

What's more, judging by, well, everything about her, Phoebe's hope for her professional future had not entirely died out.

"So," I asked, "how *is* the command-demand for industrial robots?"

"Cranking nicely. Almost like an economic bright spot. I just finished a proposal for a follow-on DCA study that would do an analysis by industry sector using much more granular data. It'd show how to best deploy various types of robotics manufacturing capabilities, complete with an interactive tool that would illustrate tradeoffs. Like if too much capacity is devoted to surveillance drones, then, say, LED grow light production suffers and too many people go hungry. Anyway, if they bite I may actually be able to sleep again for a while."

"And how optimistic are you? About them biting, I mean?"

"Cautiously." Phoebe exhaled slowly. "I know I've priced it right. The real question is how much DCA appreciates the importance of robotics in Eleven Fourteen recovery. Whether they value that kind of analytical drilldown. All depends on who the decider is, and that's a crapshoot."

Pretending not to notice the time, we talked on. Phoebe, it appeared, had no more desire to be alone than I did as we waited to hear from Duka and Isabella. So our conversation wandered. And wandered.

Mostly she did the talking. At least what she talked about was worth hearing, especially the part describing how much of the economy had been "utility-ized"—whole industry sectors quietly transformed into command-demand government-regulated public utilities. "Martial law and nationalization of industry by any other name," she quipped.

Not that private enterprise or even entrepreneurial spirit were entirely dead. Phoebe told me of one startup in Georgia, near Savannah, using robotic sensors and controls to boost greenhouse production of cocoa beans.

"Cocoa beans—you mean, like, chocolate?" I asked. "They're growing *chocolate?*"

"Actually, yes. Because they're also doing a greenhouse sugar cane crop. Have a few milk cows, too." She was laughing now. "Classic vertical integration."

"And their chocolate's for sale?"

"Trust me—we can't afford it." Translation from Phoebe-speak: Trust her—even *she* can't afford it.

"Maybe…someday…" I glanced at the greenhouse feeling a momentary surge of mindless optimism. "…We'll be able to grow our own."

Phoebe's mouth opened to reply to my idiotic idea, then shut again as she, too, looked over at the greenhouse.

"What?" I asked her.

"Why the hell didn't I think of this before?" She shook her head. "One of the Department of Agriculture women I interviewed mentioned the possibility of expanding ECASP beyond commercial growers to residential growers, which means—"

"ECASP…" I flashed on burnt scraps buried in ash, on the derelict foundations dug into those properties I'd just bought—and Phoebe chattering on about, yes, yes, this thing called ECASP. "Tell me again about that."

Phoebe started talking *very* fast, and I learned, finally, the rough outlines of the Environmentally Controlled Agriculture Support Program, wherein the federal government helps farmers with whatever can protect their crops from the cold and sustain crop production. "Mostly greenhouses, high tunnels, lighting, and heating. Sometimes water, too."

"So let me get this straight," I asked, trying to slow her down. "This program—ECASP—that helps out commercial farmers is also gonna offer help to regular people who want to shelter their backyard gardens?"

"Maybe," Phoebe emphasized. "Last I heard, nothing's decided yet." She paused while a frown etched her forehead. "They were considering grants because then they can steer how the grant money gets spent. All the way down to specific manufacturers."

Right after I insisted that Phoebe tell me more, tell me all she knew about ECASP residential any-damn-thing, my phone trilled. Duka had at last managed to send me a text:

Cold storage beach 8pm come w/my truck

Phoebe didn't say anything when I unceremoniously declared, "Gotta get ready," before abandoning her to quickly prepare a thermos of dandelion and burdock tea in the kitchen. She followed me anyway, hovering even as I proceeded to yank a jacket out of the front closet and grab Cordelia's second walkie-talkie. "Best way for Duka to communicate once *Clarus* rounds Long Point," I explained when she asked why I needed *that*.

By contrast, she did not ask to accompany me, only expressed a hope that I'd be able to drop her off at her house, which I did. By then she'd also received a text—hers from Isabella—about our 8 p.m. meetup at this lesser-known bayside Truro beach virtually guaranteed to be empty of people and especially Coasties.

Truth is, I didn't mind that she jumped in her big fat SUV and followed me, nor that she joined me in Duka's truck soon after I halted it in the small beach parking area.

We'd arrived at the sand cliff overlooking the beach shortly after the peak of high tide, a half-hour early. I'd immediately squelched the truck's headlights to avoid attracting attention, and from our perch we couldn't see where water met sand, only hear the waves crashing boisterously somewhere in front of us. Nor, as usual, could we see stars or even the moon, which one of my apps indicated was waxing gibbous.

Ever since the black cold, Truro's nights—always dark enough to intimidate our urban summer visitors—had become even darker. And yeah, the beach down there and the neighborhood around us *seemed* empty, but we'd entered an era where anything might happen, particularly in near-zero visibility.

I pulled out Duka's binoculars anyway and fruitlessly scanned westward for the boat's running lights while willing Duka's voice to come crackling over the walkie-talkie, silent on the dashboard, and wishing the wind would ease off. But judging from the way it gusted through the dead grass in front of us, briefly visible in the truck's headlights when we pulled in, the wind not only persisted, it also had begun to shift from due north to north-northeast.

Reaching Cold Storage Beach would require *Clarus* to tack almost directly into a thirty-mile-an-hour sustained blow.

And all Phoebe and I could do was wait, worry, and keep watch.

A couple of lights winked erratically off to our distant left—probably near the silted remnants of Pamet Harbor some two miles south of us—and dead ahead about five miles west across the water we could make out a bit of weakly flickering illumination in Provincetown. The sight seemed to inspire the same reaction in both of us, which Phoebe expressed with the tiniest of tremors in her voice: "It's outside at night when you realize how truly empty it's become around here…"

In that moment, I felt the chasm between me and this woman who wasn't even half my age: She, like Duka and the rest of my neighbors, faced having to figure out not just how to stay alive in this After world, but how to thrive in it. If, indeed, thriving would be a real option again anytime soon. For myself, the options were much simpler and quite evident: No— not even close to enough time to thrive again; the best I could hope for was a not-uncomfortable exit.

Seemed like Phoebe felt the chasm, too—or maybe just the darkness— and coped by asking questions about Duka. Does she have a girlfriend? Did she grow up on the Outer Cape? Does she really make kinetic sculptures? Have you seen any of them? What's her problem with Ellen Higgins, who seems basically nice if a bit stiff?

I ducked and ducked again by returning to the topic of greenhouses. That ECASP stuff sounds interesting, I kept saying as I pressed for details "to pass along to Duka."

Eventually, with a little laugh, Phoebe declared me "wicked relentless." And reminded me that, like many government support programs, ECASP had a hidden master to serve—in this case, a cabal of manufacturing companies that poured plenty of money into politicians' reelection coffers. "The deal," she noted, "is that ECASP antes up money to the manufacturers' customers, who're required to spend that money on whatever the manufacturers sell. And, so far, those customers are mostly larger-scale agricultural interests, not consumer households."

"But I thought you said—"

Phoebe nodded. "Yeah, that ECASP is considering a residential program. I was told that it *is*—because the manufacturers ECASP has to keep happy have started seeing opportunities on the consumer side. My take is they're waiting for the manufacturers to decide on the most optimal minimum size parameters."

"Like how big a greenhouse operation has to be to qualify?"

"Exactly. Below a certain threshold, an ECASP grant just doesn't pay off for the manufacturers."

"So how big is big enough?"

"Wish I knew. The woman I talked to is one of the ECASP deputy administrators, who's pushing to get the program to experiment with a few residential greenhouse grants as a way to satisfy the LED grow light manufacturers in particular. I'd forgotten that till you poked me about ECASP. Now I'm thinking I should try to get signed up as part of that experiment. So, um, thanks for the poke."

"Mmm. Think that woman might be interested in bestowing a residential grant on *several* greenhouses?"

"I—I don't know. I can try to find out."

"Good. I'll keep my fingers crossed. Because a program like that—" I halted, unwilling to give away too much too soon, then changed direction. "Y'know, Duka once told me something that's stuck with me. She said there's only one way to survive—by being part of a group of people you can trust. A community, really. Cooperation, sharing, and trading depend on trust."

"Duka said that?"

"She did."

"I like that. I guess my community's going to end up being my sister Olivia and Bill and the kids. So we'd need a greenhouse that'd be, um, let's see—"

"If you want enough to feed all of you all the time, then it's five times four hundred, roughly."

"And I'd need Duka's help building the thing—"

"Including installing grow lights and heating and ventilation, probably automatic watering, and then there's soil and seeds and—"

I stopped when I heard a small groan.

"Oh dear god." Phoebe sounded like she'd been buried under a pile of rubble. "I don't know shit…"

"The people doing this ECASP thing—you know them, yes?"

"Uh, yeah. My interview with that deputy administrator was good. We hit it off, actually."

"And you were going to make contact with her again, right?" Whereupon I talked about precisely what I'd told myself *not* to talk about—yet. "So maybe you could find out whether she'd be interested in trying out a neighborhood-wide grant for a cluster of greenhouses able to feed a number of households. Perhaps even powered by a few small-scale wind turbines."

"A whole *neighborhood...*" Phoebe sounded genuinely surprised at the notion. "That does seem pretty interesting. I'll find out." She inhaled sharply. "Yeah," she said in a revelatory hush. "Yeah, I'll find out about that."

God knows what I would have said to her next, given that I'd said way too much already. Fortunately, thanks to Duka's voice coming through on the walkie-talkie, I never had the chance.

CHAPTER THIRTY-FOUR

DUMB FUCKING LUCK

F lash the headlights three times," Duka instructed from somewhere out there. A moment after I did what she asked, her voice buzzed over the walkie-talkie again. "Yeah, we see you. We're about a mile out. Keep those lights on for us."

I refused to clock-watch, but it seemed like at least another hour before *Clarus* bobbed slowly, ghostlike into the right margin of the headlights' eerie purview. The boat showed no running lights and heaved hard to starboard despite its furled jib and reefed mainsail. As it came in close, I realized how dangerously low it sat in the water. Especially the bow.

"Oh jeezus," I may have muttered aloud.

Wave by rolling wave, Isabella and Duka managed to beach *Clarus* nearly right in front of us, which is when Phoebe bolted from the truck, flashlight waving fitfully, to scamper down the narrow road from the parking area to the sand. I watched her splash into the water to catch the line Duka threw before I followed her in the truck. While I backed its rear wheels to the edge of the pavement, she positioned herself right behind Duka and together they tugged *Clarus*'s bow into shore against a wind determined to drag the stern away from them.

Thus I didn't see Duka react to Phoebe's presence. Just as well, given the grim, squinty look she threw me a few minutes later.

"You okay?" I asked once she'd set the anchor and trudged out of the water.

She grunted what I took to be an affirmative as I handed her the thermos of tea, which she swigged. "Oh god, that's good."

"Isabella?"

"Cold an' wet but alive an' fucking kicking," Duka grumbled, then nodded oh so slightly toward Phoebe, who now helped a notably disheveled

Isabella disembark into thigh-deep water. "Don't suppose you had much choice about bringing that one along, huh?"

"Phoebe? Uh-uh." I looked Duka over again. "You're shivering."

I wanted to take her straight home, dry her off, warm her up, and feed her something. First, though, would come the small matter of offloading *Clarus*'s cargo into the back of her truck. In a near-freezing gale.

But wait…

"Duka," I inquired, "where's the dinghy?"

"Don't ask."

Instead I agreed to back the truck onto the sand and closer to the boat, all the while wondering how the hell we'd transport Isabella's cargo of thirty insulated boxes, each carrying a cubic foot of frozen meat and a slab of dry ice—too heavy to float from the boat onto dry land—without…a… dinghy…

"Seems like we'll be able to stuff all thirty of the boxes in the back," I encouraged her.

"Thirty-nine," a still-shivering Duka muttered. "An' no, don't ask. Not yet."

"Well," I offered, "good news is Phoebe brought her car—some kind of SUV, certainly big enough for nine boxes."

Duka exhaled. "Woo-fucking-hoo. I need all the small mercies I can get."

Indeed. Each box, at about eighteen inches square and weighing some thirty-five pounds, had to be wrangled out of *Clarus*'s tiny cabin to the open-transom stern, lowered off the stern to be carried above a ten-foot stretch of breaking two-foot waves, then across some fifty feet of sand to the back of Duka's truck.

We did it in a line—Duka aboard the boat offloading to Isabella standing in the water (her dry suit made the forty-eight-degree water bearable) to Phoebe at the edge of the water to me nearer the truck. I am proud to report that I was *not* the first one to wimp out. That honor went to Isabella and her bitch about "I'm just too damn cold to do this anymore." So we switched up: Phoebe aboard, Duka mostly in the water, me at the edge of the water with regular help from Duka, and Isabella whining about how hard it was to lift the boxes onto the truck.

Thus the boxes piled up on the sand—until I offered to trade places with Isabella.

"No!" Duka blared as she came stomping out of the water. "I don't give a shit what those duchesses want, Hester, no fucking way'm I letting you do any more of this heavy lifting shit!" She pivoted to face Isabella. "Screw all that overwatch crap. You get her ass down here pronto or me an' Hester are gone."

What this meant became obvious when, about three minutes after Isabella stopped gaping at Duka and decided to tap her phone, a vehicle's headlights cut a swath across the darkness above us.

Someone had driven into the small parking area atop the dune behind us. A car door slammed, and within seconds Ellen Higgins, dressed in civvies rather than a Truro police uniform, came trotting down the narrow road toward Duka's truck, her flashlight's beam seesawing in front of her. "Need some help?" she asked brightly as if what we were doing was utterly normal.

I don't recall ever seeing Isabella move so quickly, and the possessive way Ellen Higgins embraced her was unequivocal: Yessiree, they had partnered up.

"These still need to be loaded," Duka said to them, whisking her hand toward the half dozen boxes at the rear of her truck. "I'll do that while Hester takes overwatch."

Thereafter, Phoebe climbed aboard *Clarus* to do the offloading ("Since you're already wet anyway," Isabella mewled) while Isabella once more stood in thigh-deep water and Ellen Higgins drenched herself making sure Isabella didn't have to do a whole lot. At first, Duka hung back at the truck, forcing Ellen to carry each box across the sand—until Duka eventually took pity on her and did most of the cross-sand carrying before loading the boxes onto the truck bed.

I tracked all this as I stood in the parking lot above the beach keeping watch over the blackness surrounding us, ready to alert the gang below if anyone came snooping. From my vantage point, I had a sweeping view of about a third of North Truro's hilltops—and counted exactly seven lights, none of them close by. Did everyone live down in the hollows now, out of the wind, beneath my line of sight?

Or was North Truro really *that* empty?

"We got thirty boxes in the back now, the rest'll go in Phoebe's SUV," Duka declared via walkie-talkie. "So come on down, Hester. Time to go." When she signaled to the others that we were leaving, Isabella came running.

Clarus, she sniveled, would have to do an overnight on the beach, since shifting it off the sand during the ebbing tide had already become too problematic. So of *course* Duka should stay, too, because *Clarus* shouldn't be left unguarded. And no way she, Isabella, should be expected to spend the night at Cold Storage Beach—the horror! Nor, plainly, could she imagine asking Phoebe to do such a thing, and "Ellen has to work a shift tonight."

"Read my lips, Isabella: No." Duka started up her truck. "Me an' Hester are going now. You can pick up your boxes at her place when-the-fuck-ever."

Isabella blinked, then started fast-talking with a kind of petulant, you-owe-me insistence. "Okay, so, uh, uh…next high tide's a bit before eight tomorrow morning, so we can come back at, like, six, six thirty? Shouldn't take long to get *Clarus* over to Provincetown harbor."

But Duka had closed the driver-side window as soon as she heard "next high tide" and was instead persuading the truck's rear tires out of the sand where they'd sunk nearly to their rims. She made it seem easy.

As we drove home, she had plenty to say.

"Those—those *fucking* women," Duka sputtered even before we reached the crest of Pond Road. "Isabella Frenzy who knows everything an' *never* does anything wrong, plus I think she lied about what the hell she bought. Then there's Phoebe Bigshot, the world's greatest sailor who's *so familiar* with the bay an' woulda made the trip herself 'cept she had some *so important* meeting. *Why* would she think I wanna listen to her pathetic goddamn excuses? *She* can fucking take over now. Cuz I'm still looking at lugging fifteen boxes of meat into your freezer."

"*Fifteen* boxes? I thought—"

"Damn. I was afraid of that. You didn't get my message, huh?"

"Just the text about Cold Storage Beach eight p.m. How many did you send?"

"A bunch that I could tell had failed. But I thought the one I sent you this morning made it through—the one about needing more freezer space cuz Isabella can't fucking count. As in how hard can it be to understand that thirty-nine cubic feet of anything will *not* fit into one sixteen-cubic-foot freezer? Which is why I tried to give you a heads-up."

"Well, the big freezer's plenty cold now. That's eighteen cubic feet ready and waiting, plus there's some room in the smaller freezer—"

"Phoebe Bigshot has a freezer, too. Twelve cubic feet. Though Phoebe said it's about a quarter full."

"Mmm, that plus Isabella's freezer should be enough. Which leaves only one question: How good is the meat? Still frozen after, what, two days in a truck?"

"The dude showed up in a refrigerated truck, at least. Everything I saw is packed up tight with dry ice just like Isabella expected. All butchered, individually double-vacuum wrapped an' labeled, excellent dates. But we gave only the first four boxes a careful lookover. Rest of 'em are still sealed. So yeah, we oughta inspect everything that we put in your freezers."

"Any idea what Isabella paid for it all?"

"Not a clue." In the dim blue glow from the truck's dashboard, I saw Duka throw me a grin. "But at least we'll be able to pick out the best of five boxes."

"Five? I thought you said you're getting three."

"Fourth box is for dealing with those extra nine boxes Isabella pretended to look surprised about when that güey dumped 'em an' bolted instead of sticking around to help us load like Isabella said he would. I swear she knew it was thirty-nine boxes from the beginning an' didn't think I'd agree to go with her if I knew. An' guess what? She was right. We had too much fucking weight. So I told her I wouldn't touch 'em without an 'adjustment' to my fee. Fifth box is for risking my ass to retrieve the damn dinghy."

"So where *is* the dinghy?"

"Dunno—but I'm guessing it's in pieces at the bottom of Cape Cod Bay."

Finally away from the others, awash in relief, Duka couldn't stop talking. By the time we got back to the house, I'd heard all about how Isabella neglected to properly hitch the dinghy to *Clarus*'s stern after loading the boxes at White Horse Beach. How Duka jumped in the water to retrieve the line and managed to get back aboard before succumbing to hypothermia. How, halfway back across the bay, a "scary big-ass" wave swamped the dinghy and ripped not only the line clean off the boat but also the cleat it was tied to, "screws an' all."

And I heard plenty about "the transaction" at White Horse Beach.

"Right off, Isabella's guy was jumpy as hell. Had a frigging pistol in his waistband, which I didn't notice till we'd already started doing the deal. He seemed okay while we checked out a few boxes. Soon as he spotted Isabella's cash, though—well, next thing I know, he's unloading everything fast as he can right where he pulled off the road into this parking area by a buncha empty beach shacks, all while watching her count the money.

Watching like a hawk, y'know? When she's done counting, he grabs it an'—bam!—he's outta there. Like he's being chased."

I willed my voice to stay calm. "*Was* he being chased?"

Duka's shoulders rose, fell. "Doubt it. We never did see another soul except him. But he wanted to skip—fast. Left us to haul all of it four hundred fucking feet into the dinghy, drag it aboard *Clarus*, an' stuff it in the cabin."

Worried about the weight of nine additional boxes, Duka lobbied for leaving them behind. "But *no-o-o.* Isabella kept repeating her bullshit about how *Clarus* could handle the extra weight, which ended up in the bow on top of the V-berth. Coming back, the bow got buried by waves—I mean *really* buried—eleven times. *Eleven!* Dumb fucking luck we're not at the bottom of the bay right now with the damn dinghy."

When we reached the driveway, Duka halted the truck for a moment and stared at my house, now her house, too. "Sure as hell, I won't ever do that again," she said with a long exhale. "Not with Isabella. An' not to meet up with some armed dude I don't know. I figured he'd shoot us both then take off with the boxes *an'* all that cash Isabella brought along."

"I'm relieved to see he *didn't* shoot you."

While she backed the truck into the driveway, I looked her up and down once more, taking in the sight and feel of Duka when she's encountered a boundary, the kind that slams her up against her limits. My news, I decided, could wait.

"You will end up with pneumonia all over again if you don't warm yourself up," I told her. "And since we have to open all the boxes out here so we don't poison ourselves with nitrogen gas, and then we have to make sure what's inside each one is okay before we cart it to the freezer, I'll start while you take a shower and put on dry clothes and eat something."

I didn't expect her to accept that, but she did. "Then go to bed," I called to her from the truck as she went into the house. "I got this."

Twenty minutes later, though, she returned, words tumbling out of her even faster than before.

"Did you get anything to eat?" I asked.

Nope. She was more interested in talking. About Phoebe.

"Woman does not live by words alone," I insisted. "Wait here and hold that thought."

From our diminished food options I warmed up my mashed potato pone experiment and spread a generous amount of our peanut butter over it.

"Bread's sorta different," Duka observed kindly upon biting into my oversized hockey puck pone. "But I like it."

"Huh. Two for two—assuming I believe either one of you."

"We're talking about your bread, right?"

I couldn't help but smile. "Phoebe had some earlier."

"An' she liked it?" Duka sounded surprised.

"She waxed poetic about it. Too poetic, actually. But I think she meant well. And she didn't throw up or break any teeth, so there's that."

"She owns a buncha these boxes."

I nodded. "Mmm, she told me. Shortly before she met my pone. Didn't want to tell me, but something about her...she admitted it as soon as I guessed. Though I have no details—"

"Phoebe gets thirty percent of the 'original' amount. Nine boxes. Solid odds that Isabella lied to her, too—which means Phoebe sees thirty percent of thirty boxes when she should get thirty percent of thirty-nine boxes. But hey, Isabella *does* have scruples. More or less. As in endless bitching about Phoebe's so-called 'hard bargain'—cuz all the transaction expenses, mostly the boat an' me, are coming out of Isabella's share, not Phoebe's."

"Well, hard-bargaining Phoebe wants you to build her a greenhouse."

"Ha! She'll pay through the nose for that."

I almost said something then, but we had several hundred pounds of frozen meat to move into the freezer—meat so frozen by dry ice that we'd burn our hands if we touched it without gloves, meat that needed to be pulled from boxes exuding nitrogen gas, which meant doing it outdoors in a freezing northeast wind. Then we needed to check it all out to make sure it was real and not spoiled during transport.

"Looks good so far," Duka said after we'd inspected roughly half of the boxes. "I kinda worried Isabella would get ripped off, but this stuff really is okay."

About the time she'd finished selecting the meat she'd claim as her own, Isabella called her—a conversation that lasted only a few seconds during which Duka spoke only in monosyllables.

"Doubt I'll be doing any more work for the Queen of Frenzy," she said after clicking off. "Prob'ly not Phoebe either. They are—well, Isabella is—royally pissed. I have been commanded to bring over fourteen boxes an' then help with the boat in the morning."

"So besides your five boxes' worth, Isabella is asking that we store eleven of her boxes here."

"More like demanding. Whiny demanding."

"Sounds like a favor to me."

"Yeah, well, I did tell her I'd drive the boxes from the beach to her house. So fine, I will. Haven't decided yet about moving the damn boat in the morning."

"I'm going with you to Isabella's," I said. Because, I didn't say, we need to stay in Phoebe's good graces—Phoebe who lives right next door to Isabella and would likely be around for a while. Phoebe who *wants* to like you, Duka, so stop making it so damn difficult. "Ready for a bit of good news?"

Duka eyed me skeptically. "I could use a bit of good news."

Whereupon I told her about my excursion to the new Truro town hall and my adventures in property acquisition.

While she stared at me slack-jawed, I added that maybe, just possibly, we'd even be able to get a little help from a government program. "Because—surprise!—there's still a federal government. Still a Department of Agriculture that *maybe* will offer assistance to regular people investing in environmentally-controlled agriculture," I said. "Like people with greenhouses. And who knows, that may even include wind turbines, too. It's a long shot, you understand, and prob'ly later rather than sooner, but—"

"Omigod, omi*god* Hester!" she shouted. Suddenly, her arms were wrapped around me—the first time she'd ever done such a thing. "We're gonna goddamn make this work! We really *are!*"

As we drove those fourteen boxes to Isabella's, I tried to slow Duka down enough to explain that our involvement in this thing called ECASP would depend on Phoebe, of all people. I even traded the acronym for the unwieldy original mouthful, "Environmentally Controlled Agriculture Support Program"—to no avail.

Nope, sorry, that was a detail too far too soon; first Duka insisted on hearing about precisely what properties I'd bought—and then couldn't stop babbling about how each foundation might best be used, how Toby's friend Kai could maybe help figure out wind turbine siting.

"Omigod, omigod, I got so much to do," she kept saying as she veered from excitement to will-this-work worry back to excitement again.

"One more thing you need to know, kiddo—"

But no chance to explain just how critically important to us ECASP—and Phoebe—might be. Not then, anyway.

CHAPTER THIRTY-FIVE

ISABELLA'S FIRE

S omething's wrong," Duka said as we rounded the last curve on the lane to Isabella's house. "Her place is completely dark—"

"Those lights farther on—aren't they at Phoebe's? The garage maybe? I can just make out someone in—"

Wild, warbly shouting interrupted me. Half a heartbeat later came an intense burst of light and a streak of reddish-orange smoke. Then we heard a very loud bang and the sound of breaking glass.

Duka swerved the truck so its high beams illuminated Phoebe's front lawn a hundred feet in front of us—and for a long, stunned moment I just didn't comprehend the tableau before me: Isabella still in her dry suit near the top of Phoebe's driveway, semi-crouched and pointing something leftward at two black-clad figures who were running away from her while, behind her, Phoebe stood frozen at the rear of the open SUV parked just inside the garage.

Before we could react, whatever Isabella held produced another noisy burst of light and reddish-orange smoke, and we heard more sounds of broken glass just as the two guys in black she seemed to be aiming at disappeared into a thicket of mostly dead scrub between her house and Phoebe's. Several windows in Phoebe's house had begun to flicker and brighten unevenly, but Isabella seemed not to notice; she ran toward her own house, fiddling with whatever she held for a moment before lifting it level with her shoulder and aiming.

"What the *hell?*" I bleated. "She's *following* them?"

And—*bang!*—shooting at them. Again.

Behind us, a bright light ricocheted off a large black SUV lurching out of Isabella's driveway on its way toward Route Six. In its wake, a sweep of liquid flame lit up a tangle of nearby deadwood.

"Pinche pendeja!" Duka hissed. "She's burning down the whole goddamn neighborhood!"

A flare gun, I finally realized. Isabella was shooting a flare gun. And Phoebe's house, which had been on the receiving end of Isabella's first two flares, was burning.

"I'm calling for help," I said, poking at my phone. By then, Duka had already scrambled out of the truck. Oh shit, I thought—

"Isabella! Stop!" Duka bellowed, but too late.

—Isabella can see only headlights and she thinks we're more bad guys.

Panicky rage etched her brightly illuminated face as she turned, pointed the flare gun straight at us, and fired the damn thing for a fourth time.

And, thank the fates, missed for a fourth time.

But the flare she shot skidded by us like a skipping stone into the bone-dry tree debris on the property across the street from hers, igniting everything it touched before lodging among the skeletons of dead scrub pines. Within seconds, wind-whipped flames were dancing a story high on both sides of the twenty-foot-wide lane, burning like twin torches behind us on the only road out.

I struggled through several attempts to reach 911 as Duka sprinted full-tilt past Isabella toward Phoebe's garage, where Phoebe no longer stood; I finally got through just as Duka darted into the only part of the house that wasn't in flames.

"Yes, the Benevides house is on fire and it's on three sides of us!" I shrieked into my phone. "Moving toward the school. Moving fast!"

❖

What to do next.

Having emptied her flare gun and driven away the bad guys, Isabella stood pretty much in a stupor near the edge of Phoebe's front yard. I could see orange light glinting in her garage windows, hint that she'd set her place alight, too. Meanwhile, Duka had disappeared into Phoebe's burning house, presumably to find Phoebe. A quick second glance around me confirmed that although we might be able to walk out through the scrub if we stayed well east and north of the flames, we had little time left to escape by road in Duka's truck.

Tempted though I was to search out a garden hose and spray water through Phoebe's windows until the firefighters showed up, I'd seen enough of housefires to understand this one was already past saving. Saving people—all four of us—would be tough enough.

Only one other time in my life have I experienced what happened next—something I call Suddenly Being One Step Ahead Of Yourself, when the pace of your perception and thinking detaches from realtime and speeds up, which has the effect of slowing realtime just enough for you to calmly, efficiently consider your options, forge a plan, and execute it step by well-reasoned step.

From my eerily calm perch One Step Ahead, I jumped out of Duka's truck, yanked and yelled a zombified Isabella into the passenger seat, then circled the truck around to the bottom of Phoebe's driveway, knowing it could stay there for only a few minutes before it, too, risked catching fire.

"Isabella!" I bellowed inches from her frighteningly blank face. "Stay right here and honk the horn. Keep honking till I come back." I shook her shoulder hard. "*Now*, Isabella, start honking *now!*" And she did.

I didn't look forward to the prospect of running into a burning building, but at least I had an N95 mask to put over my face—worth an extra breath or two, I hoped.

I found them on their knees, coughing and choking in Phoebe's cathedral-ceilinged, smoke-filled kitchen. Phoebe had a death grip on her laptop and Duka had a death grip on Phoebe…

"This way," I croaked in Duka's ear as I grabbed her arm. I'd inhaled only once since entering the house, yet my eyes stung and my head already throbbed; I knew we had mere seconds before the poisonous air would overtake us.

After inhaling again, which made me nauseous, I shouted, "This way!" and tugged on Duka with all my strength. She responded with a jolt, lifting herself and Phoebe, too, toward me. I steered us stumbling toward the door to the mudroom, Duka's strength propelling each step through a slow-motion eternity to the garage and then out, out into fresh air.

Behind us, the overhead lights in Phoebe's garage winked out. Somewhere far, far away, a car horn blared rhythmically—two long honks, brief pause, two long honks, brief pause...

Isabella was doing her job.

"There," I wheezed, trying to point down the driveway at Duka's truck shimmering in the erratic fireglow of Phoebe's immolating house.

I was, remarkably, still One Step Ahead—so...

I noticed that flames had claimed the north side of Isabella's place...

I grasped that if Isabella was still sitting in Duka's truck dutifully honking the horn because I'd told her to, then she must be seriously out of her mind...

I understood we had very little time left to get the three of us in that damn truck and drive it beyond the reach of what I already thought of as Isabella's Fire...

Fifty feet. We were just fifty feet from the truck, but once Duka gasped out "You drive," my memory of getting there becomes a blur of coughing and careening while I forced my fingers, suddenly thick and comically clumsy, to pull Duka's keys from my jacket pocket (because sure as hell I wasn't going to leave Isabella in a truck she could actually *drive*), pick out the key that would start the truck, and fumble it into the ignition while my legs blundered me behind the wheel and Isabella insisted on reaching over to continue honking the horn.

Then, behind me, Duka quashed her coughing just long enough to thump my shoulder and wheeze, "We're both in. *Go.*"

I swerved the truck to dodge several hundred feet of whirling embers and lapping flames, almost veered off the road at the fork where I had to swing right, and nearly collided head-on with the first fire truck to arrive. No longer One Step Ahead, I also decided to keep going—onto Route Six and all the way back to Upper Hollow Circle, to Annie and Melinda, whom I'd rudely roused via walkie-talkie so they might prepare oxygen. Because it was obvious from the violent retching in the rear seat that both Duka and Phoebe needed oxygen and a medical lookover.

Next to me, Isabella hummed a sad, simple, but unrecognizable tune. Why? Because I'd told her to stop honking the horn and instead sing her favorite song. "Can't remember the words," she replied woefully—then brightened: "But I can do the melody."

"Good, Isabella," I encouraged her. "Do the melody for us."

❖

NOT ALL A DREAM

You'd have thought Annie and Melinda turned their living room into a triage station every day. They had maybe three minutes' notice (in the middle of the night), but they were ready for us, and soon Phoebe and Duka sat dully silent next to each other on their sofa breathing with the help of oxygen masks. Annie even made me use one for a bit before she departed to join the firefighters.

Our prognoses were good, and I got a pat on the back for so quickly moving us upwind of the smoke. But Isabella—well, Isabella remained in never-never land.

"I'm gonna request that she gets checked out at the hospital," an obviously fatigued Melinda whispered to me. "She has none of the usual stroke symptoms, but she presents with altered mental status—disoriented, confused. It's prob'ly not a dissociative fugue, since she knows her name and hasn't scampered off anywhere. On the other hand, when I asked her where she lived, she just shrugged and went back to playin' with Annie's baoding balls. She seems fascinated by the way they chime. And that meat you mentioned? She's clueless."

Ah yes, that meat I mentioned...

Duka's cap-covered truck bed still held fourteen boxes of dry-iced meat—dry ice that had been evaporating away for at least a couple of days in various transit vehicles.

So who do you call when you have fourteen cubic feet of frozen meat—upwards of 400 pounds—on the verge of unfreezing?

Lizbie Watts, that's who. And it helps that she buzzes you on your walkie-talkie half a second before you intended to buzz her, then shows up no more than five minutes later.

Perhaps less helpful, but inevitable, is the news she brings of the fire you've just escaped: Phoebe's house and SUV are gone and Isabella's place is going fast, but "our guys" are confident of containing the blaze before it reaches the school. And oh yeah, Toby, the senior on-scene firefighter, is asking who the hell started this one.

Of the six people in Melinda and Annie's living room, four of us knew the answer and three of us had the wit to say so, but Duka remained silent ("Not my place," she told me later), as did Phoebe, whose death grip on the laptop had not relented. Instead, they looked at me.

So first I described what Duka and I saw when we approached Isabella's, with an emphasis on black-clad men of patently malicious intent. Because meat, probably.

"All *righty* then!" Lizbie declared once I (mostly) explained about the meat and the urgency of its circumstances. "Let's find out who's got freezer space."

She didn't have to go far. Sylvie and Toby could take some of the boxes, as could she and Sam. My freezers had room for another box, maybe two. Even Melinda and Annie were good for two boxes' worth.

"Will that work for you, Isabella?" Melinda asked—but Isabella simply looked up and smiled while she kept on fumbling with Annie's baoding balls.

Melinda asked her again. And again.

"All righty then, all righty then, all righty then with me," Isabella eventually sing-songed.

The rest of us exchanged mute glances, except Phoebe, who'd been watching in squinty silence—something I noticed because I saw Duka struggling not to stare at her.

"Well," Melinda finally declared wearily, "I'd say that'll have to do."

So did Isabella relinquish control of those fourteen boxes because she'd genuinely flipped out? Because she'd stroked out? Or were those fourteen boxes the price of trying to duck and cover because she knew perfectly well that her super-sized hissy fit had burned down her own house as well as Phoebe's and several additional acres of other people's dead trees?

Melinda's request to get Isabella fifty miles up-cape to the nearest hospital quickly brought Ellen Higgins, by then in uniform and on duty, swooping in with worry and questions.

"What's wrong with her?" Ellen asked, hushed and ashen when she saw Isabella ignore her to continue playing with baoding balls.

The rest of us couldn't hear Melinda's murmured response.

"*Hospital!*" Ellen's voice spiked as she spoke the dreaded word. "Because—" She rubbed her face. "You mean like a stroke or something?"

"I can't answer that," Melinda said. "Which is why she needs a CT scan and—"

"Right," Ellen interrupted. "Got it. Thank you for not wasting time."

I'd expected questions from her about the fourteen boxes, which Lizbie and Sylvie had already begun distributing to various freezers in the neighborhood, but instead she whisked Isabella away in her police cruiser without uttering another word to anyone.

"We're going, too," I told Melinda, "so maybe you can get some sleep."

Once back at my place, I turned to Phoebe, who hadn't volunteered one single syllable since being pulled out of her burning house, hadn't let go of her laptop for one single second, and stood in the middle of my living room staring vacantly at the floor. "C'mon, have a seat," I suggested, "and I'll make us something to—"

"What the hell do I do now?" she mumbled.

I glanced at Duka, who'd also said almost nothing since escaping the fire. Her eyes swung upward to the ceiling with her tacit question, and I nodded.

"Come with me." Duka spoke softly as her hand brushed Phoebe's, then gently clasped it, and she led Phoebe upstairs.

Well, well, Aitch. I'd say that counts as progress...

CHAPTER THIRTY-SIX

BACKASSWARDS

Plans are funny things. Sometimes you're entirely aware of them; you've declared a goal and say to yourself, yep, I'm gonna do *this*, figure out how to make *that* real…

But sometimes plans happen backasswards; you act first and only later grasp that a plan had covertly formed in your head, that you'd unconsciously begun to implement it.

I suspect we all end up on the backasswards path more than we appreciate (Cordelia has whispered repeatedly that this explains a lot), and it's probably worth taking the time—when one has the time—to examine why, really, one felt the need to hide/disguise/prevaricate about one's true plans. But often enough, such self-examination is a luxury that's unaffordable until the very end, when the best you can do is greet the insight, such as it is, with a shrug of acceptance.

Compared to some, then, I guess I'm fairly fortunate: My own backasswards plan started to reveal itself early(ish) on—the day I impetuously bought those eleven properties around my house. Because within just hours the answer to that question—What the *hell* had I been thinking—had already become spectacularly obvious. To me, anyway.

When I heard Duka plod down to the kitchen around six the morning after Isabella's fire, I scurried upstairs from my basement lair to talk with her.

"Lemme guess," I said. "You're up again after only three hours' sleep to go rescue *Clarus*."

Duka's shoulders rolled upward, then dropped, which I took as a yes. "Heard from Ellen that Isabella's still weirdly out of it, even though she seems to be physically okay. So they're gonna keep her in the hospital an' watch her for a few days. I'm meeting Ellen to pick up boat keys an' a letter of permission from the owner to operate the vessel, then me an' Sam'll bring the boat over to P'town harbor. Works out nice cuz, hey, never know when we might find *Clarus* useful."

"And how're *you* doing after inhaling all that smoke last night?"

Good, she declared hoarsely as she guzzled appallingly weak coffee and rubbed tired, bloodshot eyes. Slept okay, she professed. Felt okay, too, all considered.

And Phoebe?

"Got her to take a shower before putting her to bed in the study—" Duka tossed me a Look (signaling, I assumed, that's right, not *my* bed), then gruffed, "Coughed some, but breathing pretty well. She's still asleep now, still keeping that damn laptop within reach. Secrets of the universe must be on that frigging thing, the way she risked her damn life to retrieve it. At least no one died this time, but—but ¡chingada madre!—"

I was pretty sure that more or less meant *fuck*, so I decided, what the hell, Duka was as primed as she'd ever be. "Just briefly before you go, I'd like to run a few things by you—stuff to think about while you bring the boat back to P'town…"

As soon as she nodded, I started talking as fast as I could:

Our 400-square-foot greenhouse won't feed both of us, but its yields can pretty much feed one of us…

Using that measure as a baseline, I figure if we can put greenhouses in all the foundations we'll own—okay, okay, the foundations *I'll* own in fourteen business days—then we'd be able to grow enough to feed roughly thirteen people…

But winter's coming soon—and it could well be as bad as last year—so we need to get as many of those foundations as possible converted to greenhouses and planted as fast as possible…

Which means we need to involve more people than just the two of us—so I'll contribute the land and those foundations as well as what day-to-day work I can manage, but we also need people who can help find the materials, help with all the labor of building greenhouses and planting them and harvesting and processing what we plant, people with whom we share the yields…

And there it was—my backasswards plan.

Duka didn't hesitate. "Oh yeah, I'm on board. An' I don't doubt our meatkeepers will be, too. Let's see—Sam an' Lizbie an' their kids, Toby an' Sylvie, an' Annie an' Melinda… With you an' me, that makes ten. Phoebe makes eleven—*if* Phoebe wants to be included." She gulped down the last of her coffee and squinted at me. "You were up all last night, huh? Running numbers—like which foundations have what kinda potential greenhouse square footage…"

I grinned. "Gotta start somewhere."

"I think we should keep a lid on this, Hester—till you an' me lay out some of the details so we can, like, show everybody a complete plan. After moving the boat, I got some salvage I need to do. So how 'bout we start tonight?"

My turn to nod. "Tonight," I replied to Duka's departing wave as I realized I'd neglected to mention the government greenhouse support program that Phoebe might be able to plug us into. Perhaps for the best; backasswards plans don't always play well with pipe dreams about uncertain future possibilities.

I did, however, register Duka's linguistic shift—"salvage" had replaced what I assumed had become the less acceptable (and, theoretically, less legal) "scavenge." I also pondered whether this explained Duka's hurried departure. If "salvaging" was now preferable to "scavenging," then more people would be doing it, which meant more competition for whatever was worth grabbing.

Or maybe, Cordelia suggested, *she wants to duck Phoebe after *ahem* last night.*

Tempted though I was, I did not venture upstairs to check on Phoebe, instead staying at the dining room table to resume running those potential greenhouse numbers while I listened for the sounds of my newest houseguest shuffling to the bathroom.

That worked for roughly twenty minutes. Then yes, I confess I crept upstairs to check on her—and found her curled asleep on her side in the bed in the study, her breathing steady and unstrained, one hand draped over the laptop she'd kept in the bed with her, sheets and blankets rumpled just like someone else had spooned in behind her atop rather than underneath the blankets.

To console her? Calm her down while she cried herself to sleep?

Why wouldn't Duka have mentioned this?

Du-uh, Cordelia gibed. *Take an educated guess.*

I tiptoed back downstairs to continue running numbers and wait for Phoebe, who showed up about half an hour later—without her laptop—wrapped in what had been Cordelia's lush, oversized robe until I'd bequeathed it to Duka.

She moved slowly, stiffly, her face stuck in a frown as she glanced into the kitchen. "Where's Duka?" she rasped.

I told her, then asked how she felt.

She replied silently, eyebrows lifting into her frown as she shrugged and her eyes briefly teared. "Thank you for letting me stay here last night." She exhaled, then said something about going back to her house to see what condition it was in.

Did she not understand what had been unmistakable even before we'd escaped last night's conflagration—that the house was a total loss? "How about I go with you?" I offered.

"Yeah, thank you. I'd like that," she said.

Rather than wear the same sooty clothes she arrived in, I persuaded her to put on some of Cordelia's, since she's close to the same girth and height. Seeing Phoebe walking along in one of Cordelia's outfits made for a somewhat eerie experience, but not as upsetting as I feared, especially after Cordelia's question: *So did I ever look that good in those jeans*?

"You damn well did," I carelessly said aloud—but Phoebe seemed not to notice; she was too busy trying to glimpse her house through several hundred feet of mostly dead trees and scrub.

"Where *is* it?" she asked urgently. "We're going the right way, aren't we?"

Hadn't she spotted the thin plume of smoke that wafted skyward ahead of us? "I think the damage may be pretty extensive, Phoebe. You may not recognize it."

She said nothing as we picked our way through crunchy dead underbrush—until she could no longer deny that the tangle of charred wood and mounds of debris before us were all that remained of her house. "Oh god," she rasped. Arms wrapping across her belly, she bent forward. "Oh dear god. Th-there's nothing left. No house. No car. Not even any boxes of meat. *Nothing*."

We stood side by side in her driveway while I stroked her trembling back and she slipped in and out of a daze, intermittently muttering about being burned out of two homes by two fires in less than eight months, then asking, "What does it *mean*?"

"I think," I finally said, "it means shit happens. Randomly. Arbitrarily. And I'm really sorry it's happened to you."

"My sister and her family were s'posed to move in here by Thanksgiving. What the hell do I do now?"

Obviously, this was not a rhetorical question. "Since they can't move in here," I suggested, "maybe you should stay with them in, uh—"

"Newton." Phoebe's pause was brief. "No."

"Why not? You can build a greenhouse there instead of—" I glanced toward the burnt remains of her house. "Instead of here."

Phoebe's drooping head slid slowly back and forth. She didn't speak, didn't move.

"You're afraid to go back, huh?"

"No!" she snapped, suddenly straightening. Then she slumped. "Yes." Then she sighed. "I mean—well, it's not an option."

"Your sister's place doesn't feel safe? Even though you'd be with people you know and trust?"

"No place feels safe anymore. Not for me. Not for them."

"You gotta live somewhere though, right?" I pressed. Phoebe hadn't struck me as suicidal, but damn, you never know…

She kicked her stone driveway. To avoid eye contact, I thought as I wondered what *her* backasswards plan might be—the one she couldn't yet bear to acknowledge.

In "normal" times, I'd have let it go right then, yet another instance of none-of-my-business, and Phoebe would most likely have drifted away, awash in her confusion and doubt.

"Well," I began, "if you're gonna stay here—"

"I'm not sure I should live alone anymore." Phoebe turned to gaze at me. "Maybe the fires are trying to tell me not to live alone anymore."

"Don't know about that, but I'm all for not living alone. At least not before the next bright, sunny day comes along."

This elicited a half-smile, at least. And a reminder from Cordelia: *Well, Aitch, Duka did seem open to "including" her.*

Okay then, I decided.

"Come back home with me, Phoebe," I said. "And maybe you should figure on staying for a while. You're welcomed to the bed in the study till you decide what you want to do."

Chapter Thirty-seven

Number Seven

"An'—an' what the hell kinda name is Benevides, anyway?"

"Tell me you're not *actually* asking that, Duka."

"¡Mierda!"

"You don't want her staying here, then?"

"Mierda."

"Oh. So you *do* want her staying here."

Crickets.

❖

They were going to fight. That was inevitable. Even so, I was surprised by their ferocity—and how quickly they achieved it.

Seriously, Aitch? You're surprised? Whaddaya think we sounded like back in the day?

Aw, c'mon, Deels, were we really that—?

Shh. Here it comes...

"Enough!" I heard Duka roar from the second-floor landing. "Let's just fucking drop it," she railed as she thumped down the stairs. "The age of gabacho magical thinking is fucking *over*." She stomped through the living room, then the dining room, where I was hanging out after my morning greenhouse routine, and proceeded into the kitchen without looking at me.

I'd heard no retort, but a moment later, Phoebe came downstairs, too, hesitated a moment in the living room, then walked into the dining room. Before she could say anything, I did: "I think we need to start talking about where we go from here."

"Yeah, well, *I* think I should move out," Phoebe announced. "Today."

"An' where the *hell* are you gonna go?" Duka snarled as she marched out of the kitchen.

"Anywhere *you're* not will do just fine."

The two of them had faced off a few feet from me, red-faced, some twelve inches apart, and I didn't think it was a coincidence that Phoebe couldn't get out of the room without forcing Duka to step aside.

"Ex*cuse* me, please!" Phoebe barked, but Duka didn't budge.

"Sit down," I said. "Both of you."

They turned to gawk at me but neither of them moved.

"Now, please."

So what're you gonna do about these two, Aitch? Cordelia wanted to know as I watched them circle and glare at each other over who would sit where.

Well, I'm sure as shit not gonna play matchmaker.

They don't need a matchmaker. They need a referee—and that's on you. You may not have started this, but you definitely gave it one hell of a shove.

Yeah, okay, I suppose I did. And yeah, okay, it wasn't fair to put them under such pressure nearly the instant they found themselves sleeping under the same roof. But we had no time to waste. No time to indulge in grief or anger or regret or the inevitable clashes of attitudes and tastes. Not if any of us wanted to see spring.

"Thank you," I said once they settled. "We are now going to have a calm, rational discussion about where we go from here, during which you will set aside your squabbles about who you believe ought to be on top."

Both of them straightened their backs when they heard the part about who ought to be on top, but they held their tongues, and it was all I could do not to chuckle as I watched them avoid eye contact with each other—and me.

"Let's start by assuming everybody is right," I said.

"Let's not," Duka groused, eyes flaring at me.

"We're going to assume everybody's right," I persisted, holding her angry gaze, "because even conflicting viewpoints carry elements of truth and valuable insight." I turned to look at Phoebe, then Duka again. "Our goal is to sift through it all—which, oh by the way, requires that we genuinely *listen*—in order to identify the good stuff that'll help us survive. Of course, I'm assuming we all want to survive." I paused, peering at each of them in turn. "Yes?"

They both took a few more seconds than I expected, but finally each eked out a "Yes."

"Excellent," I said. "So we start with respect. I don't care if you utterly despise each other or you adore each other or you just want to fuck each other's brains out. Regardless of all that, you *will* respect each other. If you cannot do that, we will fail. And if we fail, we will die."

They each threw the other a furtive glance, first Duka, then Phoebe— after which they simultaneously offered a slight nod. Phoebe thrust out an elbow, which Duka lightly bumped with her own elbow, and I exhaled: Progress.

Since I'd already laid out my backasswards plan for Duka, I focused on Phoebe. "If you want to move out of here," I told her, "I can show you an option right now. Close by and, potentially, quite affordable. Interested?"

Phoebe's eyebrows lifted in surprise. "Uh…y-yes."

I rose from my seat. "Now is as good a time as any." Then I led the way through the greenhouse and out its rear-facing door.

"Where are we going?" Phoebe asked. Duka followed behind her, trying and failing to quench a smile.

Duka understood we were heading to Alder Way, number seven, to the house I'd own in thirteen business days. It was, according to the documentation, a smallish 1980s ranch—two bedrooms, bath and a half, with a decent-sized detached two-car garage that had Duka beyond excited when I told her that she was welcomed to claim it ("Fuck *yes!*" she'd hooted in reply), though she said quite firmly that she had no interest in moving into the house itself unless I wanted my master bedroom back, an offer I declined.

Although Town Hall Margie had given me keys to the place—a thirty-day loan, she'd joked—I hadn't yet used them and was clueless about the house's condition. Inside, we found tired carpets, knotty pine paneling, the original kitchen, and threadbare furniture. Not that it mattered; I had no intention of upgrading anything. Nor would I be seeking any rent.

Because, as I explained to Phoebe while we walked from room to room, I hoped for a barter arrangement: Pay the utilities and the tax bite, maintain the place, feel free to fix up whatever you want, or not—and agree to participate in my backasswards plan, which, I admit, I described only in the vaguest of terms. "That might work out well for you since it *is* all about greenhouses."

To my astonishment, Phoebe started crying. Unabashedly. Right there in the middle of Number Seven's living room. I stepped toward her, opened my mouth to speak—but Duka reached her first, enveloped her in a hug, and said something I couldn't quite hear.

"I-I don't think I can live by myself anymore," Phoebe murmured into Duka's shoulder.

I shifted a couple of steps leftward into Duka's line of sight, raised my hands palms up toward her, and silently mouthed, "Whatever you want..."

"That's okay." She spoke softly into Phoebe's ear without taking her eyes from me. "You don't have to live by yourself." As I smiled and turned away, I saw her eyes slowly close. "Not anymore," she whispered, and her whisper became a kiss.

All righty then, Aitch, time to scoot outta here and leave them be...

CHAPTER THIRTY-EIGHT

THIS MATTER OF TRUST

I considered the possibility that Duka would change her mind and want to move into Number Seven with Phoebe—but before I had much of a chance to ruminate about how I'd adapt to having my whole house to myself again, I noticed the two of them tromping back through the brush from Alder Way. They were holding hands.

"Is it okay if Phoebe stays on here?" Duka asked almost as soon as they walked in the door. "Indefinitely?"

"Of course."

"An'—uh—" Duka shifted her weight from one foot to the other. "Also—"

For the third time in my life, I knew exactly what the person standing before me was about to say. Shouldn't have known. But, somehow, I did.

"You're going to ask me if—mmm, her name's Olivia, right?—if Olivia and her husband and kids can move into the Alder Way house, into Number Seven."

Duka's mouth dropped open and stayed that way. Phoebe just stared at me, eyes widening. Then—one Mississippi, two Mississippi—they nodded in mute unison.

"How'd you—?" Phoebe began before going mute again when I offered the only explanation I had: an it's-a-mystery-to-me-too shrug.

"I do want to talk about this, though," I told them, then turned to Phoebe. "Let's start with why—*really*—your sister and her husband would be willing to leave Newton for a dump like Number Seven."

"I haven't said anything to them, obviously, but—"

"But you do believe they'd be willing." I waited. Phoebe, however, had become very interested in her feet. So I gave her a nudge: "And they'd be willing because…"

"They can't stay in Newton," Phoebe finally told her feet. "It's too dangerous."

"Why?"

After she spouted a couple of the usual bromides about all the crime and instability near the city, I interrupted her. "It's pretty damn crime-ridden and unstable here, too. Plus we're much farther from essential supply chains and healthcare. So what's the real reason?"

Phoebe stumbled to the sofa and seemed to sink into it. Finally, she looked at me. "Th-They're being threatened…"

Thus she began the story of her brother-in-law's troubles, which stemmed from the collapse of his wealth management firm, staved off through the pandemic but not the aftermath of Eleven Fourteen, when losses mounted until they measured in many millions of dollars and plenty of enraged former clients.

"Bill's getting death threats. Rocks thrown through their windows. The police tell they should leave town. For their own protection. The kids are freaking out and Livvie's terrified. And now—" She stood again and glanced through the living room side windows toward where her house used to be. "They can't—they can't—"

"Am I right in supposing that they're broke and you figured on feeding everyone with the yields from that greenhouse you wanted Duka to build for you?"

"Yeah, that and all the meat I bought and the money I'm hoping I can bring in from consulting work." Phoebe's head drooped. "Maybe I can claim my nine boxes of meat from Isabella. Or maybe not, since she doesn't seem to be able to talk rationally to anyone about anything. But the greenhouse—even if there still was a house to build it onto, the whole idea was untenable."

Ha. I know an opening when I see it. "Untenable because we need to think bigger. As in four hundred square feet of greenhouse grow space *per person*. Ready as soon as possible. And our best shot for achieving that will be—"

Phoebe's head shot up. "ECASP." She turned to Duka, who looked quite puzzled. "The federal program I mentioned—the Environmentally Controlled Agriculture Support Program."

When Duka nodded, Phoebe turned back to me. "That's why I had to go back inside," she said. "There's all this ECASP stuff on my laptop that's not public yet, and I never had a chance to back it up, since backing up anything these days takes, y'know—"

"Yeah, it takes forever," I commiserated, an *oh jeezus* of comprehension beginning to rise in my chest. "If it ever happens at all."

"And without that stuff, we could miss our chance..." Phoebe rubbed her face with both hands. "The ECASP decisions are being made now, right now, and we need some of those documents on my laptop to support our case for a residential grant."

"Oh dear god," I wheezed, abruptly breathless. "You ran into a burning building for *that?*"

I reached out and placed my hands over hers. Her hands were trembling.

❖

So, despite Phoebe's actions, did I or didn't I?

My sense had been that Duka was deeply vulnerable to the sorts of women Cordelia would've called oblivious upper-crusty: well-heeled, well-educated, well-spoken—and too often titillated by trifling with those ostensibly "tough," "dangerous" girls who defiantly pretended to get off on the risks they had no hope of avoiding.

Well-educated and well-spoken certainly described Phoebe. And although recent events had diminished her status as well-heeled, this didn't seem to alter her self-perception. As for whether she was titillated by tough, dangerous women—and, indeed, whether she actually regarded Duka as tough or dangerous...mmm, let's just say it was damn obvious to anyone who looked that Duka didn't flinch, not one bit, in the face of unavoidable (and intensifying) risks.

Don't get me wrong: As someone fortunate enough to have become well-educated, well-spoken, and, eventually, marginally well-heeled, I too would have found Duka quite appealing—*if* I had been thirty-five and single rather than seventy-five and still in thrall to a figment. Which means I'm in no position to judge Phoebe.

Quite the contrary, I'm genuinely sympathetic. More than that, as Cordelia would point out (again) with a somewhat lopsided grin, by allowing Phoebe to move in, I'd actually encouraged her relationship with Duka.

True.

But...

But there's this matter of trust.

And this matter of trust is not unidirectional, nor even bidirectional. It goes (or it doesn't) every which way:

Do I trust Duka's faith in Phoebe?

Do I trust Phoebe's apparent embrace of my backasswards plan?

Do I trust, even assuming her commitment is real, that Phoebe will be able to handle the additional work such commitment will require from each of us—work which is only partly predictable, always necessary, replete with demanding physical labor that drives dirt deep beneath your fingernails, drenches you in your own sweat, and leaves your back screaming for relief?

Do I trust that even an ECASP-aided version of my backasswards plan, now our backasswards plan, can accommodate the people we'll need to pull it off *as well as* the four members of Phoebe's family and the additional 1600 square feet of greenhouse grow space they'll require—and will *their* contributions really be sufficient to earn them their greenhouse keep?

CHAPTER THIRTY-NINE

EXACTLY WHAT YOU WANTED

It started with thirteen of us in my living room. Mirrie dubbed it This Circle Thing—as in "Hester says it's okay, so can me an' Nate—oh, sorry, Mum, *may Nate and I* go down to Hester's room an' watch TV while you guys argue about this circle thing?"

I winced when I heard her say "argue." Was I a fool for hoping my neighbors might find common ground enough to use my backasswards plan both to help us squeak through the coming winter *and* to build themselves a sustainable longer-term future?

Over the last couple of days, Duka had run the backasswards plan's basics by everyone, household by household, and at least no one had outright rejected the idea. Afterward, she noted how their eyes went wide as they listened; are you sure, they asked, that Hester doesn't expect something for use of the foundations?

"An' I told 'em what you told me," Duka reported. "How no, you don't want any kinda payment, but once the greenhouses are producing yields, either they need to generate enough to pay for themselves or the people they feed need to chip in as necessary to cover operating costs. Every time, they went real quiet. So I'd say your idea's percolating."

Then, ready to tug on a guilt string or two, she ventured up the street with Phoebe to the tax-foreclosed property where the town had granted Ellen Higgins and Isabella refuge (by virtue of a perk offered to town employees, including cops). I don't know the details of what went down, but they came back smiling. "Seems like Isabella's still pretty out of it," Duka said. "But together enough to do some mea culpa, y'know? I hardly hadda open my mouth."

I counted it as a very good sign that every one of these same neighbors—including Isabella and Ellen—showed up for the meeting in my living room. We began with a discussion about contributions. "We all know what Hester's puttin' in," Melinda said. "But what about the rest of us?"

Lizbie proposed that everyone should contribute whatever they could, both up front—greenhouse building material and labor—and along the way by doing what was necessary to keep crops growing, getting them harvested, processing them. "And for that we each get an equal share of the greenhouse yields."

"Oh," said Sam with a frown, "Kinda like '*from* each accordin' to his ability, *to* each accordin' to his need.' Sounds classic commie to me."

"Or it's classic *community*," Melinda replied before Lizbie had a chance to growl at her husband, "So if—when, really—a person who started with more ability and less need suddenly needs more but has diminished ability, the community can step in to meet that need. Like what insurance does. Everyone pays a premium, and the premiums are pooled so you can tap into the pool for help as necessary."

"I like the insurance analogy," I said. "Our 'premiums' are what Lizbie talked about—the foundations, constructing the greenhouses, keeping them operating, harvesting and processing the yields."

Here, as everyone nodded and murmured (except Isabella, who'd found and begun playing with *my* baoding balls), I saw a chance to lay out some specifics. So I did: "*Not* including our own greenhouse out back here as well as Lizbie and Sam's and also Toby and Sylvie's, we have a potential for roughly fifty-four hundred square feet of grow space across eight foundations. Assuming successful year-round grows which'll provide pretty much all a person needs, my calculations show that's enough to feed thirteen people, with a tiny bit left over."

I glanced at Ellen Higgins, who sat next to the still oblivious Isabella; yep, Ellen's head had moved oh so slightly up, down. Then I looked at Phoebe; her head bob was unequivocally eager. Okay then, permission received—so I continued: "And if we include the foundations of Phoebe's place and Isabella's, once we get them cleaned out, we'll have a total of ten foundations, which will be enough grow space to feed twenty people."

Phoebe raised her hand like a timid schoolgirl. "I, uh, have something else that might help with that. Maybe not immediately, but eventually."

She took a moment to lay out why Eventually mattered: The Pentagon, she said, had just released a study reporting a bunch of climate simulations that indicated the effects of Eleven Fourteen would last for at least ten to fifteen years.

"Solar radiation—y'know, sunlight—is strengthening a little already, which will continue, but air temperatures are predicted to actually go lower for the next four years." She paused, shook her head. "We're looking at the coldest average surface temperatures the earth has seen in a thousand years. Year five will be coldest of all."

Then she described the Environmentally Controlled Agriculture Support Program. "So far, it's focused on commercial farms, but I received confirmation this morning that the ECASP people have decided to also do some residential grants, including for neighborhood groups. Groups like us. And this afternoon I received the new residential grant forms, along with some really valuable coaching from one of the program's deputy administrators about how to fill them out. Oh, and one of the things they want to encourage is the use of renewable energy sources."

"Which, around here, means wind turbines," Duka added with what can only be described as a shit-eating grin.

"Hey," blurted Toby. "I know somebody who works on wind turbines, the big ones goin' up off the backshore. I bet we could ask him to help us out."

Duka nodded her recognition. "Kai, you mean."

"Kai Geller, yeah," Toby said.

"Think he'll take tomatoes an' potatoes in payment?" Sam teased us.

"Let's hope we can do better than that," Phoebe segued, "with an ECASP grant. I've penciled in what *seems* right on the forms—but all of us here should look them over really carefully before we submit them, which we need to do ASAP. As in tomorrow."

An excited babble of *oh wow!* soon subsided into conscientious reading through of Phoebe's ECASP forms, until—

"I'm all for this ECASP thing," Toby said. "'Cept it won't deliver anythin' for weeks anyway, prob'ly months, right? But it's already mid-October. We gotta build as much as we can, grow as much as we can right now. *Before* we jump through a gazillion government hoops to get grant money. *Before* any wind turbines. We need to figure out what materials we got, what foundations we oughta work on, what else we'll need, then get to work like Phoebe says: ASAP."

By this time, he and Sam and Duka had formed a natural cluster—the builders, I thought as I watched them, already making lists and assigning tasks. Soon they'd know what they'd be able to accomplish and when.

Before Sylvie could interrupt them and drag them back into our meeting, Lizbie put a hand on her knee. "Don't bother, Syl. They'll go along with whatever we decide."

Maybe, maybe not, I mused as I noticed how Duka regularly peered over at Phoebe. Still, I mostly listened while these women danced around each other in search of a fresh balance. Some—like Lizbie and Sylvie and Annie and Melinda—knew each other well enough, but Ellen Higgins and Isabella and Phoebe were neighborhood newbies. And it would be this crew along with Duka and "the fellas"—not me—who'd make This Circle Thing a reality.

Once more, they delved into how each of us might contribute. Yes, yes, Duka and "the fellas" would handle the greenhouse building with occasional help from the rest of us—but then?

"Some of us have jobs," Ellen pointed out, "so the time we have left for greenhouse work is limited."

"But we can put in some money," Sylvie said. "And, in my case, contribute fuel for heating and transport of stuff like soil."

"I *like* gardening," Isabella wistfully informed the ceiling in a singsong. "I could do it all…day…long…"

"That's wonderful, Isabella," I told her only a tad paternalistically (because, I admit it, I couldn't quite shake a nagging sense that her New Oblivion was an act). "We'll certainly take you up on that."

Who among us, then, would best know what needed to be done when? In which order? This excursion, led by an impeccably patient Annie, entailed an itemized exploration of what running a greenhouse actually involved—and resulted in the unanimous election of Lizbie as Chief Greenhouse Operations Officer.

In addition, thanks to Annie, it also established an unspoken set of rules about how we'd all treat each other—with polite respect—as we figured out how to cope through the coming winter. Because, clearly, we weren't going to have sufficient greenhouse grow space ready by then to feed all of us all that we'd need.

My somewhat educated guess at that point held that *if* we were lucky, we'd manage to get two of our ten potential foundations transformed into greenhouses and see them planted by year end. Assuming successful grows in those new greenhouses as well as our three existing greenhouses, *and* assuming all those yields were shared by everyone at the meeting, we'd be able to provide somewhere around half of what thirteen people needed to survive—but likely not before next spring.

However—oh yeah, we had a great big whomping However—Phoebe hadn't made either of her moves yet. "We also need," she announced out of the blue, "to talk about all that meat."

Almost everyone in my living room, including the fellas (but, notably, not Duka, not me), audibly inhaled. They'd been waiting for this, wondering about this, and they stared intently at Phoebe, which seemed to disconcert her.

But she persevered admirably. "As you all know, we lost some of the meat in the fire, but we still have nine hundred pounds stashed in various freezers—"

Sidelong glances and murmurs interrupted her ("Nine hundred pounds!?")—and, this time, paralyzed her. Duka came to her rescue: "Besides those fourteen boxes that were in my truck, the rest is stored here. Thirty boxes altogether, thirty pounds to a box. An', uh—"

"Three people own the meat," Phoebe resumed, "I bought nine boxes, Duka owns five, the rest are Isabella's—and the three of us have agreed to contribute all of it to help feed all of us here his winter, but also—" Then, as murmurs floated around my living room, she hesitated. And got stuck again.

Okay, my turn. "But before you all pull out your phones to do the math," I said, "Phoebe and Duka have a request. A major one, actually. They're asking you to agree to expand this group from thirteen people to seventeen people—and two of the new people are kids just slightly younger than Mirrie and Nate."

"Jeezus!" Sam spouted. "*Seventeen?*"

"Who *are* these people?" Lizbie wanted to know.

"My sister Olivia, her husband Bill, and their two kids," said Phoebe. "Emily's eleven and David is eight."

By the time she finished, half a dozen people were poking their phones. Doing the math, which didn't take them long.

Lizbie spoke up first. "That's upwards of two hundred servings of meat per person. Certainly takes the edge off this winter."

"But that number would be higher—by, like, thirty percent—if it was divided by thirteen people instead of seventeen," Sam countered, his frown renewed.

"Except Phoebe would have to withdraw her share in order to help her family," Annie pointed out. "So the servings for the remaining twelve people actually go down just slightly—unless Duka opts to pull her share, too. And if that happens—"

"Wait. Stop." Phoebe's head was down, but her hands were up, palms facing outward in surrender. "I don't want to screw this up by asking for— for too much. I'm sorry. I'm so sor—"

"You have *my* yes vote, Phoebe," Lizbie declared, glaring at Sam. "I really like the prospect of a couple more kids around. And even with seventeen people, we'll have enough to get through this winter—"

"But these new people, they'll have to pull their weight, find ways to make a real contribution," Sam insisted.

"That's a given," Duka replied. "They know that. They want that."

"Just for the record, Phoebe, you have my yes vote too," I said.

Phoebe had yet to lift her head and look around at the rest of us, and for a brief moment that seemed to last forever, the room stayed silent.

Perhaps the undecideds were still doing the math, pondering whether Isabella's guilt about burning down the Benevides house influenced this remarkable decision to offer up hundreds of pounds of meat to a group of people who, in fact, she really didn't know very well. Perhaps they realized that if Phoebe withdrew her share and persuaded Duka to do likewise, then Phoebe's crew (even if it also included me) would end up with twenty percent *more* than if they shared with everyone in This Circle Thing.

A tiny chiming sound flitted through the room's hush as Isabella held high my baoding balls, which she now triumphantly manipulated with one hand. When we all turned to stare at her, she laughed as she touched Phoebe's arm with her free hand and her pealing laugh lilted through her words… "'And *her* heart was going like mad and yes I said yes I will Yes.'"

But…but…

Oh c'mon, Aitch, the others have agreed to include Phoebe's crew. As for trusting her relationship with Duka? Puh-leeeze! That's just so moot unless you want to try getting away with declaring yourself Emperor Queen of Upper Hollow Circle.

Dammit, Deels, sometimes I really do wish you'd just shut the fuck up.

Good luck with that, sweet cheeks. Besides, I'm merely offering an amiable reminder that you're *the one who handed off your backasswards plan to This Circle Thing. You were also, as I recall, bloody well hoping that Duka and Lizbie would emerge as the leaders—and that the decisions putting them there would be unanimous. So admit it: You've gotten exactly what you wanted.*

CHAPTER FORTY

USE IT OR LOSE IT

Duka and Lizbie wasted no time. Within a day or two after the formation of what we'd decided to call the Circle Collaborative, I'd been assigned the kind of job that my neighbors figured wouldn't be too taxing for the Old Woman, especially since I'd now get a bit of help when anything heavy needed lifting: I would make biochar.

From the biochar-producing bivouac set up for me at the center of all the initial activity—which turned out to be the edge of the Hulk foundation's driveway—I watched Duka and the fellas regularly show up with truckloads that they deftly transformed into beams and joists and glazing and planting beds and infrastructure for lighting, watering, heating, ventilation, security.

I wondered where it all came from—until I watched them dismantle and "repurpose" the long-abandoned but still intact post-and-beam house next to Lizbie and Sam's place. "Use it or lose it," Toby proclaimed one morning when he noticed my extended sidelong glance.

In my naiveté, I don't think I quite understood until that moment, at least not consciously: Duka had long since decided to build a greenhouse in the Hulk's foundation regardless of who owned the property beneath it, and now she and Lizbie and "the fellas" opened the throttle as wide as it would go. Because what the hell, who was going to stop them?

Moral hazard aside, I enjoyed watching all this. I had unobstructed lines of sight to the post-and-beam as well as all three of the first foundations Duka and Lizbie selected for transformation into greenhouses that together would provide us some 2,300 square feet of grow space. Plus two new barrel stoves kept me warm in the deepening cold, and four kids brought me the wood I needed for biochar production.

Four kids (not two) because Phoebe's relatives arrived mere days after the Circle Collaborative agreed to include them. The kid cabal formed quickly and was led by Mirrie, who was a year older and distinctly less shy than newbie Emily. Nate also found a buddy in Emily's little brother, David, who shared Nate's age and occasionally rash sensibilities. Even so, they were no match for Mirrie and Emily. So the boys (mostly) did as they were told, which (mostly) involved what Mirrie declared "men" to be good for: "heavy lifting."

Unlike their children, Olivia and Bill Kosnik struck me as dazed and disoriented (residing at Number Seven, I figured, would do that to just about anyone who'd survived puberty), but they deserved credit for both their unflagging eagerness in joining the Circle Collaborative and their ability to somehow convince their kids that they'd all embarked on a great adventure.

Olivia seemed to find her path more easily than Bill. An attorney, she was immediately enlisted to help with Circle Collaborative legal matters. She also quickly became "the other teacher," since, like Lizbie, she'd been her kids' primary home-schooling supervisor since the pandemic hit. She often shadowed Lizbie around the greenhouses, too, determined to learn as much as possible as fast as possible. Fortunately, the two got on well, though soon Lizbie expressed concern, confiding to me that "Olivia's a nervous wreck—worried about Bill, I think."

All the Circle Collaborative women worried about Bill (except Isabella, who either feigned no longer worrying about anything or maybe really did no longer worry about anything). "Thing is," Duka noted, "Outside of screw-the-minions finance, Bill doesn't know how to do shit— but he really, *really* wants to be one of the fellas. So he says 'Yeah, I can do that,' an' then he fucks it up an' everyone ends up royally pissed at him. He needs to figure out what he's good at, figure out how that can help us—an' then he needs to stick to whatever *that* is."

This struck me as a little ungenerous, since Bill had yet to burn himself when it came to wrangling the pyrolyzers. He seemed to have mastered the woodchipper, too, without sacrificing any appendages. And he managed to keep all four kids not just willing but downright excited at the prospect of hauling little wagonloads of woodchips over to our biochar bivouac.

On the other hand, I could understand Duka's complaint: She needed Bill to do more than chip wood and lift steel drums.

"Well, as an honorary 'fella' and de facto leader of the fella pack, you're in a unique position to help him," I suggested, and before Duka could convert her I-don't-have-time-for-this scowl into words, I pushed on. "Phoebe's known Bill for years, so she might be able to—"

"Uh-huh. I heard all about how Bill's a super-salesman who—what's the expression? Oh yeah: Who can sell sand to the Saudis. But he'll fucking mutilate himself if you ask him to hammer in a nail."

"Okay, then—if he's a super-salesman, he's also an accomplished persuader and negotiator. By definition. So what needs persuading and negotiating these days?"

"More like who."

Ah, a good sign: Duka was listening now. "Right. So invest in some coaching about the proclivities and weaknesses of your targets and what you want from them, then turn Bill loose on, let's see, I'm guessing Alison Perry and Greg Silva?"

"We're doing all right with those two, actually. But Bill sure as hell could earn his keep if he can figure out a way to make peace with Duncan Dorrance. Cuz I'm pretty sure it was Dorrance's goons who went after Isabella's meat."

Other than Bill, things seemed to be falling into place pretty much as I hoped they might. Phoebe had successfully submitted the ECASP applications and declared herself "optimistic." And I saw for myself just how much Duka had managed to "salvage" over the last several months; no wonder she wanted the garage at Number Seven—her unit at the Tradesmen's Center was nearly full.

But fortune can be fickle…

"Melinda's come down with pneumonia," Duka announced less than two weeks after the first Circle Collaborative meeting. "Again."

This news surprised me; I'd talked to Annie only a couple of hours earlier and she'd said nothing. "How do you know th—?"

"Just came from there." Duka held up her left hand, which sported a black splint that claimed her pinky and ring fingers, her palm, and her wrist. "Boxer's fracture," she explained, wriggling her thumb, index, and middle digits. "Not too bad. But I'm stuck with this damn wrapping for the next six weeks."

"What happened?"

"Melinda's on bedrest, so Annie fixed me up."

"I mean how did you do that to your hand, Duka?"

"My fist, uh, bumped into a hard object."

"All by itself?"

"It was motivated."

"Dare I ask by whom?"

"One of Duncan Dorrance's goons."

I looked her up and down to check for further damage, but saw none. "And...?"

Duka shrugged. "Well, um—" She rolled her shoulders. "Y'shoulda seen the other guy."

"That's it? That's all you're gonna tell me?"

"Whaddaya wanna know?"

"You hit him?"

"He swung first." Pause. "An' missed."

"But you didn't."

Duka grinned. "Left hook. Couldn't resist. Broke his nose, I think. But my angle was a little off."

"Any witnesses?"

"Nope. No cameras, either. Wasn't even driving my truck. I used one of Alison's that she keeps at the Tradesmen's Center. Plus I mudded up its license plates. *An'* I was wearing a boonie hat an' one of Mirrie's masks. Not likely he'd ever recognize me." She laughed. "Besides, he called me a prick, so I'm pretty sure he thought I was a guy."

I waited for more. In vain.

"Jeezus, Duka. Just tell me what the hell happened."

"Yeah. Well..."

She had ventured into that part of South Truro she'd taken to calling "Dorrance-land"—below the Pamet River, west of the National Seashore property—"an' that bastard thinks he owns it, but he doesn't, not all of it, not yet." And why go there? Because she'd heard about some rusting trailer hidden off Old County Road on the overgrown, sandy lane leading to Pine Grove Cemetery.

"One of those places where guys leave shit they've stolen to get picked up by the buyer. Only I got there first."

Inside she found what she expected—a stash of half-inch wire mesh. Enough for the chicken coop she'd already started constructing in the hollow east of the house, with plenty left over for Alison, who'd enlisted her to retrieve it. Worth the risk of a drive along the border of Dorrance-land, she said, because "Do you know how fucking *hard* it is around here now to come by half-inch wire mesh?"

The rusting trailer also contained an unexpected bonus: "Big buncha LED grow lights in there, too—the good kind. All we need to light the entire Hulk greenhouse an' most of the second greenhouse over at Number Twenty-four."

Dorrance's man showed up soon after Duka had turned north onto Old County Road to head home with her find snugged inside Alison's cap-covered truck bed. "Asshole crosses the yellow line, blocks me. Then he jumps outta this huge black Hummer like a goddamn cop, one hand on a gun in his waistband, an' marches up demanding to know who I am an' do I have *Mister* Dorrance's permission to be driving there. On a *public* road." Duka jutted her chin. "I told him to go fuck himself."

She shook her head when she saw my reaction.

"Don't worry, Hester. Dude was a gen-yoo-wine doofus. I never even got outta the truck. When he swung at me through the window, I ducked right real quick an' landed a solid jab, then grabbed his gun, gave him a shove—an' down he went right on his ass. Damn tempted to drive over him, but I didn't. Now we got all the wire mesh we need an' more than enough lighting for fifteen hundred square feet of grow space. Plus Alison's happy, too."

I had *so* many questions.

Was the man Duka punched one of the crew who tried to steal the meat from Isabella and Phoebe?

Will Dorrance figure out who absconded with his stolen goods—not to mention his goon's gun—and try to track Duka down?

Will he succeed?

Will he escalate?

And what the hell is happening to Melinda, now suffering through pneumonia for the second time in less than four months?

But Duka had no time for any of that. She'd come home for a quick lunch, seeking peanut butter on (my!) pone, which she snarfed while telling me the Tale of the Boxer's Fracture before departing once more with a breezy promise not to venture again onto Old County Road in South Truro "anytime soon."

CHAPTER FORTY-ONE

HE MEANT *US*

When I woke on the morning of the fifteenth business day after I signed off on buying those eleven tax-foreclosed properties, I prepared to celebrate—because for fourteen business days there'd been only blissful silence from Town Hall Margie, which meant that all the owners and mortgage holders had passed on their last chance to pay up and reclaim their properties.

So far anyway.

Just one more day to go...

Then, in mid-afternoon, my phone buzzed with a text message from Bill Kosnik that also went to Duka and Phoebe, among others:

Dude at town hall wants to pay off taxes on properties near us, says he's buying up the neighborhood.

The photo Bill attached to his message (obviously taken surreptitiously) showed a man I didn't recognize snarling at Town Hall Margie.

I gaped at the text, at the ugly image of a fifty-ish man's mouth curling with anger and contempt. Could some random guy really just walk into town hall and take away some or all of those eleven properties?

Well, maybe yes—*if* he could show power of attorney for the owners and/or mortgage holders, *if* he had enough money...

Big, seemingly unlikely ifs—but just possible enough *not* to be ignored. So what should I do?

Before I could respond to the text, Duka did:

Bill, that's duncan dorrance
STOP HIM!

Phoebe also saw the text exchange and came running from upstairs into the greenhouse, where I'd just finished the round of light weeding I'd ducked out on that morning. "Did you see Bill's message and Duka's reply?" she panted.

"God, yes. Should I go over there and try to intervene?"

Hands on the doorframe, her face scrunched as she braced herself. "Mmm." She shook her head. "No, I don't think so. I'd say Bill's our best shot."

I had doubts about Bill really being our best shot, but I knew most definitely that I was not. So I nodded and joined Phoebe in the dining room, where we sat and waited in unnerved silence. We waited for more than two excruciating hours until Bill showed up at the front door.

"Tell us," Phoebe demanded. "Everything."

"Well, I was trying to find out if there's any way to get the taxes lowered on a property with a burned-down house," he explained, winking at Phoebe. "And this guy ahead of me was all up in the lady's face about having to come to town hall in person to view property maps because the town website was screwed up. Pushy guy, loud, a real asshole."

As Bill described it, Town Hall Margie was so affronted by the man's behavior that she took her sweet time pulling up the maps. "First he turns to me and squawks about 'that old bitch of a clerk,' easily loudly enough for her to hear him. After that, he starts bragging about all the foreclosed properties he's going to pick up for almost nothing. Then he tells me where. 'That slum off South Highland Road,' he says. 'Whole streets of teardown dumps full of lowlife, trouble-making townies we need to get rid of.'

"I knew right away he meant *us*," Bill continued. "So I sent out that text and a pic of him. Then Duka tells me who he is, and shit, I'd just been checking out Duncan Dorrance—where he lives, where he gets his money. The better to make some kind of peace with him like Duka talked about, remember?

"I decided right then to play to his competitiveness, his need to dominate. So I chuckled and said I was looking for property, too—only on the south side of Truro where I'd heard the best deals were—precisely because that part of town *wasn't* a slum. Ahead of the crowd, I told him, before those guys from Weston show up with their loose change.

"I kept going like that till the maps finally went up on the screen, and by then I was standing close to him. He made this noise about how hey!, *he* was first in line—and damn if he didn't zoom right to South Truro. Ha! Wasn't gonna get bested by a cuck like me, right? While he navigated around the screen, I made sure to obviously peek over his shoulder and scribble down some property parcel numbers so he'd think I had interest in the Cooper Road area where he lives. I don't think he realized so many properties around there had fallen to tax-foreclosure.

"After a few minutes messing like that, I was tempted to leave, since at that point I sure as hell wouldn't be asking my *real* question. But I thought I should prob'ly stick around and keep up the pressure on him till the town hall office closed. And within another few minutes, he's signing documents for properties all over South Truro, with me right next to him groaning 'Hey, man, you're killing me, I had my eye on that one.' And he gloats back at me—'I'm picking up every bayside property I can between the Pamet River and the Wellfleet town line.'

"I did my best to appear disappointed—but also reluctantly admiring of his ability to whip my ass. And I made sure he saw me looking at properties just north of the Pamet right up until he strutted the hell out of there. He spent a whomping shitload, but he never did check out anything in our little 'slum' here, so we're in the clear. In a few weeks, though, there's strong odds Duncan Dorrance will own a sizable chunk of South Truro. For good or ill."

"Jeezus, Bill," Phoebe and I nearly shouted in unison. "You *did* it!"

I enjoyed this shot of relief for about ten seconds.

By the eleventh second, however, I couldn't help wonder what role that boxer's fracture run-in Duka had on Old County Road might have played in Dorrance's desire to drive us out. And I wondered whether— wondered *when*—he'd return to town hall with all he needed to buy up the rest of our neighborhood.

I'd never met the man myself, but everything I'd heard about him made me worry: What would happen to the Circle Collaborative, to our ability to survive, if we were surrounded by Duncan Dorrance and his goons?

Turns out I wasn't the only one worrying.

"You've inspired us," Sylvie told me a day after Bill's brush with Dorrance at town hall.

Sylvie, Lizbie, and Phoebe, too, had just acquired more than twenty tax-foreclosed properties between them, mostly sidelots within half a mile of my house, many that had devolved into outright ruins already thoroughly "salvaged."

"Sylvie picked up the most," Phoebe said later that day as she joined me at the biochar bivouac. "High-ground spots good for wind turbines. Someday anyway. For now, we just want to keep the area out of the hands of people like Duncan Dorrance."

All I managed in response was a sputter—so much for what I'd imagined my neighbors could or could not afford. "But—but how did you—?"

Phoebe shrugged a knowing smile. "Seems like Sylvie has plenty. Not sure how Lizbie and Sam pulled it off, although they did limit themselves to just five sidelots. Five is pretty doable, even for me now that I've seen a round of money for the follow-on robotics industry project."

"What about longer term?" I asked. "Taxes on five side lots will add up, even if you don't do anything with them. Or are you planning to—?"

"*That* is exactly what I wanna know," Duka announced loudly from the bottom of the Hulk's driveway as she glowered at Phoebe. "I thought we agreed we don't have the bandwidth right now for more properties. Is that why you came home so late last night? So you wouldn't have to tell me what you did?" She wagged her phone at Phoebe, her glower going slitty-eyed. "An' then you pretend to be asleep this morning till I'm up an' gone, an' then—*then* you tell me in a fucking *text?* With a fucking *smiley emoji?*"

Phoebe was already moving toward her. "I'm really sorry, babe. I was late because we were kind of celebr—I mean, uh, I wasn't pretending this morning. For what it's worth."

"It's worth shit," Duka growled as she spun on her heel back toward the street.

"Talk later?" Phoebe asked me. Her question was, of course, entirely rhetorical; she'd already begun running to catch up with Duka.

"Oh sure," I replied. "Any ol' time."

Damn, Aitch. A chuckle lilted through Cordelia's voice, coming from behind me. *They really are quite entertaining, aren't they?*

CHAPTER FORTY-TWO

¡ARRRRIBA!

I was in my basement lair, flaked out after several hours of pyrolyzing woodchips, when I heard the commotion above me. Another blowout, I figured. In the several weeks since they'd begun sharing the second floor of the house, brawls between Duka and Phoebe had been occurring roughly every third day, each one as raucous as its predecessor.

Especially this one. This one was *loud*.

Then I realized the sounds were wrong. So: perhaps not a fight.

I decided to venture up to the living room.

"*¡Arrrriba!*" Duka whooped while I was still on the stairs. And then she started laughing. "Talk about knowing how to push all the right government bureaucrat buttons!"

Could it be? Already? Phoebe had submitted the ECASP application a mere two weeks earlier. Not even the IRS turns around responses that fast...

"Tell me," I said as soon as I stepped into the living room.

"Phebes did it!" Duka hollered. "We're *in!*"

The email just received from the Environmentally Controlled Agriculture Support Program stated that the Circle Collaborative had not only been accepted for a grant but also fast-tracked; we'd be receiving enough ECASP money to create 4,000 square feet of greenhouse grow space and erect four small-scale wind turbines.

I smiled. I cheered. I high-fived both of them. I found myself repeating "Wow" because I suddenly felt twenty pounds lighter, breathing was easier. Wow.

"I can't believe how lucky we've been," Phoebe kept saying, looking a little wide-eyed. "Lucky I could even arrange an interview with the program's deputy administrator. Lucky her boss is so damn desperate to keep Congressional funding that they've decided now's the time to push a residential program into high gear. And super lucky that she liked me enough to add us to her proof-of-concept pilot and then send me to someone able to fast-track our application. Jeezus, the whole damn thing was luck, luck, and more dumb fucking luck."

"Call it whatever you want," Duka crowed as she wrapped her arms around Phoebe. "Thanks to you, we'll have *actual money* to buy the stuff that's tough to find around here. 'Specially all things wind turbine."

"Kinda scary, though." Phoebe spoke softly as she returned Duka's hug. "I'm not sure how many residential groups are part of the proof-of-concept pilot, but I know it's only a few, and we'll be monitored—carefully. They want detailed monthly reports—"

"An' when do we get the money?" Duka asked eagerly, hungrily.

"First round in January." Phoebe's eyes had gone wide again. "And they'll want to see how we're spending it. So we have to ante up a report—what amounts to a comprehensive video presentation—every month, starting in February. They'll use all the reports from those of us in the proof-of-concept pilot to decide by the end of the fiscal year whether the residential program is viable—or not. And since the federal fiscal year ends June thirtieth, we won't have even the whole six months to show that we've made this work. More like four months."

"That means the further ahead we are with the greenhouses by January, the better, right?" Duka asked.

"Oh yeah," Phoebe replied.

This inspired Duka's eyes to light up—something Phoebe noticed as soon as I did.

"Hey, Duka Canché," Phoebe poked, "you need to stick to supervising, okay? You're still in a cast."

"It's just a splint, Phebes. See?" Duka wiggled most of her left hand's fingers.

"It's. A. Broken. Bone."

A-a-and they were off—

"We can get a shitload done by January if we keep pushing."

"Not if you break something else, we can't."

"C'mon, admit it, the more we get done by January—"

"The more likely you'll be on your ass by February."

"I'll be fine. I'll be careful. Promise. Cuz we gotta do as much as possible as fast as possible. An' we're running outta time. First thing I do tomorrow is track down Toby's wind turbine guy, Kai. We gotta prep for those turbines even while we're building the greenhouses, y'know? Cuz it's already frigging freezing out there…"

Phoebe had plenty to say to that, but I didn't register most of her words because I'd begun a two-step retreat. First, slip into the kitchen to cobble together a small supper, then recede with it back downstairs. Thus, I hoped, the struggle of wills in the living room might follow its natural, far less verbal course all the way to a bed on the second floor.

Hurry, Aitch, Cordelia whispered. *As soon as they remember you're up here, they'll come looking for you to pick a side, which'll be tough since they're both right.*

What they wouldn't do, I was fairly sure, is follow me downstairs for anything less than a genuine emergency—or to do laundry.

But Cordelia's prodding did beg a question: Was Duka's fear of another black cold this coming winter so profound that she'd prefer dragging in a referee over make-up sex?

Maybe. I knew she was acutely aware of having to face *this* black cold without Cordelia's stash. "That saved me last winter," she'd admitted to me one day when Phoebe was over at Number Seven and we were alone. "Dunno if I ever really told you…"

She hadn't, not explicitly, but I'd guessed.

And I appreciated what she meant about running out of time. With winter would come a cold too extreme to do much more than keep whatever greenhouses we had by then warm enough and lighted enough to grow the food we'd need to survive. For that, we'd require all the dumb fucking luck we could get.

CHAPTER FORTY-THREE

SUCH A STILLNESS

How much wood would an old fart char if an old fart could char wood?

Damned if I know.

Lizbie needed that biochar "yesterday" to add to the compost that would enrich some 6,500 cubic feet of soil in the first three foundation greenhouses she hoped to have planted by early December. And that was merely the first installment; she wanted a second round of biochar before the end of January to add to the compost earmarked for the next three greenhouses' 3,500 cubic feet of soil. And more to come after that...

Count me daunted.

But I traipsed up to the Hulk's driveway every day anyway and got on with it while I watched our ever-dreary skies darken even more with winter's approach.

Then came the first Tuesday in November when, as I tended my three barrel stoves, I realized 400 days had passed since I lost Cordelia.

As far as I'm concerned, the world broke when Cordelia died. How the shards have scattered since (Eleven Fourteen included) is simply a function of—you name it—chance, fate, fortune, dumb fucking luck. All of which are utterly indifferent to persuasion or entreaty or even skill.

So yeah, Cordelia's figment reminded me yet again, *if there's any sort of lesson here, any "larger" pattern to be discerned, it's that no one any where, any time has any control over any thing. But hell, Aitch, four hundred days haven't changed that. You already know survivors are the "lucky" ones. By definition.*

Just like every damn time she said something like that to me, on this night, 400 nights after she'd gone, I couldn't sleep.

C'mon, she whispered to me as I lay in bed brooding. *Tell me what's going* well...

Okay then—

Duka and Isabella managed to bring home all that meat, rough seas and attempted robbery and Isabella's flare gun hysteria notwithstanding—so we wouldn't starve this coming winter.

My neighbors had embraced the idea of the Circle Collaborative and weren't yet squabbling about it, or about the meat.

Duncan Dorrance failed in his attempt to buy those properties out from under us and sabotage the Circle.

I haven't roasted myself alive or broken my back pyrolyzing woodchips.

Phoebe pulled off getting that ECASP grant.

And yes, it's true—thanks to Duka and Phoebe living upstairs, I felt safe in my house again. "Almost as safe as when you were still here."

Mmm, not bad, all considered... Cordelia's breath warmed the nape of my neck and I could smell her close, so close, as she spooned behind me, whispering something, something...

The next morning, on day 401, I heard from Town Hall Margie: "It's all done and dusted," she told me. "I have eleven quitclaim deeds here with your name on them that have been registered with the county and are ready for you to pick up."

I wasted no time walking the half-mile over to the former school to retrieve them, and even as I made my way through the gray, devastated landscape of tree skeletons and foundations in various stages of transformation into low-slung greenhouses and the mostly-cleaned-up ruins of Phoebe's place and Isabella's place, I heard Cordelia's words again: *Survivors are the lucky ones...*

Which perhaps explains why, as soon as I took possession of those eleven quitclaim deeds, I almost sort of relaxed.

But I shouldn't have.

I was a few feet from the school building's main entrance, heading home, when the desperate screech of locked brakes surged from somewhere behind me. Even before I pivoted to look, time went slo-mo on me...

And I turned soon enough to see a compact silver SUV that had been traveling north on Route Six veer to avoid a head-on collision with a speeding blue pickup truck which had swerved into its lane. The SUV careened into a utility pole on the opposite side of the road with such force that the pole immediately collapsed on top of it. Sounds of this violence followed half a heartbeat later: metal, wood, and glass simultaneously, gruesomely grinding clanging thudding crunching snapping groaning.

What happened next left me breathless.

The pickup never even slowed down, just kept speeding southward up Route Six. But a black Jeep right behind it halted alongside the crashed SUV and a man jumped out of the passenger side. Good, I thought—the people in the only other vehicle in sight had stopped to render assistance. Instead, though, the guy muscled the SUV's rear door open and pulled out one, then another box that he rushed into the back of the Jeep, which immediately sped off heading south almost before he managed to scramble back inside.

I had witnessed what looked a whole lot like an ambush. And someone was still inside that SUV.

Should I run to the wreckage? Should I dash back inside to alert Town Hall Margie so she could call for help on her reliable landline to the police/fire facility half a mile down the road?

And then…

Jeezus, then I recognized the small silver SUV.

I was the first person to reach it, but I don't remember anything about how I got there. Not yanking the school's front door open to yell down the hall at whoever might hear me to call for help (Town Hall Margie said I did that), not running across the old baseball field in front of the school or dashing across Route Six.

But I damn well remember fighting through the SUV's deployed airbags to find the driver somewhere in there. And I damn well remember the way her head was angled too impossibly askew—and I realized her neck, and her spinal cord, had snapped and she was dead. Not a mark on her, but Melinda was dead.

There is…*oh god*…such a stillness.

Her eyes were open. Blanked. Empty. I talked to her anyway, watching her eyes as I repeated her name, pleaded with her. I found her hand, not yet cold, and grabbed it, kneaded it as if I might massage her life back into her.

Then ambulance lights flashed into view. I knew, somehow, that Annie was with them and I told Melinda that. She's here, I said before I whispered my good-bye and exited the SUV.

When Annie saw me, she halted with a surprised, involuntary "Oh!" and her hope strengthened for a half-second—until our eyes locked.

CHAPTER FORTY-FOUR

IT'S THE EMPTINESS

I told her not to go."

For three days, this was all I heard Annie say. All any of us heard Annie say.

We buried Melinda in the Old North Cemetery less than a mile's walk from her house in a plot provided by Toby, whose family has been in Truro as long as the 330-year-old graveyard.

Annie liked that; she walked there every day, no matter how dark or cold the weather. "I feel close to Melinda here," Annie said the first time she let me accompany her. "Not because I believe Melinda's out here, or anywhere else, waiting for me." Annie splayed her hand across the middle of her chest. "Melinda is in *here*, right *here*—but..."

I nodded. "But in all the world, it's *this* spot..."

"Yeah," Annie murmured, gazing down at the grave mound, bare but for the woodchips we'd spread over it. "This is a special place. Where I left what was left of her."

And then, as I took her hand, Annie and I sat down on the cold ground and wept.

This was the only time I ever saw Annie cry, though later, on those occasions when it was just the two of us, her eyes would fill now and then while she told me some tale about the woman she'd loved so much and lost so unexpectedly. Annie and I regularly shared those sorts of moments, laughing as often as we teared up, and it was to Annie alone that I confessed having regular conversations with Cordelia.

"Me too," she replied. "Melinda has a lot to say."

This was how I got to know Melinda, because actually, really, I hadn't known Melinda well at all. She'd been an acquaintance, one of the neighbors in the Circle, a woman I was only just beginning to appreciate for her constancy, her deep commitment to taking care of whomever crossed her path. Including me, the Old Woman across the street.

I couldn't thank Melinda for the way she and Annie watched over me in those early days after Cordelia died, after Eleven Fourteen. So I thanked Annie by listening mostly, by making a place for her grief through sharing just a bit of my own.

Despite these interludes, Annie remained intensely stoic, and I wondered about how long her attachment to the spot where Melinda was buried would last. After her numbness wore off, might she decide to decamp for somewhere far from this painful place where Melinda had been, yes, murdered?

One day, I finally just asked her outright.

"Maybe someday I'll leave," she replied. "But we bought the house for the long haul using all the money we had—I mean every last cent—so we wouldn't have to carry a mortgage. No way I can get that money out of the house now. Besides, I don't want to. I feel close to Melinda here, and, god, I need that. I *need* to miss her."

Annie made one change, however. She quickly established, *very* publicly, that she would never transport any sort of opioids to or from any of the Outer Cape medical sites from which she worked or keep much of anything in her house or on her person or in the large medical SUV she drove on the job. "No matter how much anybody begs or whines or bitches. No. Just *no*." And while she wanted to find out who had attacked Melinda, she didn't obsess about it. "Won't bring back my girl," she sighed. "Nothing will. Not ever."

By contrast, Ellen Higgins did obsess about who was responsible for Melinda's death. "I shoulda gone with her," Ellen said over and over. "If she'd had an escort, nobody woulda dared jump her, not even for that much schedule-two shit." Yet for all its fervor, Ellen's investigation into Melinda's death went nowhere.

I was the sole witness, but from 500 feet away I couldn't make out license plate numbers, and my description of the only person I'd glimpsed was limited to "male, looked white." Nobody around here except Annie knew that Melinda would be returning from the hospital in Hyannis with an emergency replenishment of painkillers for the Outer Cape's medical clinics.

Melinda's drop-off at the Wellfleet site had been mundane, uneventful. But since she never made it to Provincetown, Ellen had concocted a long list of suspects, ranging from people at the hospital in Hyannis to the "more dubious Border Patrol dudes" to everyone at the skeletally staffed Wellfleet and Provincetown clinics. Yet sustained and reportedly belligerent questioning of some twenty individuals produced, as Toby noted, "nada." Nor did the cops find any of the stolen opioids anywhere.

Annie asked that we not discuss "the case" in her presence unless and until "the culprits" had been identified and arrested. So our lives shifted to a surreal pseudo-normal in which we made sure that every day Annie received a dinner care package and/or an invitation from one of the Circle households.

Initially, she mostly declined those invitations, but we persisted as much out of our own need as hers. Just before Thanksgiving, she relented (surrendered?) and walked over for an evening meal with me and Duka and Phoebe, where we kept conversation centered on the progress of our foundation greenhouses and wind turbines, the challenges of bringing in goods from off-Cape unmolested by Border Patrol goons, and whether or not today's caliginous sky really was just slightly brighter than yesterday's.

The holiday itself was subdued. The entire Circle, including Annie and Toby's friend Kai, gathered at Lizbie and Sam's because we could extend their dining area into their living room and seat us all together. I like to think Annie found some comfort in that, but she was very quiet.

A few days later, though, over another dinner with me and Duka and Phoebe, she opened up some and talked about what it was like to come home to an empty house. Depressing, she admitted.

"Focusing on work helps. Except now that all those DHS and windfarm guys have settled into P'town, they've developed a taste for fistfights and getting into accidents. So I'm told I need a teammate." She shook her head. "I'm not ready for that—though I may not have much to worry about, at least for a while. The DHS honchos want a doc, but good luck *these* days finding a physician willing to work way out here…"

As for the rest of us, losing Melinda triggered a kind of rattled restlessness. We weren't just deeply sad; we were frightened as well as damn angry.

And, in my case, haunted. Most mornings, I woke to my mind's eye staring at Melinda dead in her car. Cue ABBA's "Fernando," which would sometimes elicit Cordelia's soothing presence. Not for long usually. But every second helped.

Duka and Phoebe, meanwhile, seemed to argue less and touch each other more (gotta say, I *like* the way they kiss)—but they also paced the house more, they frowned more.

Both Lizbie and Olivia talked worriedly about their kids suffering nightmares, even though all the kids were told Melinda had died in an accident, just an accident. And maybe it was my imagination, but I'd swear Sylvie slammed things more than she used to, and Duka and the fellas made more noise every time they did anything, whether it was pounding nails or shoving logs through the woodchipper or driving by in a pickup truck.

Even Isabella changed, becoming less spacy, more attentive—and so in need of company that, notwithstanding the deepening cold, she began to hang out with me for at least a little while nearly every day at the biochar bivouac. Plus she began to speak in extended, entirely rational sentences. "It's the emptiness. Of Melinda not being here anymore, I mean," she lamented soon after joining me at the bivouac. "I'm so scared. I don't know what I'll do if something happens to my Elly."

"Ellen's strong and brave. She'll be okay."

"But what if she's not?" Isabella fretted. "What if—?"

"No, don't go there," I said. "Your job is to be strong and brave, too. And to have Ellen's back, even when it's scary."

"I—I'm not sure I can do that."

"Of course you can. Think of it as just another habit, like brushing your teeth. You make sure she's eating as well as she can, you get her to talk about what's stressing her out. You make love all the damn time. You remind yourself every day that being with her is a precious, wondrous gift."

Isabella smiled. "I can do that."

CHAPTER FORTY-FIVE

THEY'RE NOT YOU

There have been many instances since I lost Cordelia when I felt acutely sorry for myself.

But I got forty-five years with Cordelia, and months to say good-bye, months to show Cordelia how much I loved her, to revel in the *life* of her, moment by achingly beautiful moment. I remind myself of that when I look at Annie, who at forty years old hasn't even been alive as long as I had Cordelia in my life, and who never had the chance to say good-bye, to say "I love you" one last time. Instead, she got the look on my face at the wreckage where Melinda lay dead.

Annie's world exploded then. I know. I saw it happen.

The world shattered all around me, too, when Cordelia took her last breath in the guest room, now the room where I sleep, as I snugged alongside her—and then—

Then she stopped breathing.

Deels! How the fuck can you stop breathing?!

I was as ready as anyone can be, and everything broke anyway.

But even by that agonizing, disorienting measure, I count myself as (yep, I'll repeat my mantra) one of the dumb fucking lucky ones. Forty-five years, a long good-bye, and, somehow, extraordinarily, not dead yet one year after Eleven Fourteen.

Of course, I owe a great deal to Cordelia's stash. I owe Melinda and Annie, too, because their remarkably steady and even cheery presence in the house across the street put the comfort of *ordinary* into my *extra*ordinary survival.

But I owe just as much, perhaps more, to Duka, who could easily have left for parts south. She could have left anytime, could leave even now, but has chosen, for reasons that remain ineffable, to stay—although that has meant scraping by on the dregs of our formerly upscale second-home economy, supporting herself largely via barter and what an unsympathetic public prosecutor might choose to deem larceny.

In theory at least, Duka had wanted middle class, cushioned and safe; she told me that. But in so many ways, she was made for a world like the one that befell the Outer Cape after Eleven Fourteen: smart enough, quick enough, determined enough, brave enough, angry enough.

Charismatic enough.

Because, of course, she was not alone. After Eleven Fourteen, Duka, Toby, and Sam were among those who scavenged, salvaged, and repurposed many of the unoccupied houses in Truro, Wellfleet, Eastham, and even the empty back streets of Provincetown—structures the remaining year-round locals invariably regarded as "abandoned."

By autumn, much of what was worth scavenging, salvaging, and repurposing had been depleted and the four Outer Cape towns, desperate for tax revenue, had changed the rules: What little endured of those abandoned, tax-foreclosed properties now stood for sale—*cheap*. But damn, buying any of it required money. Legal tender. Not easy for someone reliant on bartering and "salvage." ·

Those who paid attention understood: A year after Eleven Fourteen, the world around us was being rearranged, from the top down—ECASP and the Nutritional Allotment Program being prime examples. "Yeah, sure, crumbs for the peasants," Duka observed. "Took the rich dicks this long to start tossing us some scraps cuz they hadda diddle the rules to make sure all their new tricks an' scams are profitable."

Yep. Rules, taxes, money. It was all back. All lopsided, all rigged. And rolling toward us like a juggernaut.

I never heard Duka genuinely bitch about it—she was far too jaded to waste breath on something so inevitable, unfightable—but she despised that world. Even though she knew she'd have to learn to dance across its landscape. Even though the woman she had a thing for (and kissed so exquisitely) came from that world, had for years thrived there, and was already working hard to thrive there again.

Instead, Duka tried breezy—like when she'd asked me, soon after the Circle Collaborative received word of the ECASP grant, to front the money for the rest of the LED grow lights in the first three greenhouses so she wouldn't have to blow her deadlines waiting for the ECASP funding—but I noticed how the tendons in her neck tensed, how her jaw clenched. How she couldn't quite meet my gaze.

Her second ask was even heftier—a fat five figures, the kind that would leave a gouge. She buttonholed me to breathlessly explain.

"We've lucked out cuz Toby's guy Kai says he can come by tomorrow to help us finalize siting the foundations, which are big, almost fifty cubic yards of concrete each. We're really pushing it with the weather, but with the right gear, which Kai says he can bring over, we still got time to get 'em all in an' then cured for four weeks before it's too cold. If we, uh, find the money to pay for 'em, we can get all four concrete pours done by early December—" Duka frowned at her shuffling feet. "But we won't see any of the ECASP grant till January, so, uh—"

I was tempted to put her out of her misery right then and just say yes. Instead, I took the opportunity she'd just handed me and poked around about Kai Geller (yes, I remembered his last name): Can you tell me again who he works for? What, precisely, are his wind turbine siting credentials?

Duka didn't know. Duka didn't care. She was in a hurry.

"It'd be a loan," she was burbling for the second time in a month, her words tumbling over each other. "Like last time. Paid back when the ECASP funding comes in."

I heard a soft chuckle from the next room, but when I turned to look, Cordelia was nowhere to be seen, though I could have sworn I heard her whisper *Now, Aitch.*

"Mmm." I nodded. "If that's what you want to do with the money—"

"An' also, the faster we—" Duka did a doubletake. "What? What did you say?"

"If…that's…what…you…want…to do…with…the money."

"Hester." Duka squinted worriedly down at me. "It's not my money."

"Come with me, kiddo." I led Duka to my basement lair and to Cordelia's rolltop desk, which she and Toby had lugged down from the second-floor study, now Phoebe's room, soon after she'd moved in. From the desk I pulled a raft of papers, stepped over to my bed, and laid them out. "This is all of it. Take a look."

But Duka was stuck in the middle of my little front room den near the desk, apparently unable to move anything but her head, which swung silently back and forth.

I smiled at her as I sighed. "In about three months, I'm going to finish up seventy-five years. So I think it's time I prepare for a future that won't have me in it." I moved next to her and nudged her elbow toward the papers on the bed. "With a little luck, though, you'll be in it. So I want to create what's called an intervivos trust that'll name you as trustee as well as beneficiary—"

"No." Duka pulled away from me as if I'd transformed into something hideous. "You can't do that. No."

Briefly, I considered explaining that Cordelia and I had already discussed it, that the idea of creating an intervivos trust was actually Cordelia's idea (*since that way what's left of our money might do some good*). When I looked at Duka again, though, I decided she wasn't ready for that particular revelation.

So I kept it simple: "I refuse to say yes or no to anything until you look at these numbers."

For what was probably only thirty seconds or so—but felt much, much longer—Duka stood statue-still, her dark eyes fixed in a thousand-yard stare until she shook her head again in what I took to be capitulation and muttered, "Mierda."

I grinned at her, then picked up one of the papers I'd placed on the bed. "Let's start with this."

❖

I confess I was concerned about how Duka would behave after I more or less shoved the intervivos trust down her throat. She needed a few days—and, I suspect, a bit of a talking to by Phoebe—before she managed to look me in the eye again.

"Are we okay?" I asked her.

She nodded. A moment later, she managed to speak actual words: "Dunno why I feel, uh…kinda guilty. Phebes says I shouldn't. Says it's like when I tell her not to feel responsible for how her parents' house burned down."

My turn to nod. "I'm with Phebes." Duka stood close enough that I could reach out and touch her forearm, so I did. "Truth is, you're doing me a favor."

"Yeah? An' how's that work exactly?"

"I'm getting tired, Duka. And there's this constant stream of—of every damn thing that needs figuring out, paying attention to, anticipating, planning, juggling, re-planning. Sometimes my head starts to scramble and all I wanna do is curl up and go to sleep and dream about Cordelia. Time's come for me to hand off. To someone I can trust."

"Mmm, I remember all that stuff you said before about trusting me. But I don't really believe that's the whole—" Suddenly, Duka's face scrunched with concern and she grabbed my hand, her dark eyes blazing. "Coño, Hester. ¡Coño! Are you—? I mean, uh…"

"I'm fine. Not dying yet, kiddo." I squeezed her hand. "But I do need to step back."

Head bowed, Duka kept hold of my hand and studied it, her fingers running delicately over its veins and creped folds and age spots. "Okay." She inhaled slowly. "So why not Phoebe? Or Lizbie? Or Annie?"

"Because they're not you."

CHAPTER FORTY-SIX

KAFKAESQUE

When Kai showed up, I watched him from my biochar bivouac as he walked the properties and staked tower locations with Duka. Even from a couple of hundred feet away, I could tell Duka liked him a lot.

I'd met him, finally, at Thanksgiving—sort of—but never actually had a chance then to talk with him, suss him out. Not until he showed up yet again to help Duka and the fellas erect the four tower foundation forms and pour the concrete, this time with sufficient "borrowed" equipment—including enclosures and supplementary heat—to protect the concrete while it cured in our increasingly cold weather.

Forty-something, in decent shape, yet obviously tired (or maybe it was stress), Kai Geller struck me as a slightly smaller, less grizzled, and distinctly gayer version of Sam Behr. And he struck me as eager, even desperate, to ingratiate himself with the denizens of Upper Hollow Circle.

Which again prompted a question that had jabbed at me on and off since Thanksgiving: What did he want from us?

Quietly, sideways like a crab, I decided to snoop Kai on my own—beyond what little about him had lodged in various internet grottos, beyond what the others tossed off in passing. Perhaps I might even be able to pry loose information from the man himself.

This didn't turn out to be as easy as I'd initially hoped, despite my almost daily biochar efforts, the heat from which invariably attracted anyone working outside or passing by—meaning everyone who was part of the Circle, as well as Kai. So far, so good. Except Kai tended to come over to warm up only when Duka and/or at least one other boy was already there. And he was adept at ducking any topic not somehow related to wind turbines.

If Duka knew anything about the rumor that Kai had two kids he wanted to bring to the Outer Cape, she didn't let on. I learned about it from a deeply ambivalent Lizbie, who found an excuse to come over and tell me as soon as Sam passed on the gossip he'd overheard in P'town from one of the offshore windfarm project guys. Lizbie liked the idea of more kids but worried about how we'd feed them.

"What makes you think we'll have to feed them?" I asked her.

"I—" Lizbie exhaled as her face tightened into an almost-frown. "Dunno. Just a feelin', I guess." Then she let out a small, jittery laugh. "I swear I can smell it on him. He's lookin' for somewhere to land."

Motivation enough to corner Kai alone, which, with the help of my old friend dumb luck, I managed to do the very next day.

"Word is you've got kids," I said after we promenaded through the usual, somewhat extended pleasantries (again), because, y'know, the Old Woman made him antsy, so he overdid everything, thus prolonging his discomfort. And mine.

Anyway, his eyebrows jiggled upward while he decided how to reply, then his head slowly bobbed. "Sarah's nine, Ariel's six."

"Do they come with a mother? Or another father?"

He stared at me. Whereupon I realized nobody had yet been as brazenly pushy with him as I was being at that moment. "Two mothers, actually. Until…well, we found out last Friday. Only one mother now."

Oh…my…god…

"Kai, I'm so sorry. What happened?"

"They're my best friends, Val and Rachel. Been together, like, forever. And they wanted kids, asked me to be the dad. So Sarah is Val's and Ariel is Rachel's. Except—" Kai lifted his head and squinched at the heavy overcast above us. "Except now Val's gone. Just fuckin' vanished one day, almost a year ago now. Took this long for the cops to figure out the body they found last May was Val's."

Of course I couldn't just leave him standing there, tears slipping into his stubble. So I took him by the hand, steered him to a seat near one of the pyrolyzers, and plied him with what passed for tea. And got the rest of his story—some of it, anyway.

"When Val went missin', Rachel was in the States—at meetings for her new job," Kai said. "She rushed back and refused to leave till she found Val. But that took almost a year, so not only had her job gone, she'd also risked her permanent resident status. Did I mention Rachel's Canadian? Upshot is that she now needs a new Green Card, or else she'll be turned back at the border. But good luck gettin' one of *those* since Eleven Fourteen and the new visa rules. As U.S. citizens, the kids can come back to the States anytime, but not Rachel."

"Why wouldn't they just stay in Montreal?"

"No way." Kai shook his head. "They barely survived last winter. The black cold was *so* much worse up there than around Boston, and this comin' winter—"

"Yeah, I've heard it's forecast to be at least as cold as last winter, prob'ly colder, even if the skies don't go dark on us again."

"Which is why they need to get the hell out. Plus Montreal is—well, it's not just fucked up and dangerous, like all the northern cities, it's makin' Rachel paranoid. She's recovered from the virus, but she hasn't worked since Val vanished, freaks out whenever the kids want to go outside, which isn't often. Because after worryin' for so long about what happened to their mother, the girls are thoroughly spooked and edgy, too."

"PTSD," I murmured.

"In fuckin' spades." Kai's face knotted into a scowl. "But now that Rachel knows Val is gone, she's willin' to leave Montreal. Eager to leave, actually. I figure I'll go up there and get the girls, bring 'em back no sweat, since I'm their father. Then Rachel can sneak in illegally. Like on one of those back roads goin' into Vermont or New Hampshire—"

"That sounds awfully dicey. How will she get work here as a doctor if she's undocumented?"

He looked stricken. "Et tu, Hester? You sound just like Rachel, who thinks it's a crime against nature if I'm their sole support. She feels trapped. Like an animal in a cage, she says. Which isn't helpin' her state of mind any."

"Have you talked to a lawyer? Someone who knows immigration law?"

"Nope. Haven't said anythin' to anyone." Kai stiffened suddenly, and his eyes drilled into mine. "'Cept for a passin' mention to a guy at work about havin' the kids join me here. Which somehow took, like, two days to get all the way back to *you*, of all people." He swung his head back and forth as though he was trying to disentangle it. "You're the first person I've talked to about Rachel. Not even Toby knows. So please don't say anythin'. Not to anyone, okay? The fewer people who know about Rachel's immigration status, the better."

"Even now, despite Eleven Fourteen, the Outer Cape has quite the grapevine," I warned him. "I heard about your kids from Lizbie, who heard from Sam, who overheard your rather talkative colleague."

And yeah, I agreed to keep my mouth shut. I also urged Kai to speak with Olivia. "Your conversation would be privileged," I reminded him. "And if it turns out that she knows squat about immigration law, she might at least be able to send you to someone who does."

He'd think about it, he told me before again making me promise to keep mum and then rather abruptly departing the biochar bivouac. I've always thought of myself as someone who can keep my mouth shut, and I did—but it was tough. Especially when Lizbie came sniffing around for whatever I might have discovered.

"Still working on it," I said to her. "Give me a little more time."

Evidently, my conversation with Kai wriggled something loose in him. Next thing I knew, Olivia visited the bivouac—at a time when it was just the two of us.

"Kai says you suggested he talk to me. So, um, thanks. I think. I haven't handled an immigration case for a while, and he may need way more expertise than I can provide. But I've gotten things rolling, already requested Rachel's files, from both the Customs and Border Protection crew—they have everyone's entry and exit records—and also the Citizenship and Immigration Services people who're the keepers of immigration records."

"How long will that take?" I asked. "I've heard such horror stories…"

"Faster if we do it piecemeal, one type of file at a time. Three weeks generally. Sometimes less. Sometimes way more."

But damn, a mere ten days later, Rachel's CBP entry and exit files showed up, followed two days after that by her immigration records— something I learned when Olivia came tromping over from Number Seven through our first significant snowfall to bang on the greenhouse door.

"I've already met with Kai about the problem, of course," she said as she stepped inside. "And he said it's okay to let you know where things stand. He went straight over to talk to Annie last night, so I expect—"

NOT ALL A DREAM

Judging by Olivia expression, I suspect my mouth fell open. "Annie?"

"They really hit it off at Thanksgiving, but I think Kai listened much more than he talked—until last night. Because this thing with Rachel is playing out very fast. Her immigration records arrived only yesterday, and my sense is that Kai's not ready to bring in the rest of the Circle. So don't say anything to anyone else yet, okay?"

"I won't. But, uh, color me intrigued. What exactly is 'the problem'?"

The problem—"and it's a biggie"—lurked in Rachel's border entry and exit records.

"Ready for a sojourn into the Kafkaesque?" Olivia asked.

"'Where you lead, I will follow'."

"As you know, Rachel's in Canada, has been since almost a year ago when she flew back to Montreal right after Val disappeared. *But* according to her CBP master crossing record, she's *not* in Canada. Her master crossing record shows her returning to the States through Vermont by car right before Val went missing."

"Are you saying that the CBP has no record of her return to Canada?"

"Yes. Exactly. As far as they're concerned, Rachel is in the United States right now. And I see only one way that could happen: The Canadian Border Services Agency somehow didn't record Rachel's entry at the Montreal airport, so the information never got sent on to the CBP for inclusion in her master crossing record. Kai confirmed that she used one of the Montreal airport inspection kiosks, which are electronic. Automated. I think the kiosk either failed to record or failed to transmit her entry data."

"So, um, what does that mean?"

"Ah, well, now we come to Kafkaesque part two. A slew of new Eleven Fourteen visa rules, clearly designed to keep out Canadians, put Rachel's Green Card status in jeopardy because she's been out of the country too long. Plus her spouse is dead. So she can't return using her existing Green Card. To get a new Green Card, essentially she has to start from scratch. That means staying in Canada and going through the U.S. consulate, which is typically a long and *very* arbitrary process, especially these days. And they might well reject her application."

"But the government believes she's here, not in Canada."

"Yep. And if she goes to the U.S. consulate in Montreal to reapply for a Green Card, they'll see the fuckup, and the fuckup will be on Rachel, not the Canadian border people. Starting with 'Why didn't you report this sooner? What are you hiding?' My own view is that if she takes that route, she'll end up stuck in Canada for god knows how long. Six months anyway. Maybe years. Maybe for good."

"Okay, wait. What if Rachel could apply for an adjustment to her Green Card status from here in the States?"

"As long as she does it reasonably soon, she'd get it automatically, no hassles, because she's the widow of a U.S. citizen and would already be residing here."

"And you told Kai this?"

"I did."

Which left me with just one question: What on earth did any of this have to do with Annie?

When I asked, Olivia just shrugged. "Haven't got a clue," she said.

CHAPTER FORTY-SEVEN

HOUSEGUESTS FOR THE HOLIDAYS

Dammit, Deels," I said out loud. "I hate when I end up in a position like this."

Where you regret what you didn't say—

"What I didn't *ask*. In this case, the questions that'd get to the bottom of what Kai's really up to. And what the hell Annie has to do with any of it."

Oooh, I like that—getting to the bottom *of what somebody's* up *to.*

"I am not amused, Deels."

Olivia had left only minutes earlier, and I'd gone back downstairs to put on a couple more layers of clothes in preparation for a few hours of pyrolyzing the mound of woodchips Bill and the kids had left me up at the bivouac.

But Cordelia didn't relent: *I know you think anyone who comes around to warm up will stick to bitching about the weather, but as soon as Lizbie sees you—and she* will *see you—she'll be in your face about Kai and his kids. Besides, it's too cold out there, too snowy, too windy. So stay inside today, in the kitchen maybe. You have quite the pile of maincrop potatoes to process.*

"Mierda." I tried to say it the way Duka did, lips pressed tight, a tongue trill in the middle, finishing with a hard snarl of contempt, all of which boosted the expletive's meaning, strength. Power. "And I don't want to hear a fucking syllable from you about cultural appropriation—understand, figment?"

Even though I'm right?

This time I opted for silence. Because, yes, my figment *was* right, about the weather, anyway, and probably Lizbie, too—though not about those frigging potatoes. I knew Phoebe would come tromping down from the study to help the instant I started on the potatoes, and that would force me into a whole new set of prevarications that, inevitably, I'd make way too elaborate because lying—even by omission—is not my strong suit.

Especially when lying involves people I've become close to, people I'd be upset with if they lied to me. Like the people in the Circle. There simply is no good solution when it comes to keeping certain kinds of secrets; any which way it goes down, *someone* is going to be exceedingly pissed off.

And yeah, I admit it: Part of me wanted to blame Kai for sticking me in the middle of all this.

Seriously? Cordelia snickered. You *started it, remember? When you decided to snoop him. "Word is you've got kids." You actually said that, Aitch. Even* you *considered yourself—how'd you put it? Oh yeah: brazenly pushy.*

"Maybe I'll just go back to bed."

And I would have—if there hadn't been a soft knock on my door.

My outside door, the one that opens from my little basement den onto the driveway. The one hardly anybody uses anymore.

"I need to talk to you—just you," Annie said in a near whisper as soon as I'd pulled the door ajar and she saw me. "Got a few minutes?"

She didn't waste a single breath on niceties or preliminaries, didn't even give me the chance to invite her to take off her jacket and sit down.

"Kai told me about Rachel and Val and the girls," she said hurriedly. "And how if Rachel can slip back across the border surreptitiously, off the books, then she can find a job here without any hassles. So I'm gonna help him."

"Say *what?*"

"Step one is the kids. Which is why I'm driving with Kai to Montreal to pick them up and bring them back."

"Back where?"

"Here. To my house. So—"

"Wait—" I put my hands to my head; did she actually mean what I thought she meant? "How well do you really even know Kai? He's—he's a newbie from god knows where—and, sure, he's helped us, but how much can we trust that he's—?"

"How well do *you* really even know Duka? Or Phoebe?" Annie smiled benevolently. "Or me?"

I sensed my eyebrows rising, my eyes widening. "Uh...point taken. Though I gotta say I feel like I know you much better than I know Kai."

Annie chuckled. "That's an illusion. Think about it: You know more about Kai—his family, his history, who he'll risk his life for—than you know about me. You've just gotten used to me over the last year, that's all. Plus you generally don't trust men a whole lot, so you need them to prove themselves. Which, by the way, Kai understands. He also thinks too many men are predators. That's why he's single and his best friends are lesbians."

Somewhere out of sight nearby, Cordelia was giggling.

"Okay." My hands, which by then had folded themselves in front of me, lifted in surrender. "But please tell me that what you're going to do is not dangerous."

"Other than a long car ride, not even a little, Hester."

"So you and Kai are just driving up to Montreal to get his kids? No Rachel hidden in the trunk or something?"

"Just the kids."

"And you're bringing them here instead of to—uh, Watertown, isn't it?"

Annie's head bobbed up, down.

"Why?" I asked. "Why *here?*"

"Kai wants them close—all of them, including Rachel. To help them retrieve their emotional balance, shore them up financially while Rachel gets back on her feet. Since he'll be working mostly in this area for several more months anyway, it makes sense to bring them here. Especially since their house in Watertown has been vandalized, stripped of all kinds of basics, like the stove, refrigerator, fixtures, copper pipes—so it's not habitable right now. Flip side of 'use it or lose it,' y'know?"

Yes—but...

There was something about Annie's expression, something. "And...?" I pressed.

Annie's tiny new smile struck me as conspiratorial. "And, well, I wanna check Rachel out in person, face to face. Cuz her credentials suggest that maybe, just maybe, she'd be right for the physician job opening at Outer Cape Healthcare."

"You checked Rachel's credentials?"

"I sure as hell did. She's overqualified, actually. Or would be if these were 'normal' times. As it is—well, I figure I'll be able to tell pretty damn quick if she's any kind of fit. And god, if she is… It'd be so much better to work with someone I know I can get along with—especially a woman. No way of telling till I meet her, of course. But based on what I've seen and heard about her, I've decided to be optimistic."

"Heard from Kai, I assume."

"That's true. I do like him, and these people are his family. When he says he wants to be around Rachel and the girls as much as possible, he means it. So I'll risk having all of them—including Kai—stay with me at least through Christmas, maybe New Year's. By January, regardless of what happens with Rachel, I figure I'll be houseguest-exhausted and they'll be ready to settle down somewhere. On the Cape, back in Watertown, wherever."

Well, I thought (but did *not* say), that's certainly one way to deal with your first Christmas without Melinda. "So when are the two of you heading to Montreal?"

"Today. Kai'll be picking me up soon. It's a seven-hour drive in good weather, which this isn't, and Kai's hoping to arrive before the kids' bedtime. He could go get them by himself, but then he'd have to leave them in a strange place with someone they've never seen before."

"You mean you. He'll be *leaving* the kids with you?" And then I got it. "Oh, because he's going back. By himself. To the border. To get Rachel—"

As Annie nodded, I watched her anxiety snowball. "I'm going with him so he can introduce me to Rachel, who needs to be okay with sending the kids off with me for a few days. We'll stay an extra night so they have a little time to get used to me, but then we'll scoot back here and Kai will leave again right away. Because of the weather—just the right conditions coming in up there, he says, so timing is everything…" Her nod withered into shrug. "I just hope they like me. Hope I like them."

"I have a really hard time imagining anyone not liking you, Annie."

"You're very kind, but trust me: I am *not* universally admired. And I've never looked after anybody's kids for more than a weekend. So I'm going for bribery while I pray nothing bad happens on Kai's second trip, the one that shall not be named. Once the kids are here, I'll focus everything on Christmas. Last Christmas never quite happened for them because of when Val went missing. I'm just hoping they'll be okay staying with me by themselves till Kai and Rachel show up."

"Can I do anything to help you out?" I asked.

"Thank you for asking that because yeah, actually, you can. My plan is to take time off while the kids are here, but I'll get calls from the EMTs and LPNs anyway and I'll have to respond, so I'm gonna need backup watching the kids when I'm not here."

"Absolutely, I can take on some of that, but it'd be good to also bring in the moms—Lizbie and Olivia. Especially if all the kids start hanging out together. Which they will if Mirrie has anything to say about it."

"I talked to Olivia already, and she's volunteered, but—"

"Yeah," I said, "Lizbie needs to be aboard, too. I'll talk to her today."

"But nothing about border crossings, okay? *Nothing*. The goal is to make it seem to all the world like Rachel's been here, in the country, for the past year. We're saying Burlington, Vermont if anyone asks."

I nodded, pinched my thumb and index finger, then made a zipping motion across my lips. "So how about your house? Have you decorated for the holidays?"

Annie snorted. "Until last night, I intended to ignore the holidays."

CHAPTER FORTY-EIGHT

I WASN'T THE ONLY ONE

A t least I didn't have to duck Lizbie anymore.

By the time I finished explaining that yes, Kai did have kids—two of them who'd only recently learned that one of their mothers, missing for almost a year, was in fact dead—Lizbie had tears in her eyes.

When I added that Annie, in a fit of almost incomprehensible generosity, had gone "up north" with Kai to retrieve his girls and bring them back to her house, whereupon he'd immediately be returning to pick up their surviving mother, and then all of them—including Kai—would stay at Annie's for a couple of weeks, Lizbie instantly approved.

"Oh," she said, "so they'll all be able to have a Christmas!" She then decided to help make it happen and enlisted a crew to prep Annie's house, a day-long effort that was much more fun than I would have expected, since everyone in the Circle showed up at some point to contribute something.

This was the first time I noticed what had become, in effect, a new chapter for me: Somewhere along the line, the decision to keep the Circle's official Old Woman—me—from "doing too much" went from kindly to over the top. As in: "Oh, Hester, let me carry that for you" and "You just stay right there, Hester—I'll go get that."

So after providing the key to Annie's house and finding Annie and Melinda's artificial Christmas tree, which we all decorated, I really didn't do a whole lot except pass on what little I'd learned from Kai about what the girls liked—chocolate and popcorn topped the list—and would likely need, such as the option to sleep in the same bed in a warm room with a nightlight...

Thus Mirrie and Emily disappeared for at least two hours into Annie's larger upstairs bedroom to make it sufficiently "girl-friendly" (I'm still not sure what that really means, other than lots of pillows), while Nate and David went from Circle house to Circle house collecting spare nightlights—"so they'll have enough."

But Mirrie wasn't done yet. "What about Christmas stockings?" she worried. "They gotta each have their own Christmas stocking!"

She and Emily ran off and returned in a couple more hours carrying seven foot-long red felt wonders they'd crafted themselves, which they attached to the fireplace mantel. Five were stuffed with a Mirrie-made facemask and festooned with snowflakes, stars, and bright gold letters— "Sarah," "Ariel," "Rachel," "Kai," and "Annie." Flanking the red stockings were two more, made of a gauzy white material with green letters—"spirit stockings," Mirrie said, one for Melinda, one for Val; inside each of these she and Emily had placed a small red felt heart.

Meanwhile, Lizbie and Isabella led the effort to ensure that Annie's houseguests would have ample food; every Circle household contributed something to Annie's larder, an exercise that revealed how the Circle itself had already begun to evolve: Some of us—Lizbie and Sam, Toby, Duka and I—brought over selections of the fresh food we'd cultivated ourselves, while those with actual incomes (Sylvie, Ellen, Phoebe) provided that which actual money could buy—grains, dairy, various forms of sugar, edible oils, any meat besides chicken.

Maybe because I was so resoundingly discouraged from "doing too much," I'd occasionally find myself dissociating to watch the activity around me from, well, somewhere else. Not quite out-of-body, but almost—a hushed encapsulation of space and time with its own distinct protocols that came for me even though I rarely moved from the comfortable chair I'd claimed in a corner of Annie's living room.

I didn't mind. At all. I was aware of seeing further than I had in a long time, maybe ever. As though my eyes, my whole self had been persuaded from the work on which I'd been so focused to see across the room, across the months since Eleven Fourteen, then to sweep out the window and perch in a nearby treetop before spinning back through the years into twinklings from my childhood, spinning higher, lower, farther, closer, and it all made sense somehow as I swung back into the moment before me, into the chair where I sat and watched...

From close up and from far away, I watched all the Circle's people but for Annie, but for Melinda. I watched our moods range across that day from quietly somber, as we remembered why we were doing any of this, to almost jolly—people laughing, eager to assist each other, showing up with a small snack, a needed tool, a useful suggestion. And I noticed I wasn't the only one who looked around gratefully at what we had and what we were able to share.

Melinda would approve, I thought, and so would Cordelia. How very sad that they never met.

Chapter Forty-nine

Another Eleven Fourteen winter

Her children were shy, innocent, earnestly polite just the way they'd been taught as Annie introduced them to me. And beautiful, of course, the way young creatures invariably are beautiful. Within about a minute, they were also in a state of high fidget; I'd arrived half a step ahead of the Circle's Gang of Four, the only other kids anywhere nearby, who were eager to resume the morning's grand tour of the neighborhood.

"Mum says we should collect eggs now," Mirrie announced. "Wanna come?"

Sarah and Ariel nodded in unison, then turned to Annie as one. "Can we? Can we?"

"Go for it," Annie replied. "But promise me you'll remember the rules we talked about, okay?"

While Sarah and Ariel solemnly nodded and scurried about for their jackets, mittens, facemasks, hats, and boots, Mirrie asked me if I'd be at the bivouac later.

"The weather's pretty good today, so yeah. I'll be up there in about an hour. And if you guys want to help out, I'll rev up all three barrel stoves."

"Oh-*kay!*" And Mirrie proffered her fist, which I almost bumped, making sure to leave an inch or two of air between us.

"What's a biv-whack?" Sarah asked. "An' what's a barrel stove?"

Mirrie grinned. "You'll see."

Seconds later, after all six kids had bounded out of the house, I noticed that Annie's eyes had filled with tears. "Those white stockings," she murmured, blinking at the fireplace. "Melinda would love those stockings—and what's inside them."

I smiled. "Mirrie, with an assist from Emily. Did she tell you she calls them 'spirit stockings'?"

"Really? She never said…" Annie sighed and her eyes slid downward as her face slumped into worry.

"Tell me," I said.

"I haven't heard a peep from them." Annie's voice was low and raspy. "Not that I expected to. Not quite yet. Not till they're truly safe on—on *this* side, y'know? Cuz that was the arrangement. But god, it's—it's rattling."

The plan, according to Kai, was to be back in Truro a couple of days before Christmas Eve. He was aiming for a five-day turnaround. Only Annie had any real notion of what that entailed, and she'd promised Kai that she'd keep mum about Rachel's immigration situation, just as I'd promised and Olivia had promised. "But I gotta talk to *someone* about this before my head explodes…"

Thus it was with me that Annie shared her anxiety about Rachel illegally crossing the border into Maine way the hell up north, where way the hell below-zero cold and feet of snow already reigned, where every inch of the border was monitored by sensors—"like infrared cameras and god knows what else"—installed every 400 feet.

Annie had been apprised of only a few of the particulars: Rachel would drive Val's car from Montreal to Quebec, then southeast into the largely depopulated farm country near the border, where she'd bundle up in clothes capable of at least partly obscuring her heat signature, abandon the car, and snowshoe through a heavily wooded couple of miles to the border. "The river's already quite frozen and Kai said he found a few spots where it's narrow and easy to cross under cover of heavy fog and a fallen tree—"

"Heavy fog?" I interrupted. "How the hell does he know there'll be fog?"

Annie grimaced. "I asked that. He said he's been closely tracking the weather up there for a while. Told me 'another Eleven Fourteen winter' is underway—very cold and a lot of snow already on the ground that far up in Maine. And now there's a front coming in that he believes will produce fog intense enough to mess up what infrared cameras can see."

"And how does he know where trees have fallen over the river?"

"Yeah, I asked about that, too. Kai has access through his job to the latest high-resolution satellite imagery, which he says shows an area where trees have collapsed across the entire width of the river, like thirty, forty feet. So once Rachel gets there, she'll pick a spot where the tree branches will help the fog obscure her crossing."

"And then?"

"Then she'll keep on snowshoeing to their designated meet-up, which Kai will have reached by snowmobile and Rachel will find using the GPS navigator Kai gave her."

"Jeezus. What if she falls down and breaks her leg or the GPS thingy fails or Kai's snowmobile goes belly up or—or the Border Patrol catches them?"

Annie shook her head. "Welcome to my world."

Another Eleven Fourteen winter. Kai's words, coming out of Annie's mouth—and echoing that Pentagon study Phoebe mentioned back when we were forming the Circle Collaborative. "Air temperatures will actually go lower for the next four years," Phoebe had said then. "Year five will be coldest of all."

From the bivouac, I gazed up at the perpetually gray-brown sky above us, its odd pinkish-orange undernotes still far too ominously dark. The air around me was some twenty degrees below "normal" and five or six inches of snow had crusted over the ground. But on this day we had little wind, no precip—as close, I concluded, as we were going to get to "mild" weather. And, if Kai was right, as good as we'd get for months to come.

I reminded myself of the starkly simple choice before me: Catch the bus now or spend every damn waking moment doing whatever I could to help us all survive our second Eleven Fourteen winter—without taking more than my share.

Oh, and don't freak out the children, who'd gathered around me within minutes of my arrival at the bivouac. We were long past the point where I needed to tell the Gang of Four what to do, so I watched them coach our new arrivals in the finer points of helping the Old Woman crank out biochar, beginning with pulling little red wagonloads of woodchips over to the barrel stoves from Bill Kosnik's impressive pile near the woodchipper.

It helped (me, anyway) that Bill had also long since relieved the Old Woman of the Circle's composting tasks, given how radically our compost requirements had grown. I admit I doubted how well he'd cope with becoming the Circle's Chief Compost Officer, but he had proved me utterly wrong: He enlisted Duka and the fellas to help him set up shop in front of the Hulk foundation some fifty feet from our three barrel stoves, which involved not only moving the woodchipper but also erecting two long rows of compost bins that he diligently managed.

Thus, over four days of comparatively benign pre-Christmas weather, all six kids lugged woodchips to the stoves and helped Bill compost. One day, he showed up with a truckload of only mildly stinky seaweed from the beach, which the kids helped him spread along one of the blacktopped driveways across the street to dry. The next day, with a combination of small rewards and lavish compliments, he ad-libbed a game of getting them to work the stuff into the compost bins—a game that turned out to be quite popular.

"Tom Sawyer meets the Pied Piper," I teased him after he sent the Gang down to Lizbie's and Duka's chicken coops to collect chicken shit and bring it back to be added to the compost bins.

Bill winked. "Whatever wears them the hell out is *so* worth it at the end of the day. But the best part is that they compete for the privilege of doing the yuckiest part of my job—they actually *like* shoveling chicken shit. And, it seems, the lovely smell of decaying seaweed."

During those four days, I had regular company besides the kids and Bill.

Our initial 2,300 square feet of grow space, occupying three Circle greenhouses (one more than I'd expected), had been constructed, filled with our meager "soil" (sand amended by Bill's compost), planted, and put on a lighting schedule, so Lizbie showed up often, sometimes with Olivia or Isabella in tow as she scurried between greenhouses. Meanwhile, Duka, Toby, and Sam were building greenhouses on two more foundations; each time any of them passed by the bivouac, they paused to ask, "Any word yet?"

For five days, all I could do was shake my head. Annie had heard nothing. As each day faded into midafternoon darkness, our apprehension deepened. "What's keeping 'em?" Duka wanted to know. Since I'd promised to say nothing of border crossings, I shrugged and mumbled something about crappy weather and dicey roads in northern New England.

On the sixth day, air temps had dropped a few degrees and the wind had picked up, but I went to the bivouac anyway since there's no such thing on Upper Hollow Circle as sufficient biochar—and I needed the distraction. Soon enough, the Gang of Now We Are Six showed up to help, and after I fired up the stoves with the woodchips they brought me, we all hunkered around the stoves' warmth—in silence.

I found this disconcerting. These kids were never silent, at least not when they were together.

"What's up?" I asked no one in particular.

Mirrie shrugged and cast her eyes toward Sarah. "We're waiting," she explained.

"Oh-kay," I responded, stretching the syllables toward a question.

"For Mae and Kaidad," Sarah said.

"Oh," I began, "Mae and—?" Of course: Kai's their Dad—so Mae (or were they saying Mère?) is likely Rachel, a conclusion I reached because I'd already heard them refer to Val as Ma. So I nodded. And had no clue what to say, since I didn't know when, or whether, we'd see Kai and/or Rachel. Maybe they'd vanish like Val did. Maybe they'd already vanished, never to be seen again.

My tongue does not tie easily, but for too long speech failed me. Even mentioning Christmas could backfire if in fact Kai and Rachel were freezing to death somewhere in Maine's north woods. I got as far as "I know it's hard" before I too fell silent and waited with them.

CHAPTER FIFTY

WITH A KIND OF GRACE

O ur meager daylight had nearly completed its surrender to darkness by the time the kids and I had shut down the biochar bivouac for the day and I was ambling back with Sarah and Ariel to the low end of Upper Hollow Circle where Annie's place, and mine too, hunkered. I'd just glanced over at the greenhouse along the back of my house, cheery bright under its LED lights, wishing (unsuccessfully) that it might inspire some sort of hopeful thought I could share, when a high-pitched scream burst out of Ariel.

"They're here! Sarah! Look! *They're here!*" she howled.

I followed her point and saw a small red SUV with the windfarm company's logo on its driver-side door pull into Annie's driveway right behind Kai's truck. By then, Ariel and Sarah both were running toward Annie's, yelling and squealing with delight.

For a second, only one really, my legs trembled: Kai and Rachel had actually done it… Umm, hadn't they? I paused for another second, listening for, hell, I dunno—sirens? Helicopters? Madly barking Border Patrol dogs psyched to chew on someone "illegal"?

Breathe, I commanded myself, because the scene before me was so supremely mundane and normal, right down to Annie emerging from the house even before anyone had stepped out of a vehicle. Like she'd been expecting them. Y'know, for the holidays.

When I reached Annie's driveway, the girls were jumping all over Rachel and Kai. "We decided to surprise you," I heard Rachel tell them. But then she glanced over at me, and I saw an entirely different explanation etched into her face.

Something inexplicable happened to me the instant I got a good look at Rachel Therrien.

Maybe it was her expression. Maybe I have an undiagnosed medical issue—epilepsy, the beginnings of dementia. Or maybe I'm more stressed, more fatigued than I've realized. Because I was quite convinced I knew this woman, knew her well, even intimately. But of course I had never seen her before, didn't know her at all, couldn't ever have known her—and I was quite aware of that, too.

"Hello," I said as walked up Annie's driveway to meet her, "and welcome—" I stopped short and literally bit my tongue to prevent myself from saying what I wanted to say, very nearly *did* say: Welcome home.

She was too pale, obviously exhausted, obviously relieved. Her children had wrapped themselves around her and I watched her relax into them as she gazed at me, then blinked at me. Was that surprise? Had she heard the words I didn't say?

I'll never know, since Annie filled the space between us with introductions. At least this gave me time to, well, look at her a little longer, as though a longer look might show me the *why* of the déjà vu that had just enveloped me. But no, she struck me as totally ordinary in all ways but one: Even in her depleted state, Rachel Therrien had the kindest eyes I'd ever seen.

Much as I wanted to, I didn't linger in Annie's driveway. I knew my chance to talk with Rachel would come soon enough.

The very next afternoon, in fact.

❖

She texted first to ask if she might drop by briefly, then showed up a few minutes later at the door to my basement lair, still pale, still very tired. But her timing had allowed me to hustle upstairs for a special version of our Eleven Fourteen tea and (mashed sweet potato) crumpets, which I set up on Cordelia's rolltop desk right before her knock on my door.

She wanted to thank me, she said softly. "I was worried about letting the girls come ahead without me, but they're having a fine time with the other kids, they love the chickens and making—what's it called? Biochar? Kai tells me we owe you and Annie a great deal."

"He's right about Annie, but he gives me way too much credit. And, I suspect, he doesn't give himself enough. Credit, that is."

"Mmm…" Rachel offered a small nod and smiled as she sat down, then sipped from the mug of tea I'd handed her. "This—" Her gray eyes went wide. "This is peppermint!"

"Almost," I said. "A little peppermint and a whole lotta dandelion and burdock."

She laughed. "Close enough. How the hell do you have *anything* peppermint?"

I chuckled. "Have you met Duka yet?"

Rachel shook her head.

"Duka can find just about anything and fix just about anything." I chuckled again. "Not quite magic, but close."

"Well, Duka's tea is truly wonderful. Thank you for sharing it with me." As her hands cupped the mug and she inhaled the tea's scent, she slipped into a silence that, to my surprise, I felt no need to interrupt—perhaps because I found Rachel's presence so calming, like a long, gentle exhale after a stretch of excruciating tension. Finally, she spoke again. "You remind me of my grandmother."

Umm…I felt my eyebrows lifting…okay. "That's a good thing, I hope."

"Oh yes. Definitely."

And then Rachel began to talk.

"In retrospect—well, I should've come home a year ago. Should've waited in Watertown for them to find Val and tried to do the job I'd just signed on for. But I—" Rachel's shoulders hunched. "I thought that was tantamount to giving up. And no way could I do that. At first, I was convinced Val was alive, that we'd find her alive. At the time, it seemed the girls felt the same way—especially Sarah—though now I wonder if they were just following my lead. Anyway, we stayed.

"Kai came as soon as I called him and stuck around as long as he could. Through the holidays. Through my giving up the job back here. Spent the whole time trying to talk me out of staying up there, but I wasn't going anywhere without Val. About mid-January, he had to leave to finish up a project in Iowa. Then came the gel noir—the black cold—and nobody with any sense went anywhere, including Kai, who was stuck in Iowa.

"So it was just the three of us for quite a while. We were in a rented place, furnished by the owners who lived in the other half of the house. During the two years we were *supposed* to be there, everything was fine, despite the pandemic. The owners' two kids were about the same age as ours, so all four of them home-schooled together. Not exactly the cultural immersion we'd imagined, but the girls learned a lot and had a great time.

"All that ended even before Val vanished, soon after le Quatorzième Novembre, when the owners went to Bermuda. No big deal, though, since the four of us were heading back to Watertown in mid-December…"

Rachel paused to sip her tea, and to gird, I think, because she seemed to stiffen and strain to draw in enough breath. I resisted an urge to touch her. *Not yet*, Cordelia mumbled. *Maybe not for quite some time…*

"At the end of January," Rachel resumed, her eyes squeezing closed, "right before the gel noir, about six weeks into Val's disappearance, I started to think maybe we *should* go home.

"Then the police found Val's car. And what was left of Val's phone. And some of Val's blood on the outside of her car. It was—well, the blood, the fact that there was still no sign of her or her wallet or her credit and debit cards, that was very bad news. I felt so damn guilty for even considering going home without her, like I was abandoning her. And it seemed like the girls felt the same way."

"So you stayed."

Her head lowered, Rachel nodded but said nothing as her eyes opened again. Was she done talking? Rather than ask her anything else, I replenished her tea.

"Getting through the gel noir—the, uh, black cold—wasn't easy," she said to the floor before looking up at me, her face drawn.

"We moved into the basement, paid a fortune to keep it barely warm enough to live in. Paid another fortune at the nearest grocery store so my food trips wouldn't take very long, since the girls freaked whenever I left them alone. And we were lucky; I only got mugged once and came out unscathed, thanks to my trusty stun gun. But I wasn't working except for writing a few academic papers and homeschooling the girls. So I spent nearly everything Val and I had saved.

"And somewhere deep in here—" Rachel splayed a hand across her chest. "I knew Val was gone. Knew it in April, like a premonition, when that asshole tried to rob me. But I couldn't tell the girls 'that's it, we're leaving' just because I had a damn *feeling*. God help me, by April I'd made a real believer out of Sarah. So I shoved that sense of doom way down deep and made myself believe like I'd made Sarah believe—that Val was still alive, that we still had hope.

"It wasn't till late in November that they told me Val was dead. Her body had been found in May in Ottawa, but she was a Jane Doe on a slab for six months until, finally, somebody in Ottawa checked out Montreal's missing persons data and made the connection."

"What happened to her?"

"Best guess is she'd been attacked. The forensics point to her dying instantly from a severe basilar skull fracture. The back of her head was hit—crushed, actually—with immense force. I figure she was jumped at her car by someone who wanted to force her to use her bank cards at cash machines. I think they pulled her into their car, then bolted out of town when they saw she was dead and later dumped her body, which was found in the Ottawa River, frozen, no trauma but for her head injury and the post-mortem effects of being tossed around in the ice."

"Oh god, Rachel." My voice refused to rise much above a whisper. "I am so, so sorry."

Tears had filled her eyes, yet she almost smiled. "For three hundred and forty-five days, I was terrified for Val. I had visions of torture, rape—every horrible, perverse harm that human beings can do to each other. I saw them all, dreamed them all, and the girls did, too—no matter how hard I worked at telling them their mama was okay. We ended up, the three of us, sleeping in the same bed, one kid on each side of me. It was the only way any of us could sleep at all.

"And when we learned what happened, yeah, it was awful. We lost Val. She lost us. But a basilar skull fracture—she experienced no pain. It happened so fast, so completely that she was dead before she had a chance to comprehend anything at all. I feel *such* relief knowing that, knowing she didn't suffer. Understanding that has helped the girls, too. They see it as Val being swept away with a kind of grace—"

Rachel shifted in the chair, like something was poking her from underneath. "Finding out how Val died kind of redeemed me. The girls, Sarah in particular, had become very angry with me. Sarah believed by then that I was lying, pretending Val was okay when actually Val must be in agony somewhere, or had died slowly, in terrible pain. And, well, Sarah was right—I *had* been pretending, I *did* fear the worst. So I needed that redemption, I needed the girls to trust me again.

"Because after we found out Val was dead, I had to get us the hell out of there. I know it's irrational. I know that. But as far as I'm concerned,

Montreal killed Val. It tried to kill me, too, and it almost destroyed my relationships with my kids. Plus it took every cent we had to get through last winter and the gel noir, so I needed to find a job. But I'm not sure I can handle a hospital emergency department again. Not yet. And not in fucking forty-below Montreal. So I knew we couldn't stay. I was afraid we wouldn't survive if we stayed.

"But somewhere along the line—I have no idea when or where—I lost my damn Green Card, which I'd need to re-enter the United States.

Which turned out to be a gift. Otherwise, I'd never have found out about the Eleven Fourteen changes to the immigration rules. And Kai would never have contacted Olivia, who would never have uncovered the airport screwup. And now that I'm back here I can apply for a new Green Card, no hassles beyond the usual BS." Rachel's soft almost-laugh sounded ragged. "Once I stop shivering."

"I knew just enough about your plan," I said, "to worry about how the hell you'd be able to get across the border without ending up in Border Patrol custody—or worse. It seemed like it took longer than—"

Rachel laughed. "Than it was supposed to? Yeah, it did. Kai wanted fog—and dear god, Kai *got* fog. The worst fog either of us have ever seen. There were times in the low-lying areas when you quite literally couldn't see your hand once you fully extended your arm. Almost like being blind.

"I was scared shitless I'd be caught by the U.S. Border Patrol at the river, figured one of their famous high-tech sensors or maybe a drone would spot me on the U.S. side and then they'd just appear and whisk me away when I couldn't produce my Green Card. But nothing happened. I just inched along using the GPS, trying to find the place where I was supposed to meet Kai, which was only about half a mile into the U.S. side.

"It all took way too long because the fog wasn't lifting, it was getting worse. By then I'd given up on the night vision monocular, which the fog had made useless. I got a bit of a mental boost from that, since maybe it meant the Border Patrol's infrared sensors were also useless. And at least Kai was right where he said he'd be.

"Kai said he expected to run into at least one logging truck, and maybe a snowmobiler or two—but we didn't see anyone, not a single soul the whole way back to Jackman. It's not like the area has ever been crowded, but it *is* a winter sports paradise. Or it used to be before Eleven Fourteen. Kai thought it was beyond strange how there were no people, no sign of human activity anywhere. Just a huge moose that appeared right in front of the snowmobile and almost caused us to roll over.

"We attempted to retrace Kai's path—less than sixty miles altogether. We were fog-blind, though, especially in those low-lying areas where we'd hoped to go a little faster, and we didn't want to travel in the dark. So we ended up out there for another night, got to Jackman late, and then stayed over in the house Kai had rented. I expected to see people in Jackman—ice fishermen and so on. It's a ghost town, though, despite having a Border Patrol station. Anyway, at least neither of us ended up hypothermic or frostbitten. But I'm still shivering."

CHAPTER FIFTY-ONE

USE MY ADDRESS

I decided that Rachel Therrien would probably be defrosting for a while yet.

"I've never lived in a place like this," she told me that first time we talked. "Been an urban girl, always. Sidewalks. Streetlights. Stores and cars and lots of people. Admittedly, way too many people when supply chains have gone to shit. But this—Annie and the girls showed me around a little this morning. This is so different. So...*quiet*."

"It used to be beautiful, too—before the black cold," I replied. "Maybe it'll be beautiful again. Someday."

Rachel dipped her head, out of sympathy perhaps, or simple acknowledgment of the unfortunate truth that Someday remained a long way off—and that while the Outer Cape might be a slight improvement over After Eleven Fourteen Montreal and her ravaged place in Watertown, she wasn't at all sure she liked it. But her daughters certainly did.

"I'd never have guessed they'd be so into making charcoal." Rachel's face scrunched. "I mean, *charcoal*? Seriously? And they love the chickens. Introduced me to each one. By name. And eggs. They can't get over how the eggs are warm and soft when they gather them from the coop."

So, um, pray tell... Cordelia's light almost-voice wafted from what seemed like the far end of an invisible tunnel. *Since* you *haven't mentioned anything to her about living here, wanna take a guess at who has?*

Before Cordelia could suggest setting up a betting pool, I decided to ask Rachel a question of my own: "Did your tour include a look inside any of our greenhouses?"

Oooh, subtle, Cordelia poked as Rachel shook her head.

"Allow me," I said and brought her upstairs so she could see how our most recent crop was coming along.

"We're still novices, but we're getting the hang of it," I told her, then began moving through the greenhouse. I got as far as the carrots when I realized Rachel hadn't yet budged from the doorway.

"Oh my god." She spoke in a near-whisper as her gaze spanned our 411 square feet of LED-lit greenery. "This is wonderful."

I extracted a ripened carrot from the soil, stepped to the sink to clean it, then offered it to her. She took it from me with great delicacy and examined it, squinting as she turned it over and over.

"It's edible," I teased her. "Promise."

She bit into it. "Izz duh-*yish*-uss!" she proclaimed as she munched.

Well, well, you made that *look positively easy*, purred Cordelia.

Made what look positively easy?

The good doctor hasn't admitted it to herself yet, but urban tendencies notwithstanding, she already wants to stick around.

Are you suggesting that I want her to stick around?

Cordelia didn't answer that, but I could hear her chuckling.

It'll work out, she insisted, *because first, barring another catastrophe, there* will *be enough food to get all of you through this coming winter. Second, none of you will say no to the kids, who love being part of the Gang of Now We Are Six. Third, it can be damn useful to have a doctor who owes you a big-ass favor real close by. And fourth, you recognize Rachel. She's your replacement.*

Two days after Rachel arrived, Lizbie and Sam hosted a potluck Christmas dinner that included everyone in the Circle along with Annie's houseguests and (to my surprise) Michael Oswald, the beekeeping mushroom guy, whom Lizbie had invited at Toby's suggestion.

"I love playin' matchmaker," Lizbie whispered to me as we prepared the sweet potatoes.

"There's a match?" I asked, glancing around. "What match?"

She stared at me like I'd suddenly lost a body part. "Kai and Michael, of course."

"Oh." Better not to mention that I'd always thought Michael was straight. "Right."

Pondering what else I'd missed, I spent most of the rest of the evening watching from a comfortable chair, hyperaware of each passing second's delicately ephemeral details, caught and crystalized like a photograph—and never mind that the photographs will fade as my memory fades and winks out, never mind that sometimes I wondered if I might be dreaming...

It all reminded me of the day we prepped Annie's house while she went "up north" with Kai to pick up Sarah and Ariel. This time, though, everyone was all together all at once. And, to my delight, they really were forming a little community able to set aside various tensions and conflicts for a larger purpose.

I knew perfectly well, for example, that Sam Behr regarded Bill Kosnik as absurdly effete, that Bill saw Sam as rough and aggravatingly primitive—but that night they joked and backslapped about how pleased they were at the close friendship their sons had developed.

Nor would you ever have understood how deeply Duka distrusted Ellen Higgins's stiff-necked copness, nor the slitty-eyed suspicion that Ellen harbored for Duka—not least because as the evening waned they stepped outside to get stoned together and then abetted each other in an extended bout of the giggles.

I watched it all: the way Sylvie smiled as she refilled Toby's glass; how the kids weaved through little clusters of jabbering adults in pursuit of yet another adventure; those moments when Annie went too quiet for too long and someone would come by to retrieve her with a touch, a soft mention of Melinda, or—in the case of Isabella—the distraction of oddness and baoding balls.

And Rachel, who'd been led by her children into Lizbie's living room understandably nervous and somewhat overwhelmed, who'd initially seemed so shy, even standoffish—until she realized her illegal border crossing had remained a secret still held tight by just the four of us while the rest of the crew found simple, casual ways to put her at ease without ever pity-prying about Val.

I watched it all, and as I watched I slipstreamed into another sort of hyperawareness—of intensifying colors, of the myriad ways light changed and shapes moved...

How do I explain the breathtaking beauty of that glimpse into the dazzling uniqueness of each moment? Nothing is mundane or ugly, not ever; mundane and ugly are merely instruments our fear deploys to blind us, deafen us, make us run and run and keep on running.

Perhaps it was only coincidence that this was the moment when Phoebe sidled up to me murmuring "I think I have some serious competition" as she tilted her head toward Duka on the far side of the room.

I turned and saw Duka drop to one knee so she'd be eye-to-eye as she engaged in conversation with a rapt, earnest Ariel, who abruptly whooped, "A crane? Can I come see?" And of course Duka smiled and said yes.

Rachel, standing close by, hid her smile behind her hand and whispered, "Looks like my girl's in love."

"Mine too." Phoebe laughed as she gently nudged Rachel's shoulder.

Whereupon I realized the Circle would never have a formal(ish) meeting to decide whether Rachel, Kai, Sarah, Ariel, and even maybe Michael Oswald would join. This Christmas gathering *was* that meeting, and a consensus of yeses had been achieved with nods and smiles and nudges and even hugs.

❖

Two days later, Annie asked me to come by without mentioning why. When I showed up—with my latest experiment in peanut-oil-fried sweet-potato chips—I found myself joining an ad hoc meeting of those who knew Rachel's secret.

Rachel should lay low, they were agreeing (that's the Kai, Annie, and Olivia "they"), until she had her new Green Card in hand. And since her house in Watertown was a vandalized mess from which mail had already been stolen, the new card should not be sent there.

Use my address, Annie proposed. "And even before your card arrives," she said, "you can apply for the Outer Cape Healthcare job. You'll get the job, too—because no one comes close to having your qualifications—and since winter's already descending, maybe you should figure on staying here till spring."

Rachel smiled. Then she nodded.

And her girls really did like my potato chips.

CHAPTER FIFTY-TWO

WHAT THE HELL IS SHE *DOING*?

It's time!" Duka declared as she gulped down a second cup of bartered coffee.

Duka rarely drank two cups in a row; coffee was way too hard to come by for such indulgence. But this morning was special: After several days of rather dramatic parts deliveries (they were quite large, those parts) and more days of prep work, she and Kai would—with the help of an enormous crane, some telecoaching from the manufacturer, and several stronger members of the Circle—raise our first wind turbine onto one of the four concrete foundations poured a month earlier that had, at last, sufficiently cured.

And, like those foundations, this first turbine and the tower on which it would perch were paid for by monies from the intervivos trust..."to be reimbursed with the ECASP funds when they arrive." Although I'd handed Duka the power to make this decision without me, she simply wouldn't, informing me with a rather sly grin that "I refuse to say yes to this until you look at these numbers." And if I thought it was a risk too far, she'd back off.

So I looked. And I do admit: Left to my own devices, I'd never have had the nerve for it. But I agreed anyway. What I'd always known about Duka—with a certainty I couldn't explain, but I felt quite sure—was that she'd never take the money out of the trust and run. She would stay. She would fight like she'd been fighting for years to stay. All I did was boost her supply of ammunition, and I would respect how she decided to use it.

"Ready?"

Even though it was still dark outside, even though my body yearned to crawl back into bed, into sleep, I was dressed, I was damn well ready. And so I trailed Duka and Phoebe as their flashlights lit the way to the edge of the Hulk property where the truck-mounted crane awaited, and Duka flipped on the temporary floodlights she and the fellas had rigged the day before to aid their early, still-dark-out start.

"Hi!" chirped Ariel Therrien as soon as the lights went up. Wearing a red jacket over her cartoon-print pajamas, yellow boots, mismatched plaid mittens, and a neon orange scarf covering her mouth and nose, she stood alone in front of the truck crane, dwarfed by one of its tires, her widened eyes flashing excitement. "Is it time now?"

Phoebe's surprised laugh came snorting out her nose, but Duka responded with a radiant, ear-to-ear smile and a resounding "Yes, ma'am! It's time!"

This inspired a squealy "Yay!" from Ariel, who ran to Duka and grabbed her hand.

"I'm gonna have some jobs for you today," Duka said. "You up for it?"

Ariel's head bobbed vigorously. "Like yesterday an' the yesterday before that."

"Excelente." Duka rested her free hand on Ariel's shoulder. "An' you gotta remember to stay exactly where I say, 'specially when the crane starts lifting the tower, okay?"

"I will. I promise."

"First, we gotta make sure everything's just like we left it yesterday. A real careful inspection. Wanna do that with me?"

And off they went hand in hand.

"Is there such a thing as achingly adorable?" Phoebe asked me in a whisper.

Before I had a chance to reply, Rachel came running up behind us.

"Ariel—" she wheezed, breathless and desperate. "Is she here?"

"She is," I replied, choosing steady calm over giggles as I pointed. "Right over there."

"Oh thank god," Rachel panted as she bent over to catch her breath. "Couldn't find—then I saw the lights—"

"They're doing a pre-tower-raising inspection," Phoebe explained with an almost straight face.

Rachel moaned. "I'm so sorry. She's not usually like this—"

"Trust me when I tell you Duka has loved every minute of it," Phoebe said.

"I can't remember the last time Ariel's been this wound up about anything." Rachel was shaking her head, but smiling, too. "She won't stop talking about hex bolts and flat washers and spud wrenches and furling cables…"

❖

The crane had already been positioned downwind from the tower foundation, the tower sections assembled, the powerhead attached, the wiring installed. As darkness gave way to murky light, the rest of the Circle clan, led by Mirrie and the Gang, began arriving. Ariel scurried around bringing tools and parts to Duka and Kai as they put together the tail boom. Soon after the other fellas helped them install the turbine blades and the spinner, Duka whispered something to Ariel, who ran toward us, arms spread wide.

"Everybody!" she announced rather officiously. "Everybody hassa move way back now! Outta the way! For—" She glanced back at Duka, who nodded reassurance. "For your own safety!"

With the help of the other members of the Gang of Now We Are Six, Ariel herded us across the street and onto what had once been a neighbor's lawn so that we stood a couple of hundred feet from all the activity. Once she was satisfied with our compliance, she took my hand "cuz Duka says I gotta make extra sure you're safe."

And then, hookups completed, the crane began lifting it all very slowly, seemingly very precariously. About fifteen minutes later, Duka, Kai, and the others were leveling the upright tower and then bolting it to the foundation.

"It's so high," Ariel murmured, staring upward. "Duka looks tiny."

I'd been talking with Phoebe, who'd rejoined the little crowd of tower-raising watchers after operating a drone that videoed the event "to impress the ECASP people." As Ariel spoke, Phoebe looked up—and gasped. "What the hell is she *doing?*"

Climbing the tower, that's what. All one hundred feet of it.

"She's, um, um—" Ariel began, then hesitated. "Oh yeah—she's gonna detach the lifting slings. An' then she'll inspect, um, all the connections an' hardware an', um, tighten as needed using a, um, accurate torque wrench. Told Kaidad it should be her cuz she'll be the main, um, maintainer person. An' then she'll come down an' Kaidad'll climb up an' check her work."

"Thank you, Ariel," Phoebe said solemnly. "I didn't know any of that."

"Yeah." Ariel frowned; one last thing to remember, it seemed. "Yeah, an'—an' then Duka an' Kaidad'll do all the, um, the commissioning checks. An' after that we can clap."

"Say g'bye to having to steal electricity," Duka whispered to me as we watched the turbine's first revolutions. "Cuz that baby'll power not only the Hulk greenhouse but also your greenhouse."

Just for a second, my chest tweaked into a cringe as I stared upward at our own crude, propeller-topped Eiffel tower barely more than two hundred feet from where I slept.

"*Our* greenhouse," I said anyway.

Duka grinned. "Happy New Year."

Chapter Fifty-three

And then I hear Cordelia's whisper

I used to be a writer, but that ended at the beginning of the pandemic. Now I scrimp and eke, and I expect to scrimp and eke for what's left of my life, mostly in and around the greenhouse out back, in the kitchen, at the pyrolyzers (where at least I regularly get to hang out with the Gang of Now We Are Six)—oh, and I participate in our various rounds of all-hands harvests and post-harvest processing…

There's high irony in this, my fate, given how intensely I dislike plunging my hands in dirt and digging weeds and anything associated with so-called "homemaking." Through my early years, I sustained an impressive distance between me and all things even vaguely domestic. These days, however, there's no part of my life that's *not* about the heart of domesticity: food.

How to get it. How to grow it. How to coax it from the earth and preserve it. How to share it and stretch it to sustain more and more people.

Assuredly, finding myself alone for the first time in forty-five years had something to do with this. As did Eleven Fourteen Anxiety, which didn't take long to shift from fears of it happening again to worries about supply chains in general and food supply chains in particular—though this took a while to infect me, thanks to Cordelia's quiet transformation from stashing extra because of the pandemic to becoming what seemed at the time like an irrationally rabid prepper.

Ultimately, she left me with enough food for at least four years—all I'd need to grieve myself out and then, when the time felt right, take myself out. Except I wasn't entirely by myself.

Only recently have I grasped the importance of that day shortly before my first After Christmas—after I lost Cordelia, after Eleven Fourteen—when Lizbie sent Mirrie over with some fresh eggs. I think Mirrie was supposed to just give them to me and scamper home, but I offered her a cup of hot chocolate, which is when I learned that the Watts-Behr household hadn't seen milk for at least two weeks. Reason enough to send Mirrie back with a couple of half-gallons of frozen fresh milk from Cordelia's stash.

Soon after that, Annie dropped by to find out if I'd gotten vaccinated yet (no, so she poked me on the spot). I fed us both a couple of grilled ham-and-cheddar sandwiches and sent her home with a big bag of soon-to-expire potato chips after she mentioned that none of the surviving stores carried them anymore.

I suppose I remember these moments so vividly because of the kindness I was shown—and because of how good it felt to have a chance to be kind in return.

And then came Duka, who seems to have an ability to, well, rally people. Or at least rally people she knows, like Toby and Sylvie, and Lizbie and Sam, and Phoebe, and Annie, and, more recently, Kai and Rachel and little Ariel. Even people like Isabella, Michael Oswald, Alison Perry, Greg Silva. Even, grudgingly, Ellen Higgins.

I doubt Duka's aware of this ability, if that's what it truly is. Maybe she's just skilled at crafting deals that benefit all parties, then honoring them, with the result that people trust her. Whether it's really about her or not, I couldn't help but notice that once she moved into my house, the something that changed shortly before Christmas became permanent.

Then it grew over the ensuing months to fill the emptiest of spaces:

From the fire that nearly destroyed our neighborhood sprang the Circle Collaborative, which actually seems to be working the way we'd all hoped...

Duka's combative wariness, and Phoebe's, too, surrendered to the gravitational power of profound physical attraction and then, yes, to love...

Annie lost Melinda but has found in Rachel more than distraction, just as Rachel has found in Annie more than a waystation, and they will, I'm beginning to believe, be able to admit this and maybe even act on it as more time passes...

My intractable worry and fatigue, born of losing Cordelia, exacerbated by the impacts of Eleven Fourteen, have ebbed ever since Duka accepted that intervivos trust, which she treats like it's something sacred...

And the effect of all this has been, well, dare I say relaxing?

Plus now that the others in the Circle worry about me "overdoing it" (Phoebe's expression, but widely shared, I suspect), whenever I venture beyond the greenhouse out back or the kitchen or the pyrolyzers or a collective greenhouse harvest—like the time I tried to help Phoebe clean out the chicken coop down in the hollow—I'm greeted with several resounding versions of NO!

Of course, on one level this is lovely. I'm not so tired, I have more time to become a better cook, to maybe ferret out what really happened on Eleven Fourteen, to take more naps...

But what does it mean that I've started dreaming about wind turbines?

It's fitting, I suppose, that the most interesting feature of my second post-Eleven Fourteen winter has been my dreams. Partly, of course, this has been because we did not suffer another *black* cold—though, marginally lighter skies notwithstanding, we did endure bloody terrible record-breaking *bleak* cold. Colder, actually, than what happened during the black cold and just as windy, almost as snowy. Way too close to what that Pentagon study predicted.

So we struggled to keep ourselves and the greenhouses from freezing through waves of the deepest freezes, which bottomed out at minus forty degrees. Twice. Despite Duka's monitoring systems, which she and Toby and Bill Kosnik installed in every one of the Circle's greenhouses, we pulled several all-nighters to make sure nothing happened to our crops.

No surprise, though, that the lack of *black* cold fostered the illusion that conditions were almost normal—so across the Outer Cape people succumbed to hypothermia and several froze to death. All of which kept Annie and Rachel plenty busy. More than once, I heard Annie express gratitude for Rachel's presence, for Rachel's skill.

Without them, the Circle's luck certainly would not have held. Annie and Rachel saved Duka's life, and Sam's, and Ellen Higgins's life, too. In separate, don't-worry-I'll-be-fine incidents, each of them dangerously underestimated the severity of the cold—"S-Sorry," Duka said as Rachel worked to warm her up, "I got f-fooled c-cuz it w-was s-so light out." After too long outside, each of them ended up with borderline Stage Three hypothermia (at its worst, Sam's body temperature registered just below ninety degrees Fahrenheit).

Even so, Duka and the fellas managed to insulate the chicken coops (we lost only two birds to the cold), erect the other three wind turbines, and complete eight of the Circle's hoped-for greenhouses—although the cold did blow away their ability to meet Duka's very ambitious deadlines, plus Phoebe's foundation and Isabella's foundation remained bare.

Still, no one lost any appendages and everyone had enough to eat.

I suppose it was precisely because we all survived that my dreams evolved and cycled the way they did. Starting with that very first one about our very first wind turbine…

Initially, I was up there with (in? on?) Phoebe's drone, staring down at spinning turbine blades until my gaze was swept across the surrounding landscape—and I began to see *two* landscapes at once, layering over each other, then weaving in and out of each other. Looping. Spiraling.

I saw the present—barren, primordially agro-industrial, always in shades of cold, windy gray. Then past-tense pastels swirled in, summer greens and blues strengthening, brightening until I was on the ground in the idyllic pretend-wilderness where Cordelia and I had lived for a quarter century.

Versions of this dream, always beginning with Duka's first wind turbine, came for me many times before I could remember more than fragments.

Finally, one morning I woke up with the whole thing still playing out, and I needed more than seconds, more than minutes even, to understand where I was—and *when* I was. I'd woken, yes, but I was still dreaming vividly, standing outside our house in a distinctly greener After Eleven Fourteen landscape, Duka's first wind turbine whirling behind me. I looked up at our bedroom windows and thought, "Jeez, I wonder if Cordelia's up there," at the same time telling myself, "No, that's impossible—Cordelia's dead."

With only slight variations, this dream repeated regularly, a recurring cycle that brought me closer and closer each time to a sense that Cordelia was inside the house waiting for me. With each cycle, each repetition, this sense grew stronger and my belief that she couldn't be there because she was dead grew weaker—until at last I decided to see for myself one way or the other.

So I went inside, up to our bedroom, and there she was, lying in our bed with an enormous grin.

"About time," she said, laughing, patting the space next to her, and I got naked and crawled in and touched her and kissed her and we made love and I was still coming when I woke up.

After that, my dreaming expanded in no particular order—cycling forward from the wind turbine to what seemed like a future not yet reached, then back to people and places and events from long ago. Memories really.

I often dreamed of dancing with Cordelia at the Saints, toking in the alley outside, driving home the back way along the Charles River, singing along to "Stayin' Alive" or "Fernando" or "Mamma Mia!" Or, every now and then, listening in comfortable silence to a Mozart sonata. And god, she looked so, so beautiful…

Sometimes, when the wind turbines in my dreams swung me into our After Eleven Fourteen landscape, I'd see the greenhouses where my neighbors' houses once stood, I'd see multiple turbines spinning enthusiastically. The land had greened with grasses, scrub oak, little pine trees and more—cedar, bayberry, beach plum.

Once I saw kids playing, eight of them now, somehow, and appearing older. I saw Duka in a large new barn-like building on the property I'd bought next to Annie's place, the doors opened wide, and she was welding something—a sculpture, I finally realized. And there was sunlight. Hazy, to be sure, but there was *sunlight!*

My most recent dream begins like the others, at Duka's first wind turbine as it spins in the dreary present. But the winter sky is not so dark; it has evolved from our usual eerily featureless purplish-orangish brown into a uniformly steel-gray that I want to believe carries hints of the blue to come. Yet it's cold again, really cold, after a too-brief respite that melted only a tiny fraction of the snow.

I'm walking and walking, all the way from the house to Cold Storage Beach and down onto the snow-covered sand, the snow crunching beneath my boots as I walk, as I gaze across the five miles of frozen, snow-topped outer harbor water stretching all the way to Provincetown in the distance.

I'm not concerned about hypothermia because I'm on my way to meet Cordelia just beyond the little boarded-up cottage ahead of me, right on the beach, where we'll hunker together into the snow-shrouded sand at the bottom of the cliff with my big bottle of amaretto and my little bottles of alprazolam and oxy.

"About time," I say aloud, eager, walking a bit faster. I know already that we'll talk about all the people who cared for me after she left, and we'll laugh and cuddle and remember and sing, and we'll watch futures unfold and refold into pasts, into presents, spiraling around us, away from us, back toward us again. I know the spirals will encompass us all, every moment, every touch, every tear, every joy…

And then I hear Cordelia's whisper—

Welcome to everywhen.

About the Author

Sophia Kell Hagin's fourth novel, *Not All a Dream*, follows three works of cross-genre/speculative fiction. The first of these, *Whatever Gods May Be*, won a 2011 Golden Crown Literary Society Award for Dramatic General Fiction, a 2010 Lesbian Fiction Readers Choice Award in General Fiction, and a 2011 LGBT Rainbow Awards Honorable Mention for Best Lesbian Debut Novel; Sophia was also named a 2011 Golden Crown Debut Author finalist. Two more novels about the same protagonist, Jamie Gwynmorgan, followed: *Shadows of Something Real* and *Omnipotence Enough*.

Sophia lives in Truro, Massachusetts, with her long-time partner. She occasionally lurks on Facebook and can be contacted via www.SophiaKellHagin.com.

Books Available from Bold Strokes Books

Bury Me in Shadows by Greg Herren. College student Jake Chapman is forced to spend the summer at his dying grandmother's home and soon finds danger from long-buried family secrets. (978-1-63555-993-4)

Can't Leave Love by Kimberly Cooper Griffin. Sophia and Pru have no intention of falling in love, but sometimes love happens when and where you least expect it. (978-1-636790041-1)

Free Fall at Angel Creek by Julie Tizard. Detective Dee Rawlings and aircraft accident investigator Dr. River Dawson use conflicting methods to find answers when a plane goes missing, while overcoming surprising threats, and discovering an unlikely chance at love. (978-1-63555-884-5)

Love's Compromise by Cass Sellars. For Piper Holthaus and Brook Myers, will professional dreams and past baggage stop two hearts from realizing they are meant for each other? (978-1-63555-942-2)

Not All a Dream by Sophia Kell Hagin. Hester has lost the woman she loved and the world has descended into relentless dark and cold. But giving up will have to wait when she stumbles upon people who help her survive. (978-1-63679-067-1)

Protecting the Lady by Amanda Radley. If Eve Webb had known she'd be protecting royalty, she'd never have taken the job as bodyguard, but as the threat to Lady Katherine's life draws closer, she'll do whatever it takes to save her, and may just lose her heart in the process. (978-1-63679-003-9)

The Secrets of Willowra by Kadyan. A family saga of three women, their homestead called Willowra in the Australian outback, and the secrets that link them all. (978-1-63679-064-0)

Trial by Fire by Carsen Taite. When prosecutor Lennox Roy and public defender Wren Bishop become fierce adversaries in a headline-grabbing arson case, their attraction ignites a passion that leads them both to question their assumptions about the law, the truth, and each other. (978-1-63555-860-9)

Turbulent Waves by Ali Vali. Kai Merlin and Vivien Palmer plan their future together as hostile forces make their own plans to destroy what they have, as well as all those they love. (978-1-63679-011-4)

Unbreakable by Cari Hunter. When Dr. Grace Kendal is forced at gunpoint to help an injured woman, she is dragged into a nightmare where nothing is quite as it seems, and their lives aren't the only ones on the line. (978-1-63555-961-3)

Veterinary Surgeon by Nancy Wheelton. When dangerous drugs are stolen from the veterinary clinic, Mitch investigates and Kay becomes a suspect. As pride and professions clash, love seems impossible. (978-1-63679-043-5)

A Different Man by Andrew L. Huerta. This diverse collection of stories chronicling the challenges of gay life at various ages shines a light on the progress made and the progress still to come. (978-1-63555-977-4)

All That Remains by Sheri Lewis Wohl. Johnnie and Shantel might have to risk their lives—and their love—to stop a werewolf intent on killing. (978-1-63555-949-1)

Beginner's Bet by Fiona Riley. Phenom luxury Realtor Ellison Gamble has everything, except a family to share it with, so when a mix-up brings youthful Katie Crawford into her life, she bets the house on love. (978-1-63555-733-6)

Dangerous Without You by Lexus Grey. Throughout their senior year in high school, Aspen, Remington, Denna, and Raleigh face challenges in life and romance that they never expect. (978-1-63555-947-7)

Desiring More by Raven Sky. In this collection of steamy stories, a rich variety of lovers find themselves desiring more, more from a lover, more from themselves, and more from life. (978-1-63679-037-4)

Jordan's Kiss by Nanisi Barrett D'Arnuck. After losing everything in a fire Jordan Phelps joins a small lounge band and meets pianist Morgan Sparks, who lights another blaze, this time in Jordan's heart. (978-1-63555-980-4)

Late City Summer by Jeanette Bears. Forced together for her wedding, Emily Stanton and Kate Alessi navigate their lingering passion for one another against the backdrop of New York City and World War II, and a summer romance they left behind. (978-1-63555-968-2)

Love and Lotus Blossoms by Anne Shade. On her path to self-acceptance and true passion, Janesse will risk everything—and possibly everyone— she loves. (978-1-63555-985-9)

Love in the Limelight by Ashley Moore. Marion Hargreaves, the finest actress of her generation, and Jessica Carmichael, the world's biggest pop star, rediscover each other twenty years after an ill-fated affair. (978-1-63679-051-0)

Suspecting Her by Mary P. Burns. Complications ensue when Erin O'Connor falls for top real estate saleswoman Catherine Williams while investigating racism in the real estate industry; the fallout could end their chance at happiness. (978-1-63555-960-6)

Two Winters by Lauren Emily Whalen. A modern YA retelling of Shakespeare's *The Winter's Tale* about birth, death, Catholic school, improv comedy, and the healing nature of time. (978-1-63679-019-0)

Busy Ain't the Half of It by Frederick Smith and Chaz Lamar Cruz. Elijah and Justin seek happily-ever-afters in LA, but are they too busy to notice happiness when it's there? (978-1-63555-944-6)

Calumet by Ali Vali. Jaxon Lavigne and Iris Long had a forbidden small-town romance that didn't last, and the consequences of that love will be uncovered fifteen years later at their high school reunion. (978-1-63555-900-2)

Her Countess to Cherish by Jane Walsh. London Society's material girl realizes there is more to life than diamonds when she falls in love with a nonbinary bluestocking. (978-1-63555-902-6)

Hot Days, Heated Nights by Renee Roman. When Cole and Lee meet, instant attraction quickly flares into uncontrollable passion, but their connection might be short lived as Lee's identity is tied to her life in the city. (978-1-63555-888-3)

Never Be the Same by MA Binfield. Casey meets Olivia and sparks fly in this opposites attract romance that proves love can be found in the unlikeliest places. (978-1-63555-938-5)

Quiet Village by Eden Darry. Something not quite human is stalking Collie and her niece, and she'll be forced to work with undercover reporter Emily Lassiter if they want to get out of Hyam alive. (978-1-63555-898-2)

Shaken or Stirred by Georgia Beers. Bar owner Julia Martini and home health aide Savannah McNally attempt to weather the storms brought on by a mysterious blogger trashing the bar, family feuds they knew nothing about, and way too much advice from way too many relatives. (978-1-63555-928-6)

The Fiend in the Fog by Jess Faraday. Can four people on different trajectories work together to save the vulnerable residents of East London from the terrifying fiend in the fog before it's too late? (978-1-63555-514-1)

The Marriage Masquerade by Toni Logan. A no strings attached marriage scheme to inherit a Maui B&B uncovers unexpected attractions and a dark family secret. (978-1-63555-914-9)

Flight SQA016 by Amanda Radley. Fastidious airline passenger Olivia Lewis is used to things being a certain way. When her routine is changed by a new, attractive member of the staff, sparks fly. (978-1-63679-045-9)

Home Is Where the Heart Is by Jenny Frame. Can Archie make the countryside her home and give Ash the fairytale romance she desires? Or will the countryside and small village life all be too much for her? (978-1-63555-922-4)

Moving Forward by PJ Trebelhorn. The last person Shelby Ryan expects to be attracted to is Iris Calhoun, the sister of the man who killed her wife four years and three thousand miles ago. (978-1-63555-953-8)

Poison Pen by Jean Copeland. Debut author Kendra Blake is finally living her best life until a nasty book review and exposed secrets threaten her promising new romance with aspiring journalist Alison Chatterley. (978-1-63555-849-4)

Seasons for Change by KC Richardson. Love, laughter, and trust develop for Shawn and Morgan throughout the changing seasons of Lake Tahoe. (978-1-63555-882-1)

Summer Lovin' by Julie Cannon. Three different women, three exotic locations, one unforgettable summer. What do you think will happen? (978-1-63555-920-0)

Unbridled by D. Jackson Leigh. A visit to a local stable turns into more than riding lessons between a novel writer and an equestrian with a taste for power play. (978-1-63555-847-0)

VIP by Jackie D. In a town where relationships are forged and shattered by perception, sometimes even love can't change who you really are. (978-1-63555-908-8)

Yearning by Gun Brooke. The sleepy town of Dennamore has an irresistible pull on those who've moved away. The mystery Darian Benson and Samantha Pike uncover will change them forever, but the love they find along the way just might be the key to saving themselves. (978-1-63555-757-2)

A Turn of Fate by Ronica Black. Will Nev and Kinsley finally face their painful past and relent to their powerful, forbidden attraction? Or will facing their past be too much to fight through? (978-1-63555-930-9)

Desires After Dark by MJ Williamz. When her human lover falls deathly ill, Alex, a vampire, must decide which is worse, letting her go or condemning her to everlasting life. (978-1-63555-940-8)

Her Consigliere by Carsen Taite. FBI agent Royal Scott swore an oath to uphold the law, and criminal defense attorney Siobhan Collins pledged her loyalty to the only family she's ever known, but will their love be stronger than the bonds they've vowed to others, or will their competing allegiances tear them apart? (978-1-63555-924-8)

In Our Words: Queer Stories from Black, Indigenous, and People of Color Writers. Stories selected by Anne Shade and edited by Victoria Villaseñor. Comprising both the renowned and emerging voices of

Black, Indigenous, and People of Color authors, this thoughtfully curated collection of short stories explores the intersection of racial and queer identity. (978-1-63555-936-1)

Measure of Devotion by CF Frizzell. Disguised as her late twin brother, Catherine Samson enters the Civil War to defend the Constitution as a Union soldier, never expecting her life to be altered by a Gettysburg farmer's daughter. (978-1-63555-951-4)

Not Guilty by Brit Ryder. Claire Weaver and Emery Pearson's day jobs clash, even as their desire for each other burns, and a discreet sex-only arrangement is the only option. (978-1-63555-896-8)

Opposites Attract: Butch/Femme Romances by Meghan O'Brien, Aurora Rey, Angie Williams. Sometimes opposites really do attract. Fall in love with these butch/femme romance novellas. (978-1-63555-784-8)

Swift Vengeance by Jean Copeland, Jackie D, Erin Zak. A journalist becomes the subject of her own investigation when sudden strange, violent visions summon her to a summer retreat and into the arms of a killer's possible next victim. (978-1-63555-880-7)

Under Her Influence by Amanda Radley. On their path to #truelove, will Beth and Jemma discover that reality is even better than illusion? (978-1-63555-963-7)

Wasteland by Kristin Keppler & Allisa Bahney. Danielle Clark is fighting against the National Armed Forces and finds peace as a scavenger, until the NAF general's daughter, Katelyn Turner, shows up on her doorstep and brings the fight right back to her. (978-1-63555-935-4)

When in Doubt by VK Powell. Police officer Jeri Wylder thinks she committed a crime in the line of duty but can't remember, until details emerge pointing to a cover-up by those close to her. (978-1-63555-955-2)